THE INVITED

Also by Jennifer McMahon

THE INVITED

Jennifer McMahon

DOUBLEDAY

New York

www.doubleday.com

Book design by Maria Carella
Jacket photograph by Edward Fielding/Arcangel Images;
(sky) Alicia Ramirez/Shutterstock
Jacket design by Michael Windsor

Library of Congress Cataloging-in-Publication Data
Names: McMahon, Jennifer, [date] author.
Title: The invited : a novel / by Jennifer McMahon.
Description: First Edition. | New York : Doubleday, 2019.
Identifiers: LCCN 2018037320 | ISBN 9780385541381 (hardback) |
ISBN 9780385541398 (ebook)
Subjects: | BISAC: FICTION / Suspense. | FICTION / Ghost. |
GSAFD: Ghost stories. | Suspense fiction.
Classification: LCC PS3613.C584 I55 2018 | DDC 813/.6—dc23
LC record available at https://lccn.loc.gov/2018037320

MANUFACTURED IN THE UNITED STATES OF AMERICA

1 3 5 7 9 10 8 6 4 2

First Edition

For Drea, again and always

THE INVITED

Hattie Breckenridge

MAY 19, 1924

It had started when Hattie was a little girl.

She'd had a cloth-bodied doll with a porcelain head called Miss Fentwig. Miss Fentwig told her things—things that Hattie had no way of knowing, things that Hattie didn't really want to hear. She felt it deep down inside her in the way that she'd felt things all her life.

Her gift.

Her curse.

One day, Miss Fentwig told her that Hattie's father would be killed, struck by lightning, and that there was nothing Hattie could do. Hattie tried to warn her daddy and her mother. She told them just what Miss Fentwig had said. "Nonsense, child," they said, and sent her to bed without supper for saying such terrible things.

Two weeks later, her daddy was dead. Struck by lightning while he was putting his horse in the barn.

Everyone started looking at Hattie funny after that. They took Miss Fentwig away from her, but Hattie, she kept hearing voices. The trees talked to her. Rocks and rivers and little shiny green beetles spoke to her. They told her what was to come.

You have a gift, the voices told her.

But Hattie, she didn't see it that way. Not at first. Not until she learned to control it.

Now, today, the voices cried out a warning.

First, it was the whisper of the reeds and cattails that grew down at the west end of the bog—a sound others would hear only as dry stalks rubbing together in the wind, but to her they formed a chorus of voices, pleading and desperate: *They're coming for you, run!*

It wasn't just the plants who spoke. The crows cawed out an urgent, hoarse warning. The frogs at the edge of the bog bellowed at her: *Hurry, hurry, hurry.*

Off in the distance, dogs barked, howled: a pack of dogs, moving closer, coming for her.

And then there were footsteps, a single runner coming down the path. Hattie was in front of their house, an ax in her hands, splitting wood for the fire. Hattie loved splitting wood: to feel the force of the blows, hear the crack as the ax head hit the wood, splitting it right at the heart. Now she raised the ax defensively, waiting.

"Jane?" she called out when she saw her daughter come bursting out of the woods, hair and eyes wild. Her blue flowered dress was torn. Hattie had sewn the dress herself, as she'd made all their clothes, on her mother's old treadle sewing machine with fabric ordered from the Sears, Roebuck catalog. Sometimes Hattie splurged and bought them dresses from the catalog, but they were never as comfortable or durable as the ones she sewed.

Hattie lowered the ax.

"Where have you been, girl?" she asked her daughter.

It was a school day, but Hattie had forbidden her daughter from going to school. And last she knew, Jane was gathering kindling in the woods.

Jane opened her mouth to speak, to say, but could not seem to make the words come.

Instead, she burst into tears.

Hattie set down her ax, went to her, wrapped her arms around Jane's trembling body.

Then she smelled the smoke on Jane's dress, in her tangled hair.

Even the smoke spoke to her, spun an evil tale.

"Jane? What's happened?"

Jane reached into the pocket of her dress, pulled out a box of matches.

"I've done something wicked," she said.

Hattie pushed her away, held tight to her arms, searched her face. Hattie had spent her life interpreting messages and signs, divining the future. But her own flesh and blood, her daughter—her mind was closed to Hattie. Always had been.

"Tell me," Hattie said, not wanting to know.

"Mama," Jane said, crying. "I'm sorry."

Hattie closed her eyes. The dogs were coming closer. Dogs and men who were shouting, crashing through the woods. It had always been funny to Hattie how men who'd spent their whole lives moving through these woods, hunting in them, could move so clumsily, without grace, without any trace of respect for the living things they trod upon.

"What will we do?" Jane looked pale and young, much younger than her twelve years. Fear does that to a person: shrinks them down, makes them small and weak. Hattie had learned, over the years, to put her own fears in a box at the back of her mind, to stand tall and brave, to be resilient to whatever enemy presented itself.

"You? You'll go hide in the root cellar back where the old house used to be."

"But there are spiders down there, Mama! Rats, too!"

"Spiders and rats are the least of our concerns. They'll bring you no harm."

Unlike the men who are coming now, Hattie thought. *The men who are close. Getting closer still.* If she listened, she could hear their voices, their shouts.

"Cut through the woods to the old place. Climb down into the cellar and bar the door. Open it for no one."

"But, Mama—"

"Go now. Run! I'll come for you. I'll lead them away, then I'll come back. I'll be back for you, Jane Breckenridge, I swear. Don't you open that cellar door for anyone but me. And, Jane?"

"Yes, Mama?"

"Don't you be afraid."

As if it could be that easy. As if you could banish fear just like that. As if words could have such power.

By the time Jane ran down the path, the dogs were coming from the east, from the road that led into the center of town. Old hound dogs, trained to tree bears and coons, but now it was her scent they were after.

Don't be afraid, Hattie told herself now. She concentrated on pushing the fear to the back of her mind. She picked up her ax and stood tall.

"Witch!" the men who ran after the dogs cried. "Get the witch!"

"Murderer!" some cried.

"The devil's bride," others said.

Ax clenched in her hands, Hattie started off across the bog, knowing the safest path. There were parts that dropped down, went deep; places where springs bubbled up, bringing icy-cold water from deep underground. Healing water. Water that knew things; water that could change you if you'd let it.

The peat was spongy beneath her feet, but she moved quickly, surely, leaping like a yearling deer.

"There she is!" a man shouted from up ahead of her. And this was not good. She hadn't expected them to come from that direction. In fact, they were coming from all directions. And there were so many more of them than she'd expected. She froze, panicked, as she looked at the circle forming around her, searching for an opening, a way out.

She was surrounded by men from the sawmill, men who stood around the potbelly stove at the general store, men who worked for the railroad, men who farmed. And there were women, too. This she should have expected, should have seen coming, but somehow hadn't.

When a child's life is lost, it's the mother who bears the most grief, the most fury. The women, Hattie knew, might be more dangerous than the men.

These were people she'd known all her life. Many of them had come to her in times of need, had asked for guidance, had asked her to look into the future; paid her to give a reading or to deliver a message from a loved one who had passed. She knew things about the people of this town; she knew their deepest secrets and fears; she knew the questions they were afraid to ask anyone else.

Her eye caught on Candace Bishkoff, who was walking into the bog with her husband's rifle trained on Hattie.

"Stay right there, Hattie!" Candace ordered. "Drop the ax!" Candace's wild eyes bulged, the cords of her neck stood out.

Hattie dropped the ax, felt it slip out of her fingers and land softly on the peat below.

Candace and Hattie had played together as children. They were neighbors and friends. They'd made dolls from twigs, bark, and wild-flowers: stick-figure bodies and bright daisies for heads. They'd played in this very bog, climbed the trees at the edge of it, had parties with bullfrogs and salamanders, sung songs about their own bright futures.

And Jane had played with Candace's daughter, Lucy, for a time. Then that had ended, as well it should have. Some things are for the best.

"In God's name, you better tell me the truth, Hattie Brecken-ridge," Candace called to her. "Where is Jane?"

Hattie followed the barrel of the rifle to Candace's eyes and looked right at her. "Gone," Hattie said. "I sent her away last night. She's miles and miles from town now."

Others were moving in on her, forming a tight circle around the edge of the bog and stepping closer, feet sinking and squishing, good dress shoes being ruined.

"If she were here, I would kill her," Candace said.

The words twisted into Hattie's chest, drove out the breath there.

"I would kill her right in front of you," Candace snarled. "Take your daughter away from you as you took mine from me."

"I did no such thing," Hattie said.

"Lucy was in the schoolhouse!" Candace wailed, her body swaying, being pushed down by the weight of the words she spoke. "They just pulled her body out not an hour ago!" Her voice cracked. "Her and Ben and Lawrence. All dead!" She began to sob.

A part of Hattie, the little-girl part who looked over and saw her once-upon-a-time best friend in such pain, longed to go to her, to put her arms around her, to sing a soothing song, weave flowers into her hair, bathe her in the healing waters of the bog.

"Candace, I am truly sorry for this tragedy and for your pain, but it was not my doing. I told you—I told everyone in town—that I foresaw this disaster. That the schoolhouse would burn. That lives would be lost. But no one would listen. I only see glimpses of what will happen. I can't control it. Can't stop it."

She never got used to it—the shock of something she'd seen in a vision actually happening; a tragedy unfolding that she had no way to stop.

"I need you to stop speaking," Candace said, gripping the gun so tightly her hands turned white. "Stop speaking and put your hands up above your head."

Gun trained on her, Hattie did as she was told.

Men came from behind, bound her wrists with rope.

"Bring her to the tree," Candace said.

What should I do? Hattie asked the voices, the trees, the bog itself. *How will you help me out of this?*

And for once in her life, for the one time she could recall in her thirty-two years here on earth, the voices were silent.

And Hattie was afraid. Deeply, truly afraid.

She knew in that moment that it was over. Her time had come. But Jane, Jane would be all right. They would not find her. She was sure.

Hattie went willingly to the tree, the largest in the woods around the bog. When they were young, she and Candace had called it the "Great Grandmother Tree" and marveled at its thick limbs that stuck out like arms in every direction, some straight, some curved.

Tree of life.

Tree of death.

Tree of my own ending, she thought as she saw the hangman's noose. There was a stool directly under it. A simple, three-legged kitchen stool. She wondered whom it belonged to. If they would take it home later, put it back at the table. If someone would eat dinner sitting on it tonight.

The men shoved her over to the stool; one of them put the noose around her neck, the rough rope draped like a heavy necklace. The rope had been thrown over a branch about fifteen feet up, and beneath it, three men stood holding the other end. She recognized them as the fathers of the dead children: Candace's husband, Huck Bishkoff; Walter Kline; and James Fulton.

"You should cover her head," Peter Boysko from the lumber mill suggested. "Blindfold her."

Peter had visited her for herbs and healing charms when his wife and children were so sick with the flu a few years back. They'd recovered well, and Peter had returned to Hattie with two of his wife's chicken potpies to thank her.

"No," said Candace. "I want to see her face as she dies. I want to watch her and know there is justice for Lucy and Ben and Lawrence. Justice for everyone she's ever harmed."

"I've harmed no one," Hattie told them. "And if all of you had listened to me, those children might still be alive."

If it weren't for my daughter, they would still be alive, she thought.

If only she'd been able to see that part. If only she'd known what was coming, she might have been able to stop it. But if there was one thing she'd learned, it was that you can't change the future. You can catch a glimpse of it, but it's not in your power to change it.

"Shut her up!" Barbara Kline snarled. She was Lawrence's mother. Lawrence had been very ill with chicken pox last year, and his mother had brought him to see Hattie, who'd sent them home with a healing salve and an infusion to drink. Lawrence had recovered without so much as a single pox scar. "The witch lies," Barbara hissed now.

"Send her back to the devil where she belongs!" a man in the crowd bellowed.

"Get her up there," another voice called, and a group of men grabbed hold of her, and then somehow her feet were on the stool. She had no choice but to stand up straight. The three men holding the end of the rope pulled back the slack, kept it taut.

The stool wobbled beneath her. Her arms were bound behind her back; the rope was already tight around her neck. She looked out across the bog, out at her cabin, saw that it was in flames. She had built it herself when she was all alone, just after the family house burned. After her mother was killed. Jane was born in that cabin, had had twelve birthdays there with cake and candles.

She thought of Jane, over where the old family house once stood, tucked quietly into the root cellar, like a forgotten jar of string beans. She'd be safe there. No one knew about the root cellar. No one knew there was anything left out there in the wreckage and ashes of the old family home.

What people don't understand, they destroy.

"Wait," someone called. It was Robert Crayson from the general store. He came forward, looked up at her. For a split second, she wondered if he would stop this madness, bring them to their senses. "Before justice is done—any last words? Do you want to beg forgiveness of these people? Of God?"

Hattie said nothing, just gazed out at the bog, her beautiful bog. Dragonflies soared over the surface, wings and bodies shimmering in the sunlight.

"Maybe you'd like to tell us where the money is?" Crayson went on. "Financial restitution for your crimes? We could give it to the families of the children you killed. Never bring 'em back, but might go a little way."

"I killed no one," she repeated.

"Where'd you hide it, witch?" someone yelled. "What happened to all your father's money?"

"Richest family in town," another man spat. "And look where it led them."

"Please," Crayson asked, his voice pleading now. "Put your family's wealth to good use. Don't let it die with you. Let your one last act be charitable. Tell us where you hid the money."

She smiled down at him, at all of them gathered below her, faces bright with hope. She smiled the smile of someone who has a secret she knows she'll never tell.

The rope tightened around her neck as the men behind her pulled. Up above, the branch it was looped over creaked. A squirrel chattered. A nuthatch flew by.

"You can kill me, but you can't be rid of me," she told them. "I'll always be here. Don't you see—me and this place, we're one."

Hattie took in a breath and waited.

She had climbed this tree as a child. Climbed it with Candace. They had dropped their flower-head dolls down, watching them flutter softly to the ground.

They'd called it the angel game.

Life is a circle, Hattie thought, tilting her head back to look up at the branches, where she could almost see the little girl that she was once climbing up, higher and higher, out of sight.

Someone shoved the stool out from under her.

Her body bucked, her feet kicked, searching frantically for something to rest on, to get the pressure off her neck.

She couldn't speak, couldn't scream, couldn't breathe.

Could only swing and twist, and for just a second, before she lost consciousness, she was sure she could see one of her old flower-head dolls drift down, its daisy face bright as the summer sun.

FOUNDATION

CHAPTER 1

Helen

The cement mixing drum turned. Fresh concrete poured down the truck's chute into the form made from wood and rigid foam insulation that rested on a thick bed of gravel. The truck belched diesel fumes into the clean, pine-scented early-morning air.

We are meant to be here, Helen told herself, trying not to choke on the truck's exhaust. It was eight o'clock in the morning. Normally, she'd be on her way in to work, or perhaps stopping for a latte, pretending she wasn't a few minutes late. Instead, she was here, surrounded by trees and northern birds whose songs she didn't recognize, watching workers pour her foundation.

The foundation was the one job she and Nate had hired out, and watching the men in their yellow boots, Helen was glad they'd left this one to the professionals. The men smoothed the concrete over rebar and mesh while Helen studied the scenery around her—the clearing they stood in, the thick woods encircling it, the hill to the west, the little path that led down to the bog to the south. Nate had argued that they could do the work, that a floating slab was easy, but Helen had insisted that a professionally laid out and poured foundation would give them the best start.

"If we're off even by a quarter of an inch, it'll screw things up big-time," Helen had said. "Trust me. This is what the entire house is going to rest on. It's got to be done right."

Nate had reluctantly agreed. He was the math and science man. If you hit him hard with numbers and facts, backed up your argument on paper in a scientific way, he'd acquiesce. And yes, in the many months leading up to this morning—in fact, even last night at the motel—Nate had studied countless books on building: *Homebuilding for Everyone, Designing and Building a House Your Way, The Owner-Builder's Guide to Creating the Home of Your Dreams.* He'd taken an owner-builder weekend workshop and volunteered a few weekends for Habitat for Humanity, coming home those evenings buzzing with the new high that building gave him, talking nonstop about the walls he'd helped frame, the electrical work they'd roughed in. "It's the most satisfying work I've ever done," he'd told her.

But Helen had grown up with a builder father. One of her earliest memories was the summer before first grade, when he brought her to a job site and had her straightening bent nails, teaching her the proper way to hold the hammer, his fingers wrapped around hers. She'd spent weekends and summer vacations pounding nails, hanging drywall, framing doors and windows. She'd helped her father repair the damage from shoddy construction: walls that weren't plumb with cracked drywall inside, windows improperly installed that had leaked, roofs that were collapsing because of rafters that weren't strong enough. She knew how hard all this was going to be. For months, Nate had gotten a blissed-out, stupidly contented look whenever he talked about building their dream house. Helen loved his enthusiasm and how he waxed poetic about roof lines and south-facing windows, but still, she got knots in her stomach and gnawed on the inside of her cheeks until she tasted blood.

She reached for Nate's hand now as the cement poured, gave him a nervous squeeze.

We are meant to be here, she told herself again. *I am the one who put all this in motion. This is my dream.* It was some shit her therapist back in Connecticut had taught her—how she could shape her own reality by giving herself these affirmations whenever she felt the ground shifting underneath her.

Nate squeezed her hand back—once, twice, three quick bursts, like a code, a secret code that said *We're here; we did it!* She could feel the excitement thrumming through him.

Two of the workmen in yellow boots carefully pulled a board over the rough surface of the slab, making it level.

.   .   .

She might have been the one to set things in motion, but they were here, really, because of Nate. Almost a year and a half ago now, Helen's father dropped dead from a heart attack, and Helen—normally so confident about every aspect of her life—felt herself floundering.

Helen began feeling stuck and unhappy, believing that there had to be more to life than waking up each morning and going to work, even though it was a job she loved: teaching American history to bright-eyed middle schoolers. Her job gave her a sense of purpose, made her feel genuinely useful and like she was making a difference—but it still wasn't enough. Her father's death had been a wake-up call—a warning that she, too, would die one day, perhaps sooner than expected, perhaps without warning, and it was entirely possible that she wasn't living the life she'd been meant to live. The thought filled her with dread, with a sinking leaden feeling that encroached on everything.

"What is it you want?" Nate had asked one evening. He saw Helen's new angst as a puzzle to unravel, a problem to solve.

They were sitting in the living room in their condo back in Connecticut. Nate had opened a bottle of wine and they were cuddled together on the couch in front of the gas fireplace, which Helen had never really liked because it seemed a poor substitute for the real thing—a crackling fire and the smell of woodsmoke. Nate bought her spruce and piñon incense to burn while the predictable gas flames were going, which was a sweet gesture but didn't do the trick.

"What would make you happy?" he asked as he refilled her glass.

She looked at him—her handsome, earnest, problem-solving husband—the absurdity of his question hitting her like a punch in the stomach.

"Happy?" she echoed dumbly. Happiness had always seemed to come so easily to Nate. He found true joy in weekend trips with his birding group (which consisted mostly of senior citizens) to wildlife sanctuaries and state parks to watch and photograph thrushes, Baltimore orioles, and goldfinches; in catching up with his favorite science blogs and podcasts. He found comfort and delight in studying the natural world around him, categorizing things by kingdom, phylum, order, class, and species. During grad school, Nate had a running guest appearance on his best friend Pete's blog. Pete wrote about environmental issues, but he roped Nate into doing a series of short videos called *Ask Mr. Science*. Readers would send in questions like "What's the deal with frog mutations?" or "What's happening to the honeybee population?" and Nate would come on, wearing a lab coat to look the part, and explain mutations, biodiversity, and evolution in a down-to-earth, totally adorable yet kind of geeky way.

The world made sense to Nate and his Mr. Science mind; there was an intrinsic order that comforted him and that he seemed to enjoy sharing with others, and he never seemed to feel the need to ask himself the big questions, like "What's missing?" or "What is our greater purpose in this thing called life?"

Now he blinked at her, nodded, and continued to watch her, waiting for an answer, clearly not going to give up until she gave him one.

She thought of how she spent her days, of her daily drives through the suburban landscape of strip malls, drugstores, restaurants, car washes, dry cleaners—so much light and noise; so many people out on little missions to do their errands, to buy curtains and antacids and pick up their freshly cleaned work clothes before hurrying off to work. It all seemed so meaningless.

What makes me happy? she thought.

The times she was happiest lately were when she did her occasional weekend stints volunteering at the Greensboro Museum, a tiny living history museum that re-created life in the mid-1800s for visitors. In her heavy ankle-length dress and bonnet, she'd dip candles and churn butter while visitors watched. She delighted in answering their questions about what life was like back then, about how the men and women spent their days. She was a historian and early America was her field of expertise, and like Nate playing Mr. Science, she loved to share her knowledge. But what she loved best were the quiet times at the museum, between tour groups, when she actually let herself pretend she'd gone back in time, that life was quiet and purposeful. There were cows to milk, gardens to tend, butter to churn, a fire to build to get dinner started.

As Nate continued to watch her, waiting, she took a long sip of wine, closed her eyes, and delved way back in her mind to the oldest dream she had, born from a childhood of reading the Little House on the Prairie books, reinforced by her college and grad school studies on life in colonial New England and the American pioneers.

She couldn't very well tell Nate that going back in time would make her happy, so she said the next best thing.

"A house in the country," she finally answered.

Nate turned to her, surprised. "The country? Really?"

"Yes," she said. "A place with lots of land. Space for a big garden. For chickens and goats maybe. And a pantry. I'd like a pantry. I want to learn to can my own vegetables. To live more simply, away from traffic and noise." As she said the words, she felt the truth in them—

this was her dream, what she'd always secretly wanted. She looked at the pathetic gas fire, adding, "And I want a real fireplace that burns actual wood."

Nate smiled. He set down his wine and took her hand. "Those sound like easy enough wishes," he said, kissing her fingers.

She didn't really think much of his comment at that moment.

How would they even begin to make a change like that? Their lives felt set in stone: a nice new condo they'd been on a waiting list for, a new Prius, monthly bills that left them with little extra each month; both of them had enviable teaching jobs at Palmer Academy, a private residential middle school for wealthy kids from all over New England. Nate taught science, and Helen history. Between time at school, commuting, grading papers and tests, and doing lesson plans at home, they easily worked sixty hours a week each. None of that seemed to fit with a quiet life in the country.

But Nate was already formulating a plan. "We're not nearly as stuck as you think we are," he said a few days later. He pointed to the pile of envelopes that had begun arriving a few weeks after her father died.

Helen understood. She nodded. She was an only child and her father, a simple man who had lived in the same ranch house for fifty years, driven a battered Ford pickup, and bought his clothes at Walmart, had left her with a surprise. She had been too numb to really absorb it in those days after the funeral when the lawyer first raised the issue, but when she finally was able to bring herself to start going through her father's files, she was shocked. Helen had had no idea that for years he'd been squirreling money away in savings and sensible investments, that he'd had two life insurance policies with generous payouts, that his modest ranch house in the suburbs, which had been paid off for twenty years, was worth a pretty penny by virtue of its location. It all added up to a generous windfall, and though she had mostly felt overwhelmed by everything, Nate was right, of course. A chunk of money this size could go a long way toward unsticking anything.

The rest of it happened in a blur. One day, Nate brought her a book on home canning. That weekend, he woke her up early on Saturday morning with a kiss and a smile. He handed her a cup of coffee. "We're going apple picking," he said. And Helen had loved being out at the orchard, breathing in the crisp autumn air. She'd come home feeling rejuvenated and, following the instructions in her new book, made six jars of applesauce and six of apple jelly. The next few weeks, Nate dove headlong into internet searches on "finding a home in the country" and spent hours on New England real estate sites.

They looked at properties in Connecticut and Massachusetts but ultimately narrowed their search to Vermont and New Hampshire. None of the houses they looked at was quite right. Helen loved the old colonials and farmhouses, but houses that were one-hundred-plus years old needed a great deal of work: they saw crumbling foundations, dirt-floored basements, old knob-and-tube wiring, leaking pipes, rotting beams, sagging roofs. Helen was enamored with the idea of finding an old house, a house with history, and bringing it back to life. Her favorite house was one of the first they'd seen: an old saltbox in a tiny village outside of Keene, New Hampshire. There were hand-hewn exposed beams in almost every room and wide-plank pine floors. She stood at the deep soapstone kitchen sink and looked out at the front yard, feeling at home immediately. But Nate—now armed with weeks of research—pointed out the dry rot, the ancient wiring that was a house fire waiting to happen, the damage to the old slate roof.

"We could save it," she said hopefully.

He shook his head. She could tell he was doing all the mental calculations. "I don't think there's enough money for that. This poor house needs to be taken apart and rebuilt from the ground up." He looked around helplessly. "We should just build our own place," he muttered.

Though it was Nate who came up with the idea, it took several more weekends of viewing a dozen more broken-down houses (a few of which delighted Helen, but he'd pronounced not worth saving) before the idea took root.

They were having dinner in a motel room—pizza, ordered in—after another long day of driving around the back roads of Vermont. "Maybe we should consider it," Nate said. "A new home, built from the ground up. That way we can get exactly what we want."

"But a new house just seems so cold, so sterile," Helen argued. She thought of her Little House on the Prairie books. She thought of her father, of the countless old houses he'd worked on—of the way he'd study a house and make a comment about its good bones or its character. He spoke of old houses like they were people.

"It doesn't have to be," Nate said. "It can be whatever we make it."

"But there's no sense of history," Helen said.

"We can base it on an old colonial design if that's what you want," Nate said. "Think about it—we get the best of both worlds! We can take something classic and make it our own. Energy efficient, eco-friendly, passive solar, whatever we want."

Helen smiled. "Have you been down a Google rabbit hole again?"

He laughed. Clearly the answer was yes. But Nate's question was still in the air and he looked at her, waiting for a response.

"I don't know," Helen admitted. "That's so much more money."

"Not necessarily," he countered. "Not once you factor in the true cost of renovating an old place like the ones we've been looking at. In fact, we might even end up saving money, especially when you look at it long term if we build it to be superefficient."

The more Nate talked, the more excited he got, the idea snowballing as he went along. They would do the work themselves—they were already discussing theoretical renovations to so many of the homes they'd viewed. Why not take it a few steps further? "Oh my god, why didn't we think of this before? We haven't found anything even close to our dream house because it doesn't exist yet—we have to build it! We'll be like Thoreau on Walden Pond!"

She shook her head, gave a *don't be ridiculous* laugh. She'd studied Thoreau in college, even took a field trip out to Walden Pond. "Thoreau built a tiny cabin big enough for a desk and a bed. We're talking about a two-thousand-square-foot house with all the modern conveniences. Do you have any idea how much work that is?"

"I'm not saying it'll be easy," Nate said. And then he threw the gauntlet down: "But don't you think this is what your father would want?"

"I don't—" She faltered. She remembered helping her father with the finish work on a house he'd built the summer before she went away to college. "This house," her dad had said, "it's gonna be here a long, long time. You can drive by with your kids, your grandkids, and tell them you helped build it. This house, this thing we built, it'll outlive us both."

"I think it's perfect!" Nate said. "Trust me! It's going to be perfect."

It was hard, really, not to get swept up in Nate's enthusiasm. Not to believe him when he had a solution to a problem. He was the rational one, the critical thinker, and she'd come to trust him on all practical matters. He'd known (after hours of research) which car they should buy, the best plan for paying off the last of their student loans, even which gym they should join.

She loved him for many reasons, but mostly because of the way he balanced her out, grounded her, took her most ethereal ideas and found a way to give them form. If he said building a house made more sense than buying one, then he was probably right. And if he said there was a way to do it and give Helen the sense of history she longed for, then she had to believe him.

Helen reached over the pizza box, picked up one of the glossy New England real estate flyers, and flipped to the back, to where the land listings were. She started looking at pictures of vacant lots, doing her best to imagine her dream house standing there, she and Nate tucked safely inside.

· · ·

This is where our house will go, Helen thought now as she watched the men work on the foundation. She could almost imagine the lines of it, the shadow it would cast, the roof reaching up to touch the impossibly blue sky. The clouds were so low, so vivid, she was sure that if she climbed the hill, she'd be able to reach out and touch them. It was like being in a child's drawing of the perfect landscape: trees, sky and clouds, happy yellow sun, and, beneath it, a square box of a house with a smiling couple standing outside.

They had discovered this piece of land back in January and made an offer that day. The craziest part was it wasn't even on their list to look at—they'd found it when they got lost looking for an old covered bridge Helen had seen signs for. They stopped at a general store for directions and there on the bulletin board was an ad for the land: forty-four acres in the small village of Hartsboro, Vermont. They called the realtor and arranged to meet him out there that afternoon. Half of the land was wooded, but the western part of the property consisted of the Breckenridge Bog. Land not useful for farming or building. Land that, local legend claimed—the realtor said this with a chuckle—was haunted. As they trudged out through a foot and a half of freshly fallen snow to look at the property, Nate chuckled with him. He said, "Do you think the seller would accept a lower offer on the basis that the land is known to be haunted?"

"I think," the realtor said, turning serious again, "the seller is highly motivated and would consider any reasonable offer."

They were in a large clearing with a hillside in front of them, woods to the right and left, the single-lane dirt road behind them. As they walked, it began to snow big, thick flakes that caught on Helen's eyelashes. Their feet sank in the perfect white snow and Helen looked at the trees, blanketed in white, softly bent with the weight of it. Helen was struck by the quiet, the serenity of the landscape.

"Haunted?" Helen asked, circling back. "Really?"

The realtor nodded, then looked a little like he was sorry he'd mentioned it. "That's what people say." He shrugged, as if he didn't really know the story, and he started telling them that the back of the property was bordered by a class three road that became a snow-mobile trail in the winter. "You folks get yourselves a couple of snow machines and you'll be in business," he said. "But seriously," he added. "What you've gotta understand is that even though this place is forty-four acres, only about four acres are suitable for building. The rest is just too hilly or marshy. That's why the low price."

Helen did not believe in ghosts. But she believed in history. "Hey, it's not every piece of property that comes with its very own ghost," Helen whispered to Nate. If there was a ghost story attached to this land, then that meant the land had a story to tell. Maybe she wouldn't get her hundred-year-old house with stories to tell, but she could settle for a place with history, a mystery even.

Nate nodded, wiggled his fingers, and made a ghostly *Oooo* sound.

Nate pointed out the sugar maples on the back hill and said they could tap the trees, boil the sap, and make syrup. "Can't get much more quintessential Vermont than that!" he said excitedly.

As they walked around the land, Helen had this strange sense of familiarity, of déjà vu almost, like she'd been there before. Silly, really.

They saw the flat area with good southern exposure that would make a perfect building site and the old green trailer that stood on the edge of the clearing.

"We can live in the trailer while we build," Nate said. Then he leaned in and whispered excitedly to Helen, "It's perfect! It's got everything we've been hoping for and then some."

And it did seem perfect. Almost too perfect—it was exactly like the land Nate had been describing that they would find, the land he'd promised her. Helen had this sense then. This land—their new home—was meant to be; it had been waiting for them, calling to them. But the thought was not entirely a warm and comforting one; no, it was more like a prickle on the back of the neck. It both drew her to the place and made her want to get in the car and race all the way back to their condo in Connecticut.

"I don't know what kind of shape that old mobile home's in," the realtor admitted. "The seller was using this place as a hunting camp, but he hasn't come up in a long time. It's got plumbing and electricity, but I don't know if it works. It's being sold as-is."

Helen looked at the vintage trailer, aluminum and faded green, and guessed it to be about thirty feet long and maybe eight feet wide, up on cinder blocks. The roof wasn't falling in, and the louvered windows weren't broken.

Nate was looking at it, at all of it—the trailer, the woods, the clearing—with an excited sparkle in his eye. He'd brought his 35 mm camera, the one he used to take photos on his birding trips, and was snapping pictures of it all.

The Hartsboro land enchanted them both, even on that frozen day in January. Helen led them down the hill, finding the path to the bog through the trees easily, like she knew the way. She loved the otherworldliness of the frozen bog. They'd walked out into the center of the bog while the realtor waited in his heated Suburban. "You folks take all the time you want," he'd said.

Nate pointed out tracks in the snow: deer, snowshoe hare, even the wing marks of an owl that had lunged down to swoop up some unsuspecting rodent from a bed of snow.

"It looks like an angel landed," Helen said, thinking of the ghost the realtor had mentioned, wondering if ghosts left marks in this world. If a ghost left a mark, she thought, it would be like this—delicate wing prints in the snow.

Nate poked around, pointed out the drops of blood. "An angel who snacks on tasty voles," he said, grinning.

Nate had spent his summers as a boy at his grandparents' farm in New Hampshire. Helen had known him only as an adult, but maybe he was secretly meant to be a country boy again, not cooped up in the suburbs where the only wildlife you encountered were the chickadees at the backyard feeder and the noisy squirrels battling them for choice black oil sunflower seeds.

The land was about a mile up a dirt road from the center of the village, which consisted of a general store, town hall, pizza place, Methodist church, tiny library, and gas station.

"We can walk to town," Nate said.

"I bet they have church suppers," Helen said.

"Square dances, maybe even," Nate said with a smile, hooking his elbow into hers, skipping around in a circle over the crusty ice covering the bog.

When they stopped, winded, cheeks pink, boots soaked through, Helen said, "I wish my dad could see this place."

Nate nodded. "He'd love it, don't you think?"

"Yeah," Helen agreed, eyes going back to the wing prints. "He definitely would."

And so it was decided. The asking price for the land was well below what they'd budgeted, but still, they put in a lowball offer just to see what the counteroffer would be. To their surprise, their offer was accepted immediately. "I guess the guy really was a motivated seller," Nate said. Two months later, they closed, never actually meeting the seller—a lawyer represented him, saying only that Mr. Decrow was down in Florida now and was unwell and not up to traveling. After the closing, Helen and Nate went out to breakfast at a little café on the outskirts of town. It was a celebration—they were now the proud owners of the land!

But Helen felt self-conscious: they were too well dressed, wore inappropriate footwear and dressy coats; they were clearly outsiders. When they came back, they'd need to work harder to blend in, to not seem so out of place. Helen pulled out her notebook from her purse and started a list of the things they'd need: sturdy leather boots, wool sweaters, fleece layers, flannel shirts, long underwear. Then she started a list of the tools they would need, putting an asterisk beside those they had already collected from her dad's basement: circular saw, keyhole saw, hacksaw, framing hammers, finishing hammers, squares, levels, a chalk line, a plumb bob, and on and on. There was comfort in making lists, in knowing just what to put on them, in checking off items accomplished.

.   .   .

They had sold their condo and Helen's father's house. Both sales were quick and easy, despite dire warnings from well-meaning friends about the crappy real estate market in Connecticut. They'd quit their nice, secure teaching jobs at the Palmer Academy, giving up not only the bimonthly paychecks but also their health insurance and the matching contributions to their 401(k)s. They'd even traded in their little Prius for a Toyota Tacoma pickup truck. They'd sold or given away a lot of their belongings, putting the things they were most attached to into a rented storage unit.

Their colleagues and friends thought they were crazy when they described their plans to build a house, grow a garden, raise chickens and goats.

"Mmm, *lovely*. Sounds like all nine circles of hell," Helen's friend Jenny had said at the going-away party Jenny and her husband, Richard, hosted. Helen had laughed.

"Did you ever think maybe you were born in the wrong century?" Jenny had asked, narrowing her eyes, topping up their glasses of pinot grigio. Helen had nodded. Yes. She thought that often.

Jenny was Helen's oldest friend—they'd known each other since kindergarten.

"Think of everything you're giving up," Jenny had said. "And what for? So you can go freeze your asses off in the middle of freaking nowhere while you act out this 1960s back-to-the-land fantasy? You'll be isolated. We'll never hear from you again."

"Of course you will," Helen had promised.

"Yeah, on the news maybe. We'll hear about how you were eaten by bears."

"Black bears don't eat people," Nate had said.

"Wolves then," Jenny said.

"No wolves in Vermont," Nate countered.

"Whatever, Nature Boy." Jenny rolled her eyes dramatically and gestured with her wine glass. "Something bad will happen, I'm telling you. You'll join a commune or cult or something, and Helen will stop shaving her armpits and Nate, you'll go all Jack from *The Shining*. Or Unabomber."

"Stop," Helen had said, laughing.

"Seriously," Jenny said. "Ted Kaczynski did the cabin-in-the-woods, self-sufficiency thing and look how it turned out for him. Please, God, do me a favor and change your minds before it's too late."

But they didn't change their minds.

When Helen expressed any apprehension about all the security they were giving up, Nate would say, "But remember, what we're doing, what we're going to create for ourselves, that's real security. When we're done, we'll have a house without a mortgage that we've built with our hands, enough acreage to grow all the food we need. It's what you've always dreamed of, isn't it? Your place in the country?"

And yes, it was. And she loved how quickly her dream had become his as well. How he'd thrown himself into it like a science project, drawing plans, making spreadsheets, spending hours doing research, even doing a PowerPoint presentation to show her their new plan, clearly laid out, step-by-step. "See, if we do this right, we have not only enough money to build our dream house and set up a self-sustaining homestead, we have a cushion to live on for at least another year, maybe more if we budget carefully. And if we find a way to earn money from the homestead—selling eggs, maple syrup, firewood, maybe your homemade jam—we may not have to ever go back to working full-time again. We can focus on the work that matters to us. Spend time outside, being caretakers of our amazing land. Think of it: walks to the bog every day, learning about all the creatures that live there," he said, eyes bright with excitement. "Maybe we could even start a blog about our lives there!" he suggested. "I can talk to Pete. I'm sure he's got lots of tips. And he actually makes decent money from links and ads and stuff on his."

"I can research the history of the land, find out why it's supposedly haunted. Maybe there was a house or farm out there once?"

Nate nodded enthusiastically. "We'll have plenty to do to keep us busy and plenty of money to keep us going for a while," Nate promised.

They made a couple of trips up in April, then again in early May, to start cleaning out the trailer and meet with contractors to survey, design, and lay out the foundation for the twenty-four-by-thirty-six-foot saltbox house they'd designed, based on old plans Helen had found in a book on historical homes. One that closely matched that first house she'd fallen in love with in New Hampshire. The front would be full of windows, south facing to get all the passive solar heating they could.

Now here it was, day one of construction. Helen watched the concrete ooze down the chute and thought, *This is it; we're stuck here now, for better or worse.* They'd assured their friends countless times they were making the right choice—"Weekends in the country for everyone once the house is up!" Helen promised—and they'd spent a large chunk of Helen's inheritance on the land, truck, tools, and building materials. The money that was left was carefully budgeted for the remaining house materials and living expenses to get them through the next year at least.

They'd spent last night in a motel, but tonight, they'd start sleeping in the trailer. Their first night on the land. Tomorrow, the lumberyard would deliver the framing lumber and they'd spend the day stacking and arranging. They'd gather supplies and work on the garden while they waited a few days for the cement to cure.

It was a chilly morning, with a rawness in the air that made it feel more like March or April than the third week of May. Helen was amazed by the difference in climate just four hours north of their old home in Connecticut. Nate stood in his new work boots, his chin already scruffy. "I'm going to grow a big mountain man beard," he'd promised whenever they discussed their new life in Vermont. She reached over, touched the stubble on his chin. He turned, smiled at her. "Happy?" he asked.

She paused, then gave him a warm smile. "Definitely," she said. There was nothing definite about it, admittedly, but . . . *Say the words and make them true,* she told herself.

"I *am* happy," she said.

She told herself that if she said it enough, then maybe this feeling of panic, of free-falling into the unknown, would go away.

"So happy."

Shape your reality. Make it true because you say it is.

Nate kissed her. It was a long kiss, and the men raking cement watched but pretended not to. And Helen was sure she could feel other eyes on them, too. Silly, really, but she couldn't shake the feeling. She pulled away, glanced at the tree line, then over toward the bog.

She thought, for a half a second, that she saw movement. A shape disappearing into the mist.

"Okay?" Nate asked.

"Yeah, it's just . . ."

"Just?"

"I thought I saw someone."

He smiled, scanned the yard and trees. The construction men and their trucks. "Well, we do have some company," he said. "Plus, there are probably a hundred animals watching us right now: mice, birds, voles, maybe even a deer or two." He seemed so excited, little boyish almost, as he looked around, imagining all the animals out there.

"Our new neighbors," she said.

And she kissed him again.

CHAPTER 2

O live

 **MAY 18, 2015**

They wouldn't stay. They *couldn't* stay.

Olive watched from her perch high up in the crook of an old maple, binoculars pressed against her face. She had her camouflage pants and jacket on. She'd smeared mud on her face so she'd blend in against the trees. Her hair was pulled back in a tight braid.

"We're gonna be late," Mike whined, voice too loud. He was perched on a branch below her, clinging desperately to the tree.

"Shh," she hissed down at him. His face was round and sweaty, and his hair had been buzzed by his mom, who'd missed a few strands, leaving him with funny little sprigs like antennae. If she were a truly good friend, she would offer to trim them. "Keep still," she said.

Daddy had been taking her hunting since she was six years old. She knew how to hold still, to blend in, to keep from being seen. Ninety percent of hunting was studying your prey: tracking, watching, holding perfectly still, and waiting, waiting for just the right shot.

"I don't get what the big deal is," Mike complained, voice lower now. "I mean, why are we even watching these people?"

"Because they don't belong here," she said. "They're ruining *everything*."

She studied the Connecticut license plate on the couple's brand-new truck through the binoculars. Noted the unblemished tan work boots the man wore, along with a crisp flannel shirt and jeans. He looked like he had walked straight off the pages of an L.L.Bean catalog. And the woman, she looked like she was ready to go to a yoga class in leggings, running shoes, a formfitting hoodie—all of it new looking, shiny, expensive.

"Flatlanders," Olive said with disgust. She knew the type. Her dad complained about them all the time. They'd post NO HUNTING signs on their property, drive all the way into Montpelier to buy organic food at the co-op, join the book discussion groups at the library, drink craft beer and eat locally made artisanal cheese. They'd complain about the black flies, the impassable roads during mud season, the smell of the dairy farm down the road. Yeah, she knew the type all right. And she knew that sometimes, they couldn't tough it out—one winter and they were putting their land back on the market and heading south.

But some of them stayed.

Some of them adjusted.

And walked around saying they'd never felt more at home.

And wasn't it wonderful to be in a place where everyone was so accepted, everyone could be their own true selves.

Talk like this made Olive want to puke.

Olive's father had warned her. He'd said an out-of-state couple had bought the land half mile down the road, filed a building permit. There had been surveyors and excavators out there. But she'd thought there would be more time. That they might not actually come. But now here they were in their shiny new truck with their shiny new clothes, watching a cement mixer pouring a foundation. It was really happening.

She dug her dirty nails into the rough bark of the tree, picked at a loose piece until it came off, then watched as it bounced off Mike's head and fell down to the ground.

"Olive, if I'm late to school again, my dad's gonna skin me."

"So leave," she said. Mike could be such a wuss. He was always chickening out on her, wriggling out of cool plans they'd made, because when push came to shove, Mike hated breaking rules. He hated getting in trouble and was one of those kids who would burst into tears when a teacher singled him out and yelled at him, despite the fact that he was now a high school freshman, not a baby middle schooler anymore. Sometimes it seemed like Mike was just begging to get his ass kicked, which happened all too often, especially since they'd started high school.

"Really," she said now. "You should hurry up and get to school." The truth was she didn't want him here anyway. He didn't know squat about holding still and blending in.

"Come with me," he begged, this totally sad pleading look on his face, all big eyed and weird like a baby doll. To make it worse, Mike's voice always rose at the slightest possibility of trouble, making him sound more like a five-year-old girl than a fourteen-year-old dude. "If you skip again, they'll, like, send the truant officer after you or something."

Olive chuffed out a disgusted laugh. There was no truant officer. If there had been, he would have been banging down her door weeks ago. She hadn't exactly been a model student this year and had lost track of how many days she'd either left early or skipped altogether. She turned in some of her assignments, showed up for tests and usually did pretty well, despite not studying.

"Look," she whispered down. "Either stay or go. I don't really care. But if you stay, you gotta hold still and shut your face."

"Whatever," Mike said, climbing clumsily back down the tree, then lumbering off once he got to the ground, heavy backpack weighing him down. The kid moved like a bear. He was built like one, too: tall, rounded shoulders, big belly. People at school said he was a retard and he got that way 'cause his parents were brother and sister, but none of that was true. Olive knew Mike was a thousand times smarter than anyone she'd ever met. Scary smart. He could read a book and remember every single thing in it and was doing math that some seniors in honors classes wouldn't even attempt. She felt a little bad sending him away like this, but what choice did she have?

She'd make it up to him later. Buy him one of the chocolate puddings he loved from the school cafeteria or leave a new comic in his locker. Mike loved the Green Lantern. When they were younger, they used to play this imaginary game where Mike was always the Green Lantern—he even made his own magic ring out of a short piece of copper pipe that turned his finger green—and Olive was the bad guy he was trying to catch. Olive knew Mike still carried that old ring— far too small now—around in his pocket, his own weird good luck charm.

Olive looked back at the out-of-state couple now, binoculars pressed against her eyes, and felt anger writhing around like worms in her belly.

"I banish you," she said, which sounded dumb, really, but it was something she'd read in a book once. A book about a kingdom and dragons and magical things, and she thought maybe they were magic words that might drive the people away. "I banish you."

She was no better than Mike and his dumb old ring. There was no such thing as magic. She was fourteen years old. Too old to believe in stupid things like wishes and magic words or rings.

Their being here would ruin everything.

She would never find the treasure if she had to sneak around in the dead of night. And she had to find it soon. Time was, as they say, of the essence.

Some people said it was all a lie, a rumor, that it didn't even exist. Even Mike didn't believe. Not really, anyway. He pretended to, just to make Olive happy. He went along with her whenever she searched for it and acted like she might find it any day, but she could tell he didn't think it was ever gonna happen.

But Mike, smart as he was at math and reciting every fact he'd ever read in any book, was also clueless about so much. And of course, most people were idiots.

Olive knew better. She knew because her own mother had told her the truth.

"Of course it's real!" her mama told her two years ago. They were in Olive's room, doing spring cleaning—taking down the curtains, washing the windows and woodwork. Olive loved spring cleaning. She always kept her room neat and organized, but it was even better after she and Mama scrubbed everything down. Everything glowed, and the lemon cleanser smell made Olive feel bright and warm.

"She knew they were coming for her, see, and she took all the gold and silver, all the jewels, and buried it in a secret place," Mama explained as she pulled back the bed so they could scrub the floor underneath. "Somewhere in the woods that border the bog. Then, once the treasure was safe, she tried to run, thinking she'd come back for it later."

"But they caught her," Olive said, dipping her mop into the sudsy bucket.

"They sure did. Her own daughter led them right to her. That's what folks say."

"I would never do that to you, Mama," Olive said, wringing out the mop.

"I know you wouldn't." Mama ruffled Olive's hair. "And there's something else I know, Ollie Girl; something I'm absolutely sure of. You and me, we're going to find that treasure. It's our destiny."

Olive loved this: knowing they had a destiny. That they were a part of something that was bigger than them, connected to events that had happened lifetimes ago. She could see it so clearly that day as they cleaned together: her and Mama finding that treasure, digging it up out of the ground. They'd be famous. Rich. Mama said they could use that money to pay off all their bills, pay off the mortgage even, then go traveling around the world—just them and Daddy. Olive pictured it: how all the kids at school would turn on the TV at night, and there would be Olive, smiling out from the evening news, because she and Mama had found the treasure that no one believed was real.

But then something changed. Mama discovered a different destiny for herself—one that didn't include Olive. It started small: she got quieter, more secretive. Olive couldn't pinpoint when it started, but Mama stopped talking about the treasure. Once, at dinner, when Olive asked about it, Mama laughed at her like she was stupid, said, "There is no treasure, Ollie. Not really. It was just a story I told you when you were a kid. But you're getting to be too grown-up for silly stories like that."

And Mama started acting like she hardly knew Olive and Daddy, like being in the house made her skin crawl. She got all jumpy, was always making up excuses to go out: they needed milk; it was a beautiful night for a long walk; a friend needed help with something. She started spending more and more time away from home. She even skipped spring cleaning that year, and when Olive brought it up, Mama shrugged, said the house was clean enough.

Olive heard her parents fighting late one night last summer, heard her daddy say, "Who is he?," followed by "Half the town knows it." Mama denied it, asked him please for the love of God to lower his voice.

Then, in the morning, Mama didn't come down for breakfast. Usually, she was the first one up and had the coffee perking, but that morning, Olive came into the kitchen and found Daddy pouring hot water over instant coffee.

"Mama's not up?"

"She's not here," Daddy said, clenching his jaw.

"Where is she?"

Daddy didn't answer, just looked away, dark circles under his red eyes. And part of Olive was glad he hadn't answered, hadn't told her the truth.

Over the next days and weeks, Olive tried hard to block out the gossip she heard around town: the hushed whispers spoken by all the adults at the general store and the library, even by the kids in school. That was the worst—starting high school last fall and hearing all the older kids whispering, "Her mama ran off with some other man. Must suck to have a slut for a mom." She walked the long, too-bright halls with her head down, pretending not to hear, pretending not to notice.

Aunt Riley, Daddy's older sister (*my bossy older sister,* Daddy called her), told her not to listen to what people said. "You know your mama better than almost anyone," Riley said. "Don't you forget that."

Riley might be older than her parents, but she was much cooler than them, and one of Olive's very favorite people in the universe. Olive always gloated a little walking around town with her, hoping kids from school might see them and it would somehow elevate Olive's status. Riley had tons of tattoos, an asymmetrical haircut with bangs that were dyed blue, and often wore blue lipstick to match it. She lived in an apartment in a funky old Victorian, worked at a building salvage yard, went to college part-time, and volunteered at the historical society and for Habitat for Humanity. She'd even gone down to Nicaragua one summer to help build houses for poor people. For a while, Riley was apprenticing to be a tattoo artist and kept sketchbooks full of designs: carefully inked drawings of skulls, flowers, and animals, and page after page of fancy lettering. Riley had this *I'm gonna be my own person and not give a crap what anyone thinks* kind of attitude that Olive totally admired and aspired to. And she really did boss Olive's dad around (or tried to, anyway). She was always telling him what to do, and he usually nodded and went along with whatever it was, whether it was something like "Time to cut the grass, Dusty," or "That shirt looks like shit, go put on a clean one." Olive knew her dad and Riley didn't have the best childhood—their mom drank and their dad was hardly ever home, so Aunt Riley basically raised Daddy and had been taking care of him and bossing him around his whole life; it was just a matter of habit now.

After Mama left, Riley suggested to her dad that maybe she could move in. "Just for a while. To help you guys out until Lori comes back." Daddy said he appreciated the offer but that they were doing fine, really.

Riley was always bringing Olive strange gifts: kumquats, a slide rule, a piece of amber with a bug trapped inside. "What can I say—weird stuff always makes me think of you," Riley would say with a wink and a ruffling of Olive's hair as she handed the gifts over.

Riley had her own collection of weird stuff in her apartment: animal bones, a crystal ball, tarot cards, and pendulums. She was always meditating and setting up little altars for various occasions, like if she wanted a new job or for some guy she liked to like her back. She liked to talk about dreams and always made Olive tell hers when she spent the night. She believed dreams were important and bought Olive a little blue journal with a sun and moon on the cover so she could write them down. Olive thought the notebook was too pretty to write her dumb dreams in, so she put it on her bookshelf to save for a time when she might have something worthwhile to use it for.

"Have you ever had an experience where you knew something was going to happen before it did?" she asked Olive once. Olive said she hadn't and Riley looked disappointed. Sometimes she'd read Olive's tarot cards, to tell her future, which always seemed hopeful and promising when Riley interpreted it—even when she got cards that scared Olive, like the Tower, which showed a tower on fire after lightning struck it and blew the top off, two people tumbling out of it to the ground.

"The Tower, that's turmoil, sudden change. Your life might feel like it's in upheaval, but really, you've got to remember that with change comes positive stuff, too. You're gonna grow from this. With destruction comes transformation, right? Sometimes you've gotta break down the structures you surround yourself with to get to the truth, to find the core strength of who you are. Does that make sense, Ollie?" And Olive nodded and they finished the reading, drinking bitter herbal tea that was supposed to help them both get centered and find clarity.

Riley tried hard, almost too hard, to make things better for Olive. She'd always been a fixture at their house, mostly hanging out with Mama. Riley and her mom went to antique shops, went out to play bingo and to hear bands perform at the Cider Mill out on Route 9. Daddy would get irritated (or at least pretend to be) when Riley showed up at the house to take Mama off somewhere. "My god, woman," he'd say. "You spend more time with my sister than you do with me!" She'd laugh as she hurried off on some adventure with Riley, saying, "I only married you so I could have the best sister-in-law ever."

But now it was Olive Riley came to take out on adventures. Olive figured that maybe Riley was lonely, too, missing Mama and looking for company. She took Olive out for milkshakes, went for walks in the woods with her, invited Olive to come stay at her place on the weekends, where they'd watch old black-and-white horror movies and eat piles of candy. Riley always got a big bag of Swedish Fish for Olive because they were her favorite. They never talked about Mama. That felt like the point; that Riley was trying to take Olive's mind (and her own, too, maybe) off Mama, to help her forget that her own mother had just up and left her and Daddy. But no amount of horror movies, popcorn, and Swedish Fish could make Olive forget.

Daddy, he pretended not to hear the rumors about Mama, either. He went to his job (he worked maintenance for the town, fixing roads and culverts and driving a snowplow in the winter) and came home each evening. He stopped playing cards with friends or going out for a beer in the evening. He stayed home and cooked microwave dinners for him and Olive. They were too bland and greasy—Salisbury steak, fried chicken, and mashed potatoes that didn't taste anything like actual potatoes—but Olive smiled and swallowed them down. The only time he actually cooked real food was when Riley came, and then it was always spaghetti with spicy Italian sausages. He even splurged and bought garlic bread and a bag of premade salad. They pretended, Daddy and Olive, that this was how they ate every night, so that Riley wouldn't worry about them.

"Your mama will be back," he promised Olive when they were alone one night, eating their crappy microwaved Salisbury steak dinners with fake mashed potatoes and little square apple pies. "And you know what I think?" Suddenly his eyes were bright again for the first time in what seemed like forever. He looked around the kitchen, as if he had never seen it before—the dingy walls with patches of missing wallpaper, the peeling Formica on the counter. "I think we should surprise her. Fix the house up real nice for her, what do you say?"

Of course Olive said yes. And this was how the renovations started.

.   .   .

The spare bedroom wall got knocked down first, her father letting Olive take the first swing with the sledgehammer. She stood looking at the wall through fogged safety glasses. "Are you sure?" she asked, testing the weight of the heavy hammer.

"Hell yes, I'm sure," Daddy said. "Knock it down, baby. Knock it all down."

She gave a few tentative swings, hating the destruction. Then Daddy took over, smashing away with a frenzy that frightened her. They were tearing down the wall to make a larger bedroom for her parents.

"Your mama always wanted a master bedroom," Daddy said between swings, plaster dust covering his arms and face. "A closet all her own." He hit the wall with renewed vigor, smashing right through to the other side.

They put in two side-by-side closets: his and hers. Olive helped her father hang all of her mother's abandoned clothing up in the closet on the left. As she handled her mother's best dress, her favorite leather coat, she believed her father, believed that her mother would actually come back. Because there was no way she would have left all this behind. Not her favorite dress and coat. Not every pair of shoes. Not the treasure. Not Olive.

Renovations aside, Olive was more determined than ever to find the treasure, sure that once she found it, her mother would return. Wherever she was, she'd see Olive on TV, hear about it on the news: about the girl who'd found the buried treasure, the girl who was now rich.

If that didn't bring her back, then Olive would have all the money she needed to find her. She'd hire an army of private detectives, do whatever it took to bring Mama home again. And Mama would see the new master bedroom, her own huge closet, and she'd never want to leave.

In the meantime, Olive kept searching.

.   .   .

Now Olive listened to Mike's footsteps as he made his way clumsily down the path. She pressed the binoculars to her face, watching the outsiders. They stood, their arms around each other, stupid smiles plastered on their faces that said all their dreams were coming true. Olive hated them. She couldn't help herself.

She bit her lip, watching the flatlanders. They were kissing now. Totally gross.

I banish you, she thought again, concentrating as hard as she could.

The woman pulled back from the man, looked right in Olive's direction.

Olive didn't flinch. Just held tight to the tree, concentrated on blending in, on being part of the landscape. Because she *was* a part of the landscape. And this place, it was a part of her. All of it: the trees, the animals, the bog, the wind in the trees.

CHAPTER 3

H elen

 **MAY 19, 2015**

Something was being eviscerated.

That's the only way she knew to describe the sound she was hearing: a horrible, keening screech. A creature being tortured, split open, and gutted. It was a desperate, high-pitched scream. At first, it sounded like it was right outside the trailer; then it seemed to move—or was it being dragged off?—farther back into the woods. Out in the direction of the bog.

She'd been awake for hours, unable to sleep in the cramped bed, listening to every strange sound—breaking branches, howling dogs, hooting owls—so unlike the hushed buzz of highway traffic that she'd heard at night back at the condo.

Now there was this terrible scream that made her chest tighten, heart pushed all the way up into her throat.

And Nate was sleeping through it. Typical.

She gave him a hard shove.

"Nate!" she whisper-yelled, trying to control her breathing, to not sound totally panic-stricken. "Nate, did you hear that?"

She sat up, bumping her head on the ridiculous shelf on the wall above the bed in the tiny bedroom of the trailer. The bedroom was wide enough only for a double bed. No closet, so there were shelves everywhere. Making the bed was a nearly impossible feat involving acts of contortion Helen hadn't imagined herself capable of.

"Hear what?" Nate asked, rolling from his side to his back.

"It was a scream. An awful scream."

He sat up, bumped his own head on the shelf, mumbled, "Shit!"

They were going to have to do something about the shelves before one of them concussed themselves or split open their head and needed stitches. The nearest hospital was forty-five minutes away. She tried not to think too hard about that when imagining all the work they were about to do: how easy it would be to slip with a saw blade, to topple off the top of a ladder set up on unlevel ground.

Nate reached up now, fumbled around on the shelf until he found the lamp, and turned it on. The little room came to life in a lightning-like explosion of brightness. Helen blinked, turned away.

"Turn it off!" Helen ordered.

"What? Why?"

"Because," she said in her best *are you an idiot or what?* tone, "whatever's out there will know we're in here."

She realized how foolish she sounded. Her fear was getting the better of her.

He gave her a *really, Helen?* look and left the light on, reached for his glasses. During the day, he wore contacts, but they were now soaking in their little plastic holder by the tiny bathroom sink.

"Helen, what you heard, it was only an animal," he said in his most soothing voice.

"An animal screaming? It sounded like someone being fucking gutted, Nate." If he'd heard the noise, there was no way he'd be this calm.

He put a comforting hand on her arm. "Probably a fox. A fisher, maybe. They make horrible screaming sounds."

"That's not what this was."

"I'll find an audio file online and play it for you in the morning," Nate said. "You'll see."

Off in the distance, an owl called, seemed to say *Who cooks for you?* over and over.

"That's a barred owl," Nate said, excited. "Is that what you heard?"

She blew out an exasperated breath. "No, *Mr. Science.* That's an owl. I know what a damn owl sounds like! What I heard was something or someone being tortured."

"I bet it was a fisher. I've never heard one, but from what I understand, it's a terrifying cry."

He turned out the light, set his glasses back on the shelf, and lay down.

"What?" she snapped, incredulous. "You're going back to sleep? Seriously?"

"It's three thirty in the morning, Helen. We've got a busy day ahead of us."

Nate had this uncanny ability to sleep no matter what. He'd be out in no time, and once he was asleep, it was nearly impossible to wake him. Alarms never worked. He proudly said that he once slept through a magnitude 6.5 earthquake in El Salvador when he was on a research trip in grad school.

Helen just wasn't wired that way. She was a terrible insomniac, especially when in a new place. And now that there was something out there screaming, her chances of falling back to sleep were slim. And it was probably best that way: one of them had to stay awake in case whatever was out there came back.

She lay there in the dark, listening to the wind, to Nate's gentle snoring. The owl hooted again. But no more screams. How, she wondered for the thousandth time, had she ever let Nate talk her into this? She remembered Jenny teasing her, saying, "Think of all you're giving up! And for what?"

Now here she was, lying awake in bed, listening for the sounds of a mysterious screaming animal—just the sort of thing Jenny had warned her about.

She closed her eyes, took a deep breath, and tried to imagine what it must have been like here when the settlers first came. When there were no electric lights. No internet to research animals that made terrible sounds in the middle of the night. When she couldn't sleep, she thought about history. Of research she'd done, of facts she knew about the past, because somehow, looking back always made the present seem not so bad, no matter what was going on.

She imagined a woman who might have come to settle in these same woods three hundred years ago, listening to the sounds for the first time: the crack of breaking twigs, the forlorn call of an owl, the wild and terrifying screams of some unknown creature. Had that woman's husband slept beside her, too, snoring and oblivious? Had she cursed him quietly in the night, wondered how she ever let him talk her into such a thing? The thought made her smile, feel not so alone.

Around 4:30, Helen gave up on sleep and scooted down to crawl over Nate's feet and out of bed. She pulled on the robe hanging from a hook on the door and walked down the narrow hall into the kitchen. The trailer was small and cramped and smelled like mice. It was basically an aluminum shoebox with tiny louvered windows, dark wood paneling, and an iffy electrical system. When you turned on a light, others dimmed. The linoleum floor was peeling up (they'd covered it with throw rugs where they could), and the fake wood paneling on the walls was buckling. There was the closet-sized bedroom that barely fit their full bed, a tiny bathroom, and a living room and kitchen that were really one not-so-big space. The kitchen was galley style, with old metal cabinets that were rusted through in places. Helen had tried to brighten them up by sticking contact paper on them, but it peeled and hung like bits of unattached skin.

When they'd first come to clean out the trailer (Nate carrying her over the rusty threshold like a silly newlywed), they found it full of stuff: ratty old furniture, food in the cupboards and fridge, clothes piled on the shelves in the bedroom; there was even a toothbrush at the sink.

"Anything worth saving?" Nate asked once she'd been over the place with her careful historian's eye. In addition to loving research, Helen adored old objects and spent a lot of time visiting estate sales and flea markets. What she was drawn to most were the small personal things—old tintype photographs, letters written in smudged and faded ink. Nate didn't understand her obsession with these objects or her reasons for buying them. "It's not like you knew these people," he said.

"No," she said. "But I do a little bit now, don't I? Now that I have a piece of their story."

She felt an attraction to the objects and believed that as long as she held on to them, looked at them from time to time, the people whose lives were captured on paper and in photographs would not be forgotten or completely lost to time.

"Nothing. It's all junk," she said, disappointed that they hadn't found any antique jelly jars, some milk glass, or one piece of well-made furniture worth keeping.

The strangest thing was the table: it was set for two, plates sticky with fossilized food remains and mouse droppings, an unopened bottle of wine and two dusty but empty glasses in the center of the table. "I guess Mr. Decrow wasn't much of a housekeeper," Nate had said. They'd hauled it all off to the dump (saving only the wine, which they stuck up on a kitchen shelf), Helen wondering what had interrupted that final dinner; what had stopped them from opening the wine?

They didn't want to put much energy or money into fixing up the trailer: they'd be there only a short time while building the house.

Then they'd have the trailer carted off. Or turn it into a chicken house, maybe. Helen liked this idea and imagined a chicken roosting in the metal cabinets she now reached into to get out the coffee.

She put a filter into the basket of the drip pot, measured in the grounds, then filled the glass carafe, looking out the window above the sink. It was a miracle the trailer had running water, drawn from a well on the property—the same well they would rely on for their new house. Nate had had the water tested and pronounced it safe.

It was still dark, but the early predawn chorus of birds had started. It was much louder than the birds in Connecticut ever had been. She could hear them through the trailer's open windows as she sat down at the table and flipped open her laptop to check her email. And maybe she'd start researching—see if she could find anything online on the supposed ghost of Breckenridge Bog, something that might give her some insight into the history of the place. She'd meant to start looking into it while they were back in Connecticut but had been too busy with the house plans and finishing up work at the school. Better to start here anyway, where she had access to the local library, records at the town hall, and local residents who might be able to tell her more about the history of her land than anything she was likely to find in old records.

She listened to the birds, thinking they sounded too loud, almost frantic, as she waited for her computer to boot up.

But there was something else, another sound. Not the tortured screaming from earlier. Something quieter.

Twigs breaking. Ground crunching.

It was the sound of footsteps.

Definitely footsteps. Coming from right outside the trailer.

She stood up and dashed down the hall to the bedroom, grabbed Nate's foot and pulled.

"Nate!" she whispered urgently. "Get up."

"Whas-it-this-time?" he slurred. "Another owl?"

"Someone's outside." She kept pulling at him.

"Animal," he said. "Fox. Fisher."

"Bullshit. There is a two-legged person out there. Now come on!"

She pulled the covers off. He reached up for his glasses, crawled to the foot of the bed.

"Get the flashlight," Helen said.

Nate always kept a flashlight by the bed, even back at the condo.

He believed in being prepared. Nate scooted back, reached up to the shelf and grabbed the big high-powered yellow rechargeable spotlight they'd bought at the hardware store for their Vermont adventure.

Nate shuffled down the hall in his T-shirt and boxers. With his round glasses, he looked like a grown-up Harry Potter, minus the scar.

"Hurry!" Helen said. She stopped at the kitchen to grab the biggest knife she could find.

Nate watched her, almost amused. "What are you going to do with that?" he asked.

"We don't know what's out there," Helen answered.

Nate shook his head. "Just be careful. Don't cut yourself in all your excitement," he said as he opened the door. He stood in the doorway, shining the beam of light around the yard while Helen perched behind him, watching. The yard was all clear. The concrete slab foundation was there, looking like the landing pad for some large spacecraft.

Or a door, she thought. *A giant door.*

"There's nothing," he said, turning to give her a *you really got me out of bed for this?* look.

"But there was," she said, pushing past him, heading down the trailer's rickety wooden steps. She kicked something, sent it rolling.

"Shine the light down here," she said, looking down at the steps.

The beam of light swung down.

There was something at the base of the steps. A small wrapped bundle of cloth.

"What the hell is this?" Helen asked. She reached out.

"Looks like a cat toy," Nate said,

Helen picked it up. "It's not a cat toy," she said. It was an old piece of white fabric, something with a touch of lace or embroidery at the edge. It had once been a dainty lady's handkerchief maybe, but now it was tattered and stained and was bundled up, the four corners pulled up and wound around with dirty string that had been tied in a neat little bow, like a present. There was something inside the bundle. Something hard.

Her stomach clenched.

"Why don't you bring it inside and we'll take a look?" Nate suggested.

"I'm not bringing it inside," Helen said. "No way is it coming into the house."

She held the bundle, fingers plucking at the string, thinking she just needed to give it a tug, unwrap it, see what was inside, but did she really want to know?

No. She did not. She did not want to see what was inside.

Whatever it was, it was awful. She knew that. She could feel it: danger flowing through her fingers like venom from a sting.

"You want me to open it?" Nate said.

"No," Helen told him. "I can do it."

The bundle, she believed, had been left for her. For her, because she was the one who'd heard the scream.

She took a deep breath, reminded herself that she was the new Helen. The Helen who was going to live in Vermont and build her own house, learn to kill her own chickens, wield an ax, grow her own food. Helen with the strength of the pioneers. The brave Helen. She could do this.

She tugged on the string, untied it, gently pulled back the folds to see what was inside as Nate shone the light on it.

"What the fuck?" Helen gasped, nearly dropping the bundle (not just dropping it, but throwing it to the ground, trying to get it as far away from her as possible).

But she held tight.

There was a bit of dried grass making a small nest, and in the center, two objects rested: a rusted old square nail and a yellowy-white tooth.

Nate leaned in, reached for the tooth. "A molar," he said. "From an ungulate."

"A what?" Helen said.

"A sheep or a deer, maybe."

"Well, what's it doing all wrapped up on our front steps?" Helen demanded.

Nate thought a minute, rubbed at the stubble on his chin, which made a faint scratching noise. "I don't know," he said, leaning back in and picking up the nail. "This is old. Looks like hand-forged iron."

"Again, I ask, 'What the hell is it doing on our front steps?'" Helen said.

"Maybe it was here all along," Nate suggested. "In the trailer. And we kicked it out."

Helen shook her head. "We cleaned. We swept. We would have noticed it."

"Maybe it's a gift," Nate said.

"A gift from whom? Who would leave us something like this?" Her voice rose in pitch, alarmed but not quite hysterical. She wondered how Nate could be so calm—as if someone had left a batch of welcome-to-the-neighborhood muffins on their front steps.

Nate rubbed his stubble again. *Scratch, scratch, scratch.* "Someone who's trying to freak us out?" He looked at her, saw the mounting panic on her face, and pulled her into a tight embrace.

"Well, they're doing a damn good job," Helen said, looking over his shoulder, scanning the tree line again, sure that someone (something) was out there, smiling a wicked little smile.

CHAPTER 4

O live

 **MAY 19, 2015**

Olive danced around the kitchen making breakfast. Daddy wasn't downstairs yet, but he needed to be out the door in half an hour, so she was sure he'd be popping in at any minute, looking for coffee. And wouldn't he be surprised when he saw the special breakfast she'd made?

A busy beaver, that's what Mama used to say when she saw Olive working hard at something. *Aren't you a busy beaver.*

Olive smiled. She was an *industrious* girl. That was a word from a vocabulary sheet a while ago, back when she did her homework regularly.

Industrious.

The old metal percolator was on the back of the stove, bubbling away. They used to have a Mr. Coffee coffeepot, but Mama liked the old-fashioned blue-and-white enameled percolator they used for camping better, so the electric one was put out at a yard sale. Mama loved yard sales—having them, stopping at them. Every spring, she cleaned the house, dragged a whole assortment of things out to the driveway, and set them up on rickety card tables: clothes, books, kitchen things, old toys, funny knickknacks. Stuff Olive was sure no one would want, but people always came and bought it. Then, over the summer, Mama would refill the house with treasures picked up from other people's yard sales. Sometimes Olive was sure her mother was buying back things she'd sold at her own sale; just this weird cycle of things coming and going from their house. Olive had a boomerang her dad had given her for her birthday. She came to believe that some objects were like that boomerang—they went out, then found their way right back where they started from. Some things didn't want to let go.

Using the percolator, hearing it bubble up like a living thing as it filled the kitchen with its warm coffee smell, reminded her of Mama.

Olive had taken to drinking coffee since Mama left; like her mother, she took it sweet with lots of milk. The first time she had it, she didn't put enough milk and sugar in, and the bitterness made her insides pucker. She had a big cup and her heart raced like a rocket engine. But she learned to pour in plenty of milk, and soon, she found her body craving the jolt the early-morning coffee gave her. She'd taken to it just like she'd taken to a lot of things: cooking, making sure the dishes got done, making sure Daddy was up and out the door to make it to work on time each morning. And the renovations. The endless ripping down of drywall, moving of walls. The way she and Daddy would change something all around, only to put it back just the way it had been a month later.

A Sisyphean task—that's what it was. She'd learned about that in school. English was the one class she was in with Mike, and he loved when they did the unit on Greek myths and knew all the stories already. She thought most of the stories were alarming and sad, especially the one about Sisyphus—that poor man rolling the boulder up the hill with a stick only to have it roll back down. That's what the renovations were like. *Futile*—that was the word Ms. Jenkins, Olive's freshman English teacher, used to describe it.

Olive poured some coffee into Mama's favorite mug: an oversized red mug that was really more like a bowl and had a chip on one side.

"When you go to a café in France, this is what all the people drink from," Mama said once.

"Have you been to France, Mama?" Olive asked.

"No," she said. "But that's the first thing we'll do when we find that treasure—go off and see the world! Sit down and have a café au lait in a French café!"

Olive checked the oven—she was baking cinnamon buns from a can. She'd bought them herself at the general store. Her father didn't go to the grocery store much these days. Riley used to bring sacks of groceries when she came over, but Daddy got mad and told her to quit doing that, that they weren't a goddamn charity case. Olive would ask him for a little cash here and there so she could pick up what they needed at Ferguson's General Store in town: coffee, milk, cereal, bread, canned soups. Nothing fancy. The cinnamon rolls, they were kind of an extravagance, but she was in a celebratory mood.

"Morning, Ollie," Daddy said, coming into the kitchen. "You had the news on at all?"

"No," she said.

He took in a breath, puffed out his cheeks as he let it go. "Terrible thing," he said in a low voice. "A bus crash out on Route 4 last night. Full of seniors from the high school coming back from a trip to Boston. A bunch hurt, three killed. Might be kids you know." He watched her, waiting to see how she'd respond.

Olive nodded. She didn't really know any seniors. Sure, she passed them in the halls, and sometimes they seemed to know her (or her story at least, and would whisper or giggle to each other as they walked by).

"Did the bus hit another car?"

"No, it went off the road. They're saying the driver swerved to avoid something in the road. An animal, maybe."

Olive nodded, wasn't sure what else to say.

Daddy looked around the kitchen, shuffled his feet.

"There's coffee ready," Olive said.

"Sure smells good in here." He smiled.

"I'm making cinnamon rolls," she said.

"Ya are, huh?" He reached for the pot of coffee on the stove, poured himself a cup. "What's the occasion?"

"Just thought we deserved a treat," she said.

He smiled at her, ruffled her hair. "You're right, kiddo. We do deserve a treat."

The timer went off and Olive took the rolls out of the oven, put them on top of the stove to cool.

"You got plans after school?" he asked.

Funny question. When did she ever have plans after school? She didn't play any sports, wasn't in the drama club or anything like that. She sometimes got invited to a classmate's house after school, but since her mom left, she always said no, made up some excuse for not going. Easier that way. Because once you went to someone's house a couple of times, they'd kind of expect to be invited to your house. And no way was she inviting any of the girls from school to her house. She didn't want people to know about the constant state of construction, to see the torn-open walls and ceiling, the exposed plumbing and wiring, the plywood subfloor, the plaster and drywall dust that covered everything. Proof that once her mama left, everything really did fall apart. Literally.

She even made excuses to keep Mike away. He used to come over all the time. Her mom loved Mike and got a real kick out of his encyclopedic knowledge of weird and random facts. He'd come over and tell her all about the life cycle of some parasite in Africa he'd been reading about, and Mama would ask all kinds of questions and tell him how clever he was for knowing so much while she fed him fresh-baked oatmeal cookies (his favorite). Olive's dad never knew what to make of Mike (a kid who neither hunted nor cared about sports)—they were weird and awkward around each other, and Olive thought it was best if she just avoided the whole scene. Also, she didn't want Mike to see how bad the house really was. He'd freak and tell his mom, who might call the Department for Children and Families or something.

But she and Mike hung out at school and in the woods. And the truth was Mike was about the only real friend Olive had these days, and Olive was Mike's one friend.

"Odd Oliver," that's what everyone at school called her—even the older kids she didn't know. The kids in her class had been call- ing her Odd Oliver since fifth grade, and she'd thought she'd lose the name when they all moved on to high school, but it carried over, got worse even. High school was so big and strange—a world where the normal rules didn't seem to apply. When she walked the halls, she was reminded of another story she'd learned about in English: the laby- rinth that held the Minotaur. Only in her version, there were Mino- taurs everywhere, around every corner, and they wore letter jackets, or cheap perfume and pounds of makeup. The high school served three towns, so there were a lot of kids Olive had never seen before, and originally, she'd looked forward to this, thought it would help her to blend in, to hide, but really it just made her stick out more. News of her nickname and what had happened with her mother spread fast during the first weeks of school.

"What ya huntin' for, Odd Oliver?" kids would tease when she came to school in her camouflage jacket and pants. *Screw them,* she thought. Sometimes she'd even mumble a quick "Fuck off," but then they'd coo and chortle and say, "You're such a freakazoid! No wonder your mom left you." That was the worst—when they brought her mother into it. Sometimes she'd get to her locker and find stuff there, stuff she hadn't put in: lip gloss, eye shadow, little notes that said, "Are you a boy or a girl?" Sometimes the notes were crueler. "Your mother's a whore. She opened her legs for half the men in this town."

Mike told her not to pay any attention to it.

"You know, I've got this game I play sometimes," he told her once, when she'd found an especially crude note taped to her locker. He pretended he hadn't seen what it said, just took it down and crumpled it up. "I come to school and pretend that I'm not one of them. That I'm this alien, from way off in some other galaxy. I've just been sent here to observe."

Olive nodded.

"But see, the creatures from my home planet are coming back soon to pick me up, and after, they're gonna destroy the Earth. One big fireball," he said, making an exploding noise and waggling his fingers. "Poof!"

Olive smiled but cringed a little. She didn't want to think of everyone all burned up like that, not even the girls who'd left the cruel notes.

"But the thing is, I get to pick people to come back with me. Everyone else will be disintegrated." His eyes glittered. "The only one I've picked so far is you," he told Olive, and gave her a big goofy smile.

"Umm . . . thanks, I guess," she'd said. The second bell rang, and they ran to class, already late.

. . .

"I thought maybe we could start in on your room," Daddy said now.

Olive blinked at him. "Huh?" she said, thinking she'd misheard him because she'd been daydreaming about Mike and the aliens.

"Your room," he repeated. "I thought we could get started with it. No need to keep putting it off, right?"

Her stomach knotted. Not her room. That was her one safe space. He had suggested making it bigger a couple of weeks ago, when Riley was over for dinner. She said her room was fine, she was happy with it the way it was.

"Don't you want it bigger? Better? A higher ceiling? A bigger closet?"

"For god's sake, Dustin," Riley said. "She said she was happy with it the way it is. Can't you just leave one room alone?"

Her dad had backed down. But after Riley left, he kept talking about all the changes they'd make someday to Olive's room, though he hadn't gone as far as suggesting they actually start work. The walls and ceiling of her bedroom remained intact. And it was clean. Dust free. It was the one place of order in the whole house. The one place that had been left exactly the same as it was the day Mama went away.

"Don't you think we should finish up in the living room first? Put the rest of the drywall up? Paint, maybe?" She tried not to show how frantic she felt. How desperate.

Not my room. Anything but that.

Her dad looked disappointed. "I just want you to have a nice room. We can make it bigger, go into the spare room a little ways. You can have a walk-in closet. You know? Like we've been talking about?"

It was Daddy who'd been doing all the talking, all the daydreaming, promising how nice, how perfect, things would be if they knocked out a wall here, put up some shelves there. As if true happiness could be brought about with a sledgehammer and new drywall.

"My closet's fine the way it is," she told him. She didn't have much clothing. Not like some of the girls in her class who seemed to have a different outfit for every day of the month. Olive was fine with her two pairs of jeans (patched in places), camo hunting pants with tons of pockets, a few T-shirts, a hoodie, and her camo jacket. She owned two pairs of shoes: hunting boots and sneakers.

"I thought—" he said, looking lost, profoundly disappointed.

"I really think we should concentrate on finishing some of the projects we've started," she said, realizing how funny it was, her talking like she was the adult and he was the little kid with his crazy, impractical ideas. "Let's work on the living room today after school, okay? That'll be the first room Mama sees when she walks through the door. Don't we want it to be perfect?"

More than looking disappointed, he looked tired. Old. He'd lost weight since Mama left. His skin looked sallow; there were dark circles under his eyes. His sandy-colored hair was a little too long. She needed to take better care of him, to make sure he ate more and to encourage him to go to bed earlier instead of falling asleep each night on the ratty old couch in front of the television in the living room.

For half a second, she thought about changing her mind, giving in, telling him sure, they could start in on her room just to make him happy, to see him smile.

She bit her lip, waited.

"Sure," he said at last. "We can finish the living room first. What color do you think we should paint it?"

Olive smiled, let herself breathe. She thought about it while she spread thick white frosting on the cinnamon rolls.

"Blue," she said. "Like the sky. Like the color of Mama's favorite dress. You know the one I mean?"

Daddy frowned hard, his brow wrinkling all old-man-like, as if the memory of Mama in her dress was just too much for him. He seemed to get visibly smaller, shrinking before her eyes. "I know the one you mean," he said, voice low and crackling. He looked down into the coffee mug, then took a sip even though it was steaming hot. "I'll pick up some paint samples on my way home and let you decide which one's closest."

"Sounds good," Olive said. She put a cinnamon roll on a plate and handed it to Daddy.

"Thanks," he said, taking a big bite as he headed back out of the kitchen to get ready for work. "Mmm! You're getting to be quite the cook."

She thought of saying, *They're from a tube, Dad. A trained monkey could make them.* But instead, she called out, "Thank you," and took a sip from her own giant mug of coffee.

. . .

She heard the shower go on, the plumbing making a not-so-comforting thumping sound. She was sure they'd put some of the pipes back together wrong when they redid the bathroom. Sometimes the thumping of the pipes turned into a low whine, sounding like there was a monster trapped behind the walls, screaming to get out. She had no doubt that they'd need to take the wall down again and replace the plumbing. Then maybe Daddy would decide that the shower should be moved to another wall and they'd do everything all over again.

Twenty minutes later, she was wrapping up the rest of the rolls when Daddy came in, smelling like mentholated shaving cream and Irish Spring soap. He filled up his travel mug. Olive handed him the sack lunch she'd packed for him: a ham sandwich, an apple, and two cinnamon rolls.

"I'm off," he said, grabbing the keys to his truck. "You want a ride? I've gotta be over on County Road this morning—they're redoing the culvert—but I can drop you off on the way."

County Road was on the other side of town from the high school. It wasn't on the way at all. She smiled at his kind offer. "No thanks, I'll take the bus."

"Better skedaddle if you don't want to miss it," he warned.

"On my way in five minutes," she said.

"Good girl," he called as he went out the front door, not looking back. She heard his old Chevy start up, cranking slowly like it wasn't sure it wanted to go anywhere, but then it caught and roared to life.

She sat back down, got out another cinnamon bun. She wasn't going to catch the bus. Odd Oliver wasn't going to school at all today.

She had other plans.

CHAPTER 5

Helen

 **MAY 19, 2015**

Nate had his laptop open and played her the terrible sounds again and again. A red fox screaming. A fisher. Both noises cruel, pained, and hideous sounding. She flinched each time he pushed the play button. He cocked his head, listened harder, like he was trying to learn their language.

"Is either of those what you heard?"

"I don't know. I don't know what I heard," she said, taking a long sip of wine. "Now would you please stop playing them over and over?"

She was tired and sore and wanted a hot bath. But they had only a tiny shower, barely large enough to turn around in, with a stained plastic enclosure and a handheld shower wand with water pressure so bad, Nate called it the spit bath. That would have to do.

"People call them fisher cats, but they're not cats at all," he explained. "They're actually a member of the weasel family."

He pushed play once more and the kitchen was filled with that horrible screeching.

"Please, Nate," she begged. "Just turn the fucking thing off."

They'd spent the morning stacking the lumber they'd had delivered under a nylon canopy, then set up a second canopy as a work area and place to store tools. The guy who delivered the lumber told them there had been a terrible accident down near the center of town last night—a school bus carrying high school kids went off the road. Three dead, twenty injured. The road was still down to one lane while the police worked the scene.

"My cousin was on that bus," the lumberyard man told them. "She's okay, but her and the others, they say the driver swerved to avoid a woman in the road."

"My god," Nate said. "Was the woman hit?"

"No sign of the woman when the fire department got there. Just the wrecked bus and a bunch of hysterical, hurt kids." The lumberman looked out at the trees, eyes on the path that led down to the bog.

"Terrible," Helen said.

"Maybe that's what you heard last night?" Nate asked. "Screeching tires? Sirens?"

She shook her head. She was familiar with those sounds; with the highway not far from their condo, she'd heard them plenty back in Connecticut.

"I doubt you would have heard anything way up here," the lumber guy said.

"Sound travels in funny ways," said Nate, more to himself than the lumberyard man, as if he was trying to convince himself that the accident might well have been what Helen had heard.

Once the lumber was stacked, she and Nate started framing one of the walls.

The work had gone well at first. They got out all their shiny new tools and had taken turns doing the measuring and cutting. They quickly found their groove, moving together, making great progress. It felt good to be doing carpentry work again; it made her think of all the time she'd spent working with her father, of how satisfied she always felt at the end of the day. And there was something meditative about working with tools: you had to clear your mind of everything else and focus on what you were doing. She felt calm. Peaceful.

Until things started to go wrong.

She started thinking about the scream she'd heard, about the bundle with the tooth and nail. It ruined her focus.

Nails bent. Boards jumped. Things didn't line up in real life the way they did on paper. Helen was put on edge by the chop saw, which they were using to cut the framing lumber to length. Each time she brought the blade down and watched it bite into the wood, she was reminded of last night's scream.

They had argued when Helen had cut something too short. "I thought you said ninety-two and five-eighths," she said.

"I did," Nate told her, checking the plans again. "That's the length of all the vertical studs."

"Well, that's where I marked and cut." She'd used the tape measure and made a careful line with the metal square and the chunky carpenter's pencil. "Just like all the others I just did."

"Maybe you read the tape measure wrong," he suggested.

"You think I don't know how to read a tape measure?" she'd snapped.

"No, babe, I'm just—"

"Cut the next one yourself," she'd said. She hadn't meant to. This was so un-Helen. She was on edge. Prickly. It was the lack of sleep. The memory of the hideous scream. The tooth and nail, which Nate had taken to calling "our strange gift."

"Hey," Nate said, coming up and rubbing her shoulders. "What do you say we call it quits for today. We can go for a little walk. Then I'll go into town and pick us up a pizza and a bottle of wine. Sound good?"

She'd agreed, apologized for being such a shit, and they'd put away the tools and walked down to the bog. It was a five-minute walk, downhill through the woods. The air was sweet and clean, and the path was layered with a thick carpet of pine needles. It really was beautiful. Along the way Helen spotted delicate, balloon-like oval pink flowers.

"What are those?"

"Lady's slippers," Nate said. "They're a member of the orchid family. But I've gotta say, it's not the foot of a lady I think of when I look at it."

Helen smiled, leaned down to study one. It was a delicate flower, almost embarrassingly sexual.

"So, I've been doing some research, and it turns out Breckenridge Bog isn't a true bog," Nate told her. "It's a fen: a boggy wetland fed by underground springs."

"A fen," Helen echoed.

"Yeah, most bogs are just fed by runoff. They have very little oxygen. A fen, on the other hand, has streams and groundwater that give it more oxygen, richer nutrients in the soil and water."

They got to the bog, which was circled with pine, cedar, and larch trees. There were a few small cedars growing up in the bog itself. The ground was a thick carpet of spongy moss floating on water. There were sedges, low bushes, thick grass that cut their legs as they walked. Their feet were sucked down. It was like walking on a giant sponge.

Everything about this place was wonderful and new, full of magic. "It's like another planet here," Helen said, leaning into Nate, who hugged her from behind.

He showed her the pitcher plants with red heart-like flowers and leaves at the bottom shaped like little pitchers.

"They're carnivorous," he said. "Bugs are drawn into the pitcher and they drown in the water there, then the plant digests them."

"Why don't they just crawl out?"

"They're trapped. The sides are sticky and have little teeth. Once they're in, there's no easy way out."

Helen shivered.

At the heart of the bog was a deep pool of dark water. Water lilies floated on the surface. Dragonflies soared over the top.

"I wonder how deep it is," Helen mused.

"Could be pretty deep. It's spring fed—feel how cold the water is here."

They got to the other side of the bog and found piles of large round fieldstone on the solid ground at the edge.

"An old wall, maybe," Nate suggested.

Helen walked around, looking. "No. Look, there are four sides." She stepped back, getting a better view. "It's an old foundation. There was a building out here once, Nate! Maybe a small house!" She walked back up to the foundation, got a little thrill as she stood there, right on the place where she imagined a front door had once opened.

"Funny place for a house, so close to the bog," Nate said, brow furrowing in that way it did when something confused him, didn't make sense to his rational mind.

Helen leaned down, picked up a rock, wondered who had stacked it, how long ago, and what had happened to them. The rock seemed almost alive to her, thrumming with history, with possibility. She wondered what else she might find if she did a little digging around the site—glass, pottery, bits of metal—signs of the people who'd once lived there.

"I bet there are old records, something that would tell us who lived here and when," she said, getting excited. Maybe this had something to do with the ghost the realtor had mentioned that first day. Seeing proof of an actual building renewed her resolve to start looking into the history of the land—history that she was now directly linked to as the current owner and steward. "I'll stop in at the town clerk's office and library this week and see what I can find out."

Nate mumbled, "Sounds good, hon." He was squatting down by a clump of pitcher plants, staring down the throat of one of them.

Helen set the rock back down gently, caught a hint of movement to the side, and turned her head.

"Do you see that?" she asked.

"What?" He looked up.

She pointed to the edge of the other side of the bog. "That huge bird."

Nate followed her finger, spotted the wading bird, and smiled. "Oh man! That's a great blue heron!"

It was a tall bird with a long neck and stork-like legs, and it wasn't blue at all but a lovely gray.

The bird turned and stared, eyes glowing yellow.

Intruders, the eyes seemed to say. *What are you doing here?*

"She's watching us," Helen said.

"How do you know it's a female?" Nate asked.

"I just do," Helen said.

Nate pulled out his phone, started taking pictures of it. "I so wish I had my camera!" he said. "When we get back, I'll look it up. Most birds have different coloration between the males and females."

The bird grew tired of watching, or of being watched, and took off, its enormous wings flapping, long legs tucked tight under its body, head and neck pulled back into an S shape.

They turned to go, and Helen's eye caught on something near the ground.

"What's that?" Nate asked, when she bent over to investigate.

"A little piece of red string," she said. It was tied around the base of a small bush.

"Maybe it just blew in there and got stuck," Nate suggested.

"No," Helen said. It was tied in a neat bow. "Someone put it here." Helen untied the string—bright red and made of nylon, she guessed—and slipped it into her pocket. As they walked back along the path, she found several more pieces of string, all tied around trees, saplings, and bushes, the loose ends hanging, waving in the breeze like little caution flags.

"Maybe the land was surveyed," Nate said.

"Maybe," Helen said, knowing this wasn't it. The red strings were too haphazard for that. And what surveyors used string and not plastic tape? Now that she was looking for them, she saw them everywhere—some weathered and frayed, and some looking bright and fresh.

When they got back, the first thing Nate did was pull out his field guide to eastern birds. "Turns out it's almost impossible to tell a male from a female," he said. He had his new nature journal open and was doing a quick sketch of the bird, recording details of the sighting. Helen had given him the Moleskine notebook as a gift when they were packing up for Vermont. "I thought it could be a sort of field journal. To keep track of your wildlife encounters at the new house." Nate loved it. And now the great blue heron was the first official entry.

He started reading her heron facts from the field guide: habitat, mating, and gestation. "Though they hunt alone, they nest in colonies," he was saying. He stopped and jotted a few of these facts down in his journal. "A female will lay two to seven eggs."

Helen was only half listening. Her eyes were on the opened bundle Nate had set on the kitchen table: the little nest that held the tooth and nail. She hadn't wanted to bring it into the house. She thought the best thing to do would be to take it out and bury it deep in the woods. Throw it into the bog, maybe. Then she had the irrational idea that it would act like a seed; that if she attempted to bury it or toss it into the bog, it would sprout, grow, turn into something powerful, something with more form, something *alive*.

"Did you know that despite their size, herons only weigh about five pounds?" Nate asked, not looking up from his field guide. "Unbelievable, right? It's the hollow bones. All birds have hollow bones."

Helen took in a breath. Her head ached. Her own bones felt solid and stiff as concrete, heavy and sore.

"Weren't you going to go get us wine and pizza?"

"Yeah, yeah, of course," he said, closing the book. He ran into the bedroom to get changed and grab his wallet.

"Hon?" he called as he walked back down the hallway. "Did you take any cash out of here?"

"No."

He shook his head. "That's weird. There's about forty bucks less than I thought I had."

"You used a bunch of cash yesterday," she reminded him. "At breakfast, then later at the store. Oh, you went out and got beer, remember?"

"Right," he said. "Maybe I spent more than I thought. Or maybe that kid at the store didn't give me the right change." He counted the money one more time, stared at it with a puzzled expression, then announced he was off. "Be back soon," he promised.

.   .   .

By the time Nate returned with pizza and two bottles of wine, Helen had taken the world's most unsatisfying lukewarm shower and changed into sweats and one of Nate's T-shirts.

"This one's from a vineyard in Vermont," he'd said proudly, holding up the bottle of Marquette.

This was to be part of their new life: buying local. Eating and drinking local.

But the truth was, at that point she didn't care if the goddamn wine was made from skunk cabbage from the bog: she just wanted a drink.

Nate had also bought a local paper. The story of the crash was on the front page. Helen saw the smiling school photos of the dead teenagers and flipped it over, unable to look. It was too terrible. She was trying hard not to take it as an ominous sign of their new lives here.

She took a deep breath, looked away from the newspaper.

We are meant to be here, she told herself. *We are living the life of our dreams.*

"There's going to be a vigil tonight at the high school," Nate said. "Maybe we should go."

Helen shook her head. "No. I can't bear it. And it would be weird. We just got here. We're not really part of the community yet. I'd feel . . . voyeuristic or something, you know?"

Nate nodded. "I see what you mean."

After they finished the pizza (which was crappy, with too-sweet sauce and canned mushrooms, but still satisfying) and polished off the first bottle of wine, Nate got out his laptop and started playing the animal noises.

Finally, mercifully, he stopped, put the computer away.

Helen was trying hard not to be annoyed with him, making herself think of all his good points, reminding herself of how much she loved him. She was just stressed. There was no need to take it out on poor Nate.

She thought back to when they met, both new teachers at Palmer Academy. It was at a faculty mixer the first week of school. Nate had worn a tie with the periodic table on it. There was another woman there, Stella Flemming, the English teacher, who kept cornering Nate, saying she wanted to put him and his tie in one of her poems. The first time Helen noticed him, she wondered why the handsome science teacher with the funny tie was looking at her so strangely. Later, she smiled, realizing that he'd been giving Helen pleading *save me* looks all night. At last, she walked over, touched his arm, and said, "You're the science teacher, right?" He nodded encouragingly. "I was hoping you could help me. I hear the Pleiades are visible in the sky this time of year, but I'm not sure just where to look."

He smiled. "Ah, yes, the Seven Sisters. I'd be happy to point them out. Excuse us please, Stella."

"Thank you," Nate whispered, once they were out of earshot.

They walked out to the back lawn near the tennis courts and he showed her the stars. "Right there," he said, taking her hand and pointing with it. "The Pleiades were the daughters of Atlas and the sea nymph Pleione," he explained. "Zeus transformed them into doves, then into stars."

"Lovely," she said.

"Your dress reminds me of starlight," he told her then. She looked down, saw the way the pale fabric seemed to shimmer in the lights around the tennis court.

"Do you think Stella will come out looking for you?" Helen asked.

Nate laughed. "Poor Stella. Maybe. She's had a bit too much wine, I think."

"I heard her saying she wanted to put you in a poem," Helen said.

Nate laughed again. "Like I said, too much wine."

"So you're not a fan of poetry?"

"Oh, I'm a big fan. In fact, I even write a bit from time to time."

Now Helen laughed. "Really?"

He nodded, and in a half imitation of poor Stella, he said to Helen, "Be careful, I might just put you and your glimmering starlight dress in a poem."

She laughed again, but the next day, she'd found a typed poem in her faculty mailbox: "Helen Talks History in a Dress of Stars." It wasn't half bad (not that Helen was qualified to judge poetry). She had it still and would tell people, years later, that it was the poem that won her over immediately, the poem that made her realize Nate was *The One.*

"We got a lot done today," he said now.

"Mm-hmm."

"We should let the concrete cure a few days, but I'm thinking we can get the first-floor walls framed and ready to go up while we wait. Start cutting the pieces for the floor, too."

"I'd like to get the garden laid out," Helen said. "Then we can get some plant starts at the farmers' market on Saturday."

"Yeah, sure. Absolutely," Nate said. Their plan was to just do a small kitchen garden this year: some greens, tomatoes, cukes, a few herbs. Next year, when they weren't busy with building, they'd expand to a proper garden, put in berry bushes, a few fruit trees. They'd laid it all out on paper: their grand plan with year-by-year goals.

"And I really want to get into town and do a little research. See what I can find out about the history of our new land."

"Sounds good," he said.

Nate cleared the dirty plates, pizza box, and empty wine bottle off the table, pulled out the house plans they'd carefully designed, and laid them out.

It was strange to see them here now, to realize that they'd actually begun to take shape—this house they'd planned, constructed on paper and in their heads and conversations.

The saltbox was a simple design. Helen loved the name *saltbox* and the history of the design. It had been popular in colonial New England and named for the lidded box people had kept salt in. Classic lines, a chimney at the center, the rear of the house a single story, the front a full two stories.

Helen thought back to the actual saltbox they'd looked at in New Hampshire at the beginning of their search; that house had sparked something deep inside her, had made her feel instantly at home. It was right in the village, down the street from a charming town green and a Congregational church. She found herself playing the what-if game—What if they were there instead of here? What if she'd found a way to convince Nate to buy that house, to not move to this land on the bog in the middle of nowhere?

Helen squinted down at the plans Nate had worked so hard on for months: the open kitchen and living room, a large pantry beside the kitchen, a woodstove in the center of the house, a half bath downstairs that shared a wall with the mechanical room, where the furnace and water heater would live, along with an eco-friendly low-energy washer and dryer. Upstairs would be the bedroom, the bathroom, and a library with floor-to-ceiling shelves. Later, as time and finances allowed, they'd add a screened-in back porch. "I took everything you loved about that New Hampshire saltbox and just made it even better," Nate had told her with a proud smile when he brought her his first sketched design.

What she'd loved most was the history of that first house: the smell of the old wood, the creak of cupboard doors and floorboards, the warbly imperfections in the old single-pane windows.

But she looked down now at what Nate had labeled DREAM HOUSE in neat block handwriting, at the carefully rendered plans done to scale: elevation drawings; close-ups of each wall, the roof, and the stairs; detailed illustrations showing how they would frame the floors and ceilings. There were materials lists calculating how many board feet of lumber they needed, how much insulation, how many bundles of shingles. Everything looked so tidy, so perfect on paper: his plan for her happiness laid out in neat columns.

And back in Connecticut, Nate managed to convince Helen that they could do this. He'd read books, watched videos, attended courses. "And you grew up building," he'd reminded her. "It's in your genes."

But none of that had prepared Helen for how unnerved she'd feel at the familiar screech of the powerful saw. Or the way Nate had looked at her when she'd mismeasured. Like she was a goddamned idiot.

"It'll get easier," Nate said now, putting his hand over hers and giving it a squeeze. "I'm not saying it'll be without its challenges, but we've just got to follow the plans. Stick together. We can do this."

Follow the plans, she thought.

She smiled, took another gulp of wine.

She thought of all the times she and her father had dealt with jobs that didn't go as planned: weather delays, bad batches of lumber, late deliveries, angles that didn't work no matter how perfect they'd looked on paper. She worried that Nate seemed to live in a world where unpredictable things didn't happen.

Her eyes moved to the little bundle with the tooth and nail, resting on the kitchen counter beside the sink now, next to the dirty dishes.

Nate rolled up the plans for their dream house.

"Tomorrow will be a better day," she said.

Say it and make it true.

CHAPTER 6

Olive

 **MAY 19, 2015**

Daddy's truck was in the driveway. He was home an hour early.

Had the school gotten in touch with him? Told him Olive hadn't shown up yet again? Had he come home to look for her?

Olive felt panic seeping in, a little dribble at first, then a steady stream as she got closer to the house.

She'd spent the day searching around with her metal detector on the northwest side of the bog. The metal detector was on the fritz—sometimes beeping when there was nothing at all beneath it, sometimes just dying altogether. It was crap, but she'd picked it up for thirty bucks at a church rummage sale last fall, so what did she expect? She was saving her money for a much better one, a hundred times more sensitive and powerful. It even came with headphones. Olive was sure that if she had this, she'd find the treasure in no time. She'd been saving her allowance, doing any odd jobs she could find. She'd even skipped eating school lunch and pocketed the four bucks Daddy gave her each day. And Mike had offered to buy the old crappy one from her for the same price she'd paid for it, which seemed unfair, but he insisted, saying he knew it would be good luck for him because it had been hers and look at all the cool stuff she'd found with it.

During today's search, from time to time, she'd take a break and go up the hill on a little path to check on Helen and Nate (she knew their names now from hearing them talking, from watching them, but more than knowing their names, she felt she knew them). She'd been watching them from behind the moss-covered root system of a tree that had fallen over—it made the perfect cover. They were trying to frame one of the walls, but things hadn't ended well—they'd started fighting as soon as things got hard. Olive almost felt sorry for them. Then they'd quit early (after getting into a fight when Helen cut a board too short) and gone down to the bog, which meant Olive's searching was over for the day. It was time to call it quits anyway, because she wanted to get home before Daddy, get dinner started, and make it look like she'd gone to school and was doing her homework like the good girl he thought she was.

But seeing Daddy's truck in the driveway wrecked all that.

She ditched the metal detector in the toolshed and scrambled to come up with a story to explain why she hadn't been in school. Saying she'd missed the bus seemed pretty lame. She could tell him she was too upset and freaked-out about the accident, about the dead kids just a little older than her, to get on the bus, go to school. That would work. It would have to. It was the best she had for now.

"Hello?" she called from the kitchen around the growing lump in her throat. She went into the living room to see if he'd started work in there like they'd planned. But she heard telltale banging from upstairs. Was he working in the hallway, which was still bare stud walls, exposed wiring?

"Daddy?" she called.

"Up here," he yelled back.

She jumped the stairs two at time, and then her chest got tight when she saw he wasn't in the hallway and that the door to her bedroom was open. This room was her haven—beautiful and pristine, with a neatly made bed and all of her treasures lined up on shelves: stuff she'd found with her metal detector (old buttons, nails, musket balls), the pelt from a fox she'd shot and skinned herself, and her favorite photo of Mama, taken a few weeks before she left. Mama was outside at the picnic table holding a plastic tumbler, grinning into the camera. She had on her lucky necklace, the one she never took off those last weeks before she left—a pattern of a circle, triangle, and square nested inside each other with another circle with an eye at the center. Mama called it her *I see all* necklace. Olive had taken the picture. It was a warm early-summer night and Daddy was cooking chicken on the grill. The radio was tuned to a classic rock station, and Mom and Dad were drinking rum and Cokes from big plastic tumblers. Olive had been happy because Mama had been home and in a good mood, and she and Daddy had been getting along so well, kissing and calling each other "honey" and "baby" and all those other terms of endearment that used to make Olive roll her eyes and make pretend gagging noises, when secretly she thought it so sweet that they were still so in love. That night, when she saw Mama take Daddy's hand after he came back from the grill with a plateful of seared chicken legs, Olive really believed they were still in love and that everything was going to be okay.

Olive walked slowly down the hall, like the way you walk in a creepy haunted house at Halloween when you don't really want to see what's going to happen next.

But it was no use. She could shut her eyes and pretend it wasn't happening, but she knew she had to look eventually. And she knew just what she'd see.

Olive walked into the bedroom to see that the shelves had been taken off the wall, the photo and all of her other things haphazardly shoved into cardboard beer boxes. Her bed had been pushed into the middle of the room and the boxes were piled on top of it. It reminded Olive of a life raft in the center of a turbulent ocean.

Daddy was standing in the back corner of her room, holding a sledgehammer, and he smiled at her. Half of the back wall was already down. He still had on his blue work pants and boots but had taken off his work shirt and was in a white T-shirt that was damp with sweat, stained yellow around the collar and under the arms, so worn it was practically see-through. She could see his wiry chest hair curled underneath it.

She hated him just then. Hated that he was a man who could do something like this. Who could betray her in such a huge, devastating way.

"Hey, Ollie Girl," he said, smiling at her in an *isn't this a nice surprise* sort of way.

All the spit in her mouth dried up. She felt like Daddy had hit her with the sledge, torn her right open and exposed her insides.

"Grab a pry bar and give me a hand," he said.

She worked to steady her breathing. To not freak out and start screaming or, worse, lose it completely and start bawling like a little kid. The room seemed to tilt and glow, everything growing brighter. She thought of that stupid old expression about being so mad you saw red and understood it now. Understood that fury brought its own fire with it, tinting the world around you.

"But you said we would finish the living room first." She choked the words out, eyes getting blurry with tears she was trying so hard to keep back. "I told you I didn't want my room changed! I'm happy with it the way it is."

He blinked at her from behind his scratched plastic safety goggles, his blue eyes bloodshot, with dark bags under them. He looked like a man who hadn't slept in a week, a haunted man.

"I thought it would be a nice surprise. I thought you wanted a nicer room."

"But I didn't—"

"Is it so wrong?" Daddy asked. "For me to want my best girl to have the best room?"

She didn't answer. Didn't speak. She was afraid if she opened her mouth, she would either yell or start to full-on cry. Why hadn't he listened to her? Why did he never, ever listen to her?

Was this why Mama had left?

Had he not listened to Mama, either? Just ignored everything she said, everything she asked for?

She rubbed at her eyes, clenched her jaw. Stared at the sledgehammer in her father's hand, willing him to drop it. Concentrating with all her might. She wanted him to drop it and for it to fall on his toes, crush them, break them maybe. She wanted him to feel pain, to be shocked by it.

Then, as she watched, the heavy hammer slipped out of Daddy's grasp, dropping to the floor with a thud, just missing the toe of his right work boot. He paid no attention.

Olive blinked down at it, not quite believing.

She held her breath.

Had she done this? Did she have that kind of power? Something awakened, brought to the surface by rage?

No way, Odd Oliver, she told herself.

It was coincidence, that's all. People couldn't control the world around them like that.

Least of all her.

"I was thinking we could put built-in shelves along this wall," Daddy said, gesturing. "Floor to ceiling. With maybe a built-in desk right in the center. A place for you to do your homework. To set up a computer."

"But I don't even have a computer." Her anger now came out as a whine. She hated whining.

"We'll get you one. To go with your brand-new room."

He smiled big and wide, and she thought, *So this is how it's going to be*. A bribe. A trap, really. But it didn't matter. It was no use fighting. What's done was done. Daddy had made up his mind. He had already taken a sledgehammer to things, torn down the wall behind where her bed used to be. The air was full of dust, the carpet covered in the rubble that was once her wall. She hated the way the walls looked without drywall—the studs, plumbing, wiring, and junction boxes exposed. It was like catching a grown-up getting undressed. It embarrassed her. Made her wish she hadn't seen.

Houses held secrets.

Her father seemed determined to expose all of their house's secrets, to strip it down and tear it wide open for all the world to see. Even in her very own room.

"You could use a computer for your schoolwork," Daddy said, giving her a sly smile. "Think how much easier your homework would be. You're still getting homework, aren't you?"

She nodded, looked down at the dusty carpet while he held her in his gaze.

She was sure, absolutely positive, then that he knew. He knew she hadn't been to school that day, that she'd been skipping regularly. He knew, but he wasn't going to say anything, wasn't going to confront her or punish her.

The world felt off-kilter, torn open.

He held out the pry bar for her, and she understood that her helping him with this, tearing down the walls of her bedroom, endlessly renovating the house, would make skipping school okay.

It was an unspoken deal.

And she knew she had no choice. Not really.

It would be different if Mama were here. But then again, if Mama hadn't gone away, none of this would have happened. She wouldn't have made a habit of skipping school; high school wouldn't have turned into the disaster that it was. The house would still be intact. Mama would never have put up with the torn-down walls, the plaster dust that covered every surface like fine snow.

Her insides twisted as she reached for the pry bar, her fingers gripping, squeezing tight, like she was trying to choke it, but the metal was cold, unyielding.

She was sure that she couldn't have made that sledgehammer drop. She was just a girl. A powerless, school-skipping, odd girl whose mother had run off and whose father was making hope where he could find it.

She was a terrible, cruel girl for wishing him harm. It was like spanking a little baby for crying because it was hungry.

He smiled at her now, his whole face lighting up. "Won't your mama be surprised," he said, "when she comes back home and finds things fixed up so nice. A brand-new house. That's what it will seem like. Won't she be happy then?"

FRAMING

CHAPTER 7

Helen

They were just finishing framing the downstairs when the sky opened up.

The house had truly begun to take shape. The subfloor was in and the four outer walls were up and braced; the interior walls framing the pantry and mechanical room were done. They were attaching the final bathroom wall when thunder shook the house; lightning struck so close Helen could feel the electricity in the air, smell the ozone. She'd never seen such a powerful storm. Was it because they were higher up in the mountains here, closer to the sky?

She stood in the center of their newly framed downstairs, surrounded by the two-by-four framed walls—the skeleton of the house—watching the storm, *feeling* the storm.

Nate was stressed because they were behind schedule. The plan was to be finished framing the entire house, including the roof, in six weeks, and it didn't look like they'd make it. Helen wasn't worried. She'd worked with her father enough to know that it was normal to be a little off schedule and over budget. They'd get it done. And they were moving a little faster each day as their skills and confidence improved.

"It's not safe out here!" Nate yelled over the downpour and rumbles of thunder. Off in the distance, they heard sirens. They got their tools under cover and sprinted down to the trailer, laughing at how soaked they got. They changed into dry clothes and Helen made a fresh pot of coffee. The thunder and lightning let up, but the rain continued. They sipped coffee and watched the rain fall, feeling cozy and content as they listened to the lovely sound it made on the old tin roof of the trailer.

"What should we do with ourselves?" Helen asked, looking at the stack of papers on Nate's makeshift card-table desk in the living room—the house plans, the building timeline, the endless to-do lists and schedules. Surely there was some rainy-day project for them to tackle.

"I say we take the rest of the day off," Nate announced, and Helen was thrilled.

"Uh-oh," Nate said, noticing a place where the roof leaked— water dripping through the thin, stained boards that made up the ceiling. He grabbed a bowl and put it beneath. Just then, Helen noticed another drip splatter onto the peeling linoleum floor. She got a saucepan. Soon, the two of them were doing a strange dance, hurrying to put vessels beneath quickly multiplying leaks.

"Better hurry up and get the second floor and roof done," Nate said. "I don't know how much longer this place is going to last."

Helen smiled in agreement. She couldn't wait to be out of their tiny sardine can of a trailer.

Nate settled in on the couch with a book on bird behavior. He turned on the lamp on the side table and the kitchen light flickered. Helen opened her laptop and checked her email to find a note from her friend Jenny, saying only: *How are things going in the Great North Woods? You ready to come back home yet? I've got martinis waiting . . .*

Helen looked around at the containers catching drips in the leaking trailer and tried to formulate a witty reply, but her attempts just sounded pathetic. She'd write Jenny back later.

The rain pounded the tin roof, adding to the percussive music of the steady drips into the pans, bowls, and cups scattered around the trailer.

Helen decided to don her rain gear and go into town. It had been three weeks since they'd arrived in Hartsboro, and she had been busy with building and starting the garden, and honestly, it felt a little selfish to take time off for research when there was so much work to do each day. And by the time work ended each day, she was too sore and exhausted to do much more than settle in with a glass of wine and early bed.

"I'm going to take advantage of the rainy weather to go check out the town hall and library and see what I can dig up on our property and local history," she announced. "Want to come?"

Nate shook his head, eyes focused on his bird book. "I think I'll stay in and catch up on some reading," he said, clearly pleased to have the afternoon to himself to read. "Have fun," he added when she paused to kiss the top of his head on the way out.

Helen stopped into Ferguson's General Store to pick up a loaf of bread. It sold everything from hunting rifles to fresh pies with labels that had clearly been made on someone's inkjet printer (Nate called them "grandma pies"—bumbleberry was his favorite). There was a teenage boy with a crew cut and a blaze-orange camo T-shirt working the register. A police scanner was squawking from a shelf behind him: chimes, followed by voices uttering codes.

"Bad weather out there," Helen said as she set her bread down to pay. There was a coffee can on the counter with a label on the front showing the photocopied faces of the three teens who had been killed in the bus accident a few weeks ago. The collection was for their families.

The kid nodded but didn't look at her. "It's been crazy. Three lightning strikes reported in town so far. One of 'em hit the old Hamilton place out on East County Road. Fire department's up there now and it must be bad, because they've called in two other towns to come help."

"Terrible," Helen said. She paid for the bread, slipped five dollars from her change into the coffee can. The boy looked at her then, but instead of looking grateful or pleased by her donation, he scowled, said, "I know who you are."

"Excuse me?"

"You bought the place out by the bog," he said.

"Yes," she said, smiling. "I'm Helen. My husband, Nate, and I bought the land. We're building a house up there. We just love Hartsboro."

The kid stared, silent.

"Well," she said at last, "nice meeting you." And she turned to go, clutching her bread in its paper bag to her chest, feeling his eyes on her back as she left the store.

.   .   .

The squat brick Hartsboro post office was right next to Ferguson's. Helen stopped in there to check the PO box she and Nate had rented. The only thing in it was a flyer for an exterminator. No house to be infested with critters just yet. A little farther down Main Street stood her true destinations: the tiny stone library and the white clapboard building that housed the town clerk's office. She tried the town clerk first, but the door was locked and had a CLOSED sign. There were no hours posted, no signs of life inside.

The rain pounded down around her, blew in sheets, as she held up her umbrella to try to keep the worst of it away. She hurried next door to the library. The smell of old books comforted her as soon as she stepped through the door.

She stopped in front of the bulletin board in the entryway and closed up her umbrella. There were signs advertising firewood for sale, a day care, rototilling services, and a poster for the high school drama club's performance of *Into the Woods*—she noticed the date was three weeks ago. There was an old poster for the vigil for the kids who were killed in the bus accident. Tucked into the left corner was a small square of white paper with an eye looking out of a cloud: HARTSBORO SPIRIT CIRCLE. LET US HELP YOU MAKE CONTACT WITH A FRIEND OR LOVED ONE WHO HAS PASSED. Then a phone number.

Helen stared, amazed. She'd moved onto land that supposedly had its own ghost and into a town with its own "spirit circle." She definitely wasn't in suburban Connecticut anymore.

Helen walked in, expecting an antiquated library with an old-fashioned paper card catalog. But there were three computers on the left with instructions above for searching the online catalog. There was also a poster explaining that e-books and audiobooks were available electronically. She said hello to the woman behind the desk and did a quick walk through the library: periodicals, audiobooks, reference, nonfiction, and then fiction.

There was a mom with a toddler playing at the train table set up in the brightly painted children's area, but they were the only other patrons. Helen went back to the computers and searched the online catalog for books about Hartsboro. The only titles she found that focused on Hartsboro itself were the VFW Ladies Auxiliary cookbook (which involved lots of maple and bacon) and a book about the flood of 1927.

She walked up to the desk. "Excuse me. I'm looking for books on Hartsboro history."

The librarian, a middle-aged woman in a Snoopy sweatshirt, told her she should check out the Hartsboro Historical Society.

"Where's that?" Helen asked, thrilled to hear such a place existed.

"A couple of doors down on the left, in the basement of the old Elks Lodge. But they're open funny hours—like every second Saturday or something. You'll want to call Mary Ann Marsden. She runs the place and she'll open it up by appointment. I'm sure I've got her number here somewhere." She tapped at her boxy computer. "Here it is!" she chirped, sounding thrilled with herself. She copied the number down on a piece of scrap paper.

"You looking for anything in particular?" the woman asked. "I've lived here my whole life and know a thing or two about the town."

"My husband and I just moved to town and I was hoping to learn a little local history. I'm a—I mean, I *was* a history teacher. In my old life." Helen laughed, but she thought, *Yes—this is my life now.* "Anyway, we've bought land out by the Breckenridge Bog and I'd love to find out whatever I can about the area."

"The Breckenridge place?" The woman smiled, showing small pearly-white teeth. "You bought it from George Decrow, isn't that right?"

"Yes." Helen nodded.

"Poor George, such a sweet man. How is he?"

"I'm afraid I don't know. We never actually met him. Apparently, he's not in great health and lives out of state."

"Don't blame him for not coming back. Not after what happened."

Helen gave her a blank look. "What happened?"

"The accident, I mean."

"I didn't hear anything about it," Helen admitted.

"Well," the librarian went on, "his wife, Edie, she nearly drowned in the bog."

"Oh no," Helen said, thinking of what Nate had said—it was spring fed, could go down very deep.

The librarian nodded. "George pulled her out, did CPR. He brought her back, but she was never the same. Brain damage." She shook her head. Clucked her tongue. "Never woke up, poor thing. After a week or so, George had them turn off the machines, let her go peacefully."

Helen's mind flashed to the table in the trailer laid out for dinner, of the two empty wine glasses. The dusty bottle of wine that still sat on the top shelf of their kitchen cabinet.

"How horrible," Helen said.

"An accident, they said, but George, he went around saying that it was no accident." The librarian waited a beat, looked around, then lowered her voice and whispered, "He said it was *Hattie*."

Helen felt a chill start at her neck and creep all the way down to her tailbone.

"I'm sorry, Hattie? Who—"

"Don't tell me you haven't heard about Hattie yet," the woman in the Snoopy sweatshirt said in a sort of chortling way, as if Hattie were some dowdy old woman who walked around town in funny hats.

"No. I don't know that name." Helen swallowed hard. Because she did know the name, didn't she? Somehow.

Be a historian, she told herself. *Gather facts. Leave your emotions out of it.* "What can you tell me about her?"

"Oh, I guess you'd say Hattie Breckenridge is the most famous resident of Hartsboro. There are all kinds of stories. People said she was a witch. Some said she was the bride of the devil himself. Spoke in tongues. Knew what was going to happen before it did."

"And she lived by the bog?"

"Oh yes, in a little cabin she built herself after her parents' house burned down. All that witch mumbo jumbo—I don't know about that. But she did live in a little house by the bog and that's a true fact."

"My husband and I found the remnants for an old foundation out by the bog," Helen said.

The librarian nodded. "That'd be Hattie's place. Folks called it the 'crooked house,' because Hattie wasn't much of a carpenter and nothing was straight or level."

Helen nodded, thinking of the arguments she and Nate still had sometimes when a measurement was off by a fraction of an inch. Would their house turn out crooked, too? She shook the thought away, remembering the beautifully straight and plumb downstairs walls they'd just finished today.

"What time frame are we talking about here?" Helen asked.

"Oh, I don't know for sure. Back in my grandmother's time. Early 1900s, I think? Mary Ann at the historical society would know."

"Do you think there are any photos? Of the cabin or Hattie?"

"Could be," the librarian said. "You talk to Mary Ann. If there are any, she'll know."

"What happened to Hattie?" Helen asked.

The librarian got quiet, looked down at the papers on her desk.

"There are all kinds of stories . . . ," she said, moving papers around. "Some folks even believe that before she died, she buried treasure on her land—her family's fortune. Me, I doubt there ever was a fortune. If there was, why didn't she leave? Or build a nicer house for herself? It's crazy, the stories some people tell."

Helen nodded. She knew how folklore worked, how stories were embellished over the years, and a true historian had to do a lot of leg-work and research to sift through those stories for the grains of truth inside them.

"One thing in the stories is always the same, though," the librar-ian continued, a little gleam in her eye. "People say her spirit haunts that bog. They see her ghost out there, walking around the water, out in the middle of it, too. If you look on some early-summer days, you can see pink flowers have sprung up where she put her feet. Lady's slippers."

Helen got another chill, remembered the scatterings of pale pink orchids she and Nate had seen while walking to the bog.

Hattie's footsteps.

The woman smiled at her, and Helen couldn't tell if she actually believed any of this (and was perhaps the sort who attended the Harts-boro Spirit Circle) or if she was just passing stories along.

Then the woman said something that answered Helen's questions. "You stay out there long enough, and who knows, maybe you'll see her, too. Go to the bog at sunset and wait. When the darkness is set-tling in, that's when Hattie comes out." She smiled vaguely again and winked. "Just, you know. Be careful."

. . .

"What's all this?" Nate asked. He'd just walked in from the down-pour outside. He'd peeled off his raincoat but was still soaked from head to toe. His bird-watching binoculars were strung around his neck.

"I've been to the library," Helen said.

"So I see." He came closer, leaving soggy footprints on the old linoleum floor.

"It's small but has a lot more than I imagined it would. I signed us both up for cards," Helen said. "But they don't actually give cards.

They just keep the patrons' names in a card catalog–looking thing. Very cute."

"I guess." He picked up one of the books piled on the kitchen table and read the title out loud. "*Witchcraft in New England*?" He glanced at the other titles, all books on witchcraft, ghosts, and the occult. "You're not planning to cast a spell on me or anything, are you?"

She smiled. "Only if you tease me about my research. Then I just might turn you into a toad."

"I'd prefer some sort of bird," Nate said. He picked up another book and glanced at the title: *Communicating with the Spirit World*. He frowned in disapproval but said nothing.

Mr. Science had never approved of anything otherworldly or unexplained.

She frowned back at him. "Those who are the victim of spells don't get to decide. And watch out, Nature Boy, you're getting my library books all wet."

Nate put the book down, took a step back. "And what, exactly, is the goal of this research?"

"Remember what the realtor told us? About the bog being haunted? And remember the little foundation we found?"

Nate nodded. "Did you find out anything at the town clerk's office?"

"Uh-uh. They were closed. But I asked at the library and it turns out this woman, Hattie Breckenridge, lived in a little house at the edge of the bog back in the early 1900s. That foundation we found is all that's left. And get this—people said she was a witch!"

"A witch?" Nate raised his eyebrows. "Like Glinda? Or like the Wicked Witch of the West?"

She rolled her eyes. "Hearing about Hattie got me curious. I didn't realize witchcraft was a thing in New England in the 1900s. The Salem trials were back 1692. As I understand it, the witch craze was all over with by 1700."

"Your point is . . ."

"I don't have a point. I'm just curious. It's an area I don't know much about."

He nodded. This he understood. The need to learn whatever you could about the things you didn't know, to fill in the gaps, to be constantly supplying your brain with new information and facts.

"And this is our new home," she added. "Her land, it's ours now. Don't you think we should learn Hattie's story?"

Nate smiled. "Of course." Then he laughed.

"What?"

"I was just thinking about Jenny—wait until we tell her our land comes with its very own witch ghost!"

"We'll tell her no such thing!" She waggled her finger at him warningly, laughing herself. "Not until I've done my research and found out who Hattie really was, what her true story is. She was probably just an eccentric woman, you know? Think about it—a woman on her own building a little house out by the bog all by herself, in that time. Of course she was shunned, called a witch."

Nate smiled, leaned in and kissed her forehead, dripping on her books. "Isn't that kind of what we are? The eccentric outsiders building a house by the bog? What will the people in town call us?"

Helen laughed, but it was an uneasy laugh. She remembered the way the kid at the store had looked at her, with suspicion, then outright loathing. *I know who you are.*

"There's something else I learned," she said, hesitating, unsure how much she should share with him.

"Oh?"

She told him about Edie Decrow.

"My god, that's awful! No wonder he let the place go for so cheap. Remember what I told you about the spring—who knows how deep it is out there in the middle of the bog. Don't go too close, okay? If you're down there on your own, stay by the edge."

She thought of telling him the rest, that the librarian said Mr. Decrow was convinced it wasn't the bog that had nearly drowned his wife, it was Hattie. But that would only annoy him, possibly lead to a lecture about how the human mind looks for explanations and patterns when terrible things happen, how it makes us prey to fairy tales and nonsense . . .

She only nodded. "I'll be careful," she said.

"I'm going to go take a nice lukewarm spit shower and put on some dry clothes," he said, giving her another quick kiss.

"Sounds good." She went back to the book she was reading, to a chapter on hexes and curses. She skimmed the pages, reading about knot magic, candle burning, anointing your enemy's door with a special oil. She found a reference to a spell that used a donkey's tooth to banish an enemy. If a donkey's tooth would work, couldn't you use a deer's or sheep's tooth?

She closed the book. A witch ghost putting curses on them from the Great Beyond? This was silly. Ridiculous even.

Helen had tucked the historical society woman's phone number into one of the books: *Spirits and Hauntings.* Now, at the kitchen table, she opened up the book and pulled out the slip of paper. She grabbed her cell phone and punched in the number.

"You've reached the home of Marvin and Mary Ann Marsden. We're not in right now, but leave us a message and we'll call you when we get back."

Helen left a short message along with her cell number.

She drummed her fingers, thought of George Decrow pulling his wife out of the bog. She dug around in her purse until she found the card of their real estate agent. She dialed and he answered on the second ring.

"Hi. This is Helen Wetherell. My husband, Nate, and I bought the land by the bog?"

"Yes, of course. How's the building going?"

"It's going well, thanks. Listen, the reason I'm calling is that we found something belonging to the previous owner in the trailer and I'd love to be able to mail it to him down in Florida. I was hoping you could give me his number?"

"I'm sure he really didn't want anything from in there," he said.

"But this looks important. It's a bunch of personal papers, letters. I'd love to call him just to ask if he'd like them. I can't bring myself to throw them away."

"Well, I'm not technically supposed to share information like that, but . . ." She heard papers rustling. He sounded distracted. "Okay, I'm willing to make an exception in this case. I'm sure I've got the number here somewhere. Hold on a sec."

He came back on the line and gave her the number, promised to stop by and see how the house was coming along the next time he was in the area.

The shower turned off and she heard Nate's footsteps thumping down the hall to their tiny shoebox of a bedroom. She tucked the little notebook she'd written George Decrow's number in into her purse.

"Babe?" Nate called half a minute later.

"Yeah?"

"Have you seen my phone?"

"No." She looked around, scanning the table and kitchen counters. "I don't see it out here."

There was the sound of rummaging, of Nate muttering something under his breath.

"Find it?" Helen called.

Nate came out into the kitchen in his boxers and a T-shirt. "No. It's crazy. I'm sure I left it on the shelf in the bedroom—the one I always put my wallet and phone on. I left it there when I went out bird-watching because the battery was nearly dead and I didn't want it to get wet in the rain."

"Maybe it's in a jacket pocket or something?" Helen suggested. "Or out in the truck?"

"It couldn't be in the truck because you had it in town all afternoon. No, I'm sure I left it in the bedroom."

"Maybe it's up at the site," Helen suggested. "You had it this morning. We used the calculator, remember?"

"Yeah, but I brought it back down, I'm sure."

"You should go check. I bet it's up there, under the first pop-up, on the table next to the saw."

Nate went and checked. He came back empty-handed and irritated.

"Where does shit go around here?" he asked. "Yesterday, the level; today, my phone."

Helen thought. It wasn't just those things that had gone missing. They'd lost the broom. Helen's favorite coffee mug. Other things had disappeared, too. Money from their wallets seemed to go missing—never all of it—just a ten here, a five there. Two days ago, Helen had splurged and bought a bumbleberry pie at the general store. When she went to get it from the fridge after dinner, it was gone.

"Maybe you left it at the store?" Nate suggested when she insisted that she'd bought a special surprise—Nate's favorite—for dessert, but it was now missing. "Or just thought about buying it, then got distracted by all the other stuff on your list?"

"Maybe," she said, beginning to doubt herself.

She couldn't recall losing a single thing back in Connecticut. Keys and phones were misplaced from time to time, sure, but they always turned up. And back at the condo, they'd had a place for everything:

a shelf for the mail, hooks by the door for keys, a charging station in the front hall for their phones. They'd lived an ordered existence. But here in Vermont, she'd somehow managed to lose an entire pie.

"Your phone will turn up," Helen said.

Nate went back to the bedroom to check the bedding and under the bed in case it had fallen off the shelf.

Helen's eyes went to the book, to the page Mary Ann Marsden's phone number had been marking. The heading at the top of the page read, "7 Signs Your House Is Haunted": unexplained noises, sudden changes in temperature, doors and cabinets opening and closing, strange odors, electronic disturbances, strange dreams, objects going missing.

She read the last sign again, then the description:

If an everyday item is not where you're sure you left it, a spirit may be playing a trick on you. Most often, these items are returned, sometimes hours, days, or weeks later, usually left in the exact same spot you last saw the object. Spirits are borrowers. They are fascinated by objects from this world.

"Can you try calling it?" Nate asked from the bedroom, his voice muffled, like he was all the way under the bed.

"Sure," she said, slamming the book closed. She dialed his number, listened to it ring and ring, then go to voice mail.

The house stayed silent. No happy birdsong ringtone.

"It's not here," Nate said, frustrated. This was followed by a bang and "Shit!"

"You okay?" Helen called.

"I'm fine. Just bashed my skull for the thousandth time on these godforsaken shelves."

"We should get rid of the shelves. Let's take them down. Right now. At least the ones right above the bed."

"Sure, but not right this second. I need to find my damn phone."

"We'll find it," she said, standing, looking around the kitchen more thoroughly. Then she walked down the hall to the bedroom. Nate was shaking out the covers.

"I've checked everywhere it could be, and it's just not here."

"You can't be sure," Helen said. "Didn't you say it was almost dead?"

"Yeah."

"Well, then that explains why we didn't hear it ringing."

"But I know I left it right here, Helen." He hit the lowest shelf with his palm for emphasis. She saw his watch, wallet, penknife, and loose change. "That's what's driving me crazy. I left it right here!"

"Are you sure you didn't take it? Maybe by accident?"

"I'm sure."

He blinked at her, and for half a second, she was sure he didn't believe her—that he thought she was lying to him.

"Why would I have taken your phone?" she said, the words coming out more defensive than she'd meant.

"Well, phones don't get up and walk away on their own," he said.

"No," she agreed. "They don't."

CHAPTER 8

O<small>live</small>

"Wow! Sure is a pricey piece of equipment," Aunt Riley, eyes wide, said when she saw the metal detector on the shelf. Riley had taken Olive up to the big hobby shop in Burlington after school. They were in the aisle with metal detectors and gold-panning supplies. The next aisle had the radio-controlled aircraft and drones, and that was where all the action was. She could hear a kid whining to his dad that he absolutely *needed* the drone with the Wi-Fi camera and anything else would totally suck.

"You got enough money for this, kiddo?" Riley asked, pushing her blue bangs back away from her eyes. "I can lend you some if you need it." Riley looked tired to Olive. Thinner, too, maybe.

"Thanks, but I've got enough," Olive said. Just barely, but she had it. Riley giving her weird but awesome gifts was one thing, but asking Riley for money was not something Olive ever wanted to have to do.

"Where'd you get all that money?" Riley asked. "Lift a little cash from your dad's wallet? Engage in any illicit activities?" Riley said this jokingly, but there was a serious questioning look in her eyes.

Olive could hide just about anything from her dad—in fact, she believed he was a willing participant in her deceptions—but Riley was another story.

"No way! I've been saving forever," Olive explained. "Then I sold my old metal detector to my friend Mike. He bought a couple of the old musket balls I've found, too. He thinks they're cool."

"So, what are you going to do with this new fancy metal detector you're spending your life's savings on?" Aunt Riley asked.

"Oh, you know. The usual. Look for coins and lost rings on the beach at the lake. See if I can find any old home sites back in the woods. Maybe find more musket balls to sell to Mike."

Riley smiled at her. "I thought maybe you were searching for Hattie's treasure."

Olive looked at her aunt, thought of telling her the truth. Riley believed in stuff like ghosts and old folktales. Riley and Mama had loved telling each other Hattie stories they'd heard, turning this woman who lived by the swamp into a witch with superhuman powers, a ghost who could come back and wreak terrible revenge. Mama and Riley agreed that that poor woman who died after nearly drowning in the bog had definitely been lured out there by Hattie, but that she must have deserved it in some way. In their minds, Hattie enacted revenge only on those who had crossed her in some way—maybe simply by trespassing or not giving her the respect she so obviously deserved. And Riley and Mama loved to tell stories of the supposed sightings of Hattie over the years, and, of course, the disappearances. As obsessed as Mama had been with Hattie, Riley might have been more so. She talked about Hattie like she'd known her, like she was an old friend no one but her understood.

"Nah," Olive said then, looking at her aunt. "There is no treasure. Mama said."

Riley looked at Olive for a few seconds. "She said that, huh?"

"Yeah," Olive said. "Mama was pretty sure. And I believe her. I mean, really, what are the chances that it actually exists and hasn't been found yet?"

"I don't know. I just think it seems kind of sad. Finding that treasure was a dream of your mom's for such a long time."

Olive remembered Mama telling her that they were the ones who would find the treasure, that it was their destiny.

There was this long, awkward pause again while Riley watched Olive, seemed to study her, really.

The kid in the next aisle had won: his dad was buying him the fancy drone with the camera he wanted.

"Dreams change," Olive said matter-of-factly as she reached for the boxed metal detector on the shelf.

"I guess they do," Riley said, and she looked so sad for a minute that Olive was sorry she'd said what she had. Sorry she'd brought up Mama at all. It was easier, safer, to not mention her, to pretend she'd never existed. Sometimes Olive got so caught up in her own grief that she forgot other people were grieving, too. Olive wasn't the only one Mama had left.

"Gonna do some treasure hunting?" the salesclerk asked Olive when she brought the box up to the register, a little gleam in her eye.

"Absolutely," Olive said.

She and Riley got into Riley's car and drove back home. In the car, Riley moved on to asking Olive all about school and how her daddy was doing. And Olive lied. It scared her sometimes, how good she was at lying. Even to Aunt Riley, who was way swifter than Daddy.

"School's great," she said. "We're learning about this thing called natural selection. Do you know about that?"

"Sure" Riley said, getting on the on-ramp for the highway. "Survival of the fittest. Charles Darwin and his finches, right?"

"It's all about adaptation," Olive said. "I like that." She loved this idea that some humans might be evolving right now, in minuscule ways, ways you couldn't even see at first.

"I guess when you think of it, that's what survival is really all about, right?" Riley asked. "I mean, not just as a species, but on a mundane, day-to-day level. Life throws shit at us and we roll with it. We adapt and evolve."

Olive nodded. Riley got it so completely.

"Of course, some people are better at adapting than others," Riley said, giving Olive this knowing, laser-eyed look. "Your dad, even when we were kids, always had trouble with change. He'd pretend to be doing okay, but when things changed, when something upset him, he'd get thrown off, sometimes go into one of his funks where he wouldn't leave his room, didn't want to eat or talk to anyone. Sometimes he'd get so mad, he'd punch holes in the walls. He broke his hand once, hitting the wall so hard."

Olive nodded; she'd heard this story a hundred times. She tried to ready herself for what she knew was coming.

"How's he doing?" Riley asked, glancing at Olive in the passenger seat beside her. "The no-bullshit answer, please."

And there it was. But Olive was ready with a smile.

"Dad's doing okay, really," Olive said. "He makes dinner every night. Helps me with my homework, even. He's getting me a computer of my very own soon."

"And the renovations? Is he still spending all of his time with that?"

Olive shrugged. "Sure, we're working on the house, but it's not too bad. The living room's nearly done. And I've decided to go ahead and do some work on my own room. Make it a little bigger, you know? So there'll be room for bookshelves and a built-in desk for the new computer."

Was being a really good liar a form of adaptation? Olive wondered. Cleverness was, she believed.

But was Olive really being that clever? She wasn't sure if Riley bought it, but her aunt pretended to, at first, and said, "That's real good, Ollie. I'm glad things are going well. I know high school can be tough—it definitely was for me."

"Really?" Olive asked.

Riley paused a minute, keeping her eyes on the road ahead, then said, "Yeah, you know, not everyone is designed to fit in. For those of us who don't, those of us destined to blaze our own paths, well, other people can be downright shitty to us. Especially in high school."

And Olive almost told her then. Almost confessed everything— how school really sucked, how she skipped more often than went these days, how her dad had started tearing her bedroom apart, how she really was looking for the treasure and hoped it would help bring Mama back.

But then Riley turned and smiled at her, and it was a genuine smile, radiating happiness and relief.

"I'm really so happy you're doing well, Ollie. I think a computer's a great idea! Let me know if you need any help picking one out or setting it up or anything. I'm not an expert, but I know enough to get by."

Olive nodded.

"And you know," Riley added, putting her hand on Olive's shoulder and giving it a gentle squeeze. "If things ever weren't going well at home, you could always come talk to me. And my guest room is always open, you know that, right? You can stay with me anytime."

"I know, thanks." Olive loved the idea of staying with her quirky aunt, but she knew she couldn't leave her dad for long. She was all he had left. "But things are fine at home now. Really."

Riley gave her a smile. "Just keep it in mind, 'kay? My door's always open. And we're still on for this weekend, right? *Bride of Frankenstein* and a double pepperoni pizza?"

"Absolutely," Olive said, giving her aunt the best happy, well-adjusted, *I'm doing fine, really* smile she could muster. "And don't forget the Swedish Fish!"

CHAPTER 9

H elen

 **JUNE 9, 2015**

Something was eating the trailer.

It was a little after two in the morning and Helen had just come to bed after sitting in the kitchen, doing research on the computer, reading her library books, and drinking two cups of herbal tea liberally laced with brandy to help her get to sleep. Country living was not doing wonders for her insomnia. Back in the condo, there had been hundreds of channels of cable TV and the constant noise of traffic from the highway to help lull Helen to sleep.

Of course her research hadn't exactly helped. She'd done a search on Hattie Breckenridge and discovered a brief entry from a collection of Vermont ghost stories written in the 1980s:

> *Hattie Breckenridge, legend had it, was the wife of the Devil himself, with a beauty no man could resist, even in death. To this day, residents of Hartsboro claim to see her in the woods and bog where she once lived, and some have been unlucky enough to follow her, to answer her siren's call, and never find their way out of the woods again.*

Helen had switched off the computer, thinking the story utter nonsense. Where were the facts? Where were the names of people who'd seen her, people who'd supposedly gone missing? She crept into the bedroom and lay down, closed her eyes, took a deep sighing breath, willing herself to fall asleep quickly—and then she heard something scratching and chewing. It seemed to come from directly beneath her pillow.

"Nate," she said, shaking him. "Wake up."

"What?"

"Do you hear that?"

"Mmm?"

It was a scrabbling, gnawing sound coming from under the bed. Steady and grinding.

There was something down there. Something with sharp teeth. Something chewing its way up to them. It would eat through the wooden slats of the bed frame, then the soft organic cotton mattress, and then—

She shook him harder, gave his shoulder a not-so-gentle punch. "Nate, there's something here, *in the trailer!*"

"Ow! God! What? Where?" he asked, sitting up, listening as he rubbed his shoulder.

"Don't you hear it?" she asked.

"Hear what?" He looked at her, puzzled. "Have you been drinking?"

"Just shut up and listen!" she hissed. This *was not* going to be like the scream their first night.

They sat together under the covers, listening.

Gnawing. Definite gnawing. Not the soft chewing of a mouse, but something much louder, much larger.

"You hear that, right?" Helen asked.

"Yeah, I hear it." He sounded worried.

"Well, *what the fuck is it?*"

"I don't know. Some kind of animal."

Helen remembered the library woman's words: "You stay out there long enough, and who knows, maybe you'll see her, too. Go to the bog at sunset and wait. When the darkness is settling in, that's when Hattie comes out."

And Helen had thought of going last night after supper, of walking to the bog by herself, but she'd been too frightened.

The mad chewing got louder, more insistent.

My, what big teeth you have.

All the better to eat you up.

She hadn't gone to Hattie. Perhaps Hattie had come to her.

"I think she's under the bed," Helen whispered.

"She?" Nate said, grabbing his glasses, flipping on the light.

"It. Whatever."

She shouldn't have been reading the ridiculous Hattie story online and the witchcraft books from the library before getting into bed. Next time she couldn't sleep, she'd pick up one of Nate's science tomes—study the anatomy of an earthworm or how evaporation and condensation cause rain.

"Hand me the flashlight," he said as he slid off the bed and dropped to his knees. She passed him the big yellow light and he flicked it on, shone the beam under the bed. Helen stayed on top of the covers, legs tucked under her, half expecting a gnarled hand to reach out and pull him under.

"What is it?" she asked. "What do you see?"

"Nothing here," he said. "But I still hear it. It sounds like it's right underneath us." He stood up, his white boxers and T-shirt glowing as he moved down the darkness of the hall.

"Where are you going?" Helen's voice was squeaky and frantic and she hated herself for it.

"Outside," he said. "To look under the trailer."

She scooted out of bed, padding behind him down the hall to the front door. She stood in the open doorway while he made his way down the steps. It was a clear night, the moon hanging low in the sky, the stars looking bright and close, the air damp and cool. Goose bumps prickled her skin.

"Be careful," she said as Nate crouched down, shone the light into the crawl space beneath the trailer, which rested uneasily on crumbling concrete blocks.

"Oh!" he said, startled. He stood up straight and took two steps back.

If whatever was under there scared Nate, it had to be bad.

"What is it?" Helen asked, nearly frantic now, and not really wanting to know what he'd seen. She wanted to grab his hand, yank him back into the trailer, bolt the door, turn out the lights, and hide.

"Nate?" she asked, voice shaking. "What do you see?"

He laughed, relieved. "It's a porcupine!"

"What?"

"A quill pig, that's what some people call it. But it's actually a rodent, of course. It's so much bigger than I thought! And he's kind of cute, honestly. Come see." Nate was talking in that fast, excited way he did when he encountered a new creature.

A porcupine. Only a woodland creature, not the wild witch of the bog. Her shoulders relaxed, and she let herself climb down the front steps.

"Will I end up with a face full of quills?"

"Not if you don't get too close," Nate said.

"Don't they shoot them out?"

"No, that's a myth. You'd have to touch him to get quilled. The quills are hollow and have little barbs. Come on, hurry up! I think I scared him off. He's heading out under the other side."

She joined him, took his hand, and together they circled around the trailer, the blazing bright beam from the flashlight illuminating everything in their path.

"There he is." He pointed. "See!"

She looked and saw a thick, squat animal the size of a large cat lumbering along. She could make out its quills. She laughed at its clumsy waddle, its complete lack of grace. Nate put his arm around her, and together they watched it disappear into the woods. "So cool," he said, and Helen turned and looked at him, saw his huge, excited smile.

"I love you," she said, kissing his cheek.

Nate went back to the trailer, got down on his knees, and peered underneath.

"Man, those teeth do a lot of damage. If he'd kept at it, he would have gone right through the floor and ended up cuddling in bed with us."

"God, I hope not!"

"I've heard porcupines like plywood. It's the glue, I think. They also like anything people have sweated on, like ax handles."

"Glue and sweat, great tastes."

"To a porcupine, yeah," he said.

"Come on," she said. "Let's get back to bed."

On the way in, he stopped in the kitchen, grabbed his nature journal to write down the details of the porcupine sighting. So far he had several pages of notes and sketches, mostly of birds, including the great blue heron.

"Come on," she said. "You can document your Mr. Nibbles encounter in the morning."

He crawled into bed beside her, put his arm around her. "Nothing like that at the condo in Connecticut," he said, clearly still excited. A supersized rodent that ate plywood and ax handles might be a nightmare to some, but to Nate it was a thrill.

She kissed his neck, gave it a gentle nibble as she pushed her body against his, heard his breathing quicken. "Still thinking about the porcupine?" she whispered.

"Not at all," he said, his hands moving up under her nightgown, tugging it off.

. . .

An hour later, she lay awake thinking of the porcupine, remembering the terrible grinding sound of it chewing. Nate, of course, was out cold, naked beside her, his limp arm draped over her stomach.

She closed her eyes, willed herself to sleep.

But she couldn't get the chewing noises from her head.

She imagined an old woman with pointed teeth chewing her way up through their floor.

My, what big teeth you have.

She woke to sunlight streaming in through their small, narrow, prisonlike rectangular bedroom window. God help them if there were ever a fire in another part of the trailer—they'd never get out.

Nate was not beside her. She looked at her watch. Nearly nine o'clock. How had she managed to sleep so late? And how had she not noticed Nate getting out of bed?

She crawled down to the bottom of the bed, slid off, and grabbed her robe from the door. There was a pot of coffee waiting in the kitchen. She poured a cup, pulled on her sneakers, and went outside to find Nate. The sun hadn't come up from behind the hill yet and the air felt cool. But the black flies were out: tiny, godforsaken creatures that swarmed, found every patch of exposed skin and left bites that itched like crazy. They'd already gone through three bottles of eco-friendly DEET-free bug repellent (which Helen was convinced the little bastards actually liked the scent of) and Nate was finally at the point of agreeing to try something a little more hard-core. As they swarmed her face, Helen vowed to go buy a can of OFF! today. And maybe a hat with an attached veil made of fine mesh netting—she'd seen one at Ferguson's in the hunting section. She'd look like an idiot, but she was sick to death of being eaten alive.

Nate was standing inside the skeletal frame of the house, right in the center of what would be their living room.

"Hey, you," she called, walking over to join him, entering through the opening that would be their front door, imagining how wonderful it would be to have an actual door there to shut out the black flies.

He didn't answer.

He was staring down at the floor, frowning.

"What's wrong?" she asked, coming up behind him, coffee mug still clenched in her hand.

Had the porcupine made his way up here in the night, started chewing up their house?

"Nate?" she asked.

There, on the plywood subfloor they'd nailed down, was one of their chunky carpenter's pencils. It had been used to write a message in big, sloppy capital letters:

BEWEAR OF HATTIE

"Hattie?" Nate said.

Helen thought back to the image that had kept her up last night: the old woman with the sharp teeth, gnawing and gnawing, coming for them.

"She's the woman I told you about, remember?"

The one who pulled poor Edie Decrow into the water.

Helen swallowed hard, then continued. "Hattie Breckenridge—the one who lived at the edge of the bog."

Nate shook his head, frowning. "I think our witch ghost needs some spelling lessons," he said.

"Nate, you don't think . . ." She couldn't even finish saying it—that it might really be a ghost who'd left the message.

"I think some locals are messing with us. Probably kids, probably drunk or high. Scare the flatlanders, ha-ha."

Nate turned and went back to the area where they'd been keeping their tools.

"Have you seen my hammer with the blue handle? I can't find it anywhere."

"No," she said.

"Jesus. It's like there's some mysterious vortex. My cell phone, the level, my hammer. Maybe the kids are taking our shit, too."

"If we were being robbed, wouldn't they take more than a couple of random tools?" Helen asked.

"Not if they were just doing it to mess with us," Nate said grimly.

"I'm sure the tools are around here somewhere," Helen said now. It was the logical, adult thing to say. She didn't tell him that when he'd said "vortex," she'd immediately thought of the deep center of the bog and all that could be hidden there.

CHAPTER 10

O live

 **JUNE 10, 2015**

"I can't believe how much better this one works," Mike said. Olive was letting him try out the brand-new metal detector, and he was waving it over the ground at the edge of the bog.

Mike was right: the new metal detector was amazing. It was so much more sensitive than her old one and could find things much farther down. So far, she and Mike had found two metal buttons, some coins, an old hinge, and bullet casings. And that was from working on only one square of her grid.

"I think I should go back and redo all the areas I already searched," she told him. "The treasure might be too far down for my old machine to pick up on. But this one will get it."

Mike nodded but kept his eyes on the ground. He didn't believe in the treasure. He'd never come right out and said that, but it was obvious to Olive.

He was wrong, though. Hattie's treasure was real. She felt it in her bones, especially when she was out here in the bog; she knew she was close. And Mama had been right: they were going to be the ones to find it. Now, without Mama, it was all up to her.

The treasure called to her, whispered, pulled on her, told her not to give up. That this could be the day.

Keep looking, it seemed to say.

You're so close.

Some people, they were afraid of the bog. They said Hattie's spirit was out there, and she was angry, looking for revenge. They said that if you went after dark, you'd see her walking across the bog, that the pink lady's slippers that bloomed in the woodlands around the edges sprung up in the places where she'd stepped.

Olive had seen plenty of lady's slippers but never a ghost. She'd come at night, setting her alarm for one a.m. and keeping the clock under her pillow so her dad wouldn't hear it. He was a heavy sleeper and was always sound asleep by midnight. She'd come on full moons and sat by the edge of the bog, begging Hattie to show herself, begging her to leave a clue about where the treasure might be. But the only figures who ever materialized there in the bog were very much alive: hunters and hikers sometimes; but at night, it was older kids who'd come out on dares to get high, fool around, drink beer, and piss on the old foundation of Hattie's house, daring her to come forward.

"Come on and show yourself, witch!" a boy hollered once while Olive watched from her hiding spot behind a big tree. Olive held her breath, wished Hattie would come forward, scare the crap out of the kid and teach him a lesson. No such luck.

"Careful, she'll put a curse on you," the girl who was with him squealed.

The boy laughed, cracked open another can of beer. "Let her try. She ain't nothing but a pile of bones sunk down at the bottom of the bog."

Olive picked up a rock then and threw it deep into the center of the bog, where it landed with a huge splash.

The girl screamed.

"The fuck?" the boy said.

"Let's get outta here," the girl said in a trembling voice, and the boy didn't argue.

Olive waited for them to go, then cleaned up the crushed beer cans they'd left behind—it didn't seem right to leave them there. It seemed . . . disrespectful.

"Mike?" she said now.

"Yeah?" He looked hopeful. Expectant. It made her cringe a little, deep down inside, when he looked at her this way. When all she ever seemed to do lately was hurt his feelings and disappoint him.

"You don't believe the treasure exists, do you?"

"I—"

"Ya gotta tell the truth. I'll know if you're lying." She would, too. His left eyebrow always went up a little when he was lying. It was a funny thing, but she noticed it every time. It helped her beat the crap out of him whenever they played poker for pennies in Mike's old tree house. He also got all sweaty when he was even a little bit nervous, his ears got red when he was mad, and he chewed his top lip when something was worrying him.

"It's not that I don't believe," he said.

"Well, what is it then?"

"I think the treasure might exist. I mean, it's definitely possible. But I'm just not sure that anyone should go digging it up."

"Why not?"

" 'Cause. It's Hattie's, right? Are you sure you want to go messing around with anything that belonged to her? It's probably, like, cursed or something."

Olive chuffed out a laugh, picked up the metal detector, and slipped the headphones back on. Mike sat down on a fallen log and pulled a bag of Skittles out of his backpack, offering some to her. She shook her head and went back to work.

They were searching the northwest corner of the bog. Even with the headphones on, she heard hammering and Helen's and Nate's voices. Olive and Mike weren't technically on their land, not way over on this side of the bog, but still, Olive didn't really want them to catch her. But she had their routine down by now. They worked every morning, took a break for lunch, then worked until just before dinner. They'd usually take a walk down to the bog either before or after dinner. And they couldn't see the bog from their house. They were uphill, up a steep path through a little strip of woods. So Olive felt safe. And even if they caught her, she wasn't doing anything illegal. She'd just smile real big, introduce herself as a neighbor, and tell them she was fooling around, looking for old coins and stuff.

She'd been watching Helen and Nate enough to know things had been tense lately. They snapped at each other when they were building, accused each other of misplacing tools. This morning, Nate had a big freak-out about his cell phone, which had been missing for days.

Olive smiled, thought they'd be gone soon. They'd realize they couldn't hack it, then pack up and leave. She'd also been buoyed by the rumors she'd been hearing in town. People were saying that Helen and Nate should never have come. Olive liked the idea of the whole town being against them, making them feel unwelcome; this would drive Helen and Nate away for sure.

Olive marked her map with a big, satisfying no-treasure-here X and tagged the corners of the grid with tiny pieces of red string tied around saplings—something no one would notice if they weren't looking. Then she moved on to the next part of her grid: a six-by-six-foot section along the northern edge of the bog. Her sneakers were already soaked, so she didn't mind working on such soggy ground. Her feet sank into the mossy carpet, the water well above her ankles in places. Tall rubber boots would have been better. There was always the chance that Daddy would notice her wet sneakers and ask how she'd gotten so soaked going to school and back.

She was playing hooky more and more these days—she figured with just days of school left before summer vacation, it didn't really matter all that much. As long as she did decently on her final exams and turned in her papers, she figured she'd pass ninth grade. She'd been ripping up the notes they gave her to bring home for her dad, asking to set up a special meeting, saying Olive's truancy had become a serious issue. Deleting the messages from the school on the digital answering machine (yeah, they still had an answering machine—something her mom had picked up at a yard sale—and the weirdest part was hearing Mom's voice on the recording each time someone called: *You've reached the Kissners. We're not home right now, but leave a message and we'll get back to you;* neither Olive nor her father could bear to erase it). Sooner or later, if he didn't already know how much she'd been skipping (*of course he knows, dumbass*), he'd find out. But by then, she'd have found the treasure, and it wouldn't matter anymore. He'd be so happy, so proud, that he'd understand completely why conducting her search had been way more important than showing up for freshman biology and English each day.

Mike was giving her a lot of shit about missing school, too. He'd cut out early himself today, sneaking out after lunch to come meet her here in the bog. But he'd been trying to make her feel guilty about it all afternoon—like if his dad found out, he'd get hell and it would be all her fault for being such a bad influence. Like he didn't have a choice. Like she actually had that much power.

Olive looked out across the bog. "Maybe Hattie's here now, watching us."

"Quit it, Kissner," Mike barked.

It always amused Olive, how easy poor Mike was to scare.

"Are you here with us, Hattie?" she called out. "Give us a sign."

"Shut up," Mike said.

"Okay, Hattie," she said now as she stood with her metal detector. "If you are here, help me out, okay? Show me where the treasure is!"

Mike gritted his teeth. "You shouldn't be talking to her like that," he warned.

She held the metal detector out in front of her like some heavy dowsing rod, pretending to be pulled right, then left. Mike's eyes got bigger, more frantic.

Odd Oliver, she thought. *Being cruel to her one and only true friend. Talking to ghosts.*

She wondered if there were people who really could talk to ghosts. Aunt Riley said there totally were. That mediums were real and had a special kind of gift.

"Can *you* talk to ghosts?" Olive had asked her once.

"I know people who can. I haven't been able to myself, not yet, but I keep trying."

Now Olive wondered if being able to talk to ghosts was something you were born with. Like people who had a photographic memory or were supertasters. Which brought Olive back to thinking about natural selection again. About Darwin sailing around on his boat, the *Beagle,* and writing notes, drawing pictures of birds.

Everyone's looking for something, she thought. *Ghosts. Scientific explanations of the world around us. A new and different life somewhere else.*

Buried treasure.

She started sweeping the metal detector over the ground in front of her, through brush, tall grass, and sedge. Nothing. She startled a moth, which came fluttering up from the grass. A damselfly darted down in front of her. A junco chattered from a nearby cedar. She continued slogging forward, sweeping carefully, making her way through the thick brush at the edge of the bog. Then the high-pitched beep of a signal. A strong one. Her heart banged in her chest.

The gauge on the detector said it wasn't far down.

"Mike, I got something!" she called out.

"Are you messing with me?" he asked.

"No," she said, and Mike trotted over.

She got down on her knees, pants soaking through because the ground was so wet here, the carpet of moss deep and spongy. She pushed back the tall grass, cotton sedge, and old dead leaves. She had a trowel and a small folding camp shovel in her backpack.

But she didn't need them.

There, right on the mossy surface, silver glinted up at her.

Maybe it really was the treasure and that one piece had worked its way up from underground, a marker meant for her and her alone to find.

X marks the spot.

She reached for it, brushed away the leaves.

It was a silver chain. She picked it up, pulling it up slowly and carefully from its camouflaged place in the dead leaves.

But this wasn't treasure.

No, this was a necklace that she recognized immediately.

"What is it?" Mike asked, leaning closer. "A necklace?"

Olive's skin got all prickly, charged up, feeling like lightning had struck somewhere close-by. Like danger was near.

The silver chain was broken, but the clasp was fastened. Near the clasp hung a delicate silver circle with a triangle inside it, a square inside that, and inside the square another circle with an eye at the center.

"It's my mother's," she managed to say even though her throat felt like it was closing up. "Her favorite. She never took it off."

Olive held the necklace, now tarnished, caked with mud. The eye looked back at her.

I see you.

I know things.

"Weird," Mike said, biting his top lip, lower jaw sticking out like a bulldog's. He stepped back, like the necklace scared him the way Hattie's cursed treasure might scare him. "So . . . what's your mom's favorite necklace that she never took off doing out here in the bog?"

CHAPTER 11

Helen

 **JUNE 15, 2015**

It was 3:33 a.m. That's what Helen's light-up digital watch showed when she pushed the button.

Nate was not beside her in bed.

"Nate?" she called sleepily. The trailer was dark and quiet. "Nate?" she tried again, listening.

All she heard was the dull thud of her own quickening heartbeat.

Her worrying, anxiety, and paranoia were getting the better of her. Whenever she went into town to pick up a box of screws or a new hammer to replace one they'd lost, she was sure everyone was watching, whispering. She told this to Nate, and he laughed it off, said she was imagining things. But she hadn't imagined it when she heard a woman at the post office say to another, "It's her. The one from the Breckenridge place." And the other woman had shaken her head in disgust, very clearly said, "Should never have come, disturbed Hattie like they did," then scuttled out of the post office like she was frightened of Helen.

"I'm telling you," she'd said to Nate. "I don't think they want us here. They think we . . . stirred up Hattie's ghost or something."

"I think you're taking your own worries, your own dis-ease, and putting it on other people," he said, setting down his new hammer. They were nailing down the upstairs plywood subfloor. "Sure, folks in Hartsboro may be a little leery of outsiders, but saying they don't want us here is a bit of a stretch. And don't even get me started on the ghost stuff."

Now she reached up on the shelf for the flashlight, fingers groping, spider-crawling along the dusty wood.

It wasn't there. She swept back and forth with her hand but found nothing. Nate's glasses were missing, too.

Helen slid her way off the bottom of the bed, her feet hitting the cold linoleum of the floor. It was spongy in places, giving just a little under her bare feet.

Like walking on the bog, she thought. *And at any moment, I'll fall through, down into a deep dark spring, into the place Hattie came from.*

She thought of turning on the light but was too frightened. She didn't want whatever might be out there to know she was up, to see her through the tiny trailer windows.

Nothing's out there, she told herself.

She tried to steady her breathing, but it still came out in jagged puffs.

She crept quietly down the hall, through the living room to the front door. There was a window just to the left of it. She looked through the dusty glass, past her own dim, frightened reflection. The night seemed impossibly dark. A sliver of a moon. A cloudy sky. Not even the pinprick lights of the stars overhead.

As her eyes adjusted, she could make out shapes in the darkness: the sharp angles of the two pop-up canopies they stored their tools and wood under. And there, beyond them, the strange skeletal walls of what would one day be their home. There was something inside it, within the cage of walls, moving across the floor. A pale figure, writhing, dancing. This wasn't Nate with his sure gait, his broad shoulders.

This was a woman.

A woman in a white dress.

This, Helen knew at once, was Hattie Breckenridge.

And there was a reason Helen could see her figure so well—there was a flickering orange glow behind her.

"Shit, shit, shit, shit," Helen gasped.

A ghost! An actual for real ghost. And she was dancing around flames.

Their house was burning.

This was not some imagined horror born from panic or a bout of paranoid thinking.

This was actually happening.

Helen wanted to drop down on her knees, to hide and stay hidden. But Nate was out there, maybe in danger. And their house, the house of their dreams that they'd only just begun, was burning.

She felt Hattie beckoning her, saying, *Come closer, please.* Saying, *I dare you.*

Helen held her breath, turned the knob, pushed the front door open as quietly as she could, not wanting to draw attention to herself. The cool air hit her, her skin turning to gooseflesh.

Then, once she reached the steps, she ran.

Her bare feet pounded across the grass, past the truck, up the newly graded driveway.

She ran toward the acrid, stinking smoke. Toward the figure in white, twisting and contorting, giving off a low, droning moan.

Helen thought about history, about how places held memories, and how maybe ghosts were just a magnification of that force. Maybe ghosts were like an echo.

"Hattie?" she called as she came upon the building.

"Like hell," a voice roared, and a blindingly bright light hit her face, illuminated the floor of the house, the girl who was trapped there, her foot encircled with rope. She hadn't been dancing. She'd been trying to get away.

And this was no ghost, Helen understood now, but an actual flesh-and-blood girl. A girl with white makeup caked on her face, wearing camouflage pants and a matching shirt with a lacy white nightgown on top of them.

Helen guessed the girl was only thirteen or fourteen years old, all elbows and knees with a thin, pointed elfish face and dark, tangled hair that looked like it hadn't seen a brush in a while.

"Nate?" Helen called, shading her eyes, trying to look past the girl and the beam of light at her husband. "What's going on?"

"This is our ghost," Nate said. He stood at the other end of the house, aiming the spotlight at them. He was holding the other end of the heavy rope that was looped around the girl's foot. The ground was strewn with tools, more rope, and the nylon netting they used to cover loads in the back of the truck.

"What's all this rope and netting?" Helen asked.

"I knew someone was coming and messing with our stuff," Nate explained, "and that it sure as hell wasn't any ghost. So I set a trap. I laid some snares out. And the netting. Put a pile of tools right in the center of the floor. Then I hid and waited. This girl shows up, all dressed in white, and starts a freaking fire in the middle of our house. I couldn't believe what I was seeing!"

Helen leaned down and untied her. The girl was shaking like a frightened animal.

Nate came forward, standing next to the pile of smoldering rags that lay in a metal pot on the floor. "She was trying to burn our house down!"

"I wasn't," the girl said, her chin shaking as she struggled not to cry. "I'm sorry."

"I'm calling the cops," Nate said, voice crackling as he tried to contain his fury. "Arson is a crime." He turned to Helen. "Do you have your phone on you?"

"No," Helen said. "I didn't . . . I thought . . ." She gestured lamely at the scene before her.

"Go get it," Nate said. "Get it and call the state police. Tell them we caught a kid vandalizing our new house. I'll keep her here."

"Wait," the girl said. "Please, you don't understand. Let me explain." She looked so young, so genuinely scared.

"You have about twenty seconds and then my wife goes down to call 911," Nate barked.

Helen stepped between them. "Let's all just slow down," she said. "Nate, let's hear what she has to say."

"I just wanted to scare you," the girl said. "See, I built the fire in a pot so it wouldn't burn anything else. I thought if you saw the flames, if you saw me dressed like this, you'd think I was Hattie. And you'd be freaked out and . . . leave."

Helen saw the girl was right. The fire, nearly out now, had been burning in a cast-iron Dutch oven, like a mini-cauldron. The fire wasn't actually very big at all, just bright in the dark night.

"Are you the one who's been taking our things?" Helen said, understanding slowly dawning.

"*Of course* she is," Nate answered.

At first, the girl said nothing.

"Yes," the girl admitted. "Okay, you're right. It was me. It was all me."

"Our tools? Our money?" Helen said.

"My cell phone?" Nate asked.

"Yes," the girl said, looking down at the ground. "All of it. But I'll give it back!"

"You went in and took things from the trailer?" Nate asked. "Jesus. That's breaking and entering!"

"I didn't break in or anything—the door was always unlocked."

"You opened the door, entered our home without our knowledge, and took shit," Nate said. "I'm pretty sure that still counts. People go to jail for what you did."

"Please!" the girl said. She was crying now.

"What is it? Drugs?" Nate asked. "You took our stuff to sell and get cash for what . . . OxyContin, fentanyl, some meth? What is it you guys up here are all into?"

"No!" The girl was shaking her head. "I don't do drugs. It's nothing like that. I have all your stuff still. I didn't sell it. I just wanted to scare you. I swear that was all. I wanted you to think it was her."

"Her?" Nate asked. "The ghost? Who's going to believe in a ghost that steals money and cell phones?" He laughed harshly.

Helen winced. She didn't think Nate saw, but she thought the girl might have.

Helen had wanted to believe in Hattie, to believe it was possible for someone from the past to somehow open a door and reach into the present and make contact—one misunderstood outsider to the other.

"I'll give it all back," the girl said. "I promise. I'll make it up to you, just please don't call the police. My father, he . . . he's been through so much. This would kill him."

"Guess you should have thought of that before pulling these stunts," Nate said.

Helen put a hand on the girl's arm. "Okay, you're not a ghost. We've got that straight. So, who are you?"

"My name's Olive. Olive Kissner. I live about half a mile down the road with my dad. We're in the old blue house at the top of the hill."

Helen nodded. She'd walked by the house. Waved to a man in blue work clothes who drove a banged-up half-ton pickup.

"How old are you, Olive?" Helen asked.

"Fourteen."

"So what, are you a freshman?" Helen asked.

Olive nodded. "Yeah. I go to Hartsboro High."

"And it's just you and your father?"

The girl nodded. "Just us now." Helen almost asked more, but the pained look on Olive's face stopped her.

Nate spotted a camouflage backpack, set down his spotlight on the floor, and grabbed the bag. He unzipped it and peeked inside. He pulled out a can of lighter fluid, some matches, then his hammer, a measuring tape. "These are our tools," he said. He reached in again. "My phone!" He tried turning it on, but the battery was dead.

Olive nodded. "I've got the rest of them at home. I'll bring them all back. I promise."

Nate slipped his dead phone into his pocket and reached back into the bag, pulling out a graph-paper notebook this time and flipping through it, holding it in the spotlight beam. There were maps on the pages, maps of the bog with all the trees and large rocks marked. The maps were outlined in red grids with Xs over some of them.

"What's this?" Nate asked.

"A map," the girl said.

"Oh, really? You are *so* not in a position to be sarcastic, okay?" Nate said.

"I know! It's just . . . it's hard to explain," the girl said.

Nate was studying the notebook, frowning hard at the map with the tiny Xs. Helen could see that the drawing was a good one, the bog accurately rendered, right down to the path leading to her and Nate's house.

"You said you were trying to scare us?" Helen asked. "Why? Why did you want us to leave?"

Olive chewed her lip, looked down at the plywood floor.

Nate set the notebook aside. "Better start talking, Little Ghost Girl, or I'm calling the police and driving down the road to knock on your father's door."

"Okay, okay," the girl said, sounding frantic. "See, this land, it all used to belong to Hattie Breckenridge."

Helen nodded. "We know. She lived in a house on the other side of the bog. But the house isn't there anymore. Only the old stone foundation."

"Right," Olive said.

"So, you're what—protecting Hattie's land? Trying to keep it safe from outsiders?" Nate asked. He'd picked up the spotlight again and kept shining it right at Olive, blinding her, making her close her eyes. "Why? Because her ghost told you to?"

"No," Helen said, understanding. She suddenly got it. The marked-up map in Olive's notebook, the little bits of red string she'd found, Olive's desire for them to leave the land. "You're looking for the treasure, right?"

Olive looked away, bit her lip.

"What treasure?" Nate asked.

"It's a story I heard in town," Helen said. "Hattie Breckenridge supposedly buried treasure somewhere around the bog."

"Treasure?" Nate scoffed. He rocked back on his heels, held out his arms in an *I can't believe this* gesture. "First, we've got a witch ghost, now there's a buried treasure? Is this *Scooby* fucking *Doo*?"

Helen put a gentle hand on Nate's arm and squeezed. She got how absurd it all sounded. "The librarian said it was just a story people told, town legend."

"It's not a story," Olive said. "The treasure is real."

"And you've been looking for it? Around the bog? Here on our land?" Helen asked.

Olive nodded. "It's real and I'm gonna find it. I *need* to find it."

"So much that you had to break the law? To spy on us, steal from us?" Nate said.

"You don't understand," Olive said.

"Help us understand, Olive," Helen said.

The girl drew in a deep breath. "See, my mom and I, we used to hunt for the treasure. She always said it was real. And she said she knew we'd be the ones to find it. But then last year, my mom, she . . ." Olive faltered. "She took off, okay?"

"Took off?" Nate repeated.

Olive nodded. "She left us. Me and my dad. We haven't heard from her since. And I think—no, *I know,* that if I find the treasure, my mom will hear about it, 'cause it'll be on the news and stuff, right? And if she hears, she'll come back. If not, I can hire someone to find her. A private detective."

Helen flashed Nate a *this poor kid* look. Helen had lost her own mother when she was just eleven. She knew firsthand how hard it was to be motherless. How back when she was Olive's age, she would have done anything, anything at all, to get her mother back. She looked back at Olive, dressed up as a ghost in the old nightgown—her mother's probably—and her heart just about broke.

"I wish you'd just asked if it was okay to go poking around on our land," Nate said, voice softer, calmer now. He'd lowered the light so the beam was pointing down at the floor. "You didn't need to try to drive us off with this whole crazy ghost girl thing. And you certainly didn't need to steal."

"I know," Olive said. "I know and it was really stupid . . . and I'm really sorry."

"Nate's right," Helen agreed. "If you'd just asked if you could search our land, we would have been fine with that."

Olive looked down at the plywood floor, eyes on the charred

remains in the cast-iron pot. She began to pick at the frayed edge of the left sleeve of her nightgown.

"So what are we going to do here?" Nate asked, looking from Helen to Olive.

Olive looked up, twisting the sleeve of her nightgown now. "Like I said, I can give all your stuff back. Well, not the pie. My dad and I ate that."

"I knew it!" Helen said, looking over at Nate. "I told you I'd brought that pie home and put it in the fridge! You made me think I was nuts, telling me I must have left it back at the store or that maybe I didn't buy it at all."

"Sorry," Olive said, looking small and sheepish. She toed the floor with a ratty sneaker. "And I can't exactly give back the money, either. I . . . I kind of spent it."

"Of course," Nate said, his voice taking on an edge again. "Are you sure drugs aren't involved in this in any way?"

"I swear! I used the money to help buy a new metal detector. A really nice one. So I could look for the treasure. I guess I can sell the metal detector and use the money to pay you back."

"How much money of ours did you take?" Helen asked.

The girl looked up, thinking, then counted with her fingers. "About eighty dollars, I think. Actually, maybe closer to a hundred? I'm not sure 'cause I didn't do it all at once. It was a twenty here, five or ten there, you know?"

"Jesus," Nate said again, shaking his head, rubbing his eyes.

Helen was amazed that she'd taken so much. They'd been careless with their cash—she and Nate sharing money, passing it back and forth, sticking it in pockets, and both running off to the general or hardware store several times a day for little things they needed.

"Wow," Helen said. "Well, the stolen money is definitely a problem. We're going to need you to pay us back somehow."

"At the very least!" Nate added.

They were silent a minute, both of them watching Olive, who continued to twist at her nightgown worriedly.

"What if I work it off?" Olive suggested.

"What?" Nate scowled at her.

"I'm a really hard worker, honest! And I know a lot about building stuff. My dad and I, we've been renovating our house for a long time. I'm really good with tools and I'm a lot stronger than I look. I can frame walls and hang Sheetrock. I can even do some electrical and plumbing."

"I don't know," Nate said. "I don't think—"

"We could definitely use some help," Helen said, turning to him. "We're behind schedule, right? And if Olive's got building experience, the work will go faster if there are three of us."

Olive nodded, looked hopefully at Helen. "I can come after school tomorrow. A trial. To prove that I'm not messing with you—I'm actually really good at building. And if it works out, if you want me to keep helping you, school's out for the summer next Wednesday, then I can come all day. Until you feel like I've done enough to pay you back. I'll work all summer if I have to, just to make it up to you. And if it doesn't work out, I'll sell my metal detector and get you the cash."

"What do you say, Nate?" Helen asked.

"I don't know," Nate said. "The kid just tried to burn our house down."

"Let's not exaggerate," Helen said. "She wasn't trying to burn the house down."

"Look," Olive said, looking right at Nate, "I know what I did, it was really wrong and downright shi—I mean downright crappy. I thought . . . well, who cares what I thought? I'm so, so sorry. Please, let me make it up to you."

Helen looked at Nate. "What do you think?"

"We don't know anything about her," Nate said.

"She's our neighbor," Helen said. "She's a kid, she made some bad choices, but she's trying to do the right thing. Right, Olive?"

The girl nodded enthusiastically.

Nate sighed. "No more stealing?" he asked. "No more tricks, no more sneaking around?"

"I promise! Everything aboveboard from now on," Olive said. "And hey, I saw all your field guides inside. I know everything about the animals in these woods. I can show you a bear's den, a beaver dam, and where the bald eagles nest. I even know where a bobcat's been hanging out lately."

Nate couldn't quite hide his interest. "A bobcat? Really?"

"Totally. I can tell you all about the land. I've been hunting around here since I was a little kid."

"And about Hattie?" Helen asked.

"I'll tell you everything I know," the girl promised. "And if you want, I can take you to meet my aunt Riley. She knows a lot more. She's kind of an expert on local history. And she loves all that ghost and ghost story stuff, too."

"What do you think, Nate?" Helen asked again.

He was quiet, still shining the light on Olive's face, trying to make up his mind.

"Nate?" Helen said in way that she hoped he'd hear as *You'd better go along with this.*

"Sure," he said, still looking skeptical. "You come back tomorrow after school and we'll see what kind of a worker you are. But if you don't keep up your end of the bargain, or if you pull any more tricks, I go right to your father and the police."

"You won't be disappointed," Olive said. "I promise."

"But right now, you should get back home before your father finds out you're gone," Helen said. "I can't imagine how worried he'd be."

"Right," Olive said, happy to be dismissed. "See you tomorrow then."

"Olive," Nate said, "one more thing."

Great, Helen thought. *Is he going to make her sign a waiver or something?*

"It was a deer tooth, wasn't it?"

"Huh?" she said.

"The little bundle with the old nail and tooth you left on our steps? I'm just wondering what kind of tooth it was and where you got it. It looks old and I can't figure out what animal it might have come from."

The girl shook her head, looked confused. "Whatever it was, it didn't come from me. I took plenty of stuff, but I never left anything."

"You're sure?" Nate asked.

She nodded. "Positive. Cross my heart."

Helen opened her mouth to say something more, but no words came.

"Okay if I head back now?" Olive asked.

"Sure," they both said in unison, Helen's answer gentle, Nate's more of a harsh dismissal.

They watched as she ran off into the woods, moving quickly and surely through the trees, the white of her old nightgown glowing like the ghost she'd tried to be.

Closing in

CHAPTER 12

O live

 JULY 8, 2015

Olive knew Nate didn't really like her. He didn't trust her, that was for sure. As helpful as she'd been over these last three weeks, as much work as she'd helped them accomplish (they'd finished framing the walls and roof and had moved on to putting plywood sheathing up), he kept looking at her like he was just waiting for her to screw up, to try to slip something in her backpack when they weren't looking. He even went through a show of making her open up her backpack each day before she went home. Once a thief, always a thief.

Helen, she'd been great. Olive heard her snap at Nate, "Christ, Nate, what's next—are you gonna strip-search the poor kid?" when she thought Olive was out of earshot. Helen had been a history teacher back in Connecticut, but Olive could tell she hadn't been the boring kind of teacher at all. Olive wished Helen was one of her teachers. The way she talked about history, about how people used to live back before there was electricity, before cars, it made Olive feel like she was right there, like she could really imagine what it must have been like.

And she did it so naturally, just working all these cool facts into everyday conversation. Like now, they were driving through town in Helen's pickup, passing by one old house after another, Helen pointing out the different architectural styles in a typical New England village like Hartsboro.

"That house on the left, it's a classic colonial. See how it's a simple two-story box—no eaves, shutters, porches? Such a clean design. The saltbox, what we're building, is a variation on the style. And see that one across the street?" Helen asked, slowing as she pointed at a huge white house with peeling paint. "Greek revival. Look at the columns, the way the peak of the roof faces the street. All the cornice detailing. It's really a work of art."

A car behind her blew its horn and Helen sped up.

"It's amazing that all these old houses were built in the days before electricity," Helen said as they drove. "Just think of it—no power tools. Everything was cut with a handsaw. And they used axes to hew the lumber. Chisels to do all that finely detailed carving on the columns and trim."

"Building a house must have taken *for-ev-er,*" Olive said.

"Sure, things might have taken longer, but there was more of a level of craftsmanship. There was real skill involved in shaping posts and beams and joining them, in doing all the delicate trim work by hand. Builders were artists."

Olive liked this. She doubted folks back then would be so quick to tear down a wall and put up another the way she and her dad did constantly. Part of her kind of wished to go back to a time without power tools and plywood and drywall.

Along with all the cool stories she told, Olive also loved that Helen was really interested in Hattie. Not just in all the creepy ghost stories, but in the real woman behind them. Helen had been doing research—looking online and asking around in town—but was frustrated that she hadn't yet learned any real facts. Olive had told her that her aunt Riley might be able to help—she volunteered at the historical society and could get Helen in. Today, they were on their way to the salvage yard where Riley worked.

"You're gonna love this place!" Olive promised as they pulled up in front of the Fox Hill Salvage Yard. "And you're also gonna love my aunt Riley."

Olive led Helen into the big salvage warehouse, past the old hand-hewn beams and milled lumber, the rows of old bathtubs, racks of plumbing fixtures and copper pipes. Helen stopped to look at sinks and tubs.

"You were right," Helen said as she walked up to a deep soapstone sink like she was being pulled by a magnet. "This place is amazing! Oh my god, look at this sink!"

"I'm gonna go find my aunt," Olive said. "You look around."

Olive found Riley behind a big desk on a raised platform in the middle of the store.

"Hey, Ollie!" Riley called out. She came around the desk, jumped down, and enveloped Olive in one of her bone-crushing hugs. "This is a nice surprise! What are you doing here? Where's your dad?" She looked around.

"He's working. I came with my neighbor Helen, you know, the lady I've been telling you about?"

"Cool! Can't wait to meet her."

"She's over by the sinks, I think. She kinda has a thing for old stuff."

Riley smiled. "Well, she's in the right place! Hey, I've got something for you," Riley said. She went back up to the desk, pulled her messenger bag out from underneath it, and rummaged around for a minute. "Here it is!" she chirped, coming back down and presenting her gift to Olive.

It was a small brass compass, tarnished and scratched.

"I picked it up at a yard sale."

"It's amazing," Olive said.

"It's for helping you find your way," Riley told her, and Olive had a feeling she meant a whole lot more than just getting in and out of the woods.

"Thank you," Olive said. Olive looked down at the compass in her hands, the needle spinning, wavering, until it settled on north. She told herself to be brave, to just ask—it was now or never. "Hey, Aunt Riley, can I ask you something?"

"Sure, kiddo. What's up?"

"It's about my mom."

This seemed to catch Aunt Riley off guard. She smiled a worried smile. "What about her, Ollie?"

"I'm wondering if you can tell me anything about those last couple of weeks. If you knew what she was up to. Who she was seeing."

Riley let out a long, deep sigh. "Have you talked to your dad about this?"

Olive shook her head. "No way! We don't talk about that. Only about how things will be when Mama gets home."

"That's for the best, maybe."

"I know. Dad can't handle it. He just . . . can't. But if you know anything, if there's something you've been keeping from me, I want to know. Please. I can handle it, whatever it is. I'm not a little kid anymore."

Riley reached out, took Olive's hand and gave it a squeeze. "I know you're not, Ollie. You're growing up fast. I can't believe you're going into your second year of high school in the fall. I remember the day your parents brought you back from the hospital, how tiny you were, how perfect. Where does time go?"

"You're kind of doing it again, Aunt Riley," Olive said.

"Doing what?"

"Changing the subject like you always do when Mom comes up. I'm sick of not talking about her, about what happened—aren't you sick of it, too?"

Riley looked at her for a few seconds, thinking and frowning.

"Look, I'll tell you what I told your dad," Riley said at last. "The truth is I don't know what your mom was up to. She was real secretive all of sudden. I could tell something was up. Something was different."

"Me, too!" Olive said. "She was like that with me, too."

It felt good to be talking about it at last, to get everything out in the open.

Riley nodded. "There was definitely some kind of change in her."

"Do you remember the last time you saw her?" Olive asked.

"Yeah. She was at Rosy's Tavern. I stopped in with some friends after work and she was there."

"Was she alone?" Olive asked.

Riley hesitated, bit her lip. Olive gave her a pleading *come on, we've gone this far* look.

"No," Riley said. "She was with a guy."

"What guy?" Olive asked.

Riley looked away. "No one I know."

"Well, what'd he look like?"

She looked back at Olive, shrugging her shoulders. "I don't remember exactly. Dark hair and eyes, maybe. A leather jacket."

"Do you think maybe Sylvia knows who he was?"

Sylvia tended bar at Rosy's and was one of Mama's best friends, going way back before Olive was born.

"I don't know, Ollie, and honestly, even if she did, what good does it do?"

"'Cause maybe he's the guy she ran off with? And maybe if we know more about him, we can figure out where they might have gone?"

"Oh, honey," Riley said as she gave Olive *The Look*. The pitying *poor little girl* look Olive knew so well. Olive clenched her jaw. She didn't want anyone's pity, especially her aunt Riley's. She didn't want to be *that girl*.

"Here's the thing, honey," Riley continued. "If your mama wanted us to find her, she would get in touch."

"But if we—"

"I know it hurts, believe me. But we've got to be patient. She'll come back when she's ready, Ollie." She raised her eyes, looked up behind Olive, and smiled.

"Hi, there. You must be Riley," said Helen.

Helen joined Olive at her side.

"Aunt Riley, this is Helen. Our new neighbor I've been telling you about," Olive said, forcing a smile even though she felt broken and frustrated by the conversation they'd been having. How could Riley think it wouldn't do any good to follow clues, to try to figure out where Mama had gone? "She'll come back when she's ready" wasn't good enough for Olive, and she couldn't believe that it seemed to be good enough for Riley.

"Ah, yes, you live out by Breckenridge Bog!"

"That's me—the one living on the cursed land, stirring up ghosts!" Helen said with a chuckle.

"Wonderful to meet you," Riley said enthusiastically, holding out a hand for Helen to shake.

"Wait!" Olive said to Helen. "What did you say?"

"Nothing," Helen said. "Sorry. Just some silly stuff I heard in town."

"So you've heard it? What they've been saying? How you brought Hattie back?"

Helen looked at her, narrowed her eyes. "I've heard a bit. And it sounds like you have, too. Why didn't you say anything?"

Olive shrugged. "It's just dumb stuff people are saying. 'Cause you live out by the bog, I guess," Olive said. "And then there's all the witch books you checked out of the library."

Helen shook her head in disbelief. "You're kidding, right? People know what library books I checked out?"

Olive nodded. "Brendan at Ferguson's, he's even going around telling people that he thinks you might be a witch yourself."

Riley laughed. "In a little town like Hartsboro, you have to be careful what you check out of the library. Check out one book on the occult and you're in league with the devil himself."

"Don't librarians take an oath or something?" Helen said. "Isn't there a code of honor?"

"Not in Hartsboro, apparently," Riley said.

"It's more than the library books, though," Olive went on. "They're saying you, like, woke Hattie up or something. Made bad things start happening."

"What?" Helen asked. "What bad things? Like the bus accident?"

Olive nodded.

"Let me guess, Hattie and I caused the lightning and fires, too?"

"Maybe." Olive shrugged. "That's what some people are saying anyway."

Riley smiled. "Probably even the traffic light going out again and again," she said. "It's usually just Hattie who gets blamed for anything bad that happens in Hartsboro, but now all the old gossips are over the moon because they have someone new, an actual flesh-and-blood person to blame."

Helen stood stunned, shaking her head.

"I wouldn't worry too much about it," Riley said. "It'll burn itself out. Some teenage girl will get pregnant or a guy will leave his wife for another guy and the whole town will have something else to chatter about."

"Yeah," Olive agreed. "Take it from me, the best thing to do is ignore it."

"Damn. I thought maybe I should start dressing in black and drawing mystical signs on the sidewalks," Helen said, and they all laughed.

"I hear that in addition to being the new town witch," Riley said with a mischievous wink, "you're building an amazing house out there."

"It's really cool," Olive said. "They're doing all the work themselves!"

"Impressive," Riley said.

"Or crazy," Helen added. "Idiotic maybe, even?"

They all laughed again.

"Olive's been a huge help," Helen said.

"She's a good worker, that's for sure," Riley said. "She's learned a lot from working with her dad on their house. Have you met my brother, Dustin, yet?"

Helen shook her head. "Not yet."

"I've been talking to dad about having Helen and Nate over sometime for a cookout. You'll have to come, too, Aunt Riley!"

It was something they used to do all the time back when Mama was around—have cookouts and invite a bunch of people. Everyone would bring something—extra beer, potato salad, watermelon—and

Daddy would shoot off fireworks in the backyard once it got good and dark.

"Absolutely, Ollie," Riley said. "Name the date and I'll be there." She turned to Helen. "So, what brought you in? Are you looking for anything in particular for the house?"

"Yeah, actually, I am. I want that soapstone sink you've got over there."

"It's a beauty. Let's go mark it as sold and I'll get a couple of the guys to load it for you."

"Also, I'm looking for a beam to use as a header. Something old, hand-hewn. Maybe four by four or four by six?"

"We'll take a look at what we've got," Riley said, leading them back across the vast warehouse of a store.

"Olive tells me you're kind of a local history expert," Helen said.

Riley shrugged. "I wouldn't say an expert. Not by any stretch. But it's definitely a passion of mine."

"I told Helen you could let her into the historical society so she could do some research," Olive explained.

"I'd love to check it out," Helen said. "In fact, I got the number of a woman named Mary Ann, hoping to get in and take a look around, and I left her a message, but she never called me back."

"Yeah, she and her husband are in North Carolina—their daughter and her family live there. She's about to have another grandchild and Mary Ann and her husband are down there waiting for labor to kick in. But I'm afraid the historical society is temporarily closed anyway. A water pipe burst and there was some damage. They have to redo the floor. A lot of stuff got frantically packed into plastic boxes and totes. It's kind of a mess. But I can let you know as soon as we get the all clear to open up again."

"That would be great!" Helen said. "I hope nothing was damaged."

"No," Riley said. "Everything was up out of the way, thankfully. It was just the floor. The carpeting has to be torn out and replaced, and there's some question about the subfloor."

They got to the sinks, and Riley pulled a tag from her pocket, wrote SOLD in big letters, and attached it to the sink. Olive's eyes just about popped out when she saw the price: it was $799. It was a large, deep double sink made from smooth cut slabs of slate-gray stone.

"The sink's from right here in town. And my guess is that the stone itself was quarried right here in Vermont."

"Really?" Helen said, looking even more excited.

"The sink came from an old farmhouse out on County Road. A couple bought it last year and are doing all kinds of upgrades, making it more modern."

Helen shook her head. "I can't believe anyone would give up a sink like this."

"I know, right? They probably put some new, shiny stainless steel sink in to match their appliances," Riley said. "Now let's go find you the perfect beam."

Riley led them over to the other side of the store, where the large beams were piled and stacked on racks. They all had white tags and were written on with yellow chalk.

"This place is so amazing," Helen said. "And I can't thank you enough for offering to open up the historical society for me." She started looking at the tags on the beams.

"It's no problem. Is there anything in particular you're hoping to find?"

"Anything about our land, really. But mostly, what I'm hoping to find is anything about Hattie Breckenridge."

"I don't think there's all that much, sadly. There are a couple of pictures. There might be an old land deed with her name on it. There could be more I haven't seen yet—we can look together."

"Do you know what happened to her?" Helen asked, turning away from the beams, looking at Riley. "I haven't been able to get any real answers out of anyone in town."

"I'm sure you haven't," Riley said. "It's kind of a gruesome story and not one folks in Hartsboro are all that proud of."

"Gruesome?" Olive said. "Awesome! Tell us!"

Olive had never heard the true story of what happened to Hattie. She'd asked her mom, but her mom had said no one knew for sure. Olive couldn't believe she'd never thought to ask Riley. Of course Riley would know what really happened, and more important, she could trust Riley to tell her the uncensored, no-bullshit truth.

Riley leaned against a stack of wood, pushed her blue bangs out of her eyes, and began. "Well, people believed Hattie was a witch, right? That she had the power to see what was going to happen before it did. Her predictions often came true and it scared people. They believed that maybe she wasn't just looking into the future but changing it somehow. That things happened because Hattie said they would."

Olive tried to imagine having this kind of power over people—the ability to make them believe you were capable of seeing into the future, shaping it even.

"One day, she warned everyone that the old schoolhouse would burn down. When it did, three children were killed. Hattie's daughter was fine—she'd kept her out of school that day, which made Hattie look even more suspicious, right? So Hattie was blamed for the fire, as she'd been blamed for every bad event she'd predicted. See, people then, like now, I guess, are afraid of the things they don't understand. They want something, *someone,* to blame."

"Isn't it interesting," Helen said, "how little some things change?"

"Yeah, yeah," Olive said impatiently. "So what happened to Hattie?"

"They hanged her."

Helen made a little gasping sound. "Really?"

Riley nodded. "Half the town showed up after the fire at the schoolhouse. Kids had died and they were really pissed. They declared Hattie a witch and they hanged her from an old white pine that stood near the edge of the bog."

"What year was this?" Helen asked.

"Nineteen twenty-four," Riley said.

"Wow!" Helen said. "I've never heard of anyone being hanged for witchcraft that late. Most of the trials and executions were back in Puritan times."

"I think it was pretty well covered up. People in Hartsboro weren't exactly proud of what they'd done."

"Where's she buried?" Helen asked.

"No one knows for sure," Riley said. "Though folks say she was dragged into the center of the bog and weighted down. That she lies there still and that's what makes it a haunted place."

"So, she's in the bog?" Olive asked.

"Maybe," Riley said.

"And the hanging tree? What happened to that?" Olive asked, trying to think of which tree it could be. There weren't any big pines along the edge of the bog.

"They cut it down soon after," Riley said. "Milled it into lumber. They actually used the beams to rebuild the schoolhouse."

"The one they tore down last year?" Olive said.

"Yeah. Actually, I think I've still got a couple of the beams from it right here for sale." She turned back toward the wood stacked on heavy steel racks.

"No way!" Olive said. "Like, from the actual hanging tree?"

"That's what people say," Riley told them as she started looking at the tags stapled to the beams. "This one," she said, pointing.

Helen came up, reached out to touch the beam, hesitated a second, then placed her hand on it, gave it a soft caress.

"This came from a tree from our land? From Hattie's time?" she asked.

"I can't prove it or give you a certificate of authenticity or any-thing, but I'm reasonably sure it did, yes. Then it helped frame the old one-room Hartsboro schoolhouse."

The beam looked like all the others to Olive—old, a rich brown color, full of ax marks.

"It's perfect," Helen said. "It's just what we need to be the header between the living room and kitchen."

"No way!" Olive said. "You're going to put the hanging tree beam in your house? What if it's, like, haunted or something?"

Helen laughed. "There's no such thing as ghosts," she said. "But this beam . . . remember what I was telling you about, how they used to make lumber with just an ax? That's what all these marks are from." She ran her fingers over the face of the beam. "You can practically feel the history in it, can't you?"

Olive put her hand on the beam, too, trying hard to imagine the tree it had once come from, standing at the edge of the bog; trying to imagine Hattie with a noose around her neck, how that tree was one of the last things she ever saw. And that tree had seen Hattie, too. Had held her weight, felt her last movements. Olive imagined there was some piece of Hattie in that tree, like a stain somewhere deep down inside it.

CHAPTER 13

Helen

 JULY 12, 2015

"It's perfect," Helen said.

She and Nate had just installed the beam as the header framing the opening between the living room and the kitchen.

It was a rough-hewn beam about four by eight inches, and it spanned the top of the six-foot opening between the two rooms perfectly. It tied the rooms together and added a wonderful old-wood warmth.

It was amazing how the rooms were beginning to feel like rooms, like an actual space they might soon live in. The framing for the walls was up, the plywood subfloor nailed down, and all the outer sheathing in place; they'd put marks on the floor and stud walls to show where the counters, cabinets, and big soapstone sink would be installed. The sink was being stored under one of the pop-up canopies in the yard. Nate had balked a bit at the price but agreed that it would go perfectly in their kitchen.

Helen was already starting to look at the inside of the house and think about where their couch and favorite reading lamp would go; what it would be like to make coffee in their kitchen. She felt like a little kid playing house with imaginary furniture as she moved from room to room.

"Let's just tell people the beam came from the old Hartsboro schoolhouse and leave out the hanging tree bit, okay?" Nate said, blinking up at it like it was something he was still trying to understand.

Nate had found the beam's history a bit disturbing, unsettling even, but had agreed it was a beautiful piece of wood.

"You can't buy wood like this these days," he'd said, running his fingers over its surface, feeling the rough edges left by the hewing ax. "Sturdy old heartwood from the center of an old-growth tree like this."

The beam seemed to give a warm glow compared with the new, pale spruce two-by-fours underneath it.

"I love the way it makes the house feel," Helen said now, as she took Nate's hand, led him around the downstairs. "The way it brings in this real sense of history."

Nate laughed. "Kind of a morbid history, but yeah, I get what you're saying."

"It's pretty amazing that it came from a tree right here on our land. Imagine the stories it would tell if it could," Helen said. "I really want to incorporate more old building materials—more stuff with local history. You should see that salvage yard, Nate! So many beautiful things just waiting to be given new life. My dad would have loved the place!" She remembered going to barn sales and flea markets with him, picking up old windows, doors, sinks, and hardware for him to use in his renovations. "They had stained-glass windows, claw-foot bathtubs, old farmhouse sinks, and so much lumber. And all of it had stories to tell!"

Nate nodded, rubbing his beard, which had filled in substantially and was now looking more beard-like and less *I forgot to shave*–like. Helen wasn't sure whether she liked the new beard yet. She thought it made him look more like a serial killer than a woodsman.

"I think that's an excellent idea," Nate said. "We wanted to build green, right? And you can't get much more green than reusing and recycling. And it's a definite bonus when the materials are of higher quality than what you can buy new. Plus, I imagine it's cheaper in a lot of cases. Maybe with the exception of that massive stone sink you brought home. Overall, it's a win-win."

"I'm going to go back to the salvage yard, check online sites, just be on the lookout for other things we can use."

"Okay," he said with smile. "You're officially in charge of acquiring salvaged materials."

"Artifact hunting!" she declared.

"I love it," he said, giving her a kiss. "And I love that you're so excited about this!"

"Riley will be a big help. She's so great, Nate. I can't wait for you to meet her. She looks like this Goth girl with crazy hair, tattoos, and piercings, all dressed in black, but she's a total history nerd! And in the summer, she builds houses for Habitat for Humanity. I told you she offered to come give us a hand, right?"

"Mm-hmm."

"I think we should take her up on it. Maybe I'll schedule a work day and have her and Olive come; maybe we can invite Olive's dad, too. We can get pizza and beer for after. What do you think?"

"Sounds great, hon."

"Nate? I just had an idea."

He smiled. "You're on a roll today."

He was right, her mind was whirring. She felt so good. Keyed up.

"What do you think about sleeping in here tonight?"

He laughed. "What, on the floor between the sawhorses? Make a bed from bundles of insulation and sawdust?"

His *you've gotta be kidding* smile turned to a frown. "You're serious?"

She put her hands on his shoulders, gave them a little convincing massage. "Come on! It'll be fun! We can clear a spot in the living room. Bring our sleeping bags. Light some candles. It'll be like camping, only better. The first night in our new house!"

"I don't know. I—"

"First sex in the new house," she whispered.

"Okay, I'm in," he said, stepping toward her, giving her a scratchy kiss.

.   .   .

They'd had two bottles of wine, which would explain Helen's pounding headache and terrible thirst. She woke up naked, disoriented. She turned her head. They were in the bare bones of the unfinished new house. On the living room floor. In the spot where their old braided rug would one day go.

One of the candles in the glass votive jar was still flickering dimly. Nate snored softly beside her. They'd zipped their two sleeping bags together, making one large bag, which now felt suffocatingly hot and damp with sweat. The plywood floor beneath them was hard, too hard to sleep on comfortably. Her back and neck ached. And she had to pee.

She unzipped her side of the sleeping bag and crawled out, searching around on the floor until she found her T-shirt and panties. The air felt startlingly frigid. She rubbed her arms, trying to brush the goose bumps away.

Something creaked behind her. The house settling, maybe?

Did brand-new, totally unfinished houses settle?

There it was again, a loud creaking sound.

Jesus. What *was* that?

Her damp skin turned even more cold and clammy.

Turn around, she told herself. *Just turn around.*

She took in a breath, then slowly turned so that she was facing the kitchen, looking at it through the framed opening with the new beam up above. The beam from the hanging tree.

It's the beam making the sound, she thought. *The beam remembering the weight of Hattie hanging from one of the tree's sturdiest branches.*

She recalled something she read once about hangings: how unless the victim's neck was broken with the initial drop, she would hang and slowly suffocate. A terrible way to die.

Helen felt her own throat tightening as she reached down to grab the candle and forced herself to shuffle forward, passing under the beam, moving into the kitchen, which was all shadows. The windows in the house had all been framed, but she and Nate hadn't cut through the plywood that covered them yet, so they were dark. No views. No moonlight coming through.

It was like being in a tomb with only a dimly flickering candle.

And she wasn't alone in here. She felt that instantly.

She could hear something.

Not creaking this time, and not Nate snoring in the other room, but the quiet breathing of someone trying not to be heard.

She turned to her right and looked in her blind spot, and her bladder nearly let go.

There was a woman there.

She was standing just to the right of the wide doorway, her back against the wall, her body right where a set of kitchen shelves would go. She wore a dirty white dress, black lace-up shoes. Helen saw the woman's wild inky-black hair, the dark circles like bruises under her eyes, and knew exactly who she was. She knew, just looking into her eyes. She would have known her even without seeing the heavy hemp rope looped around her neck: a coarse noose like a macabre necklace, the frayed end of the rope hanging to the woman's waist.

Hattie was here for real this time. Not some little girl playing dress up.

Helen froze. Hattie's eyes—for this must be Hattie—were black and shimmered like the dark water at the center of the bog.

Helen wanted to speak, to say something—Hattie's name maybe, or just a simple hello—but there was no air in her chest, and when she opened her mouth, no sound came. She felt like a cartoon fish letting out little bubbles of air, bubbles that rose to the surface and popped without making a sound.

The air felt heavy and cold, as if Helen were wrapped in a blanket of fog. And the smell! The peaty, primordial smell of the bog with something sweet and rotten behind it.

Hattie looked up at the beam above them, the beam from the tree she'd died beneath; the tree whose branch had borne her full weight, the tree that remembered her as she must remember it.

Hattie touched the noose around her neck, ran her pale fingers over each knob of the braid like a woman praying the rosary. And, like a woman praying, Hattie moved her lips—she was speaking, whispering softly, silently almost, and Helen couldn't make out what she was saying. She looked more and more distressed as she whispered to herself, her fingers moving along the rope, her eyes still locked on the beam.

Then she looked right at Helen and said one clear word: *Jaaane.*

Her voice sounded like breaking glass—no, that wasn't quite right; it was the sound of glass being ground up, being tumbled and smashed. It was a broken, screaming, hissing sort of sound that made Helen's bowels go icy. The sweet, rotting stench intensified.

"Jane?" Helen croaked back, her throat dry. She wanted to turn and run. To not be here with this . . . this creature who looked human but was clearly not of this world. Not anymore.

"Babe?"

Helen whirled around.

Nate was sitting up, looking at her. He could see Helen, but his view of the corner where Hattie stood was blocked by the wall.

"Whatcha doing?" he asked, voice thick with sleep and wine.

Helen drew a jagged breath. "Nate," she said, trying to keep her voice calm. "Come here."

"What is it?" He unzipped the sleeping bag and staggered forward, naked, his body pale and glowing in the dark. "Don't tell me that porcupine found its way in here."

"Look," Helen said, pointing to the corner. But when her own eyes followed her finger, she saw that Hattie was gone.

"Look at what?"

"She was here!" Helen said. "She was right here, standing in the corner."

"Who?"

"Hattie."

"Oh man." He smiled. "Is our little ghost girl playing tricks on us again?"

"No! This wasn't Olive. This was the *real* Hattie. She had black hair. An old dress. A noose around her neck."

"Sweetie," Nate said, taking her hand. "You imagined it."

"She was here! I know what I saw. Don't you smell that?"

"Smell it?"

"That rotting, boggy smell? She was here, Nate!"

The smell was fading, she thought, but still distinct.

He paused, studied her, his face full of concern—the way he looked when she ran a high fever. "It's the crazy stories you've been listening to. The books you've been reading. And all the wine we had. You were probably dreaming about her. You woke up and part of your brain was still stuck inside the dream."

"Nate—"

"Come on, Helen. You really expect me to believe that there was just a ghost in our house?"

She didn't answer. How could she answer? She'd just seen the proof with her own eyes. And if Nate didn't believe her, she knew there was no way to convince him.

She tried to imagine what would happen if it were the other way around: if he were the one saying he'd seen a ghost. Would she believe him?

Yes, she told herself. Yes, of course she would.

"Let's go back to bed, huh?" Nate said, talking to her like she was a child who'd had a bad dream. "But I've gotta pee first."

"Me, too," Helen said.

They went back to the trailer to use the bathroom and Nate headed for the bedroom after.

"No," Helen said. "Let's go back up to the house."

"Are you sure?" Nate asked, brow furrowed. "Wouldn't you rather sleep in a real bed?"

"I think it's cozy up there. Besides, we left a candle burning. We have to go up anyway."

"Okay," Nate agreed, and as they walked back up, hand in hand,

Helen kept her eyes on the house, but of course it was a solid box—no holes where the windows would be—so she couldn't see what was happening inside, if maybe Hattie had come back.

Nate settled into the sleeping bags, and Helen went into the kitchen one more time to check the corner. It was still empty. No sign at all that anyone or anything had been there.

But it hadn't been empty.

She knew what she'd seen.

She reached up, touched the header beam in the doorway. She imagined it had a pulse like a living thing. A living thing with a memory of its own. And maybe, just maybe, the power to call someone back.

A historical artifact turned talisman.

What if objects didn't just hold memories but held traces of the people who'd touched them, threads that connected them still?

It was a crazy thought, one she knew better than to share with Nate.

"Come to bed," Nate called, holding open her edge of the sleeping bag.

She went over and crawled in beside him, trying to get comfortable on the hard floor. He wrapped his arm around her, nuzzled the back of her neck.

"You know what I love about you?" he asked. "I love the places your imagination takes you. That's what makes you such an amazing history student and teacher. Because you can read about a time and place and put yourself right back there."

She listened to him as she lay in the dark, her eyes on the opening to the kitchen, on the beam at the top of the frame.

"It was not my imagination. And it wasn't the wine, either."

She knew it was pointless to argue but couldn't help herself.

"There's no such thing as ghosts," Nate told her as he stroked her hair, and part of her longed to believe him. To believe she'd imagined it. Because that would make sense. That would be simple.

But the world was not simple.

She knew this.

Soon, Nate was asleep again.

"I know what I saw," she whispered once more, to herself, to the night, to whoever (or whatever) might be listening.

Helen woke up on the floor of the house, body stiff and sore. She was sure she could hear the faint sound of creaking, swaying: the sound a body hanging from a noose would make.

She stared up at the beam, squinted her eyes, searching for a shadow, a sign that Hattie was there. But she wasn't.

And neither was Nate.

His side of the sleeping bag was empty. His clothes were gone from the floor. Helen looked at her watch. Six in the morning. Too early for Nate to be up and out of bed normally. Maybe he'd gone back to the trailer to sleep. She unzipped the sleeping bag and climbed out.

"Nate?" she called.

Nothing.

The windowless house was dark. It was like being sealed in a wooden box. A coffin. Buried like Hattie.

But Hattie hadn't been buried in a coffin, had she?

Helen thought back to what Riley had told her: *folks say she was dragged into the center of the bog and weighted down. That she lies there still and that's what makes it a haunted place.*

That's where the smell came from. That horrible, sweet rotting smell layered with the damp earthy smell of the bog.

She's down there and she's still got the noose around her neck.

Then, knowing it was silly to check, but unable to stop herself, she stepped into the kitchen, passing beneath the beam, and looked in the corner. Empty.

"Hattie?" she said, voice low, unsure of itself. "Are you here somewhere?"

She waited, listening, watching, feeling a little self-conscious, a little crazy even. Was she really talking to a ghost? What would Nate say if he heard her?

Maybe he was right. Maybe she'd imagined it. She'd had too much wine, and maybe she'd had a nightmare, a nightmare come to life.

But that smell, she told herself. Could she really have imagined that smell? And the sound of the creature's voice. Ground glass on glass. The sound of pain.

It was real and she knew it.

She pulled on her jeans and got the hell out of the house, walked down the hill to the trailer.

"Nate? You here?"

Not in the kitchen. No coffee had been made. No granola left out. And he wasn't in the bed.

The truck was parked in the driveway, windshield covered in dew; the keys hung on the little brass hook next to the front door. She pulled her phone out of her pocket and called him. It went straight to voice mail.

She clenched her jaw, felt the air around her grow thin, the walls moving in a little closer.

No need to panic, Helen told herself. *He must have gone for a walk. Early-morning bird-watching maybe. That's a Nate-like thing to do.*

"Nate is fine," she said to the empty trailer.

Say the words. Make them real.

She made coffee, ate some cereal, checked her email, telling herself everything was fine. Everything was normal. An email from her friend Jenny greeted her:

> Glad to hear you're making progress with the house. Love the pic of Nate's mountain man beard! And the story of your "ghost" visitor. Olive sounds like quite the kid. Still though . . . maybe I'm reading between the lines, or maybe it's just my best friend super-psychic powers, but are you doing okay up there? Really?

Helen closed her laptop, looked over at the pile of library books on the table. She kept renewing them. She picked up *Communicating with the Spirit World* and opened to the first page:

> *Do you ever feel that you are not alone?*
> *Do you sometimes look over your shoulder, sure there was just a figure standing there?*

Helen slammed the book closed, hands trembling, and left the trailer and stood in the yard calling for Nate. Nothing. Only the morning chatter of birds.

She walked down the path to the bog, sure she'd find him there sketching early-morning birds. But there was nothing. No one.

She looked out into the center, where the deep part of the water was, and imagined George Decrow pulling his wife out, dragging her to the edge, her body cold and lifeless as he started CPR. She imagined it was her doing the CPR, Nate beneath her, lips blue.

Helen shook the image away, trudged back up the path to the trailer, poured herself another cup of coffee.

She grabbed the little notebook in her purse, found the number the realtor had given her for George Decrow down in Florida. She dialed it and waited.

"Hello?" A crackling old-man voice, a little out of breath.

"Yes, good morning. Mr. Decrow?"

"Yes?"

"My name is Helen Wetherell. My husband, Nate, and I bought your place in Vermont out by the bog."

The line went dead. He'd hung up.

Helen pushed redial. He answered on the first ring. "What is it you want?"

"Mr. Decrow, I heard what happened to your wife and I'm so, so sorry. And I hate to bother you, but it's just that weird things are happening here. My husband, he thinks I'm imagining things, and I'm starting to wonder if I'm going a little crazy." She paused, worried that she'd said too much.

She heard his raspy breathing, was sure he was about to hang up. But he didn't.

"Have you seen her?" he asked.

Helen held the phone tight against her ear, listening to George Decrow breathing. She thought of lying, of playing dumb, but this might be her one and only shot with this guy and she thought honesty was her best hope of keeping him talking.

"Yes. I saw her last night."

"Edie saw her, too. I didn't believe. I didn't believe until it was too late."

"Mr. Decrow, I know this might sound crazy, but I think maybe she wants something. She said a name last night—"

"She wants something, all right. She wants *you*. The best thing you can do, you and your husband, is leave right now. Leave and don't ever go back. I'm sorry."

And there it was again, that sound of dead air. He'd hung up. She tried calling again, but the line was busy. He'd taken his phone off the hook.

Shaken, she sat down at the table, opened her laptop, then closed it. Where the hell was Nate?

Work. That's what she needed to do. Go to work like this was just a normal day. Like she hadn't seen a ghost last night. Like Nate hadn't disappeared into thin air.

He's gone for a walk, that's all, she told herself. *He's gone to look for birds.* She said this last bit while trying to ignore the fact that his binoculars, bird book, camera, and nature journal were sitting on the table right beside the front door.

She went back over to the house, stood outside staring up at it, entirely framed now and sheathed in plywood. It was the first step of the process her father always called "closing in," where they sheathed the house, put in the windows and doors.

Helen continued to study the unfinished house; it looked more like an abstract painting of a house than an actual house. The shape was there, the geometry that said *house.* She tried to envision the house finished, sided with clapboards, the windows in, a warm light glowing behind them. She tried to imagine Nate peering down at her from up in the library: Nate holding a book in one hand, waving to her with the other. But soon that image was replaced by another figure: Hattie in her white dress, hands pressed against the window glass, peering down, waiting for Helen. Helen blinked, looked up at the unfinished plywood nailed to the studs.

She remembered Nate's words last night: *I love the places your imagination takes you.*

She went into the dark house, half expecting Nate to be there, but he wasn't. Only their empty sleeping bags, burned-out candles.

She went to work, getting out the tools she'd need to start cutting out the windows. She started on the first, the relatively small bathroom window, drilling holes in all four corners, just inside the two-by-sixes that made up the window frame. Then she guided the blade of the reciprocal saw along the inner edge of the frame. She popped the rectangle of plywood out, and she had an open window. The edges were a little woggly here and there, but it didn't matter; once they got the window in and put up the trim and siding, it would look perfect. Most of their windows had been delivered and were being stored under one of the pop-up canopies. According to Nate's schedule, they should have put them in two weeks ago.

Nate. Where the hell was Nate?

She set down her tools, went outside and did a walk around the perimeter of the yard, calling. Then down to the trailer. No sign of him.

She imagined him coming back from a walk, smiling, teasing her for having been worried.

Helen went back up to the house and went to work on the second window, telling herself she was sure he'd be back by the time she finished. Then, still no sign, she started on the third. With each section of plywood cut out, more sunlight poured into the house, chasing the shadows away. She felt her body relax as she got into the work. Helen was nearly finished with the fourth window when she decided this was ridiculous. She needed to find Nate. She'd take the truck and drive into town—maybe he'd walked down to the store? If she didn't find him there, she'd drive to Olive's, see if she and her dad could help her search.

She was on her way out the door to get the keys from the trailer when she saw Nate coming up from the direction of the bog.

Thank God!

But as he got closer, she saw that he was all scratched up, soaking wet, walking slowly, and he seemed to be favoring one leg.

She heard George Decrow's warning: *The best thing you can do, you and your husband, is leave right now. Leave and don't ever go back.*

Helen ran to meet him.

"Nate! My god! What happened? Are you all right?"

"I'm fine," he said, snappish, looking away. "I fell into a deep spot in the bog."

"What were you doing out in the bog?"

"There was a deer," he said. "A pure white doe. An albino. I woke up this morning and went outside, and there she was, right in our backyard. I tried to get a picture on my phone, but she bolted. So I followed her into the woods."

"You followed a white deer into the woods?" It sounded absurd. Like the beginning of a fairy tale. Maybe the deer would lead to a well where there would be a magic talking frog.

He shrugged. "I know it sounds crazy, made-up, but it happened. She was only a little ways ahead of me, and I stayed right behind her. She led me in a big circle, and we ended up at the bog. She walked right out into the middle. It was the craziest thing—she knew just where to step, avoiding the deep parts, finding footing. Me, I was stumbling, in up to my knees in places. The bog sucks you down, holds on to you."

Helen nodded. She knew what he meant, that sucking feeling like something underneath was grabbing hold, pulling at your feet, wanting to keep you there.

"But I kept following her. I got great photos on my phone, a video even. But then I went to get closer and must have stepped into a spring; I thought I was safe because I was still a ways away from the center. But the ground just wasn't there anymore. It was deep. I couldn't feel the bottom at all. Coldest water I've ever been in, too."

She thought of Hattie's bones lying down at the bottom of the bog, of a skeletal hand reaching up for Nate as he flailed around in the water . . .

She didn't get you. She didn't get you this time.

Helen shook the thought away. "But you're okay?" she asked.

"Yeah. Can't say the same for my phone, though." He held up his iPhone with a shiny, dead black screen. "I'm pretty sure the swim killed it. I'll try sticking it in a bag of rice, but I'm afraid it's a little beyond that."

"You should go get a hot shower, dry clothes," Helen said. "I'll make a fresh pot of coffee."

"Sounds good," Nate said. He started to leave, then turned back to her. "I wish you could have seen that deer, Helen," he said wistfully. "She was the most beautiful creature I've ever seen. I hope she comes back."

Helen smiled and nodded. "I hope so, too." But really, as she watched him limp away, leaving wet footprints behind, she thought he'd been very lucky.

She wants something, all right. She wants you, George Decrow had said.

Helen hoped this was the last they'd see of the white deer.

CHAPTER 14

O live

 JULY 13, 2015

Rosy's Tavern wasn't really the kind of place a kid stopped by for
lunch (maybe kids weren't even allowed in there?), but Olive went in
anyway.

She pushed open the heavy wooden door with a dartboard painted
on the outside and a sign advertising that Back in Black, an AC/DC
tribute band, would be playing Friday night. She'd tried to talk Mike
into coming with her, but he'd wimped out.

"No way," he said yesterday when they were hanging out in his old
tree fort. Since summer vacation had started, he wasn't around much.
His mom dragged him off to work with her most days. She ran a sewing alterations shop; she also took in dry cleaning and had it sent out.
So Mike spent his days filling out dry cleaning slips, hanging dresses
and suits in plastic bags, and doing receipts. "My dad and his buddies
hang out at Rosy's. If any of them saw me there, I'd be in deep shit!"

"Suit yourself," she'd said, climbing back down the ladder and not
stopping when he shouted down, "Olive, don't go! Please?" She hadn't
picked up the phone when he called later, just let the machine get it,
her mom's voice echoing out: *You've reached the Kissners. We're not home
right now, but leave a message and we'll get back to you.*

The dark tavern smelled like beer and cigarettes, even though
Olive knew you weren't allowed to smoke inside anymore. Not in
any store, bar, or restaurant. State law. But maybe people cheated.
Maybe they snuck smokes in the bathroom, or maybe the people who
worked there lit up once the place was closed down for the night. Or
maybe there were just so many years' worth of cigarette smoke in the
place that it permeated the floorboards, walls, and ceiling, clung like
a ghost the building would never be rid of.

It was a Monday afternoon and the place was dead. Two sports
announcers were doing a pregame baseball show on a TV mounted in

a corner up above the bar. There was an older couple in a booth sharing a plate of chicken wings, a pile of chewed-up, sucked-on bones between them. Two young guys in Red Sox jerseys played pool in the back room. One of them looked up at her, puzzled. A man with really bad posture sat nursing a beer at the bar, his body curled in a funny question mark shape.

Olive walked up to the bar, passing the question mark man, who gave off a raw onion smell. "Do I know you?" the question mark man asked.

"No, sir," Olive said. "I don't think so." She moved down to the other end of the bar.

"Aren't you a little young to be out drinking?" the woman behind the bar said. She wore a tank top and had a blue apron tied around her waist. Her hair was dry, frizzy, and dyed red, with blond roots showing.

Olive stood as tall as she could and placed two hands on the polished wooden bar top, between two cardboard coasters with beer logos on them.

"You're Sylvia, right? I'm Olive. Lori Kissner's daughter."

Sylvia squinted at Olive. "Sure, yeah. You look like your mom, anyone ever tell you that?"

Olive shrugged. "Sometimes, I guess." Actually, more than sometimes—at Quality Market, where Mama worked, all the cashiers teased her, called her Lori Junior. And Amanda, the woman who cut her and Mama's hair—she said, "You're the spitting image of your mother, you know it? You haven't grown into it all the way yet, but you will. Then Lord have mercy on the boys!"

She didn't think she looked much like Mama at all. Sure, they both had dark hair and eyes, but Olive was skinny and bony, with arms and legs that felt too long for her body; Mama was all perfect curves and grace. One time, Mama sat Olive down at her dressing table, put some of her makeup on her—a little blush, some bronzy eye shadow, mascara, wine-colored lipstick that tasted like wax. "Don't you look all grown up?" Mama had said, and Olive had been startled, because when she looked in the mirror, she saw a strange version of Mama looking back; a Mama imposter, that's what she'd become. She couldn't wait to take the makeup off and go back to being plain old Olive.

Now Sylvia studied Olive while she polished a pint glass. "Last time I saw you, you were a whole lot shorter. You've shot up like some kind of weed. How old are you now?"

"Fourteen," Olive said.

"Fourteen," Sylvia said wistfully. "Where does the time go?"

Olive didn't know what to say. She stared down at the shiny bar top.

"So what can I do for you, Little Miss Kissner? Want a Coke or something?"

"No thanks," Olive said, reaching into her pockets, which were empty. She hadn't brought any money. Didn't have any to bring.

Sylvia poured her a Coke anyway, put a cherry in it. "On the house," she said, setting it down on a beer coaster in front of Olive.

"You hear anything from your mom yet?" Sylvia asked.

"No," Olive said, touching the glass, watching the bubbles rise to the surface and pop, disappearing. "Not yet."

Sylvia made a grim face, polished the glass in her hand extra hard. She held it up so that she was looking at Olive through it.

"I was hoping you could tell me something, though," Olive said, taking a sip of the sweet, cold Coke. "I heard my mom was in here with a man not long before she took off. A man with dark hair and a leather jacket. My aunt Riley saw them sitting at a table together. I was hoping maybe you might remember that and know who he was. Or really anything else about who she was spending time with before she left." She watched Sylvia, waiting, trying not to look too hopeful. The last thing she wanted was to get the *poor pitiful Olive* look from Sylvia.

Sylvia put down the glass she'd been holding, twisted the white polishing rag in her hands. "Olive, your mom, she—"

"I know what people say," Olive said. "That she saw lots of men. I've heard her called a lot of horrible names. Not much you can say would shock me, so it's okay. Really. I just want to know the truth."

Now Sylvia just looked sad. Much older all of a sudden. Olive noticed the wrinkles around her eyes and at the corners of her mouth.

"I think a lot of people misunderstood your mother . . . I mean, sure, she came in here and would sit and have a drink with whoever was buying." Sylvia leaned down, polished at the counter with her rag, rubbing one spot in hard, tight circles, like there was a mark that just wouldn't come out. "She liked meeting new people, especially if they were just passing through. Tourists and hunters and long-distance truckers—people with stories about other places. Men and women. You know how people around here are about outsiders—distrustful."

Olive nodded, thought about Helen and Nate. How she'd heard the buzz around town about the new flatlanders who'd bought the land by the bog; how they were blamed for all the trouble in town, for stirring up Hattie; how some even said Helen was a witch herself.

"So the rumors would fly," Sylvia continued. "But your mother—as far as I know—wasn't hooking up with strangers all the time the way people go around saying she did."

"But she had a . . . like, a boyfriend, right?"

"I don't know, Olive. If she did, she didn't tell me. And I never saw her with anyone here who seemed like a boyfriend."

"But she met men here, right?"

Sylvia stared at Olive a minute, looking like she couldn't quite believe what Olive had just asked. "Like I said, she had drinks with lots of people in here. Including the weirdos in that ghost club she was in."

"Ghost club?"

"Yeah. The 'spirit circle,' or whatever they call it."

Olive drew in a breath. *No way! Her mom was off trying to talk to spirits?*

"Don't look so freaked, kiddo. It's basically a bunch of folks drinking bad wine and having séances and stuff at Dicky Barns's old hotel. Then they go into trances and charge old ladies money to talk to dead people."

"Wait. You're saying my mom actually went there? To Dicky's place?"

Sylvia nodded. "She went more than a few times. For a while, I think she was something of a regular."

Dicky Barns was a fifty-something man who had once been a rodeo star in Texas. That's the way he told it anyway. He walked around like he was Hartsboro's biggest celebrity, a huge silver rodeo belt buckle glimmering on the waistband of his Wranglers and a leather holster with an old Colt revolver. He'd corner anyone he was able to and yammer on to them about the old rodeo circuit: horses he'd ridden, steer he'd roped. His favorite stories, the ones he liked to tell the kids, were about the horrible injuries he'd seen: men gored by bulls, cowboys with skulls crushed, missing fingers. Mike said Dicky had dropped off some fancy Western shirts to be dry-cleaned at his mom's shop earlier this summer. "Do you have any idea how many bones I've broken, son?" he asked.

Mike admitted that no, he did not know.

"I got more metal plates and screws than Iron Man in those super-hero movies."

Dicky had grown up in Hartsboro but left home at sixteen to head for Texas to learn to be a cowboy. His dad had been the town doctor, but he got lost while hunting with Dicky way back in the '70s, when Dicky was just a kid. Some people said it was Hattie who got poor Dr. Barns, which Olive didn't take too seriously. Besides, her daddy said that Dr. Barns had been a heavy drinker and it was no wonder he'd wandered into the woods and couldn't find his way back out.

After a few too many broken bones and concussions, Dicky quit the rodeo life and came back home to Hartsboro in his thirties and bought the old Hartsboro Hotel, turned it into a used furniture and antiques shop. Olive had heard about the séances. People said he was trying to make contact with his father, which seemed just plain sad to Olive. Kids at school said Dicky was mental, that he'd landed on his head one too many times after being thrown off horses. Olive had seen the signs around town, heard stories about the ghost parties at the old hotel. Some kids, they said they'd seen it for themselves: Dicky moving from room to room in there, surrounded by the shadows of ghosts. But for the most part, people made fun of Dicky, including Olive's parents, who liked to tell the story of how Dicky was kicked out of a town meeting in the elementary school gymnasium a couple years ago for showing up with a loaded six-shooter.

"The guy never takes his gun off. He thinks he's an actual cow-boy," her mama said when they got home from the town meeting.

"A cowboy who talks to dead people," her dad chortled. "He's got a permit and it's registered, but you can't bring a gun into a school like that."

"No exceptions, not even for John Wayne—I mean Dicky Barns!" Mama said back then, laughing, shaking her head.

Now Sylvia leaned against the bar so that she was real close to Olive. She smelled like roses, only it was off somehow, more chemi-cal. Like a kid's rose-scented perfume. "Lori went to those meetings hoping to make contact with Hattie." She kept her voice low, nearly a whisper. "She wanted to know about the treasure."

"Did she? Did she make contact? Did she find out anything?" The words tumbled out fast.

Sylvia smiled at her. "You don't just look like her, you get all wound up like her, too!" She shook her head and considered for a moment, then went on. "I don't know if any ghosts turned up, but I do know this: Lori showed up late here at the tavern one night. After everyone else had gone home. She was all shaken up and she asked if she could spend the night at my place, said she couldn't go home, that Dustin—your dad—was real mad at her for something. I asked her what for, and she said it didn't matter, that none of it mattered anymore." Sylvia looked over at the men watching baseball stats flashing on the TV. Then she leaned in closer, lowered her voice and whispered, "Your mom, she had a few drinks here with me that night and, to be honest, she got a little tipsy. She told me that she had a secret, and I had to swear not to tell a living soul. Of course I promised. And she told me she'd found it. Hattie's treasure. She knew just where it was, but she hadn't dug it up yet."

"What?" Olive nearly tipped over her Coke. "When was this? Did she say where it was? Did she dig it up?"

Sylvia smiled again. She was enjoying herself now, enjoying the reaction her story got.

"It wasn't long before she went away. And no, she didn't tell me where it was. I don't know if she dug it up. Hell, I don't even know if she really found it. You know how your mama is. Always telling stories. Especially with a few drinks in her. She likes to pull your leg, you know? See what she can make you believe."

Olive nodded. Mama did like to fool people, to tell tall tales. She was always testing people, to see how gullible they were, what crazy story they might believe.

"Did she stay with you that night?" Olive asked.

"Yeah. But she was gone when I got up the next morning."

"And did you see her again after that?"

Sylvia frowned, the lines around her mouth deepening like little canyons. "No. That was the last time. Like I said, it was just a day or two before she took off."

"And you haven't heard from her? Or heard anything about her from anyone?"

Sylvia shook her head, dangly turquoise earrings swaying. She reached up, touched one, tugged on it a little. "No." She stared out across the room, her eyes on the glowing EXIT sign above the door. "Sometimes I think that maybe she did find it. Hattie's treasure. I never believed it existed, but maybe it did and your mama found it and she took that money and got as far away from here as she possibly could."

Without me, Olive thought. She took a long sip of her cold Coke, trying to concentrate on the sweetness, to give herself something else to focus on other than the horrible empty feeling this idea left her with.

All she got was brain freeze.

CHAPTER 15

Helen

 JULY 13, 2015

They spent the remainder of the afternoon cutting out the rest of the holes that would be windows. Helen went around with the drill, making holes in each corner, and Nate followed her with the saw, making the cuts, letting the pieces of plywood fall out to the ground below. They didn't talk about the deer or what Helen had seen the night before. They didn't talk much at all, just worked steadily, power tools whining, sawdust flying.

"Feels more like a proper house now, doesn't it?" Nate asked once they were finished, standing back to admire their work from the front yard.

"Getting there," Helen said. "But we've still got a long way to go. Let's bring in one of the windows and see if we can get it in."

Riley arrived just in time to help, pulling up in an old battered Honda Civic.

"Thought I'd come check out this house I've been hearing so much about," she said. "Wow! I love it! Classic saltbox!"

Helen gave her a grateful hug. "I love that you know it's a saltbox! And that you're here!"

Helen introduced her to Nate, whose first words were "You don't know anything about installing windows, do you?"

She laughed. "Lots," she said. They led her into the house.

"That beam looks amazing there!" she said, stopping below the header between the living room and kitchen. "It's perfect!"

"Too bad it's from a hanging tree," Nate said, laughing. "And that it seems to be haunted."

"Haunted?" Riley said, looking from Nate to Helen.

Nate laughed, and Helen said, "He's just joking. Come on, let's see if we can get our first window in. Let's start small—the bathroom?"

Riley helped them fit the window into the frame, then shim,

square, and level it and nail it in place. When they finished the first window, they went on to do four more, in what seemed like no time.

"Wow," Nate said, admiring their work. "If we had you here more often, we might even get back on schedule."

"Big project like this is bound to get a little behind," Riley said. "I'm happy to swing by and help out when I can. And if you want to break down and hire a pro for a week or two to help speed things along, I've got lots of names."

Riley was wearing a tank top, and Helen was struck by the woman's tattoos. She was covered in designs, all in black ink only, ranging from delicate to bold: an eye, a fish, a pentagram, a crystal ball, a winged horse. She had a black snake in a perfect circle on the back of her neck, its tail tucked into its open mouth, just visible under her angled bob.

Helen saw Nate looking at the tattoos and knew he didn't approve—he couldn't understand why anyone would want to do that to their body. Helen had toyed with the idea of getting a tattoo once, back when they were first together, but Nate had advised her against it, warning that she'd be sure to regret it at some point.

"I think we owe you a beer," Nate said.

"Sounds great! And I've got a little weed if either of you are interested," Riley said.

Nate shook his head. "None for me thanks, but I'll go grab some beers." He gave Helen a raised-eyebrows *you're not really going to do that, are you?* look that helped her make up her mind.

"I'd love some," she said, sitting down on the front steps of the new house beside her new friend. Riley produced a joint and a lighter from her bag, lit the joint, took a hit, and handed it to Helen. Helen inhaled the smoke, let it seep into her lungs. She looked out across the yard to the tree line, to the path that led down to the bog. She was sure she could smell the bog, the dampness and earthy scent of peat, when the wind blew in their direction. It was as if the wind from the bog was telling her: *You are meant to be here.*

And: *I chose you.*

She hadn't smoked pot since college, but it seemed like the right thing to do—part of who the new Vermont Helen was. She felt loose and relaxed for the first time in days.

She imagined the shit she'd get if her friend Jenny back in Connecticut could see her now—*Embracing your hippie self, Helen? First step weed, second step unshaven armpits, then you're commune-bound for sure.* And if Jenny had any idea Helen believed she'd seen a ghost—her old friend would be up here in four hours, shoving Helen into her Land Rover to go back to the safe predictability of life in Connecticut. *An intervention,* she'd call it.

Helen imagined having a dinner party with Jenny and Riley—pictured Jenny staring at Riley's tattoos, piercings, and blue bangs. Helen got a little thrill out of the idea of introducing them, showing off Riley like an exotic pet—*look at my new friend, look at my new life.*

Riley's skin seemed almost alive to her. "I've been thinking about getting a tattoo," Helen found herself saying.

"Awesome! I can hook you up with someone. There's this guy, Skyler, I apprenticed with him once upon a time when I thought maybe I wanted to be a tattoo artist. He's amazing. Most of this is his work." She held out her arms and Helen saw things she hadn't noticed before: images and faces within the designs.

"Do you know what you want?" Riley asked.

What did she want? Her mind drifted, spun. She stared into the empty black eye socket of the crow skull on Riley's forearm. Nate would like that one, Helen decided. It was like something he might draw in his nature journal.

"Do you have a design in mind?" Riley asked.

Nate came back with a six-pack of beer.

"What are we designing?" he asked.

"Helen's tattoo," Riley said as Nate passed her a beer.

"Is that right?" he asked, his tone carefully neutral, but he shot Helen a look of concern—or was it derision? He pulled up a folding camp chair and sat facing them on the lawn in front of the house. Helen felt a twinge of guilt, like she had betrayed him somehow. The weed was making her paranoid, surely.

"Nate," Helen said, as he settled into his chair and cracked open a beer. "You should tell Riley about the deer you saw this morning."

Nate had a good swig of beer, then told Riley the story of the albino deer.

Riley smiled and nodded, happy for him, but not seeming the least surprised.

"Wait," Nate said. "You know about the white deer?"

"That was Hattie you saw," Riley said.

Helen's stomach clenched.

"What?" Nate laughed.

Riley laughed, too, but comfortably.

"Oh yeah! There are tons of stories that go back for decades about a white doe in these woods. A couple of hunters back in the late sixties swear they found a naked woman out here by the bog. She ran, and while they chased her—they say to help her—she transformed into a white doe." Riley's leg was pressed against Helen's as they sat side by side on the steps.

Nate laughed so hard he snorted beer out his nose. "And how much had they had to drink?" Nate asked, once he'd pulled himself together. "Or maybe it was something stronger—nothing goes with a hunting trip like a little LSD, some magic mushrooms maybe. I've heard how Vermont was in the late sixties and seventies."

Riley shrugged her shoulders. "I guess you never know. However, as I said, there are dozens of stories going back years and years. People seeing her, following her deep into the woods."

Nate took a long sip of his beer and looked at Riley, his eyes moving from her face to her tattoos. "Interesting. I mean, albinism has always been linked with mystical stuff. In folklore, the 'pure white animals' often have magical abilities. In some cultures, albinos are considered cursed and are shunned. But really, it's just a genetic mutation—an accident that causes melanin to be improperly produced or distributed. Beautiful, unique, sure . . . but just genes."

"It's weird, though," Helen said. "Don't you think? That there are so many stories about a white doe in these woods going back years and years? I mean, if hunters were seeing her in the sixties, it can't be the same deer, right? How long can one deer live?"

Nate scooted his chair a little closer to Helen, put a hand on her knee. "I'd have to look it up, but I doubt more than ten years, probably less," he said. Helen reached down, took Nate's hand, gave it a squeeze, then removed it from her knee.

"I'm telling you, it's Hattie," Riley said, rolling another joint. "Got to be."

"Maybe it's not just one," Nate said, pushing his chair back again. "Maybe it's hereditary. Maybe there's a whole population of them out there. A colony of albino deer! Like the black squirrels in Toronto!"

Riley relit the joint and passed it to Helen. Nate gave her a quick frown. She took a deep hit, let the smoke seep out of her lungs as she smiled at Nate. "A colony of albino deer?" Helen said. "I hate to say it, but a ghost almost seems more likely."

Riley smiled.

Nate narrowed his eyes, shook his head, and stood up. "I'm gonna go look it up. Do some research."

"Sounds good," Helen said. "Enjoy."

They watched Nate jog back down the hill to the trailer, like walking wasn't fast enough.

"Nate's not a big believer in the supernatural, I guess," Riley said as she lit a second joint, then took a hit.

"He's very evidence-based. Scientific."

"Not everything can be explained with science," Riley said, passing the joint to Helen. Helen looked at the tattoos on Riley's arms: a crow skull, an Egyptian ankh, a dragon encircling her left upper arm. Or was it a gargoyle?

"I agree completely," Helen said. She thought of Hattie appearing in her kitchen last night. She was contemplating telling Riley about it when Riley changed the subject.

"I think it's great that Olive's spending so much time with you two," Riley said.

"She's a good kid," Helen said. "And she's really been a huge help with the house."

"The truth is I'm kind of worried about her," Riley admitted.

"How so?"

"My brother, her dad, Dustin, you've met him, right?"

Helen shook her head. It was a little strange. You'd think he'd be interested to see where his daughter was spending so much spare time, would want to stop in just to make sure she and Nate weren't obvious perverts or drug addicts or anything.

"Not yet," she told Riley. "We told Olive we wanted the two of them to come to dinner, but it sounds like he's kind of busy lately so we haven't found a time to make it work."

Olive had offered one excuse after another: her dad was too tired, he was working overtime, he was busy with house renovations. Helen had started to wonder if there might be something else going on. Maybe he was an alcoholic? Or just antisocial?

"Busy?" Riley quipped, shaking her head. "I doubt it. The truth is Dustin hasn't really been the same since Lori took off. He's kind of a mess, actually."

Helen took the joint again, said, "Oh no. I had no idea. Olive hasn't told us much about her mother."

That was an understatement. Olive hadn't really said word one about her mom at all, except to repeat a couple of stories she'd heard from her about Hattie. Helen knew Olive's mom wasn't in the picture but hadn't yet figured out why.

"Yeah," Riley said. "I'm not surprised. I mean, it's one thing to leave your husband, right? But your kid? Poor Olive. My heart freaking breaks for her."

"Was there another man?" Helen asked, worried she was crossing the line, but the pot loosened her tongue.

Riley nodded, looked away.

"No one's heard from her?" Helen asked.

Riley shook her head, blue bangs falling into her eyes. "No. It's fucked up. She and I were like—like best friends. Did everything together. It was like *The Lori and Riley Show,* you know? That's what Dustin used to say. Then she just . . . took off."

She looked away, eyes shining with tears. Then she took a deep breath and went on.

"Anyway, Dustin's been a wreck. He spends all his free time tearing his house apart and putting it back together again. He says he wants to fix it up to surprise Lori when she gets home. Like she's coming home. And like having a bigger bedroom and a brand-new living room is seriously going to get her to stay, right?" She rubbed at a small hole in her jeans, worrying the fabric, making it bigger.

"That seems so sad," Helen said, imagining the poor guy constantly fixing things up, thinking that if he just gets it right, maybe his wife will come home and will want to stay this time. She wondered if Olive believed this, too, or if she was just going along with all the work to help keep her dad busy, to give him hope.

"Yeah, but the worst part is he's so caught up in his grief over Lori leaving him that he's not really paying much attention to Olive. I hear she barely showed up at school the whole final semester. She somehow managed to ace most of her tests and handed in homework from time to time, so she got passing grades, but from what I hear, it's lucky they're letting her move on to tenth grade in the fall. I've got a friend in the guidance department there."

"And Dustin doesn't know this?"

"If he does, he's not doing anything about it. He's made it pretty clear that it's not my place to step in and give my opinion. I'm actually heading over there after this to check in with him, see what Olive's up to. Make sure they've got food and stuff." She sat up straighter, pocketed the baggie of weed and the lighter.

"Wait, they might not have food?" Helen said.

"Last time I went over, Olive was having frozen French fries for dinner because that's all there was in the house. It's not a money thing. Dustin works. He just doesn't have it together enough to shop and cook and be a single dad. Lori, she kept that house together. Dustin and Olive, they're kind of floundering."

"Wow, I had no idea," Helen said. She thought about Olive stealing their stuff, setting the fire in the middle of the night on a school night, obsessed with buried treasure like a much younger kid—of course she didn't have a good home life. How wrapped up in her own shit was she to have missed it?

They were quiet a minute, staring out at the yard, at the line of trees beyond it, the path that led down to the bog.

"Nate and I will try to do more to help. Ask Olive to stay for supper whenever she's here. She's such an amazing kid. So smart and helpful." Riley nodded at her, looked grateful. "I hate to think of her not doing well in school," Helen continued. "Maybe there's something we can do to help with that, too. Nate and I were both middle school teachers, so we're certainly up to doing some tutoring. We can offer to catch her up if she's missed a lot of school."

"That would be so great," Riley said. "I worry about her a lot, but I don't know how to help. I've offered for her to come and stay with me for a while, but she always says no. Besides, I don't think Dustin would go for it. Olive's all he has now. Honestly, I think if she wasn't there, he'd lose it completely. Back when he was younger, before he married Lori, he was a big drinker. Suffered from bouts of depression. I'm afraid he's slipping back into his old self. Which makes me so, so worried for Olive. She's all he has, but he's all *she* has, too. Well, her dad and me." She paused, smiled at Helen, put a hand on her knee and gave it a grateful squeeze. "And now you and Nate!"

Helen nodded. She looked over toward the trailer, thought about telling Nate all of this. Surely he'd want to help Olive, too. He still didn't trust her, called her "Little Ghost Girl" when she wasn't around, but once Helen told him what was going on with Olive, he'd want to help. How could he not?

Riley saw her looking toward the trailer. "Nate should be careful," she said.

"Careful?"

"Yeah, there's a story I didn't mention when he was here 'cause I could tell he'd dismiss it as pure bullshit."

"What is it?"

"Well, there used to be this guy, Frank Barns. He was the town doctor, and he loved to hunt. He lived over by Carver Creek. One day, back in the seventies, I think it was, he caught sight of the white doe out in the woods and became totally obsessed. He went out looking for it every weekend. One time, he was with his son, Dicky. Dicky was just a kid then, ten or eleven years old. They were over by the bog hunting quail. And Frank caught sight of the doe and took off after it. Dicky tried to keep up but lost sight of him. Frank Barns never came out of those woods."

"No way!" Helen practically yelled. "He disappeared?"

Riley nodded, eyes widening, caught up in the story and Helen's response to it. "Search parties looked for him for weeks. Hound dogs, a helicopter even. Nothing. The man vanished without a trace."

"What do you think happened?" Helen asked. She was good and stoned now. Her thoughts felt strangely fluid.

"Hattie got him," Riley said matter-of-factly.

Helen felt cold all over. "You know," she said, feeling brave, emboldened by the weed. "I saw her, too."

"The white deer?"

"No, the person. Hattie in human form. If I tell you, will you think I'm totally nuts?"

"Oh my god, not at all," Riley said, reaching over, giving Helen's arm a squeeze. "In case you haven't noticed, I'm a big believer in this kind of stuff! Please tell me."

"Well, ever since we got here, I've had this feeling, this sense." She stopped.

Riley watched her. Not like she was crazy, but openly. She was genuinely curious.

"This feeling," Helen continued, "that someone was watching me. I've almost caught sight of her a few times, just a hint of movement out of the corner of my eye, you know?"

Riley nodded excitedly.

"And I think . . . I think maybe she left something for me. A sort of gift."

"What kind of gift?"

"A cloth bundle with an old rusty nail and an animal tooth sitting in a little nest of straw. Nate thinks the tooth came from a deer or a sheep maybe."

Riley frowned. "Do you have it still?"

"Yeah, it's in the trailer."

"So when you say you saw her, it was just a shadow, a little hint of movement?"

"No. I mean, at first, yes. But then last night—I actually saw her. She looked like a real person. As solid as you look now sitting here beside me."

"Did you see her out in the bog?"

"No." Helen shook her head. "Here in the house."

"No way! Here?" Riley turned and looked back at the house right behind them. "Wait, is this what Nate was talking about before? About the haunted beam?"

Helen nodded. "We installed that beam yesterday and spent the night in the new house last night. I talked Nate into it. I thought it would be fun—like camping out. I got up in the middle of the night and walked into the kitchen and she was there, standing in the corner. A dark-haired woman with dark eyes, a rope around her neck."

"Shii–it!" Riley said, drawing the word out slowly. "What'd she do?"

"She . . . spoke to me."

"No."

"Yes!" Helen said. She looked around to make sure that Nate was still out of earshot.

"No way!" Riley looked both shocked and excited. "She actually spoke? And you heard her?"

"It was kind of a horrible sound. It made me feel cold all over."

"What'd she say?"

"She said one word: *Jane.*"

"Jane?" Riley was leaning close now, her face flushed. "That's her daughter."

"Her daughter." Helen repeated.

If Hattie's daughter's name was Jane, this was proof that Helen hadn't imagined the whole thing. It wasn't any wine or nightmare that had given Helen that piece of information. She had seen Hattie's ghost, and the ghost had really spoken to her, told her something she had no way of knowing.

Jane.

"Jane was about twelve years old when Hattie was killed," Riley said. "She disappeared right after."

"Oh my god. What happened to her?"

"No one knows." Riley shrugged dramatically. "She was never heard from again. There were rumors—she changed her name and moved south, or went up to Canada. Some say she never left, that she drowned herself in the bog so she could be with her mother."

"There has got to be a way to find out what happened to her," Helen said. "What's the latest on when the historical society might open again? I'd love to get in there and see if we can find any leads. Anything about Jane, about Hattie. I feel like there are so many unanswered questions."

"I talked to Mary Ann last night. Sounds like the damage was a little worse than she thought. It's going to take a couple more weeks to get it cleaned up and renovated."

"Oh no!"

"I guess the old wood floor under the carpet is ruined, and when they started ripping it out, they discovered some structural rot underneath. Mary Ann says we can't go back in until we get the all clear—insurance regulations. Fucking sucks."

"Okay, that's okay. I'll keep doing what I can online in the meantime." Helen was nodding, rocking slightly to and fro like she couldn't contain the energy buzzing through her mind and body. What if Jane had moved away, had kids of her own? What if there were living relatives, direct descendants of Hattie, who might hold important pieces of family history?

"Wow," Riley said. "I still can't get my head around this. You actually saw her! What else did she say?"

"Nothing. I called Nate over, wanted him to come see, but she disappeared."

"She didn't want him to see her," Riley said. "Not like that anyway—she appeared to him as the white deer. I can't believe she came to both of you guys. This feels huge. Most people, they just get a glimpse of her out in the bog. I've never heard of anyone saying she spoke to them."

"Do you think it was the beam?" Helen asked. "I mean, do you think it's possible that installing it, if it really was a piece of wood from the hanging tree, that maybe it helped her come back somehow?"

Riley thought a minute, then said, "I've heard that sometimes objects act as conduits, you know? Like if you hold your grandmother's wedding ring, you might call her back enough to be able to smell her perfume."

"I've always had this idea that objects hold history," Helen said.

Riley nodded. "But maybe it's more than that. Maybe they don't just hold it—maybe it flows through them, you know? Gives the dead a kind of . . . touchstone; something to pull them back to this world."

MECHANICAL

CHAPTER 16

O live

 AUGUST 3, 2015

Olive had never been inside the Hartsboro Hotel. It was a big, creepy three-story building with sagging porches and Gothic arched windows with leaded glass. The gray paint was peeling; the black shutters hung crooked. A hand-painted sign hung from a chain on the front porch: USED FURNITURE AND ANTIQUES. Olive and Mike stood on the other side of Main Street from it. The old hotel was a good half mile from the center of town, where the general store and post office were. There were some houses scattered here and there along this part of Main Street, and School Street ran off Main and curved back behind the hotel. School Street didn't have a school on it. Not anymore. It's where the old one-room schoolhouse they'd torn down used to be.

"I don't think this is such a good idea," Mike said, shifting nervously from one foot to the other. There was a broken beer bottle there in the road and he kicked it, scattering the bits of brown glass.

"So don't come with me then."

The truth was Olive wasn't sure it was a good idea, either, but she was going in. She'd put it off for weeks now, trying to convince herself she was waiting for a good plan, but really, she was just being a chicken. She'd even called Dicky once and asked when the next spirit circle meeting was, thinking she could just join in, pretend to be interested in the spirit world and see if anyone would say anything to her about her mom having been a member.

"Who is this?" Dicky had asked, sounding angry, like his hissing voice was sending tendrils through the phone to identify her, to stop her.

Olive had hung up without saying anything more.

"It looks creepy as shit," Mike said now.

To Olive the hotel looked like a neglected old woman—someone who'd been popular and stylish once but was now slumped over and sitting in her own pee. "It looks more derelict than creepy to me," she said.

The kids at school all said the hotel was haunted, that Dicky lived there with the ghosts he'd called up with his spirit circle. That his dead father lived there with him—his father who'd gone into the woods years ago and disappeared. Now they ate dinner together every night. Kids said that if you watched the hotel from across the street at midnight, you'd see the place was full of the shadows of people, moving from room to room. Some said they heard music, the clinking of glasses, chortling laughter.

"My mom came here once," Mike said. "To one of Dicky's gatherings."

"No way!" Olive said. "How come you never told me?"

"She made me promise."

Olive gave him an appreciative nod. She knew Mike took promises seriously. Him telling her this? It was kind of a big deal.

"Anyway, about six months ago, she went to try to talk to her sister, Val, who died back when they were kids. She drowned."

"Shit, Mike. You had an aunt who drowned? How come you didn't ever tell me?"

He shrugged. "It's not like I knew her or anything. She was, like, twelve when she died."

Olive nodded. She'd been younger than they were now. It was weird to think about.

"So what happened at Dicky's? Did your mom talk to her sister?"

"Yeah. She *says* she did." He rolled his eyes. "That Val told her she was all right, that she was watching over us, that she was never far." He said this last bit in a warbling imitation medium voice. He shook his head, disgusted. "My mom told me all this after a couple glasses of wine—you know how she gets. But she seemed so, like, happy about it. Happy that this pack of quacks gave her this fake message from her dead kid sister."

"How do you know the message was fake?" Olive asked.

He bit his lip, looked over at the old hotel across the street. "My dad says that Dicky and his friends, they offer this great service. They tell people exactly what they want to hear, then they pass a hat and ask for a few bucks to help keep the circle going. It's a racket. He was real pissed off at my mom for going."

"But maybe it's possible, right? Maybe there are some people who can actually talk to ghosts, call them back."

Mike blew out a breath. "Maybe. My mom sure believes it. And she told me half the people in this town have gone slinking into that old hotel at one point or another, trying to make contact with some dead friend or relative. But then, out in public, they all make fun of Dicky and his weirdo friends. No one ever admits to having gone. It's a funny thing."

"Well, maybe we'll get lucky in there and see a ghost."

"No way! Don't wish for that!"

"Come on, chicken," she said, tugging on his sleeve, leading him across the street. Main Street didn't have a whole lot of traffic—locals passing through, dairy trucks loaded with milk or manure from nearby farms. If you looked up to the left, you could see where Main Street intersected with Route 4—up where the bus accident had been months ago. Olive could make out the white cross someone had nailed up, the piles of stuffed animals and flowers and cards people had been leaving there since the accident.

They got to the old hotel and climbed the steps. They walked up behind the USED FURNITURE AND ANTIQUES sign, which swung slightly from the rusty chains that attached it to the edge of the porch ceiling. There were three mannequins on the porch: pale plastic women with movable limbs like giant Barbie dolls. They'd been dressed in old-fashioned clothes—ratty mink stoles, pillbox hats, moth-eaten dresses, velvet coats. Their faces were flat, blank, and featureless—no eyes, noses, or mouths. Yet they seemed to stare at Olive and Mike, to emit a buzz from unseen lips, a warning that said, *Go away. You don't belong here.*

"Well, that's not creepy at all," Mike said, looking at them.

Olive made her way across the warped and splintering porch floor to the heavy front door, Mike skulking along behind her. A crooked COME IN, WE'RE OPEN sign hung in the window of the hotel's front door.

Mike pointed to the sign above the door that said, THIS PROPERTY PROTECTED BY SMITH AND WESSON, and raised his eyebrows at Olive.

"We are so gonna get shot," Mike said.

"Don't be a wimp."

"You're not scared of that big old gun Dicky carries everywhere?"

"Guns don't scare me," Olive said. And that was true. She'd been hunting forever, had passed the youth hunting course and had her license. She'd gone to the range with her daddy and his friends and shot all kinds of rifles and handguns.

"It's not the gun you should be scared of—it's the crazy man *with* the gun," Mike said.

Olive took in a breath, wondered if Dicky was even inside. Dicky lived in the hotel, on the top floor. People said his apartment was where the old ballroom had been. Olive thought it was strange that Hartsboro once had a hotel with a ballroom. But that was back when the passenger trains stopped here. Back when the lumber industry was big. Way back in Hattie's time. The old train station building was still there, but now it was Depot Pizza and Subs, the one and only restaurant in town these days.

Olive pushed open the heavy door of the old hotel. A bell jingled. She stepped into what was once the lobby. It was now crammed full of junk: a battered rocking horse missing one of the rockers, ugly lamps without shades, unidentifiable objects made of rusty metal. Surely no one would pay money for this stuff. To the right was a long wooden counter, which must have been the front desk back when the hotel was running. It was covered with haphazard piles of junk mail and folders spilling papers. On the wall behind it, a few rows of old room keys on diamond-shaped placards with room numbers hung from hooks. Some of the keys were missing. Olive wondered what all these rooms held now.

Ghosts, a little voice told her. Which made it the perfect place for the ghost club to gather.

She thought she heard something, faint footsteps, a tinkling sound like glass breaking.

"Hello?" she called, her voice timid and lost sounding in the clutter. "Mr. Barns?"

She pictured him watching from the shadows, his gun trained on her.

"I don't think we're supposed to be in here," Mike said. He was about two inches behind her. She could feel his breath on her neck. She waved him back impatiently.

"It's a store, Mike. Of course we're supposed to be in here."

There was another sound from upstairs. A dragging sound.

Mike grabbed her hand, squeezing hard, his fingers warm and sweaty. "Let's go, Olive. Please?"

She pulled her hand away and moved through the narrow aisles, between dusty tables covered with old postcards and towers of stacked plastic buckets, and came to a massive, curving staircase on the left.

The banister was loose, hanging from the staircase at a funny angle, like a broken limb.

Had her mother really come here? Had she climbed these stairs, wary of the broken banister?

"Hello?" she called again, slightly louder this time. She heard a noise from the floor above her, that dragging sort of sound again. Furniture being moved, maybe. Or something shuffling, dragging a limp limb (or entire body) across the floor.

"Sometimes a vivid imagination is a curse," her mama used to tell her.

"For real, though. Let's get out of here," Mike pleaded, voice low, desperate.

Olive crept up the stairs, staying to the left, next to the wall and away from the failing banister.

"Olive, don't!" Mike called from the bottom. "What're you *doing*?" But she kept going.

There was a loud *thump* from up above them.

Mike bolted back to the entry. Olive heard the jingling bells of the front door.

"Chickenshit," she muttered.

She hoped the stairs were not rotten like the boards on the porch floor. It made her so sad, to see all this beautiful wood in such terrible shape. If she lived here, she'd fix it up. Turn it into something special. Maybe a fancy hotel again. Something that would really draw people to Hartsboro. And Aunt Riley could help her fix it up, find all kinds of vintage materials for it. Her dad would have something to renovate besides their little house. And Mama, Mama would definitely come back then, if she learned Olive had a whole hotel . . .

Sometimes a vivid imagination truly was a curse.

She got to the second floor. The wall-to-wall burgundy carpeting was stained, worn through in places, exposing floorboards. She held still, listening. "Mr. Barns?" she called again. "Are you here?"

This seemed like a bad idea. Maybe Mike had been right to run. But if her mother had been here, if Dicky knew something that might help, she had to find out.

She moved down the hallway, passing guest rooms on the right and left. Some of the doors were closed. The ones that were open revealed rooms full of furniture, paintings, old clothes hung on racks. Boxes and trunks. An old piano with a water-stained top and peeling keys. Light passed through the leaded-glass windows; shadows stretched across the floor with fingers that seemed to reach for her, to pull her in.

The hallway ended with a set of heavy wooden double doors, one of which was propped open like a gaping mouth, musty darkness behind. BAR AND LOUNGE, read an old, faded sign above the doors.

She crept into the room, thinking she should call out again but afraid to make a sound in this place. Afraid because she had the strong sense that she wasn't alone. That someone, something, was watching her.

The lights were out, but dim sunlight filtering through the dusty windows gave the room a hazy glow. There was a bar along the back wall, long and made from a dark wood coated with dust and grime, decades of neglect. Behind the bar, shelves. On the shelves, a random assortment of objects: a baseball, Christmas ornaments, old cigar boxes, and a bottle of tequila still half full. The bottle of tequila felt sad to Olive somehow, like the bar was longing for the old days, beckoning for one more customer to come up and have a drink.

She turned from the bar, went over to the other side of the room, which was dominated by a massive old fireplace surrounded by bricks and a crumbling hearth. There was a mantel above the fireplace littered with candlesticks and half-burned candles. There were little brass bowls full of ashes. Above the mantel, a black cloth was draped over something that hung from the wall. A mirror, maybe? Didn't people sometimes cover mirrors when a person died? Olive thought she'd seen that in a movie once.

But why?

Maybe so you wouldn't see the dead person looking back at you.

The thought, which came from nowhere, gave her chills. She looked away from the cloth-covered mirror, then back again. Had the cloth moved? Rippled slightly as though something was pushing from behind it?

This place was giving her the big-time creeps. She hated to think of her mother lurking around here with a bunch of weirdos, looking for dead people in the mirror, maybe.

Half a dozen chairs had been pushed back in a rough circle in front of the old fireplace. The chairs were in bad shape: broken arms, stuffing coming out in places, covered in dark mysterious stains. Olive thought she'd have to be pretty darn worn-out before she'd sit in one of those.

Then she noticed the floor.

The stained and worn maroon carpeting had been pulled up, cut out in this part of the room. The bare wooden floor was exposed: old wide pine boards held down with rusty nails. But there, on the floor in front of the fireplace, someone had done a drawing in yellow chalk. Olive saw the piece of thick chalk resting on the mantel with the candles—it was like what kids used on the elementary school playground to draw courts for hopscotch or foursquare.

But this hadn't been done by a kid playing hopscotch.

The design on the floor was a large circle. Inside the circle, an equilateral triangle. In the center of the triangle, a square with another circle inside it. And in the center of the final circle, an eye.

The same design as Mama's necklace!

I see all.

This was proof! Proof that Mama had been here. Had she done the drawing?

Olive stepped toward it, then back again. She had a really bad feeling that if she stepped into the circle, something terrible would happen.

It was a door, maybe.

A door to the mirror world.

Jeez, she told herself. *Enough with the crazy thoughts.*

"What are you doing up here?" a voice barked behind her. She jumped like an idiot, like a girl in a movie who is easily frightened. She nearly stumbled into the chalk drawing (doorway) but stopped herself.

She turned.

It was a man with a little potbelly that hung over his too-tight jeans, which had been tucked into shiny black cowboy boots with toes so pointy they looked dangerous. His salt-and-pepper hair was pulled back in a greasy-looking ponytail. He wore a denim shirt with silver snaps that was tight over the bulge of his belly. He had an angular, chiseled face with a big cowboy-style handlebar mustache. And strapped to his waist was a fancy tooled-leather holster holding a single-action revolver. He put his fingers on it now, just resting there, just making sure the gun was there, and making sure Olive knew it.

The infamous Dicky Barns.

CHAPTER 17

H elen

 **AUGUST 3, 2015**

"You're going to do what?" Nate said.

"Riley's bringing her Ouija board over. We're going to bring it up to the house and try to contact Hattie."

Nate was crouched over his laptop, reading about deer and albinism. He'd had a couple more sightings of his white deer in the last two and a half weeks but still hadn't managed to get a picture of her. His nature journal was open to the spread where he'd drawn the deer and taken notes. The shiny, heavily penciled-in eyes of the doe gazed up at Helen.

Nate stared at her. "This is a joke, right?"

Helen laughed. "I know, it's a little crazy, isn't it? Riley suggested it. You know she's into all that occult stuff."

Even though Nate had seen his deer several more times, there had been no more ghost sightings. Helen went up to the house almost every night to sit below the beam, looking at the corner where Hattie had once appeared. But nothing ever happened. When she'd expressed her frustration to Riley that afternoon, Riley had suggested the Ouija board. Riley had come over to help them with plumbing. All the windows and doors were in, the house wrap was on the exterior walls, and the tar paper was on the roof. Last week, Riley had talked them into outsourcing the installation of the propane furnace and hot water heater and they'd called in a friend of hers—Duane, who owned Ridge View Plumbing and Heating. He'd not only installed the new units for a fair price, but he'd helped them get started with roughing in the plumbing. Between Duane, Riley, and Olive, they were done with the basic work in the kitchen and upstairs bathroom, the copper and PVC pipes all in place, ending in stubs where they would eventually connect to a sink or a toilet or a bathtub. Only the downstairs bathroom was left to finish. Then they'd move on to the electrical work.

Once all that was in place, they'd be ready to drywall. It seemed so close and yet so far.

"Riley thinks that maybe if we call to Hattie, she'll show herself again," Helen explained to Nate now.

"Yeah, and maybe Santa Claus and the Easter Bunny will show up, too," Nate scoffed. "Bigfoot, too. Hell, maybe Elvis." He shook his head, looked at Helen the way she'd seen him look at his students when they'd disappointed him in some way. "I think all that weed you've been smoking with Riley is messing with your common sense, Helen." He took a breath, reached for her hand. "Don't you get how totally fucking nuts this is?"

"I think—" she started, wanting to finish her true thought: *that you're being an asshole,* but instead, she took a breath and said, "—that we need to be open to the possibility that there's more to this world than meets the eye. I know you think I imagined it, but I know what I saw, Nate. I trust the evidence of my senses. It was Hattie. And if she showed herself once, she might do it again."

He looked at her. "I'm getting a little worried here, Helen. I don't want you to lose your shit completely out here in the woods and turn into this total *I see dead people and read auras, and let me tell you about my past lives* kind of person."

Helen took a deep breath. "No losing my shit completely," she said. "Just keeping an open mind. I promise."

"I know this hasn't been a cakewalk," he said, voice softening. "The move here, the house-building, living in this crappy trailer—it's been way harder than we'd both imagined."

Harder than you'd imagined, she thought. *I fucking tried to tell you, but you knew better.*

"Few things in life ever go the way you imagine they will, Nate," she said, then left him to go up to the house to wait for Riley.

. . .

Riley pulled into the driveway twenty minutes later with the Ouija board and more pot. Nate was down in the trailer, thinking about his white deer, no doubt. It occurred to Helen that she had never questioned the existence of the deer, even though she'd never seen it, and Nate had failed to get a photo of it. She filed that away for their next argument about whether she'd really seen Hattie in the kitchen. Helen led Riley into the new house and showed her the strange bundle with the tooth and nail. She'd been meaning to show it to her for days but wanted to wait until Nate wasn't around. "What do you make of it? Is it a curse or something? A binding spell, maybe?"

Riley raised her eyebrows.

"I checked some books on witchcraft out of the library," Helen explained. "Remember? I thought everyone knew about my reading habits . . ."

Riley picked up the bundle. "I don't think it's a binding spell. It looks more like an amulet of protection. Both the tooth and the nail, they're used in spells to protect and ward off evil. Where did you say it came from?"

"It was left for us on our front steps our first night here. I don't know what to think."

Riley looked at Helen like Helen herself was a puzzle Riley was trying to solve.

They sat on the floor across from each other, directly underneath the old beam. Their legs were crossed, the Ouija board resting on their knees, fingers of all four hands resting lightly on the plastic planchette. The candles they'd lit in a circle around them flickered.

Helen hadn't used a Ouija board since she was a young girl at slumber parties asking about crushes, whom she would marry, when she was going to die. But back then, the spirits were vague, just giving teasing answers, never really telling her just what she wanted to know.

"We call to the spirit of Hattie Breckenridge," Riley said. "Are you here with us, Hattie? We wish to speak with you."

Helen closed her eyes and listened to the wind blow out across the bog and up the hill, push in through the windows at the front of the house that they'd left open. All she could think of was Hattie Breckenridge and how much she wanted her to appear.

She wanted Riley to see her, too, to have some other human being know she wasn't nuts, she wasn't losing her shit completely, as Nate had said.

She just didn't want to hear her voice. No, she didn't ever want to hear that sound again.

"Please, Hattie," Helen said. "Let us know you're here."

Prove I'm not crazy.

Prove I didn't imagine you.

Come back.

The planchette twitched to life under her fingers.

Helen had found a section in one of the library books—*Communicating with the Spirit World*—about Ouija boards. The book warned to be very careful—that using a board was like opening a door and you could never be sure what might come through.

"Be clear of your intentions," the book had said.

But what were her intentions?

To make contact. To learn about Hattie. About this place. It was more than intentions: it was a need, a compulsion that she felt pulling her along, begging her to work harder, to find out all she could by whatever means necessary, even if it meant talking to ghosts with a Ouija board.

"Is that you?" Helen asked Riley as the plastic zigzagged around the board. "Are you moving it?"

"No," Riley whispered. She was studying the little clear window on the planchette, noting which letters it rested on for a moment before swooping off to the next.

"B-C-A-W . . . ," Riley read out. The planchette slid almost off the corner of the board closest to Riley, Helen having to stretch to keep her right hand on it. The temperature in the room seemed to drop. The planchette looped back to the alphabet and continued to spell. Now Riley and Helen read in unison.

"O . . . F . . . U." The planchette sketched out a final large circle and then settled on the image of the moon in the upper right corner and was still. There was a damp, rotten smell in the air that clung to the back of Helen's throat.

"That doesn't spell anything," Helen whispered.

Riley repeated the letters again, trying to pick words out. "B caws . . . of u," she said. "Holy shit, Helen, she means 'because of you'!"

This wasn't happening. It couldn't be real, could it?

The damp rotten smell intensified.

"Be wary when using a spirit board," the library book had warned. "Remember that spirits, like the living, can easily lead you astray."

Riley spoke again.

"Because of who, Hattie? Because of Helen?"

The planchette slid swiftly left, stopping at the word *Yes*.

"What's because of Helen?" Riley asked.

The planchette moved quickly now and they read the letters together: *C-O-M-B-A-K.*

"'Come back,'" Helen said quietly. Her mouth was bone-dry and her voice sounded creaky to herself. "You came back because of me?"

Yes.

The thrill of it hit Helen like a jolt, making all the hairs on her arms stand on end. And it wasn't just that Hattie was speaking directly to her; it was the change in the air—the coldness, the crackling hum like the whole room was full of strange electricity.

She was talking to a ghost. The spirit of a woman who had lived and died here, on these lands.

"The spirit board is one of the most effective methods for communicating with the spirit world," the book had told her, but she hadn't dared to believe it would actually work. Not like this.

"Was it because we put up the beam?" Helen asked. "The wood from the hanging tree?"

Yes.

The planchette moved again, making Helen's fingertips tingle. *P-L-E-E-Z.*

"Please?" Helen said. "Please what? Is there something you need? Something you want me to do?"

What would Hattie ask? More important, what was Helen willing to do for her? *Anything,* she thought right now. *I'd do anything she asked me to.*

Riley was watching her with a mix of awe and worry. "Helen, I'm not sure . . . ," she started to say, then the planchette moved beneath their fingers, gliding smoothly around the board. Helen watched as it stopped with the little window over letters, Riley reading each one out loud.

"*G-O-T-O-D-O-N-O-V-O-N-A-N-D-S-U-N-S.*"

Then the planchette moved to *GOODBYE.*

"Does that mean anything to you?" Helen asked Riley.

"Not sure," Riley said.

"'Got odono von and suns . . . ,'" Helen said.

"'Go to,'" Riley said. "It could be 'go to.'"

"'Go to donovon and suns'?"

"Oh my god! Donovan and Sons!" Riley said. "Maybe it's the old mill. Is that what you mean, Hattie? The old mill in Lewisburg?"

The planchette did not move.

"I don't think she's here anymore," Helen said.

"Hattie?" Riley said again. "Are you with us?"

No. The planchette held still, no longer full of the thrum of energy Helen had felt, just a piece of lifeless plastic. The damp rotten smell had dissipated. The air felt warm and thick. Used up.

Hattie was gone.

CHAPTER 18

O live

 **AUGUST 3, 2015**

"Mr. Barns," Olive said.

"That's me," he said, squaring his broad shoulders. "But who the hell are you and what are you doing up here?"

"I was looking for you," she said.

But now that she'd found him, she wasn't sure what to say, what to do. Seeing him there with his gun, the strange symbol chalked on the floor, the covered mirror, she felt her nerve slipping away.

Maybe she should tell him she was looking for something, an "antique" of some kind? She looked around for inspiration but nothing seemed plausible—a chair? But what if he tried to sell her one of those chairs in the circle . . . ?

"You're not supposed to be up here," he said. His teeth were straight and perfect, like movie-star teeth. He looked like he could have walked straight off the set of some old Western. Like those Clint Eastwood movies her dad sometimes watched.

"I'm sorry. I thought this was a store," she said.

"Downstairs only. Didn't you see the sign?"

There hadn't been any sign telling her to stay downstairs, no roped-off area or curtain.

"No. I'm sorry—I guess I missed it? I came in and called out, but I guess you didn't hear me."

"I'm closed anyway," he said, scowling at her.

She remembered the OPEN sign on the front door. But she didn't want to argue. Not with a man who had a gun strapped to his waist.

"I'm not here to shop," she admitted.

"Well, what is it you want, then? If you're doing some school fund-raiser, selling cookies or raffle tickets or some shit like that, I'm not interested."

"No. Nothing like that. I'm Lori Kissner's daughter." She watched him, hoping these would be the magic words, the key that unlocked the door; that he might even smile, say, *Oh, of course, you're Lori's girl, what can I do for you?*

He stared at her, poker-faced and silent.

"I heard," she said, "uh, I heard you two were friends. That she came here sometimes?" She hated how small and unsure her own voice sounded. And it seemed absurd, really. The idea that her mother actually came here, spent time with this man she and Daddy had always made fun of.

Her eyes went to his gun again.

She thought of what Mike had said earlier: *It's the crazy man with the gun.*

"A gun is a tool," her daddy always told her. "But it's also a deadly weapon. Guns deserve our respect. They demand our focus. When there's a gun in the room with you, you give it your full attention, Ollie."

So this is what she did now. She gave that gun her full attention while trying real hard to pretend that's exactly what she wasn't doing. She kept it in sight at all times without looking right at it.

"I know Lori, sure. Everyone knows Lori," he said with a sly smile that made Olive's skin crawl. "But I wouldn't say we were friends."

"But she came here sometimes, right?" Olive persisted.

Was it her imagination, or did he flinch a little here?

He looked from her to the covered mirror, like maybe the answer was there. Maybe the mirror would speak, voice strange and muffled from the heavy drapery-like cloth that covered it. The mirror would tell her the truth.

This man, she knew, was going to lie. She felt it in the way her skin tingled, like she had her very own built-in lie detector. And what was she supposed to do, tell a grown-up who carried a loaded gun everywhere he went that she knew he was full of shit?

"Lots of people come here looking for lots of different things," he said.

"To talk to dead people?" Olive asked. "Isn't that what you do here?"

He narrowed his eyes, squinting at her like he was trying to make her smaller and smaller, like if he closed them enough, she might just go away completely.

"Sometimes people come looking for the perfect armoire," he said. "And sometimes because they have unfinished business with those who have passed." He started walking, gesturing with his arms, moving in a slow circle. "They have questions they want answered. One final thing they want to say. We offer that opportunity."

"Is that why my mother came?"

"Your mother," he said, voice soft at first, then hardening, "she didn't come here. The only time I ever saw Lori Kissner was when she bagged my groceries over at the market."

She looked around the room and smiled. "Sorry I bothered you," she said. "I can see you're real busy." She turned to go.

"I'll walk you out," he said, following her out of the lounge, down the hall and the curved stairs with their broken banister, through the crowded mess of the lobby, and all the way to the front door, making damn sure she was leaving. She didn't turn back to look, but she heard him behind her, his footsteps heavy, his breathing raspy. He smelled like stale cigarette smoke and spicy-sweet cologne. When they were out on the porch, he pulled a pack of Marlboro Reds from his shirt pocket and shook one out. Then he pulled his phone from his pocket, started to look at it, the three mannequins behind him seeming to peer over his shoulder.

"Mr. Barns?" She stopped on the rickety front steps and turned back to him.

"What is it?" He took his eyes off his phone and looked down at her, clearly irritated.

"I don't know if you've heard, but my mom isn't around anymore. She left me and my dad."

He nodded. Of course he knew. Everyone knew.

"People in town, they say all kinds of terrible things about my mother. But I just . . . I just wanted you to know that most of that stuff, I don't think it's true."

He looked at his unlit cigarette, seeming more interested in it than in Olive.

"You said before that the reason people come here, the reason they want to make contact with dead people, is that they have questions they want answered. That's why I came here today. Not to ask any ghosts or spirits or whatever, but to ask you, an actual living person, if you can help me figure out the truth about my mother."

He lit his cigarette, took a drag, and watched the smoke that drifted out of his mouth. "Sorry," he said, not sounding sorry in the least. "I can't help you."

"Okay," Olive said. "Sorry to bother you." She hopped down the steps and headed for Main Street, back toward the village, half thinking she'd see Mike hiding and waiting for her. But he was long gone. "Coward," she muttered.

When she got to School Street, she turned and doubled back to the old inn, sneaking across people's backyards. She came up behind the building and walked along the side until she was almost to the porch. She could hear Dicky pacing across the rotten floorboards. She peeked around the corner and saw he was on his phone.

"Well, her daughter was just here!"

Olive's heart thumped hard in her chest.

"I don't know," Dicky said, agitated, practically shouting. "But she was asking questions. She knows something. I don't know who she's been talking to, but she knows Lori used to come here."

Olive continued to watch, crouched down, peering around the corner. Dicky's boot heels banged against the worn floorboards as he paced back and forth.

"I don't think so. No. We need to meet again and figure out what we should do. All of us."

He waited, listening.

"I know what we agreed to! I'm not a fucking idiot! Don't give me this unsafe shit. Don't you think we're already unsafe?"

He listened again.

"Well, how much time do you need for that?"

He paced faster, boot heels clicking.

"Jesus! That's too long. I'm telling you, this kid is suspicious and who knows who she's been talking to."

She heard his lighter flick, an inhalation, then smelled the sharp tang of cigarette smoke.

"Okay. Okay. I guess I don't have a choice. I'll have to trust you, but you better be right about all this. I'll wait till then, but I'm not happy. Yes, the second Sunday in September. Yes, here, where the hell else? Okay. Yes. Same time as usual. Spread the word. Get everyone here. *Everyone.* And make sure you bring the diary!"

Olive pressed her back against the building, listened to the front door open with a jingle, then slam closed.

The second Sunday in September. She had to be here, to find a way to sneak in and hide. To see who was coming and what they were up to.

And what they might say about her mother.

CHAPTER 19

Helen

 **AUGUST 4, 2015**

"Did you tell Nate what happened with the Ouija board last night?" Riley asked when Helen called her the next morning.

"Oh god, no," Helen said. She could only imagine his derision, talking about unconscious micro-movements of the muscles and whatnot. She pressed the phone against her ear. "But I've been think- ing about it all night, and I want to drive out to that Donovan and Sons place. How far is it?"

"It's about an hour away. It's been closed for ages. I'd actually be interested in taking a ride out there to take a look, but I can't go with you this morning. We had two guys call out sick at the salvage yard and I've got to go in. But you should totally go check the mill out. It's really easy to find—you basically take Route 4 all the way up to Lewisburg and it's right in the center of town." She gave Helen direc- tions, then went on to say, "I did a little research online last night. The Donovan and Sons Mill used to make heavy canvas—they had a big military contract. There was a terrible fire there back in 1943. A dozen women and one of the foreman died. The mill closed right after, stood abandoned for ages, but it looks like they're turning it into condos now."

"I'll take a ride up there and let you know what I find," Helen told her, hanging up and looking out the window to see if there was any sign of Nate yet. He'd crept off early in the morning with his bin- oculars, camera, and wildlife notebook while Helen was still in bed. Bird-watching, or maybe out looking for his white deer.

That was Hattie. Riley's words echoed in her brain. *Nate should be careful.*

Helen wrote him a note saying she was going to do errands and would be back by lunchtime and that she thought they could finish up the plumbing.

She couldn't very well tell him she was going to visit a mill because the Ouija board told her to. He'd be making her an appointment with the nearest shrink, talking about stress and delusions and Riley being a bad influence. She felt a little pang of guilt. This was the first time she'd ever told a little white lie to him, ever omitted the truth.

But it was for the best, really.

.   .   .

The drive was pretty and didn't take nearly as long as she'd expected. On her way out of town, she passed Ferguson's, the pizza and sub shop, and, on the outskirts of town, a place she and Nate hadn't ventured into yet: Uncle Fred's Smokehouse—advertised by a sign with a smiling cartoon pig holding a plateful of bacon, which seemed profoundly wrong to Helen.

She drove through forests, past green fields full of white-and-black Holsteins grazing, and through tiny, picturesque villages with gazebos and little white churches. It was all postcard perfect: a land-scape without the billboards, big-box stores, strip malls, and eight-lane highways she was used to in Connecticut. She thought of her father and how he always talked about building a cabin out in the woods, someplace where he could hear himself think. He would have loved this: all the forests and fields, how the air smelled fresh and green. It was like going back in time. She imagined the landscape had changed little since Hattie's time. There were paved roads and power lines now, but the hills, mountains, and fields were no doubt the same. Had Hattie ever come this way, riding in a Model T perhaps, or on the train, along the old tracks Helen spotted running beside the road here and there?

After forty-five minutes, she saw the sign welcoming her to Lewisburg, HOME OF THE STATE CHAMPION LEWISBURG LIONS! She found the old mill without any problems: a sprawling brick complex along the riverbank. There were construction vehicles of all sorts: a bulldozer and crane, trucks full of lumber, a fleet of electrical con-tractor vans. Helen pulled up alongside a sign advertising one-, two-, and three-bedroom condos and commercial spaces for rent. She parked the truck and got out.

"All right, Hattie," she muttered to herself as she stood looking at the brick building nearest her. "What am I doing here?"

She walked down a brick-lined path to one of the buildings, where a sign on the front door warned, HARD HAT AREA. AUTHORIZED PERSONNEL ONLY.

"Applications are over at the office," a voice behind her said.

"Huh?" She turned, saw a tall, wiry guy in a white hard hat. He was wearing clean khaki pants and a blue button-down shirt and carrying a clipboard. A foreman or manager, she figured.

"There's an office set up in that blue trailer back there," he told her, gesturing with his thumb. "You can pick up information and an application for the condos, apartments, office spaces."

"Actually," Helen said, "I was just hoping to have a look around. I'm interested in local history and I understand the mill was once an important part of the town."

He nodded. "It sure was. Until the fire anyway. I suppose you can look around, if you want. Just steer clear of the work areas, okay? It's not safe." He started to turn away.

"Do they know what caused it?" Helen asked. "The fire?"

"I'm not sure they ever found out," he said. "The worst of the damage was down at the north end."

"Where's that?" Helen asked.

"Here, I can show you," he said. "I was heading down that way anyway."

She followed him down the walkway to the right. On their left, the massive old brick mill loomed. It was a beautiful building, three stories tall with large windows, a big bell tower over the front entrance. There were men on the roof, and she could hear power tools and hammering inside. Beyond it, she heard the murmur of the river. The man in the white hard hat walked quickly, speaking as he went along.

"The story goes that management was tired of the girls sneaking out for smoke breaks or to meet their fellas or whatever it was they were sneaking out for. So they took to barring the doors from the outside once all the workers were in. Let 'em out when the bell rang for lunch, then at quitting time."

"They locked them in?" Helen was horrified. Her eyes fell on the tall doors leading into the mill, imagined fists pounding on them, the crushing weight of all those women trapped inside pushing, desperate for escape.

"That's what folks say. The ones who remember. The ones who

made it out of the fire. I'm from right here in Lewisburg, so I grew up hearing the stories. That day, maybe someone was having a smoke inside because they couldn't go out anymore? I guess we'll never know how it started, but they say the building went up fast. Dry timbers, all that cotton."

They got to the end of the building, and Helen could see that the whole last quarter of it was redone in new brickwork, the bricks a more vivid red, the mortar more pale.

"This whole end of the building was gutted. We had to tear it down, rip everything out, and rebuild."

Helen looked over to the right, down along the river where a massive amount of rubble had been bulldozed into a pile: burned and snapped boards and timbers, rusted machines and gears, a small mountain of bricks with black fire marks.

"Since they couldn't get out the doors," he said, "they broke windows, jumped through. Some made it. A bunch didn't." He shook his head, the hard hat shifting a little. "Hell of a way to go."

Helen imagined what it must have been like to be trapped inside, lungs filling with smoke, the heat from the fire growing stronger, screams and chaos all around you. Hopefully it was the smoke that got them, not the flames.

"You know," he said, "between you and me, it's probably a good thing you're not interested in a condo."

"Why's that?"

He looked around, lowered his voice. "You couldn't pay me to live here."

The skin on Helen's arms prickled.

This was it, she thought. This was why she'd come.

"Yeah, I had a whole crew, the HVAC contractors, quit on me last week. These weren't wimpy guys, and they weren't stoned teenagers— not the sort to get spooked easily, if you know what I'm saying."

"What happened?" Helen asked.

"They were down in the basement, the lower level, working where the turbines used to be. They came tearing up the stairs, screaming. Three big dudes—they'd dropped their tools; they were pale and shaking and totally flipped out. They said they'd seen someone down there—a woman. Her face and arms were all burned up, skin just hanging off like loose wallpaper. That's what they said."

Helen said nothing, just waited. He went on.

"We went down to look, me and some other guys. There was no one down there, of course. But you could smell something. Kind of like burnt hair . . . or burnt flesh. No reason for a smell like that down there."

"Wow," Helen said. "Incredible."

"Yeah, that HVAC crew never came back. And lots of other freaky stuff has happened. Guys seeing and hearing things. Tools going missing. Lights turning on and off. The place is haunted. No doubt." He looked at the building long and hard. "I mean, when you think about it, how could it not be?"

Helen looked, too, then her eyes moved from the newly rebuilt section to the junked materials from the original mill.

Helen took a few steps forward, picked up one of the discarded bricks that hadn't made it to the large pile. It was old and worn, most likely made from red clay and kiln fired, and one side was stained black. She could almost smell the smoke. Feel the heat. Hear the screams of the women as they beat on the latched door.

"What are you going to do with all this?" Helen asked, gesturing at the rubble, still clutching the brick, not wanting to let it go. It felt almost alive to her: alive with history, alive with the things it had seen and heard, the tragedy it had been a part of.

He frowned, surprised by the change of subject, or maybe by the stupidity of the question.

"Have it carted off to the landfill."

It seemed terrible to her, to have materials with such history just thrown away. They should be in a museum. Or used to build a memorial for the people who died in the factory fire. Not just thrown in the dump.

"Even the bricks?"

"All of it."

"Mind if I take some? My husband and I, we're building a house, trying to incorporate local materials—things with history. These bricks would be perfect."

He gave her a puzzled, slightly amused grin. "Sure, Madame Historian. Knock yourself out," he said. "Take 'em all if you want. I guess they are a one-of-a-kind item."

"I appreciate it."

. . .

Nate came out of the house to meet her when she pulled into the driveway. He looked excited. "Look what I found in the hunting area at the general store," he said, holding up a box. "I walked into town to grab a sandwich for lunch and spotted this."

Helen looked. "An outdoor wildlife camera?"

He nodded enthusiastically. "It's got night vision! It's motion activated. And I can set it up so that it sends the images and videos right to my laptop."

Helen looked at the orange price sticker: $110.

"Great," she said, thinking that she could only imagine the rumors going through the town now. Witchcraft books, night-vision cameras—she could almost understand why people were freaked out by the two of them.

"Oh, and I got most of the plumbing finished in the downstairs bathroom," he said. "All that's left is the flange for the toilet."

"Fantastic," Helen said. She'd been amazed by how fast Nate had picked up working with the copper pipes. He had a real knack for soldering—all his joints were perfect every time. "I think maybe you were a plumber in a past life!"

He grinned at her. "How were your errands?" he asked.

"Look what I got for us," she said, showing him the pile of bricks she'd loaded into the back of the truck.

"Wow! Where'd they come from?"

"An old mill. They're renovating it, turning it into condos and offices. I got the bricks for free."

"Cool," Nate said. "How'd you find them?"

Hattie sent me.

"Craigslist," Helen said without missing a beat. "I thought we could use them for the hearth for the woodstove."

"I thought we were going to use slate from the quarry in town," Nate said, frowning a little. They'd visited the quarry, and Nate had loved the texture and gray-green color of the stone.

"We can still get that and use it for something else. Maybe the kitchen floor?"

"I think that might be a little pricey," Nate said. He was already worried that they were over budget. The money they'd inherited from Helen's father had seemed like so much at first, more than enough to build with and live on for at least a year. But there had been unexpected outlays: the price of lumber up here was higher than they'd originally budgeted for; the professional furnace and water heater install took a huge chunk of money; the ongoing expense of all the beer, wine, and take-out food because cooking in the trailer was depressing and difficult. The money was going fast. Faster than they'd imagined and planned for. Helen looked at the accounts and was sure they'd have more than enough to finish the house, but she worried that Nate might be right—if they kept going at this rate, they wouldn't have much left over to live on. They hadn't thought much about what they were going to do for income when the time came—it seemed so far away.

Of course, it didn't help that Nate was splurging on hundred-dollar night-vision cameras. She shook the thought away, told herself she was being petty.

"Maybe we could get the rejected slate pieces for cheap, you know? The weird shapes that broke and aren't square. I think it could work. We could do like a funky mosaic thing." Her dad had done a floor like that for an artist friend of his and it had turned out beautifully.

"Maybe," Nate said.

"These bricks—they were just so cool, and I love knowing that they came from a real mill up the road. Think about it. It's like I pick one up and feel this instant connection to the past. I can practically smell the grease, hear the hum of the looms, feel the cotton dust in the air."

Smell the smoke of the fire, she thought.

If installing the beam had helped Hattie come back, would installing the bricks draw one of the mill workers back? The burned woman with skin hanging off that the contractors had seen in the basement, maybe?

She shivered.

Nate smiled at her, kissed her nose. "I love you. I'm not at all sure that cotton dust is a thing, but I love that you imagine it is. And saving these bricks from the landfill by reusing them in our house—can't really complain about that."

"Cotton dust is definitely a thing," she said. "Wanna help me unload these?"

"Sure," he said.

She moved the truck up closer to the house and pulled down the tailgate, and they started pulling the bricks out, putting them in a stack next to the house.

"These are in pretty good shape. They'll have to be cleaned up," Nate said. "All the old mortar scraped off."

Helen nodded.

"Some of them look like they're from a chimney stack or something. They're all black on one side."

Helen said nothing, feigning ignorance as she continued to stack the bricks. At last, she said, "You were up and out early this morning."

"Went for a walk. That heron was in the bog again. Such a beautiful bird." There was that wistful look he got again, the one that reminded Helen of his deep love and respect for nature. "I got some good shots of it. I was thinking I'd print the best one, maybe have it framed? We could start a sort of gallery up in our library with photos of the local wildlife. Maybe even some of my sketches as I get better at it?"

"I love it," Helen said, gathering an armload of bricks to bring to the house. "Did you see your white deer?"

He hesitated a moment, then said, "No."

He was leaving something out, she was sure of it. And she felt oddly comforted, knowing that she wasn't the only one who wasn't telling the whole truth.

"But I do wonder if maybe there's a group of them. I've been reading about these white Seneca deer in New York. It's really interesting— there's a population of about two hundred of them living on a protected reserve that was once an old army depot. They're white-tailed deer, but they're leucistic, which means they lack pigmentation in the hair. They've got brown eyes, not pink like true albinos."

"Leucistic, huh?" Helen said. She loved how excited Nate got when he learned something new like this, like he couldn't wait to share it. Mr. Science in action.

"Wouldn't it be amazing if we had something like that here? A whole population of white deer! I was thinking I could do a study, write a paper."

Nate had been talking about one day writing articles and papers for scientific journals since she'd met him, but back in Connecticut he'd never had the time or found a subject inspiring enough.

"Sounds great, hon," she said, only half paying attention because her mind was on other things. She was working out the best way to get the bricks into the house as soon as possible, to test out the theory and see who, or what, they might call back.

She was dreaming about the fire. She was in the factory beside other women who had to shout to be heard over the deafening thrum of the looms, the machines making the walls and floor vibrate, turning the mill into a living thing.

"Fire!" someone shrieked. "Run!"

And then she smelled the smoke, turned and saw the flames, how they licked up the far wall like the tongue of a great demon, gobbling the dry wooden beams, the painted floor and ceiling. She ran to the front doors, her and a throng of women and girls in their plain dresses with work aprons over the top, hair pulled back. They pushed, they pounded and clawed and screamed, but the heavy wooden door did not budge.

Trapped. They were trapped.

She thought of the windows. Thought that if they were calm, if they could all get to the windows and break through them, they could escape. But the women, in full panic now, screaming, choking on the smoke, which had grown black and thick, kept pushing at the doors, at the women between themselves and the door. She was pinned there, pressed tight by the bodies around her. She could not move.

Helen opened her eyes, took a gasping breath of cool air.

She was not in the factory being crushed against the locked door while flames overtook the building.

But where was she?

Who was she?

I am Helen, she told herself, taking a deep breath, trying to slow her racing heart. *I'm married to Nate. We used to live in Connecticut, where we were both middle school teachers. Now we live in Vermont and are building our own house.*

She reached for Nate beside her, but he was not there.

She rolled over, realized she was not in her bed but on the plywood subfloor of the unfinished house.

Her head ached and felt foggy.

It was the smoke. The smoke from the mill.

But that was only a dream.

There was a little pile of half a dozen bricks from the mill beside her, one side of each stained black. There was a flashlight beside them, turned off.

She'd snuck back up to the house after Nate had gone to bed and brought the bricks into the house, hoping that they might trigger something, that they might pull someone back. But after sitting in the dark with the bricks for a while, she had realized her mistake. Hattie had come back not just because of the beam but because she had a connection to this place. What reason would one of the mill workers have to show herself to Helen? To come back to a little half-built house at the edge of a bog in Hartsboro, forty miles from where the mill once stood. She'd been debating going back down to the trailer but decided that she'd stay a little while in case Hattie decided to show up again. Maybe Hattie would give her a sign about what she was supposed to do next. She must've dozed off on the floor, waiting in vain.

She sat up, pushed the button on her watch: 3:33 a.m.

She was in the opening between the kitchen and the living room, under the hanging tree beam, facing into the kitchen. She studied the corner where she'd seen Hattie three weeks ago. She looked up at the beam, at the dark shape in the dim moonlight that filtered through the windows.

There were voices behind her. Whispering. Talking so low, it sounded more like radio static than human voices, but she knew that was what they were. She could recognize the ebb and flow of conversation, of two people trying not to be heard.

Was Nate here?

She had an absurd thought then: that she would turn and he'd be there, talking with his white doe; that the deer was actually Hattie, just like Riley said. They'd be sitting together, and the deer would be whispering to him, speaking perfect English, singing him a little song maybe . . . *Mares eat oats and does eat oats and little lambs eat ivy.* Or maybe something else. Something strangely romantic—*Don't sit under the apple tree with anyone else but me*—as she looked up at him with her big, glossy doe eyes.

She heard a giggle, but it was all wrong—low and crackly, like it was coming through a far-off AM radio station. She didn't want to see, didn't want to know what was there.

Slowly, she forced herself to turn her head and look, to see who, or what, was behind her.

There, sitting in the living room in the place the new brick hearth would go, was Hattie. She was on a stool. *Where does a ghost get a stool?* Helen wondered. Hattie was wearing the same white dress she'd had on the last time Helen had seen her, but there was no rope around her neck. She was smiling, laughing. And at her feet, a young woman sat, having her hair braided by Hattie. The woman shared Hattie's dark hair and eyes. Helen saw the young woman wore a plain blue dress, but it was tattered and burned, stained brown and yellow from smoke. And she carried the smell of smoke on her; Helen caught a whiff of it in the air.

This must be Hattie's daughter, Jane. The one no one knew what had happened to.

But Helen knew.

The pieces clicked into place. She didn't know the details yet, but she was sure of one thing: Hattie's daughter, Jane, had died in the fire at the mill.

"Jane?" Helen said, and the woman looked up at her, opened her mouth to speak, to tell Helen something, something important, Helen knew, but no sound came out.

The room flickered with light; the beam of a flashlight dancing through the window.

"Helen?" Nate called, coming through the door, shining his light on her. "Helen, my god! What are you doing out here?"

"I . . ." She glanced to the center of the living room. Hattie and Jane were gone.

I don't know what I'm doing here. Maybe I'm going crazy.

"I couldn't sleep," she said. "So I came up here. Thinking about the kitchen. What kind of countertops do you think would work with a slate floor?"

"Well, come back to bed, okay? It's, like, three in the morning. I was worried sick when I woke up and couldn't find you."

"Sure," Helen said, "of course. I'm sorry, I'm just . . . excited, I guess." She smiled what she hoped was a reassuring *everything's fine* smile.

As they walked out the front door, she looked back over her shoulder and thought she just caught the outline of a simple stool sitting in the darkness. She closed the door.

CHAPTER 20

Jane

SEPTEMBER 3, 1943

When Jane woke up, she didn't know it was to be her last day on earth. She roused her children and husband, made coffee and oatmeal just like every other morning. Her husband, Silas, read the paper.

"More news about the war, Daddy?" her son asked.

"We sunk a Japanese submarine," her husband said.

"Boom!" shouted the boy.

"No shouting or explosives allowed at the table, please," Jane pleaded.

Her daughter scowled into her oatmeal, whispered to her doll.

Jane looked at the photographs of the people in the newspaper and thought she herself was not unlike them: a paper woman, one-dimensional. That's what her family saw. But really, she was more like the chains of paper dolls her daughter would cut from leftover news-paper: folded together, she looked like one, but once you opened her up, you saw she contained multitudes.

There were stories, she knew, about people who led double lives. Spies. People who had affairs.

Everyone had secrets.

Everyone told lies.

She comforted herself with these facts. She told herself she was not alone.

Her husband, he knew nothing about her. Not really. He called her a good girl. She had told him she was an orphan and he had taken pity on her, said, "How terrible to have no one in the world." And she had cried. It wasn't just for show. She had cried because she knew he was right.

She missed Mama.

She missed her with the dull ache of a phantom limb, like some basic part of her had been ripped away.

And almost every night, in the darkest hours, she was back in that old root cellar in Hartsboro.

She would remember, with chilling detail, how she'd hid in the root cellar for what felt like days, though surely it was only hours. Time moved slowly in the dark, when you were alone with just your own grim thoughts and spiders to keep you company.

Crouched down on the bare dirt of the root cellar floor, listening carefully for the scuttle of a rat, she went over everything that had led her there to that moment. The root cellar was the only thing left from her mother's family home, which had burned to the ground, killing Jane's grandmother years before Jane was even born.

"Someone from town started that fire," Mama told her once, when Jane had asked about the fire that had killed her grandmother, destroyed everything her mama knew and loved, leaving nothing behind but a cellar hole lined with rocks, some charred wood, lilac trees in the dooryard. And the old root cellar off behind the house. The fire didn't damage that at all. Over the years when she was growing up, Jane would go there and just sit, look at the jars of canned goods her grandma had put up long ago. It was like going to a museum. The museum of *What Came Before*. Of the Breckenridge family house. Of glass jars full of applesauce and string beans labeled in her grandmother's careful hand. She never stayed long and never closed the door, because there were spiders and rats living down there.

"Why did they start the fire, Mama?" Jane had asked.

"It was me they were trying to kill."

"But why?" she asked. "Why would they want to burn you up?"

"Fear is a funny thing," her mother said.

"Why are they afraid of you?"

"People fear anything different, anything they don't understand."

Jane knew this to be true, even at a young age.

Her mama had a gift, but not everyone saw it that way. It was funny, though—even the people who spoke ill of her, called her a witch and the devil's bride, they'd come sneaking out to the bog, asking Mama for love charms, healing spells, asking her to tell them their future or looking for a message from a spirit who had passed. People were afraid of her mother, but they also depended on her, sought her out in times of need (though they would never admit this out loud).

Jane herself had been ridiculed, called the devil's daughter. She'd been held down in the schoolyard, stuck with pins to see if she would bleed. Jane had none of her mother's powers. The spirits did not speak to her. She did not see signs of what was to come in tea leaves at the bottom of the cup. She longed for the voices, the signs, but they did not come. What she did have, what she held on to fiercely, was fury. Fury that she had not been born special like her mama. Fury at the way she and her mother were treated. Fury at what the people in town had done to her grandmother.

All her life, she carried a box of matches in her pocket, waiting.

Earlier that morning, when the children had circled her in the yard outside the school, Lucy Bishkoff had pulled up her dress and pulled down her underthings to see if she bore the mark of the devil on her skin. Jane felt something breaking inside. A dam letting go, her fury pouring through, overtaking her. And then, for the first time in her life, she heard a voice, loud and clear: not the voice of a spirit, but the voice of her own rage. *Punish them,* it said. *Punish them all.*

When everyone was still outside, she went into the schoolhouse, snuck back to the supply cupboard, made a nest of crumpled paper, lit the edges with a match. Then she went back out and waited. Once everyone was inside, sitting down for lessons, she used the strongest branch she could find to bar the door.

Crouching in the root cellar hours later, her heartbeat pounding in her ears, she smelled the smoke on her clothing. Heard the screams of the children. They screamed and screamed and screamed in her mind. But she told herself they deserved what they got. The whole town deserved to be punished.

She waited in the dark root cellar, listening to the echoes of the screams, waiting. But Mama did not come for her.

Eventually, she grew tired of waiting; her legs had turned to pins and needles and she was cold all over. She cracked open the door, stepped outside, the afternoon sun blinding. She staggered, squinting like a mole-girl, and moved toward home, willing herself to be slow and cautious. Where was Mama?

When she got to the bog, she saw that what was left of their little house was smoldering. Gone. All gone. There was a crowd gathered at the opposite end of the bog, by the big white pine. She moved closer, stealthily, and saw what they were all looking at.

.   .   .

At first, when she ran away from Hartsboro as a girl of twelve, she didn't know who she was without Mama.

She'd spent her whole life being Jane Breckenridge—daughter of Hattie, the witch of the bog, the most powerful woman in the county.

Then she was a no one. A street urchin with no last name. *Smith,* she said when she had to make one up. *I'm Jane Smith. I come from downstate. By the Massachusetts border. My parents, they died when I was a baby and I was raised by an aunt, then she died. Now I've got no one.*

People take pity on you when you are young and pretty and have a sad story to tell. People are drawn to sorrow.

She was taken in by a kind Baptist family in Lewisburg—the Millers. They had a large farm outside of town. Jane learned to rise in the dark hours before dawn to milk the cows, gather eggs from the hens, collect wood for the old cookstove in the kitchen. She went to church and prayed, read the Bible each night. Learned to fit in. To be someone else.

And now, now Jane was a married woman with children of her own. Her son, Mark, he was a good boy. At eleven, he looked more and more like his father every day. He took after him, too—did well in school, was strong and well-liked. But her girl child, Ann, Jane worried for her.

And, if the truth be told, Jane was actually frightened of her.

The girl *knew* things. Things no six-year-old should know. Things that she said her toys and dolls told her. She had a favorite doll that she was always whispering to. It was a doll Ann had made herself from rags and scraps from her mother's sewing basket—she loved to sew, Jane's girl. The doll was a funny-looking thing: a patchwork of colors with a pale face, an embroidered mouth like a red flower petal, and two black button eyes. Her hair was a tangle of black yarn braided together.

"What's your dolly's name?" she'd asked Ann, not long after she'd made her.

"She's Hattie," Ann said.

Jane stepped back, clapped a hand over her mouth to keep from screaming. Ann giggled, thought Jane was laughing, too. "It's a silly name, isn't it?" she said, grinning. "It must mean she likes hats!"

Jane had never told her about her grandmother. About her real name or where she'd come from. No one living knew the truth about Jane.

"Hattie says hello," her little girl told her. "She says she knows you."

Jane felt as if she'd been submerged in cold water—the water back at the center of the Breckenridge Bog. She felt it pulling on her, sucking her down.

"Of course she knows me," Jane said, forcing the words out through her too-tight throat. "She's your doll. She lives here in our house."

"No," she said. "She says she knows you from *before*."

Jane didn't respond. How could she?

Before.

Before.

Before.

She tried to remember before, and what came back strongest was the smell of that damp root cellar she hid in, waiting for Mama to come. But she never did.

And what she saw when she got to the bog and peered through the circle of people gathered there:

Mama was hanging from a rope tied to a branch of that old pine, dangling, lifeless. She swung in small, slow circles like a strange pendulum.

Jane had to cover her mouth with her hand to keep from screaming back then as well. She bit down, chewed at her palm until she tasted blood.

She sat there, crouched down in the bushes, and watched as the men cut her mother down, stuffed her dress full of rocks, and dragged her out into the middle of the bog, the deep place where the spring came up.

"The spirits will protect us," Mama had always promised.

Now, years later as an adult with children of her own, Jane felt her chest grow cold and tight as she remembered her mother saying those words. And how earnestly she'd believed them.

"Hattie says she loves you," her daughter told her, clutching the terrifying doll in her arms. "Do you love her, too?"

"Of course I do," Jane said.

When she went in to tuck her daughter in at night, she covered the doll's face with a blanket; sometimes, if Ann was already asleep, Jane would take the doll out and hide it under the bed or in a dark corner of her closet.

But somehow, each morning when Ann woke up, Hattie the doll was beside her once more, peering up at Jane with her shiny button eyes when she came in to draw back the curtains and say "Good morning."

"Hattie says you shouldn't go to work today," Ann announced this morning as she clutched at her gruesome little doll. Its button eyes seemed to watch Jane, to give a familiar little glint when she dared look in her direction.

"Whyever not?" Jane asked, spooning more oatmeal into Ann's bowl. Mark and his father had gone outside to feed the dog and chickens.

"Something bad is going to happen," Ann said, pushing the bowl away. "She says you're going to make something bad happen."

"Me? All I'm going to do is run those old looms."

"Please, Mama," she said, her brow furrowed like an old lady's, not like a little girl's.

"Don't be silly," Jane told her. "Eat your breakfast and get ready for school. I'm going to work, just as I do every day."

But when she got to the mill, Jane realized she should have listened.

Tom Chancy, the foreman, told the women they were behind—they'd gotten too lazy, too slow, and if it kept up, he was going to dock their pay. "No more midmorning breaks," he announced when he gathered them all in a circle for a meeting before the first work bell rang. There were murmurs of dissent. "And no one," Tom said, voice rising above all the mumbled complaints, "I mean *no one,* is to leave their workstation until the bell rings at noon!"

"What about cigarettes?" Maggie Bianco asked.

"You'll wait till noon. If any one of you is foolish enough to try to sneak a smoke in here, you'll be fired instantly."

The women wouldn't dare. They all knew how flammable the very air was, full of cotton dust that could ignite, send the whole mill up in a great ball of flames.

"Well, what if we've got to use the john?" Mildred Cox wanted to know.

"Then you'll hold it."

"And if we can't?"

"Then you'll piss down your leg, I imagine," Tom said.

The bell rang and the women went to work, annoyed, sure—but

there was no point in grumbling. They quickly settled at their stations, running the looms. The sound was deafening but comforting to Jane. The whole room vibrated, smelled of hot grease and warm cotton. Their fingers moved quickly, deftly, over the machines. About ten o'clock, Tom came by Jane's loom, stood behind her, said he needed to speak with her a moment. In the office. He took her into his office, a tiny box of a room with shelves and a desk covered with piles of paper. Tom shut the door and Jane's heart grew cold.

"I've been watching you," he said.

"Oh?"

"The other girls look up to you," he said.

She nodded. It was true. She was older than most of them, had been here longer. That counted for something. She'd learned to get by. To keep walking when Tom gave her bottom a pinch or when he stood so close behind her that she could feel his privates pressed against her. She recalled her first day on the job over ten years ago now, how Tom had seemed so kind, had said he knew her husband's family and was happy to hire her despite the terrible state of the economy. "We're in a depression, you know," he reminded her. She told him she understood and would work hard, that he wouldn't be sorry he'd hired her. And she had kept up her end. She didn't smoke or gossip. She did good work and showed the new girls how to do good work, too. She didn't reckon she'd been late to work one day in ten years.

"I'm going to be making cuts," he said this morning, "letting some of the girls go."

Jane stiffened.

"Do you want to keep your job, Mrs. Whitcomb?"

"Yes, of course."

She needed the job. Silas was not bringing in much pay. He'd lost his job at the bank and was logging now—work that didn't suit him and didn't pay nearly as much. Everyone in town knew this, Tom included.

Tom came toward Jane, put his big, dirty hand on her hip, pulled her to him.

Jane pushed away.

"I thought you wanted to keep your job?" he asked, coming closer. He smelled like sausages and tobacco. His teeth were brown.

He put one hand at her waist and began tugging at her dress with the other, and just like that, she was back down on the ground of the schoolyard in Hartsboro, a circle of children around her, taunting, tugging at her clothes, exposing her, looking for the devil's mark.

What they didn't know, what she herself didn't fully understand until that day, was that mark was not out on her skin but somewhere deep inside her.

She felt it surface once more as she gathered all her strength, planted her hands on Tom's chest, and shoved. He stumbled a step backward, his rump hitting his desk. Jane lunged for the door but stopped when he spoke.

"You'll finish up your day today," he snarled, eyes furious. "And then you're fired."

"You can't do that!" she said.

He smiled a sickening smile. "Are you sure about that, Mrs. Whitcomb?"

"I'll tell my husband," she said.

He laughed. "Tell him that you made improper advances toward me in a pathetic attempt to keep your job after I told you cuts would have to be made? Do you really want to go stirring up that kind of trouble, letting the whole town hear about the sort of woman you really are?"

Tears blurred her vision. She hurried back to her looms, blood pounding in her ears. She began to work, walking around the looms, checking the warps, watching the thread unspool, feeling the quality of the cloth as she always did. But a rage boiled inside. She pictured Tom Chancy's face, his filthy hands, and imagined terrible things. She imagined him suffering. Screaming.

Jane remembered her daughter's words: *Something bad is going to happen. You're going to make something bad happen.*

And she felt for the matches in her pocket. They were always there, waiting, making her feel safe, powerful. A talisman.

Punish him, the voice inside told her. *Make him pay.*

She went over to the corner, to one of the bins of cotton just outside the door of Tom's office. She glanced around—none of the other workers were watching, all focused on their looms, perhaps hoping to avoid getting involved in whatever trouble Jane Whitcomb might be in. They certainly wouldn't hear the quiet *scritch* of the match striking over the din. She lit the match, held it to the cotton, watched it catch.

Just like that, she was a little girl again, hearing her mother's voice: *The spirits will protect us.*

She saw a little curl of smoke drift up from the bin and walked calmly back to her loom, doing her best not to smile.

"Fire!" someone yelled not three minutes later. And in an instant, the place was alive with panic, all the women scrambling, surging toward the doors. Jane wasn't worried. The foreman's office was on the far end of the cavernous space—they all had plenty of time to make it to the doors and out before the whole wretched place went up in flames. Still, she shrieked and ran as the others did, grabbed Maggie Bianco's hand as she passed when she saw Maggie standing frozen, looking around in confusion, and urged her on—"Let's go, Mags! You'll be all right, but we've got to go!"

But something was wrong.

Instead of following the other workers out of the mill into the fresh air, she and Maggie ran smack into a throng of women pushing, shoving forward, crying out, "For God's sake, move!"

The doors wouldn't open.

"They've bolted them from the outside!" someone yelled.

The women, they pounded and screamed and wept. Jane lost hold of Maggie. She felt the press of bodies behind her, crushing her.

There was another scream, too. A different one.

Tom Chancy was screaming. Jane could turn her head just enough to see the walls of his office fully engulfed.

At least there was that.

CHAPTER 21

O live

 **AUGUST 5, 2015**

As soon as Olive saw Daddy's truck leave the driveway, headed to work, she was out the door, making a beeline for the old maple at the edge of the yard.

He'd taken yesterday off so they could make some progress on the house together, and honestly, she couldn't wait for him to leave and go back to work. She wanted some alone time. Time to go over everything she'd seen and heard at Dicky's and time to do some serious detective work.

She got to the maple at the edge of the yard and looked around, making sure no one was watching—silly, really, because there wasn't anyone out in those woods, ever, except for Mike sometimes. He hadn't shown his face or called since he'd ditched her at the hotel the other day.

There was a hollow spot about four feet up in the old tree, a place where a branch used to grow. Now there was the perfect little cavity tucked into the trunk, about four inches high and two inches across. She and Mama used to leave each other secret messages and gifts there: chocolate coins, acorns, pennies flattened out on railroad tracks. When Olive was very little, Mama told her the gifts were from the fairies.

Olive reached in now, feeling for the treasure she'd stashed there: Mama's silver necklace with the broken chain. She pulled it out and took it into the house. She brought it to her room, where she took the silver amulet off the broken chain and polished it with toothpaste (she'd seen Mama polish silver this way). She didn't have a new chain for it, but she had a thin leather cord left over from a leather craft kit Mama had given her. She put the silver pendant onto the cord, tied a knot at the ends, and slipped it around her neck, tucking it under her shirt.

After seeing the symbol on the floor at Dicky's hotel the day before last, she felt that the necklace, the symbol itself, was important. She couldn't stop thinking about it. And Olive had this idea then that wearing it might help act as a magnet, might pull Mama closer to her or at least bring Olive closer to finding out where Mama had gone.

Mama had called it her *I see all* necklace; maybe, just maybe, it would help Olive see things, too.

Aunt Riley would understand. She believed in things like having visions and magical necklaces. But no way could Olive tell Riley about finding her mom's necklace. Not yet anyway. She'd keep it a secret for just a little while.

Necklace tucked safely under her shirt, guiding her in some new strange way, she went down the hall to Daddy's room. Like it or not, she now thought of it as *his* room, not *their* room any longer. It was partly because her mother had been gone so long and partly because it was a completely different room now. It had bigger closets, a door to the bathroom right from the bedroom. A new, much larger window.

"Your mama always loved the view of the mountains from here," Daddy had said when he planned it. And Olive remembered her mother looking out at the mountains, saying they looked like a sleeping giant.

"Don't you think, Ollie?" she'd asked. "Look, there are his feet, his legs, his round belly. And there are his shoulders, his chin and nose."

And Olive saw the shape of the man in the mountains but was frightened, because she was little and the idea of a giant right outside their door scared her. "How long has he been sleeping?"

"Oh, a long, long time, I think," Mama said. "Maybe since back before there were people here, even."

"What if he wakes up, Mama? What if he wakes up and finds out that everything's different? What if he's angry?"

Her mother had smiled. "I don't think that's anything we have to worry about, Ollie."

Her father had placed their bed against the north wall so they could look out the new picture window. As with all the other renovations, the bedroom was not finished. The floor was still bare plywood because Daddy didn't know what Mama would like best: carpeting or hardwood, or painted wide pine planks maybe. And the inside of his own closet had no drywall, no ceiling, just exposed framing and wires, a light fixture screwed right to the open junction box. He had only a few things hanging up in there: a couple of flannel shirts, one good white dress shirt, a blazer and a pair of nice pants he wore to funerals.

She stood in the bedroom now, saw the unmade bed with the new comforter her daddy had bought—it was covered in ducks and hunters in red flannel with guns. She looked around and realized that with the exception of the clothes that had been placed in her new closet, all traces of her mother were gone. The room no longer smelled like her perfume. The top of the dresser had been cleared of Mama's makeup and stack of magazines. Olive wondered, not for the first time, what Mama would really think when (if) she came home. Wouldn't it be unsettling to find that everything had changed, that nothing was the way she remembered? Daddy believed it would be this big, wonderful surprise, but Olive couldn't help but imagine how shocked Mama would be. How the changes might actually make her angry, make her think they'd moved on to new things without her, tried to erase all traces of the way their lives had been before. It would be like the sleeping giant waking up to find everything changed.

Feeling like a trespasser, Olive started with her mother's closet. What she was looking for exactly, she couldn't say. A clue. Something unusual. Something to give her some insight into what had been going on with Mama in those last weeks. She went through the pockets of pants, shirts, and jackets, found nothing but breath mints, a Rosy's Tavern matchbook, receipts from the grocery store and gas station. Nothing out of the ordinary. Nothing that told Olive anything new.

She continued to look, listening carefully for the sounds of a car or truck coming up the driveway. Daddy should be at work until six tonight, but he sometimes came back because he forgot something—his lunch or Thermos usually. Riley would occasionally pop in unexpectedly, just walk right in and take a look around just to check up on them, to make sure Olive was doing okay. She'd say she just dropped by to say hello, but Olive caught her opening the fridge and cabinets, as if she was making sure there was food. She'd caught her poking around in the rest of the house, too—opening drawers, going through closets. Maybe she was looking for clues, too; something to tell her where Mama might have gone.

Riley and Olive's dad had argued the other night when Riley came by, but Olive had caught only the end of it.

"I'm not talking about forever, Dusty," Riley said. She was in the kitchen putting away a load of dishes she'd just washed. "I'd just move in for a little while. I could help with the renovations. Do the shopping and cooking. Be there for Olive."

"Olive's fine," he said sharply. "We're both doing fine. We don't need a goddamn babysitter."

Olive had walked in then, and they'd changed the subject, starting talking about what color Daddy and Olive should paint the kitchen.

Now Olive dug farther back in her mother's closet and found two clean green aprons that Mama wore when she cashiered part-time at Quality Market. One of them still had her name tag attached: LORI, with a little stick-on flower with a smile in the middle. A happy *have a nice day* daisy.

Her mother's old purses were on the top shelf and Olive went through those next, found change, old lipstick, an unlabeled key that could have gone to anything. They never locked the doors on their house, and this was not a car key. Olive looked at it, ran her finger over its teeth, then slipped it into the pocket of her jeans. She kept looking, sure there had to be something that would help.

Tucked up in the back corner of the top shelf was the mauve-and-tan box that held Mama's best shoes. They were her special shoes; her "fairy-tale slippers" is what she called them. They were ivory-colored leather with silver beads embroidered across the toes in a flower pattern. They had a low heel and a delicate strap that fastened with a tiny silver buckle. Olive remembered one night, not long before her mother went away, how she'd awoken late at night, unable to sleep. She'd gone downstairs for a glass of milk and caught Mama sneaking in. It was nearly two in the morning. Mama was all dressed up and had her fancy ivory shoes on and much more makeup than she normally wore. "Shh," she'd said, putting a finger over her lips. "Don't tell your father." Then she'd slipped the shoes off and carried them upstairs, creeping up the steps in her stockings.

Olive reached for the box now and could tell before opening it that there was nothing inside. She pulled off the lid, found only a crumpled piece of tissue paper and a single silver bead that must have fallen off. She took the bead out, tucked that into her pocket beside the key.

Olive looked through the rest of the closet, through the jumble of other shoes at the bottom, but the ivory shoes weren't there, either.

Her mother must have brought them with her or been wearing them the night she left. Olive looked and didn't notice that anything else was missing. All her mother's other shoes seemed to be there: her cowboy boots, black heels, flip-flops, sneakers.

Olive searched the closet for other missing things but didn't notice anything special. Mama seemed to have left all of her favorites: her old Levi's jacket that she'd had since high school and still wore, her suede boots, the purple silk top she wore to job interviews and meetings at Olive's school, her favorite black jeans. If Mama had been planning a trip, why hadn't she packed any of her favorite things?

A hard knot formed in Olive's stomach.

Maybe she found the money and just took off. Why pack clothes when you can buy a whole new wardrobe, a whole new life? It made sense in a terrible way: If you wanted to start over, wouldn't you rather leave every trace of your old life behind? Or maybe there were things she'd taken, clothing that Olive just didn't notice was missing.

Olive continued her search, moving faster now, just wanting the whole thing to be done and over with. It was too much, being in the closet, surrounded by all of Mama's things.

She found more receipts stuffed in jacket pockets, all for regular things: milk and eggs, a haircut and color at House of Style, a cup of coffee and a candy bar at a gas station up in Lewisburg.

Lewisburg.

That was weird. It was a tiny town in the middle of nowhere as far as Olive knew.

She looked at the date on the receipt. It was from May 10 of last year. Just a couple weeks before Mama left. The knot in Olive's stomach tightened.

Went missing, a little voice told her. *She didn't leave. She went missing.*

Receipt in hand, Olive jogged down the steps and into the living room, searched the bookshelf, and pulled out the worn Vermont road atlas they had. She flipped to a page toward the front that showed the whole state. Using the index, she found Lewisburg, J-10 on the grid.

Someone had drawn a tiny star next to it in red ink.

She put her finger on the town and couldn't imagine what would bring her mother there. It was totally off the beaten path, wasn't on the way to anywhere. Then she noticed other red stars. One in Elsbury. Then another, here in Hartsboro.

Olive blinked down at the stars, trying to make sense of what she was seeing.

The three towns—Lewisburg, Elsbury, and Hartsboro—formed almost a perfect equilateral triangle.

The image reminded her of the triangle in the necklace she was wearing and the same image she'd seen chalked on the floor of Dicky's old hotel. But the necklace and drawing had a freaky triangle with a square, and a circle and an eye at the center.

The necklace under her shirt seemed to grow warmer against her chest. The whole room felt warm, too warm. She looked down at the triangle of red stars on the map.

She thought about the Bermuda Triangle, a place where people disappeared, boats and planes just fell off the map.

That's what people said anyway, but was that what really happened?

Was it possible to lose people, a whole boat or plane even?

Was there an edge of the world, or a doorway, that you could fall through and be lost forever?

Was that what had happened to her mama?

CHAPTER 22

H<small>elen</small>

 AUGUST 5, 2015

"I've got good news," Riley said when she called. "They've finally finished the repairs to the historical society. Mary Ann gave me the okay to go back in and start putting the place back together again. I'm heading over this afternoon. Want to join me?"

"Definitely!" Helen said. "I've got news, too."

"About the mill? How'd your trip go?"

"You're not going to believe it. Hattie's daughter died in that fire," Helen said on the phone.

"What? No way!"

"I'm sure of it!" Helen was pacing back and forth in the tiny trailer kitchen. "I can't prove it exactly, but I know it was her."

Helen looked out the trailer window, saw Nate carrying boxes of electrical supplies into the house: rolls of cable, metal junction boxes, plastic boxes for all of their outlets and switches. She'd promised she'd be up to help him get started in a few minutes. She'd told him nothing about what she'd seen in the house, about her research this morning. When he saw her on the computer, she told him she was looking for roofing materials. Nate had been advocating for basic gray asphalt shingles. He said they'd be easiest to acquire and install, and they were affordable—he'd long ago calculated how many bundles they'd need and put it in the budget. Helen was hoping to find something more unique: reclaimed tin roofing, slate, maybe cedar shakes.

"Tell me everything," Riley said.

Helen took a breath and started at the beginning. She told Riley about her trip to the mill, the bricks, the stories the foreman told her, and what she'd seen in the house last night.

"It was Jane. I'm sure of it. And I think bringing the bricks here helped her come back. I know it sounds crazy, but I think Hattie wanted me to go to that mill to bring something back to the house."

Riley was quiet for a few seconds.

"Doesn't sound crazy at all," she said.

"I think you were right—if they have an object, a physical thing connecting them to their lives, to the way they died maybe, it acts as a kind of doorway—a way back into our world."

"It would be nice if we could confirm it," Riley said. "You know, prove that Jane really did die in that fire."

"Agreed. I found this website that lists the names of the people who died at the mill that day and there's only one Jane—a Jane Whitcomb. I did a little more research—checked out genealogy sites and public records—and found marriage records for a Jane Smith and Silas Whitcomb in 1934. They lived right in Lewisburg. According to the records I found, they had two children, Ann and Mark. I haven't looked into what happened to them yet. After Jane was killed in the fire, Silas remarried and had several more children. Do you think the historical society might have more information on Jane? Photos, even? I found a photo of the mill workers taken the year of the fire. Jane's in it. I just know it's the same woman I saw last night. Maybe we can match her to an old photo of Jane Breckenridge?"

"I think there are a couple photos, but Jane was just a girl when her mother died and she disappeared, so I'm not sure we'll be able to recognize her," Riley said. "Let's plan to meet at the historical society at three. We'll see what we can find."

"See you at three."

. . .

It amazed Helen how little could be left when a person was gone. A human being lived an entire life full of family and friends, dinner parties, work, church, and what was left? A couple of photos, a line or two in a town newspaper, an obituary usually, a tombstone with a name and dates and little else. Unless you kept digging. This is what she loved about history: the thrill of filling in the blanks, digging for and finding the hard evidence—birth and death records, marriage licenses, census data, photographs, diaries, and letters—and then using hunches and intuition to put it all together into a cohesive narrative. Studying a person or an event from long ago was like trying to solve a mystery: following clues, piecing things together.

There was no gravestone or obituary for Hattie Breckenridge. No mention of her or what had happened to her in the local paper. Very little proof that she had existed at all.

"It's like she was a ghost even back when she was alive," Helen said. She sat across from Riley at a big table in the center of the historical society. The space was in a disheveled state because of the flood—boxes and plastic totes were piled up on desks and shelves, files and documents haphazardly thrown in to save them from water damage.

Riley had arrived earlier to attempt to start putting things in some semblance of order, and she'd pulled what little she'd found on the Breckenridge family aside, started making notes. Helen had her own little notebook out now, hoping for a chance to jot down some solid facts about Hattie and Jane, something that might tell her where to go from here, how to find out more. Seeing them together in her house last night had made her more determined than ever to learn their stories, to follow the family tree and see if there might be more information, living relatives even.

"I know, it's crazy," Riley said. "We have whole boxes full of stuff on some families in town: letters, diaries, photographs. But there really isn't much on the Breckenridge family."

She pulled down another box and opened it up.

"Like I said, you've gotta bear with me here. Things aren't usually in such disarray."

"How'd you get involved with the historical society?" Helen asked.

Riley smiled. "I've been a volunteer here forever. Mary Ann roped me into it years ago when I was practically living here doing research on my own family. When I was in college, I did this project on Vermont in the Civil War and I found out some of my relatives had fought, not just for the Union army, but for the Confederates, too. I don't know, I guess it made me feel like I was part of something so much bigger, you know? I feel like studying the past helps me to frame the present. I guess I've always been a bit of a history geek—I love all the old stories, the way what came before shapes who we are now. Sometimes I get all caught up in my own little bullshit life dramas, like trouble with boyfriends or money, and then I think about those relatives, cousins fighting each other in the Civil War, or people who went through the Great Depression or the Holocaust, and it just puts things in perspective." Riley's eyes blazed and Helen recognized a kindred spirit.

"Absolutely," Helen said.

"I mean, just look at Hattie's life—everything that happened to her, the bullshit she must have had to endure. Imagine walking through town, being called a witch, the hatred hurled at her, building day after day, year after year, until they eventually killed her, then weighed her down and sank her in the bog. All because she was different. Because she was special."

Helen thought of the looks and sneers she got in town, the whispering behind her back. Her, the outsider, the one who'd stirred up Hattie's spirit.

Riley took a few seconds to compose herself, then looked back down at the boxes. "Okay, moving forward. We've got no death records. Let me show you what we do have."

Hattie's father's name, James Breckenridge, was on an old deed for the land around the bog.

"And here's her father's death certificate," she said, pulling out a copy. "He died back in 1899. Struck by lightning, just days after Hattie predicted it."

Hattie's name was there on the census from 1900 when she was an eight-year-old child. And there were three photographs of her that they could find: one as a girl, with her schoolmates, in 1899, their names written in careful cursive on the back. Helen didn't need to check the names to find Hattie, though—she recognized her immediately. Seeing her—finding proof that she'd existed as an actual flesh-and-blood person, a student in the Hartsboro one-room schoolhouse, and wasn't just a ghost in Helen's kitchen—gave Helen a feeling of deep satisfaction. Helen looked down at the school photograph: Hattie was in the back corner, a shadow of a girl with dark hair that fell down to cover her eyes. She was frowning into the camera, scowling really. It was an *I hate you all* kind of look. But still, even as an angry little girl, there was something stunningly beautiful about her. Something captivating. It nearly took Helen's breath away.

"Folks say that Hattie couldn't read or write very well because she left school in the third grade, got kicked out, really. Strange things happened when she was at school—books jumped off shelves, desks shook. And one time, the stories go, she was writing in her primer and the teacher came over to look. There were three pages written in Latin." Riley paused here, eyes widened for emphasis.

"Latin?" Helen asked. "How does a girl her age in Hartsboro, Vermont, learn Latin?"

"That's the thing about Hattie. She knew things she shouldn't have. Things the spirits told her. That's what the stories people passed down say anyway," she added.

The other two photos of Hattie were group shots at a town picnic and were dated 1909. Hattie was a teenager then and stood at the edge, away from the others. She was tall, her dark hair pulled back in a long braid, her eyes dark and stormy.

"Those pictures were taken around the time her family home burned," Riley said.

"And her mother was killed?"

"Yeah, listen to this. It's from 1909." She pulled out an old article clipped from the local paper and read it out loud: "'A fire of unde- termined origin took the life of Mrs. Lila Breckenridge of Harts- boro on Tuesday, October 12. The Breckenridge family home was destroyed. Hattie Breckenridge, Mrs. Breckenridge's daughter, escaped unharmed.'"

"'A fire of undetermined origin'?" Helen asked.

Riley looked up from the clipping. "I've heard that a group of men from town went out and set that fire. They'd been drinking at the pub and got it into their heads that it was up to them to save the town from Hattie Breckenridge."

"Jesus. She was the one who needed saving, not the other way around."

Riley nodded.

"Okay, so Hattie's mother is killed and Hattie's left homeless. Those are two facts we know for sure."

"Right. So she builds her little crooked house down by the bog. And let's not forget the money," Riley added. "Her parents were very well-off—her dad had owned a stake in the local railroad—and she was their only child. There aren't any surviving pictures of the family home, but they say it was deluxe. The Breckenridges were probably the richest family in town."

"So what happened to the money?"

Riley shrugged. "That's the great mystery. Supposedly, Hattie took it all out of the bank and brought it home with her, buried it out near the bog. Not far from the little house she built herself. People have looked for it over the years but never found a thing."

Helen smiled. "Olive thinks she'll be the one to find it."

"Does she? I thought she'd given up on the treasure."

"No. She's still looking. Going out to the bog with her new metal detector. Working the grid. She's very methodical."

Riley nodded. "That she is," she said.

"What I don't understand," Helen said, "is that if Hattie had all that money, why didn't she leave? Get on the first train out of here and start over someplace where no one knew her name? It doesn't make sense that she would stay here and build a tiny little cabin on the bog."

"If I had to guess, I'd say it's because she was connected to this place: it was a part of her, for better or worse. And maybe there were other reasons. Maybe there was a man."

"Jane's father? What do we know about him?"

"Nothing at all. Hattie never married. She lived alone in that little house by the bog. Then, not long after the fire, she was pregnant. Like she wasn't enough of a pariah before. Imagine being a single mother back then. Holy shit. The woman had guts, that's for sure. Staying here. Raising that girl on her own."

"Do we have anything on Jane?" Helen asked.

"Not a lot," Riley said. She reached into a box on the table, grabbed a photo there and handed it to Helen.

It was another school photo, showing about fifteen children ranging from tiny to almost adult in front of a one-room schoolhouse. *Hartsboro School, 1924,* said a neatly penned note in the corner. Helen flipped it over, and someone had written the children's names in now-faint penciled letters. Jane Breckenridge was the third girl from the left in the back row. She looked to be about twelve in the photo and was a near exact replica of Hattie at that age. Same dark hair and eyes, same haunted look. As with Hattie, Helen recognized her immediately— after all, a grown-up ghost version of Jane in a singed dress had visited her about twelve hours before. She could almost still smell the smoke.

"That's the last photo of the schoolhouse before it burned down," Riley said.

Burned down. She'd forgotten that's what happened. First, Hattie's family home burns, killing her mother. Then a fire at the schoolhouse. Another at the mill years later. A coincidence? Or something more?

"And Hattie was blamed for the fire?" Helen asked.

"She'd predicted it, kept Jane out of school that day. Three children were killed. Let's see." She looked through some notes on the table. "Lucy Bishkoff, Lawrence Kline, and Benjamin Fulton."

Helen turned the photo over again, searched for the names of the dead children. Benjamin and Lawrence were two little boys in the first row. They sat side by side with mischievous smiles. Lucy Bishkoff stood in the back row, right beside Jane. She had blond hair, pale eyes, and a warm smile.

Helen studied the photo, looked at their smiles, and thought, *None of you have any idea what's coming.* She felt like the Grim Reaper now, pointing a finger at the photo, at the little faces.

"Did they determine what caused the fire?" Helen asked.

Riley shook her head. "No, but they say the fire spread very quickly. And apparently the kids and teacher had trouble getting out of the building."

"Oh?"

"The door was stuck. Not just stuck, but people said someone had wedged it closed with a tree branch. It took some time, and a great deal of force, to get it open."

Another strange coincidence.

"That's so terrible," Helen said, studying the black-and-white photo of those schoolchildren, wishing she could go back in time and warn them, warn them all, like Hattie had tried to warn them. Tell them the danger was real.

That was the cruelest part about history, whether your own or a stranger's from a hundred years ago—there wasn't a damn thing you could do to change it.

Helen reached into her bag, pulled out the picture she'd printed from her computer of the workers at the Donovan and Sons Mill, taken just months before the fire.

"Meet Jane Whitcomb," she said, pointing to the woman in the back row with dark hair and eyes.

"My god," Riley said. "It's her. It's got to be. She looks just like Hattie, right?"

Helen looked down at the mill worker version of Jane, then the photo of young Jane outside the schoolhouse, then Hattie as a girl and Hattie as a teenager. They could have been sisters.

"Too bad we don't have anything of Hattie as an adult," Helen said.

"Just wait," Riley said with a sly smile. "I've saved the best for last." She stood up and went to a large wooden cabinet with long, narrow drawers. She pulled one open and lifted out a painting, keeping it facing toward her. Helen guessed it to be about two feet by four feet.

"What is it?"

"May I present: Miss Hattie Breckenridge," Riley said, slowly turning the painting so that Helen was face-to-face with the subject.

Helen's eyes locked on the framed portrait. Hattie stood in a bloodred dress and had her long raven-black hair held back with combs. Her lips were painted the color of the dress. Her eyes sparkled, teased, taunted, and seemed to glisten, to move, watching Helen.

Helen felt the air pulled out of her lungs, as if Hattie were sucking it in, inhaling the very life out of her.

I know you, the eyes said. *And you think you know me.*

Helen studied the neat signature in the bottom right corner; it was only two initials: W.T.

"Who's the artist?" Helen asked.

"If only we knew," Riley said. "We've researched, asked folks who are experts on artists in the area during that time period, but no one can tell us anything."

"Lost to history," Helen said.

She thought about all that was lost, all that she would not and could not ever know about Hattie Breckenridge. But she knew there were still some things to find. Like living relatives. The idea of finding an actual descendant of Hattie's sent an electric charge through Helen. Would they look like Hattie? Would they know any of her story, passed down through generations? Maybe they'd have something more: photos, letters, things that might have belonged to Hattie herself. What might happen if Helen found a relative, invited them to her house? Wouldn't Hattie be pleased? So pleased she'd show herself? Was this where Hattie had been leading her—to learn her whole story, not just the bits and pieces she could glean from her life, but the story of Hattie's legacy, of what came after?

She thought of the ways her father had shaped her, the things he'd taught her and stories he'd told her that she carried still: her house building, the tales he told about his own boyhood, about relatives long gone. What might Hattie have passed on to her descendants? What stories might they still be able to tell?

"Okay," Helen said, looking down at her notebook. "Let's see if we can figure out what happened to Jane's children, Ann and Mark."

"I'll see what I can dig up," Riley said, carefully setting the painting down on the table, leaned against the wall. Then she sat at the computer on a desk in the corner, fingers flying over the keyboard.

"You and Nate get the plumbing done?" Riley asked.

"Yeah. We started on the wiring today actually. Got a lot of the boxes in place. Drilled holes in the framing and started running cable."

"I'm booked up tomorrow, but I can come out and give you guys a hand for a bit the day after," Riley offered.

"That would be great," Helen said.

Helen turned back toward the painting.

Hattie was wearing an unusual necklace: a silver circle with a triangle inside it. At the center of the triangle was a square, then another circle with an eye in the middle.

Third eye, Helen thought.

"Okay if I get some photos of the painting?" she asked Riley.

"Sure," Riley said, still tapping at the keyboard.

Helen took pictures from different angles. Wherever she went, Hattie's eyes followed her.

"Hey, listen to this," Riley said. "Jane and Silas's son, Mark Whitcomb, died in 2000. He was married. Can't tell if there were kids." More rapid clicking on the keyboard, then, "Oh! This is interesting!"

"What is it?" Helen asked, moving closer, coming up behind Riley.

"Looks like I found Jane's daughter, Ann."

Helen moved closer to the computer and glanced down at a photo of a couple. The woman had dark hair pinned back and dark, haunting eyes. Hattie's eyes. The man was shorter than the woman and had receding hair and a mustache. They stood with their arms around each other in front of a Christmas tree. Above it was the headline: "Murder-Suicide Shakes the Town of Elsbury."

Helen squinted down at the article, dated May 24, 1980.

Police are calling the deaths of Samuel Gray and his wife, Ann Gray, a murder-suicide.

Vermont State Police colonel Gregory Atkinson gave this statement: "At approximately 5 p.m. on Friday, Samuel Gray shot and killed his wife, Ann, and then himself with a handgun registered in his name. This happened in their home on County Road, where Gray ran a dairy farm. Their two minor children were witnesses to the crime but were not harmed. The children are currently in the care of relatives."

It is the worst crime on record in this small town of 754 residents. "It's just a horrible shock," said Town Clerk Tara Gonyea. "It's shaken the community to the core."

Friends and neighbors expressed sorrow at the horrific events that transpired at the old Gray farmhouse, but neighbor William Marsh said he was not surprised. "Sam had a temper and he was a drinker," Marsh explained. "He's had trouble with the farm, making ends meet. I think his wife and kids bore the brunt of it. I've seen bruises and black eyes on 'em. I've heard the yelling and screaming."

Police declined to comment on whether there was a known history of domestic violence in the home.

"Ann was just an angel," neighbor Penny Stromberg said. "Full of life, always smiling. Such a good friend and neighbor. And those poor children. Can you imagine? It's heartbreaking, what they've had to endure."

Family members could not be reached for comment.

Helen stepped back, skin prickling, feeling suddenly cold all over. Gone. Ann was gone.

"It's so fucking awful," Riley said out loud. "Terrible things happened to all of those women: Hattie, Jane, Ann. It's like the women in that family were all cursed. Doomed to have their lives end in violence."

Helen nodded, eyes still on the picture in the article—the smiling faces of Ann and Samuel in front of their Christmas tree. "Where's Elsbury?" she asked.

"Southeast of here. Probably a little over an hour away."

"I think I'll take a ride down there. Take a look around."

Riley looked up at her, squinting a little. "You want to bring something back, don't you? For the house? For Hattie?"

Helen nodded. "I feel like it's the least I can do. A way to pay tribute."

And maybe, just maybe, it would be enough to bring Ann back. Helen let herself imagine it—three generations of Breckenridge women in her kitchen.

Riley looked at her a minute. "It's like you're creating a sort of family tree with objects," she said. "It's such a beautiful idea. A real way to honor those poor Breckenridge women."

Riley turned back to the computer, typed again, scanned the screen, then found what she was looking for. "202 County Road, Elsbury," she said, writing it down on a scrap of paper. "That's where the old Gray farmhouse is. Where the murder took place."

CHAPTER 23

O live

 AUGUST 7, 2015

"You got these from where, exactly?"

Olive was kneeling on the ground outside with a hammer and chisel, cleaning the old cement off the bricks. They'd spent the morning inside, working on the wiring. Riley had come by to help for a bit, and they'd finished the entire downstairs. Then Riley left to get to work, and Nate ran down to the trailer.

Olive scraped at the brick with the chisel. She had her new *I see all* necklace tucked under her T-shirt.

Helen and Nate were going to use the bricks to build a hearth in the living room, underneath the woodstove. Helen explained that instead of the traditional fireplace at the heart of the old New England saltbox, they'd have a much more efficient high-tech woodstove. They should be able to heat the whole house much of the time and use the propane heat for backup on really cold days. Olive nodded thoughtfully. She liked the little history lessons Helen incorporated into everyday conversations and had learned a lot about colonial New England and how the first settlers survived. Those were the stories that interested her the most. She didn't care much about heat sources or how energy efficient a woodstove was. She wanted to hear about chopping wood, killing animals, how there were no refrigerators so people cut ice in blocks out of lakes.

"I picked them up at an old mill that's being renovated," Helen said. She was working on her own brick with a wire brush. "They were just going to throw them away—I got them for free."

She smiled proudly. Olive had been around Helen and Nate enough to know that the house budget was an issue. Nate seemed super stressed about it and was always holding up spreadsheets and stuff to show to Helen. Helen was a little more laid-back and had this *don't worry, everything will work itself out* attitude.

It reminded her a little of her own parents—how her dad would sit down at the end of the month with all the bills and a big calculator and get all stressed out, and Mama would bring him a beer and massage his shoulders and promise that things were going to change one day soon.

"The bricks look old," Olive said, holding one in her hands. "And some of them are all black and stained like they're from the inside of a chimney."

"There was a fire at the mill. It destroyed part of the building."

"Cool. Where was the mill?" Olive asked.

"Up in Lewisburg."

Lewisburg. The name sent off a ping in Olive's brain. The receipt she'd found for coffee and a candy bar, the little red star on the map, the bottom left corner of the triangle.

"The mill was once the center of the community up there, until there was a big fire in 1943."

"What happened?" Olive asked.

Helen gave Olive a protective, worried sort of look that Olive's own mother might have given her. "It's a pretty terrible story," she said.

"Then I definitely want to hear it," Olive said. "Come on, it can't be worse than the stuff Aunt Riley has told us about Hattie and what happened to her, right?"

"Well, this is terrible in a different way," Helen said. "The people who ran the factory had barred the doors from the outside so workers couldn't sneak out on their shifts. They couldn't escape when the fire started."

"Holy shit," Olive said, then remembered she was with a grownup, a teacher no less. "Sorry," she said, embarrassed.

"It's okay." Helen smiled.

"So what was it like up there in Lewisburg?" Olive asked. "Is it a big place?"

"No, it's pretty small—smaller than Hartsboro. Not much to it at all. The mill is the main thing. They're fixing it up. Turning it into condos, shops, and offices."

Olive nodded. But why would her mom have gone up there? It's not like she was in the market for a new condo or had this great interest in old mills or anything, unless . . .

"Wait, so is anyone living there? Like are any of the condos done?"

Did she dare hope it? That maybe her mom had moved there? That that's where she and the mystery man were living at this very minute?

"No," Helen said. "It's all still under construction and looks like there's a long way to go. It's nice that they're giving it a new purpose—it's a great old building. The man I talked to up there claimed that it was haunted."

Maybe that's what it was. Maybe Mama went up because of her ghost club. Hell, maybe she and Dicky and all the members went up to have a séance or to try to record spirit voices like the ghost hunters on TV did.

"Wow, haunted?" Olive said. "For real?"

Helen nodded. "He said so."

"You believe in stuff like that?" Olive said. "Ghosts and hauntings?"

Helen concentrated extra hard on her brick. "I do," she said at last. "I didn't used to, but I do now."

A history teacher who believed in ghosts. How cool was that? Olive smiled at Helen.

"I wish I could see a ghost," Olive admitted. "Any ghost, really, but the ghost I'd most like to see—Hattie Breckenridge."

Helen scrubbed harder at her brick, opened her mouth like she was going to say something, then stopped, looked down toward the trailer. Nate had just come out the door and was heading toward them.

Nate spent a lot of time looking for the white deer he kept seeing. Olive thought it was strange that she practically lived in these woods, had been hunting in them all her life, and she'd never seen a white deer, and now this guy from Connecticut had seen one a bunch of times. She had heard the stories, of course. Warnings to never shoot the white deer if you saw it. Stories of hunters following a white doe deep into the woods and never coming back again. Like something from a fairy tale.

Nate was coming toward them and he looked pissed.

Olive braced herself, wondering if maybe she'd done something wrong. Nate was still so suspicious of her, and he seemed to go out of his way to find fault with her.

The truth of it was, Olive worried that maybe he was starting to go a little off the deep end himself. This white deer, or ghost deer or whatever it really was, seemed to have consumed him.

Nate had put up wildlife cameras in the yard. He'd started with one he got at the general store, then had gone online and ordered two more crazy-expensive motion-activated night-vision cameras that he'd set up in the trees at the edge of their yard—to "maximize coverage," he said. It seemed a little weird that he'd blow what must have been over a thousand bucks on this setup when they were supposedly over budget with house stuff, but far be it from Olive to understand what made grown-ups do the things they did. He'd connected the cameras to his laptop wirelessly so he could constantly check the feed. He'd hung salt licks and put out special deer pellets. He was determined to catch the deer on video or get a photo of it. But so far, he hadn't been successful. He'd gotten some great shots of skunks, a porcupine, even a coyote. But no deer.

"I know where the bricks came from," he said as he reached them now. His face was serious, his mouth a tight little line.

"What?" Helen asked. Olive looked down at the brick she was holding, like she was concentrating extra hard on getting every speck of old mortar off.

"You left the search engine open on your laptop, Helen. And the pages you've been looking at are all right in the history. Donovan and Sons? That's where the bricks came from, right? The mill where there was a fire that killed all those women?"

Olive looked at the brick she was holding in her hand, looked at the black sooty stains, wondered if bricks could be haunted.

"Well, yeah, but—"

Olive snuck a look at Helen, saw she had this *I've been caught* guilty kind of look on her face that made Olive squirm. Olive shrank down, hunching her shoulders, scrubbing hard at the brick. She wished she could disappear altogether. Get up and run away, but that would be too weird. She hated when grown-ups fought. There were too many times when her mom and dad were arguing and there was Olive, sitting right at the table, sinking lower and lower into her chair, practicing becoming invisible. She'd seen her mom fight with Aunt Riley once, too, which was weird because they were like best friends. Riley came to pick her mom up for something, but her mom said she wasn't going, that she had other plans. "You have to go," Riley had said. Mama had refused. "There are some things you don't bail on and this is one of them," Riley had hissed, and she was all pissed off, like going out to hear some crappy band play on two-dollar beer night was the most important thing that had ever happened. But Olive understood now it probably wasn't *what* they were going to that was important, but the fact that they were doing it together; that her mother was blowing off Riley.

Mama had refused to go, and Riley had slammed the door on her way out. It was the only time Olive could ever remember seeing her aunt totally lose her cool.

Nate stood over them now, looking down at Helen, eyes blazing with their own fire. "That's why you went there, right?" he demanded. "You knew about the fire. And you wanted the bricks *because* of the fire, because of the people who died."

"Nate, just calm down. I think there's a possibility that—"

"Jesus, Helen," he spat, interrupting her. "Why can't we just use bricks from Home Depot? What's this sudden obsession you have with filling our house with these things steeped in dark history?"

Dark history.

Olive liked that. She touched her T-shirt, feeling for the necklace underneath.

I see all.

"Bricks from Home Depot don't tell a story," Helen said.

He let out a long, dramatic sigh. "You know I love that you want to put things in the house that have history, that tell a story. But do the stories have to be such awful ones? Do they have to center around death and tragedy?"

She didn't answer.

Maybe Nate wasn't the only one going a little crazy. Maybe Helen was, too. The thought hit Olive like a cannonball in the stomach.

Helen had been keeping secrets.

Olive's mother had been keeping secrets, too, and look where they got her.

Nate didn't wait for Helen to respond or reprimand him for swearing in front of Olive. He just stalked through the front door of the house, calling back, "I'm going to go start wiring the upstairs."

Olive kept scraping at her brick even though all the cement was gone. She wanted to say something—felt like she should say something—but no words came. This was an adult. A teacher, even. Helen was really nice to her, and she guessed they were kind of friends—but to try to comfort her, to say, *I'm sorry your husband just yelled at you like that,* it felt all wrong. Finally, when she couldn't stand the silence any longer, she asked, "So did a bunch of people die in the fire?"

Helen startled a bit, as if she'd forgotten Olive was there. Then she nodded. "One man and twelve women died. Mill workers. And I think . . . no, I'm sure—that one of them was Hattie's daughter, Jane."

Olive got a tingle at the back of her neck. And the necklace gave a warm pulse under her T-shirt.

That's what her mother was doing there. She must have figured it out, must have known about Jane. Must have thought that learning about Jane might lead her to find a clue about the treasure.

Helen

 AUGUST 8, 2015

Helen left home at eight and headed for Elsbury in search of the farmhouse where Ann had been killed. She'd plugged the address, 202 County Road, into the GPS. She wasn't sure what she'd do once she found it—knock on the door, greet the current owners, and say she was interested in anything they might have that had once belonged to Ann, anything that had been in the house when she was killed, anything haunted?

Right. That was a sure way to get the door slammed in her face and the cops called.

Hattie will show me what to do, she told herself.

She'd promised Nate that she'd be back by one to help with the upstairs wiring—told him she had a couple of places to check out, places that had used roofing materials. She felt guilty lying, but she couldn't exactly tell him the truth. Letting him know she was doing anything connected to Hattie would just start another argument. And they'd had enough of those lately. It seemed they fought over everything, from the color of the tile they should put in the bathroom to what to have for dinner. Nate had insisted they stop eating out and getting pizza, start keeping a strict budget for groceries. Yet he frowned at her when she came home from food shopping with cheap store-brand coffee and gave her a lecture about how they should drink only fair trade, organic coffee because everything else was poison and a disaster for the environment and the local people.

About an hour into the drive, her phone rang. Nate's ringtone. She reached over and answered the phone, left hand still on the wheel of the pickup. "Hello?"

There was only dead crackling air.

"Nate? Hello?"

"—elen?" His voice sounded echoey, far off, like he was calling from the bottom of a well.

"I can barely hear you, Nate. Where are you calling from?"

"The house," he said. "I wanted—"

He was gone again, his voice replaced by a crackle, a sizzling sound, like meat on a grill.

"Can you—" he said.

"What?" she asked. "I can't hear you."

"Because of you."

"Nate?"

"Because of you." It was a woman's voice that came through loud and sure. A woman's voice that sounded like glass being ground up in a blender. A jagged, grating sound.

Helen nearly swerved off the road. Heart pounding, she pulled over, turned on her blinkers.

"Hello?" she croaked out. "Who is this?"

She held her breath, afraid of what the voice might answer. The phone felt hot in her hand, like the circuits were overheating, might just burst into flames.

"Sorry, hon, you're breaking up," Nate said. "You there?"

"Yes," she said. "I'm here."

Nate. Only Nate. Just a bad connection. She must have misheard.

"I was just calling to see if you could stop at the farm supply store on the way home and pick up some deer feed. Hello? Can you hear me?"

Deer feed. Of course that's what he wanted.

For his elusive white doe.

He thinks you're going crazy, and you think he is, too.

Stop it, she told herself.

No money for pizza or decent beer or wine, but plenty of money to feed the wildlife.

She hated thinking of him like this, feeling bitter and resentful. She took a breath. Remembered how just last night he'd cooked an amazing dinner—coconut curry soup with sweet potato biscuits— then made her close her eyes before he pulled out his surprise dessert, a cute little saltbox house made from graham crackers and frosting that looked nearly identical to theirs. His way of apologizing for freaking out about the bricks, though he didn't say it out loud.

"Yeah, Nate, I hear you," she said now. "I'll stop."

"Thanks," he said. "See you when—" He cut out again.

She put the phone down on the passenger seat, pulled back out, and continued on. Half an hour later, the voice on the GPS cheerfully announced, "You have reached your destination."

But there was no farmhouse in sight.

She was in front of a large expanse of lawn with a narrow driveway that led up to an enormous, glass-fronted log home with a wraparound porch and a pond beside it. There was no mailbox, no visible address. She drove on, scanning both sides of the road for a dairy farm and an old farmhouse. She passed fields of low-growing corn and even a pasture with some Holsteins grazing, but there was no sign of a farm or farmhouse. She had to be close to the old Gray place, though. Riley must have gotten the address wrong, or the GPS wasn't doing well with Vermont directions (it often didn't). Maybe there was an old County Road and this was the new County Road. She'd have to stop and ask someone. She continued on, hoping she'd come to the center of town. She only passed more fields, some grown over, abandoned.

Had Ann passed these fields often, walked them, even?

At last, Helen spotted a large red barn up ahead on the right. HAY BARN ANTIQUES was painted in tall white letters on the side. Perfect. She'd stop in, ask about the Gray place, get proper directions.

Helen parked, went through the front door and found herself in a room crowded with furniture and knickknacks. Classical music played from a back room. She passed an old schoolhouse desk with an abacus on top, a stuffed fox, an ornate cast-iron coal stove (FOR DECORATIVE USE ONLY, warned a hand-lettered sign), couches, chairs, mirrors, and tables of all sorts. At the end of the room, a mantel leaned precariously against the wall.

It was a reddish hardwood, polished to a shine with straight sides and carved brackets. There was something beautiful about the simplicity of the design. The price tag said $200, but it had been crossed out, marked down to $100. Helen felt drawn to it, imagined it in the living room of the new house, above the woodstove.

"It's a lovely piece," a voice said.

Helen turned, saw a gray-haired woman in a turtleneck with little Scottie dogs all over it. A real-life Scottish terrier trotted up behind her, squeaking a rubber hedgehog in its jaws.

"This is Mulligan," the woman said. "He's the real owner of the place. I just work for him. My name's Aggie."

Helen smiled at the woman and the dog, who was now sitting by her feet, torturing the rubber dog toy.

"The mantel is solid maple. I'd let it go for seventy-five dollars—I've got another load from an estate sale coming in at the end of the week and I need to make room."

"It's beautiful," Helen said. "You've got a lot of lovely things." She walked around a bit, stopping to pick up sad irons, to touch a treadle Singer sewing machine. Then she approached Aggie.

"Looking for anything in particular?" Aggie asked.

"I actually stopped in hoping you could help me with directions," she said.

"Sure. You on your way to the college? Or out to the bed-and-breakfast?"

"No, actually, I'm looking for the farmhouse the Gray family used to own. I've got an address, 202 County Road, but couldn't seem to find it. Maybe the address I've got is wrong, but—"

"No, you've got the address right. The house isn't there anymore. Stood empty for a long time, no one wanted to touch it. People said it was haunted. I imagine if any place was going to be haunted, it would be that house. I think houses hold memories, don't you?"

Helen nodded, said, "Absolutely."

"Anyway, it fell into neglect, then a doctor from out of state bought the place last year, had it all torn down—the house, the barn, everything—so he could build a fancy log house with a whole wall of windows."

"Oh yes, I saw that," Helen said.

Aggie nodded, stepped over to a table full of knickknacks. "One of those big prefab things trucked in. He put in a pond, stocked it with trout so he can fish whenever he wants. He comes up a few weekends a year. Place sits empty most of the time." Aggie's voice dripped disdain. She began to fiddle with a collection of old brass bells on the table, arranging them from largest to smallest.

Helen nodded sympathetically, said, "That's too bad. People should be fixing up the old farmhouses, not tearing them down."

"It's a rotten shame, if you ask me," Aggie continued, still moving the old bells around. "The Gray place, it had history. Some of it a bit dark, mind you, but that house, it had character." She leaned down, gave Mulligan a pat on the head. The dog leaned into her. "Isn't that right, Mulligan?" Then she looked up at Helen and asked, "Why were you looking for it, anyway?"

"I'm doing a history project. A family tree of sorts. I'm trying to trace any living relatives of the woman who used to live on the land my husband I bought in Hartsboro. Apparently, Ann Gray was her granddaughter."

Aggie shook her head. "Terrible what happened. It's kind of local legend around here. The worst crime ever to happen in Elsbury—well, the only crime really, if you don't count a few breaks-ins and the gas station being robbed."

Mulligan squeaked his toy, and Helen leaned down to give his ears a scratch.

"Do you know any details about what happened?"

Aggie gave a deep sigh. "Oh, sure. I guess everyone around here knows just about every gruesome detail . . . Sam was an alcoholic, for one. And the farm was going under. It was the family farm and it fell to him to keep it going, but he couldn't manage. He'd sold off most of the cows, even subdivided the back acreage and sold some off, but he still wasn't able to pay the bills. Not that those are excuses for what he did, but they provide the background."

She'd moved over to a desk and was neatening a pile of old photographs now—sepia-toned portraits of people no one could name.

"It was a murder-suicide, right? Did it happen in the house?"

Aggie nodded. "He shot his wife, then himself. Right in the living room. She was an odd one, his wife. Some said she was crazy. And of course it didn't help that she went around calling herself a witch."

"A *witch?*" Helen practically shouted. "Really?"

Aggie nodded. "She actually made a little business out of it, you know. People would come visit her in her parlor and she'd read their tea leaves, palms, do spells to help them with love or money. She even self-published a little book about the spirit world and divination. If only she'd been able to see her own future, to know what was coming and find a way to stop it."

"Maybe it doesn't work that way," Helen mused. *Maybe it's like everything else,* she thought; *it's hardest to see what's right in front of us.*

"I guess not. A shame, though. Just terrible. He shot her right in front of their kids."

"Do you know what happened to them? The kids?" Helen stepped closer to Aggie. "Are they around here still?"

"The poor things—neither of them could have been much older than ten when it happened. Jason. That was the son's name. And the daughter, let's see, I can't say I recall her name. They didn't stick around. Went off to live with relatives."

"Do you know where?"

She shook her head. "Afraid not. Out of state, I think, but I'm not sure." There was a pause. "You know, it's a funny coincidence, but that mantel you noticed when you first came in? It came from the Gray farmhouse."

"You're kidding."

"My husband and I managed to salvage a few things out of it before the contractors tore it down—some shelves, all the doors, and the mantel. We've got a set of shelves and a couple of doors left, too."

Helen went back to the mantel, touched the wood.

Right in the living room, Aggie had said.

Shot right in front of the mantel, Helen imagined.

"My husband, Phil, always said that whole family was cursed. I'm not sure I believe in curses, but you have to admit the poor Gray family had more than its fair share of horrible things happen."

Runs in the family, Helen thought.

Closing her eyes, Helen could almost see it: the mantel covered in knickknacks and family photos of Samuel, Ann, and their two children smiling into the camera. Then everything splattered in blood. The screaming of the children.

"I'll take the mantel," Helen said, before she could think it through. "It'll be perfect for my living room."

Aggie smiled. "One second," she said, and went back into the room the classical music was coming from. When she came out, she was carrying a thin paperback book. "I'll throw this in with it," she said.

Helen looked at the title: *Communicating with the Spirit World,* by Ann Whitcomb Gray.

"Wait . . . this is Ann's book?"

Aggie nodded.

It was one of the library books she'd been holding on to all summer. Her head spun at the thought of it—that a book written by a direct descendant of Hattie had been sitting on her kitchen table for

weeks, a book she'd turned to to help her understand what was happening between her and Hattie.

Aggie smiled. "I've collected a few copies and I pull them out for
the right customer. This copy goes with you."

"Thank you so much," Helen said as she flipped to a chapter
toward the end, read:

> Spirits, like living people, can come with an agenda. Some come in
> peace, just seeking to make contact with the living, especially those they
> have a connection to. For others, it may be more complicated than that.
>
> A spirit may come to pass along a message you may not wish to hear
> or even to warn you of something.
>
> Sometimes they return to exact revenge.

INSULATION AND DRYWALL

CHAPTER 25

Olive

"I still can't believe you actually went into Dicky's," Mike said, shaking his head. Olive hadn't seen him since then—his mom had been keeping him busy, and between that and Olive still being pretty pissed at him for abandoning her, they hadn't managed to find time to hang out. As soon as he met up with her, he asked her to tell him the whole story, every detail of what had happened once she went up those old stairs at the hotel. So she'd told it, but in a vague, rough-outline kind of way.

"And I can't believe you ditched me. You are *such* a wimp," she said. "You could have waited for me. I actually looked around for you when I came out. I thought maybe you'd at least stand guard or something."

He said nothing, just looked down at his dirty sneakers.

They were out in the bog, near Hattie's old house. Bullfrogs sang in a strange angry-sounding chorus, voices raised, like they were shouting over each other.

It was quiet up at Helen and Nate's. Olive had spent the morning helping them fill the walls with rolls of pink fiberglass insulation. Even with gloves, long sleeves, and her jeans tucked into her boots, bits of fiberglass found their way to her skin and made her itchy, just like when she'd helped her dad with insulation. She'd kinda hoped Nate would use hay bales or milkweed fluff or recycled Patagonia fleece to insulate—no such luck. Probably too expensive. She went home, took a shower, and met up with Mike. Helen and Nate were hoping to finish the insulation today and start hanging drywall.

"What if someone had seen you going in?" Mike asked, reaching down, picking a handful of sedge grass. "What if your dad had found out you went there? He'd be pissed."

"Well, he didn't, right? My dad isn't exactly paying a whole lot of attention to where I go and what I do these days."

Mike scowled, picked apart the grass in his hand, ripping it into tiny pieces. "Maybe he should. I mean, that guy Dicky is a legit weirdo. The dude lives with ghosts and carries a loaded gun everywhere! And don't tell me you didn't think that old hotel was creepy as hell."

Olive had told Mike only what Dicky had told her: that her mom hadn't been there. She'd decided to keep the phone call she'd heard to herself. And right now, she was realizing what a smart move that had been. No way was she going to tell Mike that she planned to go back next month, that there was some connection between her mom and Dicky and his ghost club.

"Did he have his gun when you saw him?"

"Sure," Olive said.

"Oh man, oh man!" He dropped the grass, looked at her in wide-eyed amazement that soon morphed into this stupid, furrowed-brow reprimanding-parent kind of look. "Olive, do you get how dangerous that was?" There was spittle on his lower lip.

"Like he was going to shoot me for coming to his store in the middle of the day. Quit trying to act like you're my dad," Olive said.

"That's not what I'm doing," Mike shot back.

"Oh, really? 'Cause that's what it seems like."

"I don't want to be your dad," he said.

"Well, what is it you're trying to be? A boyfriend, maybe? Because I *so* do not need a boyfriend."

His cheeks turned lobster red and he stood up, glaring at her. "I am trying to be your *friend,* Olive." He was wheezing a little, giving his words a whistling sound, like a freaking talking prairie dog with big sad eyes. "I'm, like, your *only* friend. If you're too dense to get that, then maybe we shouldn't be friends at all."

He looked at her, waiting. Blood rushed in her ears. "Maybe not," she said, glaring at him.

He turned his back and walked away.

She sat on the edge of the old stone foundation, her metal detector beside her, eyes on Mike's back as he made his way along the edge of the bog to the path up through the woods.

"Scaredy-cat asshole!" she yelled after him when he was almost out of sight. "Think you're so smart, but you don't know shit!"

She got up and started working the grid in a halfhearted, half-assed way.

She didn't need Mike. She didn't need anyone.

She rubbed away tears with a balled fist, let the metal detector fall to the ground.

She wasn't even sure what she was looking for anymore.

The treasure, sure.

But more than that, she wanted answers.

What had her mother been up to? What had she found in Lewisburg? Something about Jane? Something that led Mama to find the treasure? Something that got her in trouble? And what had she been up to with Dicky and his friends at the old hotel? What did the chalked drawing of Mama's necklace mean?

She felt like the pieces were all there in front of her like loose beads waiting to be strung in a pattern that made sense. Maybe if she'd told Mike everything, he could have helped her figure it out.

Too late now. He would've just gone running to her dad anyway, blabbed everything.

Her head ached. Her eyes stung. She sat heavily back down on the short wall of stones that had once been a part of Hattie's foundation.

Olive took Mama's necklace off, pulling it out from its hiding place under her shirt. The necklace hung, the thin leather cord pinched between her index finger and thumb. She stared at the eye at the center, which seemed to wink at her as it caught the light. She imagined it hanging from her mother's neck. She pictured her mother's shoes, the fairy-tale slippers, and imagined her mother dancing in them slowly, languidly, across the bog, floating out over the water, leaving pale pink lady's slippers in the places where the magic shoes had touched down.

The pendant hung at the end of the cord, swaying slightly on its own, as if remembering what moving with her mother had been like.

Spin, Olive thought as she watched it start to spin.

Faster, she told the necklace, and it picked up speed, twirled in the air at the end of the line.

I'm doing this, Olive thought as she sat perfectly still. *I'm doing this with my mind.*

She stared at the necklace, concentrated.

Move clockwise, she told it. And it stopped spinning and began to loop in a circle clockwise, slowly at first, then faster, faster.

Stop, she commanded, and all at once, as if an invisible hand had come down and closed around the charm, it held perfectly still.

"Jump up and down," she told it, saying the words aloud this time, because all of a sudden, it felt like it was alive, this silver symbol, and it didn't seem strange at all to be talking to a necklace.

The charm moved, dancing, leaping up and down like a puppet on a string.

A dark, doubtful part of herself said, *You idiot. You're moving it. Of course you're moving it and you're not even aware of it.*

She thought of her science teacher Mr. Pomprey, who'd taught the class about natural selection. Earlier in the year, they'd covered the scientific method. Make observations, propose questions, come up with a hypothesis, test your hypothesis.

Olive looked at the necklace.

The silver charm at the end is bouncing up and down, she observed, *as if the cord is being jerked repeatedly, like a yo-yo. There is no breeze. I'm holding my hand perfectly still. Something else must be moving it. What hypothesis would explain this phenomenon? I hypothesize that I legitimately have teleki-nesis, like a character in a movie or comic book.*

Was she going crazy?

This wasn't possible. People couldn't do things like that. It didn't happen in real life, only in made-up stories.

Her head felt foggy, and the pain in her temples was coming on strong. She was tired and thirsty.

Hattie had been able to make things move, make objects around her fly through the air. That's what Aunt Riley had said. So maybe it was being here that did it. Maybe it was the place, the bog, that was responsible somehow.

Or maybe Hattie was helping her.

Her head hurt more.

"Am I making this move?" she asked aloud, looking at the neck-lace. All at once, the bouncing stopped. The cord hung straight and still, the pendant motionless.

No, dummy, it seemed to say. *It's not you at all. How could you have thought such a thing?*

You're just Odd Oliver. What powers could you possibly have?

"Hattie?" Olive said, her throat tightening a little around the name. "Are you here? Are you the one making it move?"

The necklace began to swing in big clockwise loops.

Olive's hands felt prickly, her whole body humming with a strange electricity. Her body was a conduit. A conduit for Hattie to come through.

"Okay," Olive said. "So, does clockwise mean yes?"

The charm moved in clockwise circles again.

Yes! Yes, yes, Hattie was speaking with her. Actually communicating.

"What's no?"

The necklace stopped, then began to revolve in the opposite direction, counterclockwise.

"Right, got it," she said as her heart hammered and her palms grew sticky with sweat.

So she could ask yes or no questions.

Her mind was going so fast, she had trouble coming up with her first question.

"Is this really Hattie Breckenridge?"

Yes, the necklace said, swinging clockwise.

Of course, she thought. *Of course it is. Who else would it be?*

She tried to calm her thoughts, to stay focused. What was it she most wanted to know?

"Is the treasure real?"

Yes.

Olive laughed out loud. "I knew it!" she said.

"Can you show me where it is?"

Counterclockwise this time: *No.*

"Did my mother find it?"

Yes.

"Did she take it with her when she left?"

No.

"Did my mother leave? Did she run off with a man?"

No.

Olive held her breath, eyes on the necklace, which was now slowing to a stop.

"Do you know where she is?"

Yes.

"Can you help me find her?"

The silver charm hesitated, then swung clockwise.

Yes. Yes. Yes.

CHAPTER 26

Helen

 AUGUST 19, 2015

Helen was in the new house, curled up on the floor in the living room. The framed walls were stuffed full of fluffy pink insulation. With the windows and doors closed and insulation in, it was much quieter. She and Nate finished the insulation this afternoon and had even gotten started with the drywall. Hanging the drywall had been a slow, cumbersome project—maneuvering the heavy four-by-eight sheets into the house, making the necessary cuts, and then Nate holding the pieces in place while Helen screwed them to the walls with the cordless drill. The downstairs bathroom was covered in grayish drywall screwed to the studs and was ready to tape, compound, and prime. It felt good to have one room with solid walls instead of the cage of two-by-fours.

Now she blinked in the dark. Her head felt heavy, her thoughts slow. She'd gone to bed in the trailer next to Nate. It had been raining out, absolutely pouring, and the roof was leaking again. They'd put cooking pots and bowls around to catch the drips, and Helen had tossed and turned while listening to the percussion of water hitting metal pots, empty tin cans, plastic bowls. That, combined with the rain pounding down on the metal roof, created a taunting, angry symphony of rain, with the occasional rumble of thunder thrown in. She hadn't been able to sleep, so she'd gotten up, gone into the kitchen, and read *Communicating with the Spirit World* again. She'd been through it several times but kept going back to it.

At one a.m., Helen had given up on the idea of going back to bed, slipped on her sneakers and a sweatshirt, and headed down to the bog. Back at the beginning of the summer, she wouldn't have dared go out walking through the woods at night and would have jumped at every noise. But she'd grown more comfortable with her surroundings, with the nighttime noises. She was nervous still, yes, but the feeling of being drawn to Hattie overpowered that fear. And she had this sense, irrational as it may have been, that Hattie wouldn't let anything bad happen to her. Hattie would protect her.

The rain had let up from the downpour to fine sprinkles. She'd made her way across the yard, feet squishing in puddles as she left the shadowy house and trailer behind. She'd descended the path through the little stretch of woods, listening to the noises around her: raindrops on leaves, frogs calling, a splash from the bog. The path had opened up and the bog had come into view. There had been a pale mist over the water that seemed to waver and shift as if it were trying to take form.

"Hattie?" she'd called quietly. The only answer she'd received was the dull croaking of a lone frog. She'd stood watching the water, thinking about what might be underneath. The rain had picked up, soaking through her sweatshirt. She'd gone back up to the unfinished house. She'd sat on the floor, beside the mantel, waiting, hoping. But nothing had happened. And she'd fallen asleep.

She sat up now, stretched. It was still raining. Helen could hear it upstairs, hitting the roof of the new house, the roof that had been covered in tar paper roofing material but had not yet been shingled.

(*Because you haven't found roofing materials. You've been going off to get haunted bricks and a mantel, to learn about Hattie and her family, instead of bringing home something you actually need to finish your house.*)

She heard Nate's voice in her head: *I'm worried about you, Helen.*

She looked at the mantel—her latest victory. They'd placed it inside on the floor, wrapped up in a tarp to keep it protected until the walls were done and they could hang it. She peeled back the tarp now and looked at it.

She had been right—it was perfect. It was the missing piece their living room needed, another way to give their new house a sense of history.

"But we don't need a mantel," Nate had said when he'd first seen it. He walked away from the mantel in the back of the truck and looked in the cab. "Where's the deer food?"

"Shit, I'm sorry. I forgot it."

He sighed, rubbed his face. "What are we going to do with a mantel? We don't have a fireplace."

"I've been thinking," Helen said. "Maybe we should have one

built—put a big brick chimney right in the center of the house. That would make it more of an authentic saltbox design and add thermal mass—"

"Helen, that's not part of the plans! That is not a do-it-yourself project—do you have any idea how much a skilled mason costs? As it is, we're over budget!"

"Okay, okay," Helen said. "So we go with the woodstove and metal chimney for now. Maybe later, we can talk about a real brick chimney? For now, we put the mantel on the wall behind the woodstove."

Nate squinted, trying to visualize it, and shook his head.

"But the stovepipe will run in front of it. It'll look weird."

"Maybe we can run the pipe out the back of the stove, through the wall, then run the metal chimney up behind the living room wall," Helen suggested. "That would look better anyway, right? Instead of a shiny metal chimney running straight up to the ceiling?"

Nate blinked at her. "I don't know, Helen. I'd have to look at the plans, see what might work. It might involve rethinking the pantry behind that wall. I don't think we want warm stovepipe running through the pantry, do we? We'd lose storage space, and that heat would be wasted. It wasn't part of the original design." He gave a frustrated sigh.

"The mantel's over a hundred years old, Nate. And it's solid maple," she said. "I got a great deal on it. Once I clean it up, you'll see just how beautiful it is."

"I just wish you'd checked with me," he said. "A mantel isn't in the plans. *Or* in the budget."

"It was seventy-five bucks, Nate." Her voice came out a little sharper than she'd meant.

"But now that's seventy-five dollars we don't have for other materials, things we really need, like roofing materials." His voice was slightly raised. "I thought that's what you were doing today. Going to check out a lead on old metal roofing."

She looked away, took in a breath, told herself to be calm. Just one more little white lie. "It didn't work out. It was in rougher shape than the ad described."

He looked at her quizzically. Could he tell she was lying?

When had it gotten so easy, lying to her husband? She would have never considered lying to him back in Connecticut. Back then, they'd told each other everything. It was only a few months ago, but it felt like lifetimes.

She looked at him then, his full beard, his tired eyes, and thought how different this man was from the man she'd been married to back in Connecticut—how different everything was.

"I'm sorry, Nate. If I don't find anything that'll work soon, we'll just go ahead and order the shingles you want from the home center."

Nate nodded, still frowning at the mantel.

"Nate, can't we just bring the mantel in, put it against the wall, and see how it looks?" she asked. "Please?"

"Fine," he said, and she got that little ping of satisfaction she got when she'd won a round.

Nate had agreed it did look great in the house, done some figuring, and decided they could put the stovepipe behind the stove, go straight into the wall, and then run the chimney up through the pantry so the mantel would not be obscured. They'd laid the mantel out on a tarp and Helen had cleaned it up, used some lemon polish on it, rubbed at the scuffed and scratched places, trying to imagine all the mantel must have seen: the years of Christmases, birthdays, celebrations; the coming of television; the decline of the farm; the fights; the murder and suicide.

.   .   .

Now, tonight, the mantel seemed to shine, to almost glow, in the dark of the empty house.

But the house was not empty. Helen understood that.

She held perfectly still and waited, listening. She heard footsteps on the plywood subfloor, felt the air grow colder around her. Her skin prickled. Keeping her eyes fixed on the mantel, she stared without blinking until her eyes teared, until a figure moved into view, came to stand beside her. Helen raised her eyes slowly.

The woman was wearing jeans; her dark hair was cut in a bouncy bob, the front of her pink sweater soaked with dark red bloodstains. Helen could smell gunpowder and the rich iron scent of fresh blood.

This isn't real, Helen thought. *I'm dreaming it.*

She closed her eyes tight, then opened them wide, and the woman was still there. Helen could see the box of nails Nate had left on the floor beside the mantel. And there was his hammer. There was an unused roll of fiberglass insulation.

This was no dream.

"Where are the children?" the woman asked, looking around, eyes frantic. She seemed to be speaking loudly, shouting even, yet Helen could barely hear her; her words came out like a cicada buzz. Then she looked down at her front, reached a hand up to touch the bullet hole, and started to scream. It was the most anguished, high-pitched keening sound Helen had ever heard.

"Please," Helen said, trying to raise her head but finding it too heavy. "It's all right."

But as soon as she spoke, the woman faded like a gust of smoke being blown by a sharp wind.

She was gone.

But the sound remained.

Outside, the screaming went on and on.

It was the same sound Helen had heard that first night. The sound Nate had insisted was a fisher or a fox.

Helen curled herself tight into a ball, put her hands over her ears, tried to silence the screams.

CHAPTER 27

Ann Whitcomb Gray

 **MAY 23, 1980**

Miss Vera with her blue hair in a tight perm comes every Friday at three, asks me to read the tea leaves, the cards, to gaze into my scrying bowl and see what the future holds for her, to see if she has any messages from the beyond.

"What do you see, Ann?" she asks. "What do the spirits show you?"

I gaze into the black water of the bowl, concentrate, furrow my brow and let my eyes go glassy by not blinking.

"Is my darling Alan trying to reach us?" she asks.

"Oh yes," I say, peering into the bowl as if Alan were a goldfish circling in the murky water. "He's calling from the Great Beyond. He wants you to know how much he loves you and that he's okay."

I don't really see any of this, of course, but I've learned to tell the ladies of Elsbury what they most want to hear. Especially the old, the lonely. Poor Miss Vera with her humped back, her swollen arthritic fingers. The diamond engagement ring and white gold wedding band that rattle around, loose now, clearly fitted for a plumper, younger finger. And though I don't see any spirits of the present, I can clearly picture the past: Vera as a young woman on the altar, beautiful and happy with Alan by her side. He slips the ring on her finger, takes her in his arms and kisses her, and that kiss transcends time and space, fills the air in this room now, nearly sixty years later. The kiss that came before everything else: before four children, the oldest of whom would die in a car wreck; before Vera's breast cancer, which she survived; and before Alan's lung cancer, which he did not. Two packs a day for sixty years will get you in the end.

"He's here now," I say, gazing into the cut crystal bowl filled with water and black dye—a few drops of RIT poured from a bottle.

"What does he say?" the old woman asks. "Does he have a message for me?"

I squint down into the bowl and am startled by what I see. It's not Alan's face looking back at me (real or imagined), nor is it my own reflection.

It's *her* again. The woman. She's come back to me, this woman from my dreams, from my nightmares. Sometimes I think she's just a part of me: my dark side, the place all my powers come from. She's the one who gives me my visions, whatever knowledge I may have, I understand that. My spirit guide. She's so familiar to me, with a face that isn't my mother's but has certain similarities. She has the same eyes as my mother but a longer face; same dark curly hair but kept long, not cut short like my mother's. And this woman wears a necklace, a strange design with a circle, triangle, square, and circle, with an eye in the center. I've been dreaming of her since I was a little girl. Since before my mother was killed in the fire, before my father remarried and carted my brother, Mark, and me off to Springfield to start another life with his new wife, Margaret, whom we were made to call "Mother," and soon our new flock of half siblings, all blond and blue-eyed and freckled like their mother. They pretended to love us for Father's sake but were always slightly suspicious of our dark hair and eyes, of the tragedy we wore on our sleeves.

The woman from my dreams is speaking now, trying to tell me something, but I can't hear the words. I lower my face closer to the bowl. I can smell the alkaline scent of the black dye. My breath is making the water ripple slightly, distorting her image.

The woman in the water speaks urgently, though without sound. Her eyes bore into mine. She's got something in her hands, something I can't make out at first; then the image clarifies, the object comes into view.

It's a gun. A handgun. Small and silver, like the one Sam owns.

Sweet Melissa. That's what he calls his gun. Silly, to name a gun and to name it something you might call a lover. It gives a strange power to the object, imbues the cold metal with warmth, with emotion.

Sam is out plowing the fields now, but he'll be home by suppertime. If Miss Vera pays me well, we'll have a nice roast tonight. No pasta primavera with Alfredo or Cajun rice and beans—giving a dish a fancy name doesn't make it fill your belly more or disguise that it's a cheap meal, that we couldn't afford better.

No money for meat, but there's always money for Sam's bourbon. He sees to that.

He isn't a bad man, Sam. Just a man who's run out of luck. Out of choices. Last year, we sold off thirty acres to pay the back taxes. Now we're underwater again.

I hear Sam's voice, clear as a church bell in my mind (though I know he's out plowing the east fields, getting ready to plant the corn).

Finished, he says.

We're all finished.

I glance down and see my own reflection in the rippling water, but there's blood on my chest, blooming like a flower.

I gasp, totter backward, nearly falling out of my chair.

"What is it?" Vera asks. "Is it my Alan?"

"Yes," I say, sitting up, collecting myself, looking back down at the front of my sweater, which is clean, spotless.

"He came to me with such force, it caught me off guard," I tell her. "He really loves you. He misses that cake you used to make."

A guess on my part, but I'm good at this, and the smile on Vera's face shows I've gotten it right again.

"Oh!" she cries. "The brown sugar cake! Heavens, yes! I haven't made that in ages! I think I'll go home and make some this afternoon."

"He'd like that," I tell her, daring another look down at my bowl. I see only my own dim reflection. "He's smiling at you. Can you feel him smiling down at you?"

"Yes," she says. "Yes, I can."

She reaches into her patent leather purse, pulls out forty dollars and passes it to me. Then she grabs another ten and slips it into my hand. "Thank you, Ann," she says, her hand dry and powdery in my own. "This means so much to me."

And at moments like this, I think, *Is it so wrong, what I do? Lying, pretending, inventing small fictions based on little flashes I may or may not receive?* I see how happy I make Miss Vera, the spring in her step as she hurries out the door to make her cake, and I think, *I am doing good work. I am shining a positive light on the world.*

. . .

I'm busy making dinner in the kitchen when Sam comes in later. "Daddy," the children chirp, crowding him like hungry birds. I see that even though it's not yet five, Sam's been drinking. He totters on his feet, leaning this way and that, trying to correct his balance, to remain upright. He's got a bottle stashed in the barn. One in the workshop, too. They're all over, so he'll never be thirsty.

"Don't pester your father," I tell the children. "He's been working all day. Go on in the living room. I'll call you when supper's ready."

They mind so well, my children.

They've learned.

Learned to be a little fearful of their daddy, to keep their distance when he's drinking.

Once they've left, I look him in the eye. "Everything okay?" I ask. I hate how timid my voice sounds. How quickly I turn into a little mouse around him.

And he laughs. He laughs a bitter, mirthless laugh, and his hot bourbon-fueled breath fills the kitchen, turns the air into a dangerous, combustible thing. All we'd need is a match and we'd all go up with a bang.

He staggers out of the kitchen, bumping against a chair, hitting the wall as he careens around the corner toward our bedroom. I hear him in there, opening drawers. Maybe he's putting on his pajamas. Maybe he's tired and sick and sick and tired and just wants to lie down, wants the day to be over, mercifully over.

But then I hear his footsteps move into the living room.

And Jason, he says, "Daddy, what're you doing with Sweet Melissa?"

And there's that laugh again, that empty haunting laugh that fills the hall as I start to run, run from the kitchen toward the living room, over the carpet; I'm going faster than I ever have in my life, past the door to the cellar, the bedrooms, the bathroom with the leaking faucet, and into the living room, where Sam is standing by the mantel, holding his little silver pistol. His laugh turns into a hum, a little song, and at last I can make out the words:

"Finished," he says. "We're all finished."

I step toward him, hands outstretched. "Sam," I say. "My darling."

And he raises the gun and fires.

CHAPTER 28

O live

"Dad," Olive said through the dust mask she was wearing. They were tearing down the old plaster and lath wall in her bedroom, and the air was thick with dust. It was funny, because she'd spent all day yesterday helping Helen and Nate finish putting up new drywall in their house. Today they were starting the process of taping and compounding. And here she was, tearing down an old, perfectly good wall. It was the one they'd thought they were keeping, but Daddy insisted they redo it anyway—that it would look funny to have smooth, new drywall on three walls and bumpy old plaster on the other. She'd told him it was fine, preferable even, to keep the old wall (she even suggested accentuating the difference by painting it a different color), but he insisted. "Your mama always says 'No point doing a job if you're not going to do it right.'"

And who was she to argue with Mama?

Olive was determined to work quickly, to hurry up and get her room taken apart so they could put it back together. It was taking forever. They'd had to put her room on hold while they tore out the bathroom wall and redid the plumbing, which had begun to leak. Then her dad decided they really needed to paint the living room, and they'd gotten two coats done before he announced that the color was all wrong and Mama wouldn't like it at all, so they'd tried a paler shade of blue, which he said wasn't right, either. Olive put her foot down, insisting that they had to leave the living room and go back to working on her bedroom. If her dad wouldn't help, and just abandoned the work like he had with so many other rooms before they were done, she'd finish it herself. She'd been camping out on the lumpy living room couch since before school ended and needed the sanctuary of her own room back. She could live inside a house that was a construction zone if she just had one finished place to take refuge in, one room where everything was in its place. An eye in the center of the storm.

"What's up, Ollie?"

"I've been thinking. You know, about—" She hesitated, not sure she could go on. Knowing this was the one subject she wasn't supposed to bring up, the thing that hurt her father the most. But she had to. She needed to know. "About Mom. About how things were just before she left."

He clenched his jaw. He did not wear a mask when he worked, so she could see the muscles working under his taut, unshaven skin that was now coated with a thin layer of plaster dust. He looked like a ghost.

"Yeah?" he said, holding the sledgehammer, ready to swing again, but waiting now.

"I remember how she was gone a lot. Did she ever tell you where she was going, who she was spending time with?"

"No, Ollie, she didn't. And when she did tell me, it was real vague. 'Out with Riley' or 'friends,' that sort of thing." He paused. "Part of me knew she was lying. But I didn't want to face the truth."

"What truth is that, Dad?"

He scowled, shook his head. He wasn't going to say it out loud.

"But what if that wasn't the truth? What if that was all just rumors?"

"Drop it," he said.

"But, Dad, what if that's not what happened? What if she—"

"She would go out with one set of clothes on and come back in another!" Daddy's eyes blazed. "She'd tell me she was with Riley when I knew damn well she hadn't been because Riley called the house looking for her, wondering if she wanted to go out. There were nights she didn't even bother to come home at all, Ollie. I'd catch her sneaking in at dawn. How else do you explain it?" He shook his head. "I'm sorry, Ollie. I'm really sorry, but it's the truth."

"I talked to Sylvia—you know, Mom's friend who tends bar over at Rosy's—and I know Mama spent at least one night over at her place."

He turned back to the wall, ripped off a chunk of loose plaster with his hand. "Is that right?"

"Sylvia also said something about a club Mama might have been a part of. Do you know anything about that?"

She considered mentioning Dicky Barns but decided that was a lousy idea—she already knew what her daddy thought of Dicky, and she thought that might just send him off on a rant and that wasn't the way she wanted this to go.

"She was probably talking about a dance club or something," he said, sounding kind of disgusted. "Loud music, cheap well drinks. Your mama loves places like that." There went his jaw again, tightening, like he was clamping something between his teeth, holding it tight.

Olive remembered how sometimes Mama and Daddy would go out for a date night: dinner at the steak place in Barre, sometimes a movie after. Sometimes they'd go out to Rosy's to watch a Red Sox game on the big screen or meet up with some of Daddy's friends from the town team after a softball game. Daddy used to play on the team but didn't anymore because of his bad knee. But she couldn't think of a single time they ever went out dancing or to a place that called itself a club. Those trips were reserved for Mama and Riley's nights out. Or Mama on her own, meeting up with other friends. Other boyfriends maybe even, if you believed the rumors.

Olive shook her head. "I don't think that's what Sylvia meant."

"Well, your mama never said anything to me about any club. She's not exactly a joiner kind of person, know what I mean?" He turned back to her, looked her in the eye.

Olive nodded. She knew exactly what he meant. Her mom had never volunteered to help on field trips or to make brownies for the school bake sale. When Olive had begged to join the Girl Scouts in third grade because her best friend, Jenna, was in it, her mom had said no. "What do you want to go and do that for, Ollie? Sitting around making macaroni necklaces and selling cookies with a bunch of girls in identical uniforms, competing for badges. Groups like that, they're just training kids to lose their individuality, to be like everyone else. That's not what you want, is it?"

Olive had shaken her head then. But it was a lie. Secretly, part of her did want to be like those other girls, to blend in, to feel like she belonged.

Mama was her own person. Her own unique individual who spun and glittered and shone when she walked into any room. But Olive just wanted to blend in, to disappear in the scenery.

"Do you have any idea how special you are, Ollie?" Mama had asked her one night, not long before she went away.

Olive had shrugged, thought, *Not me. I'm not special at all,* but she didn't want to contradict her. Mama was sitting on the edge of her bed, tucking her in even though Olive was too old to be tucked in, really.

"Some people, they have magic in their veins. You're one of them. You and me both. Can't you feel it?" Then she reached down and touched the necklace, the *I see all* necklace, and smiled real big.

.   .   .

Now Olive stared at her dust-covered father, knew she had to keep going, that he might know something, might be carrying some crucial piece of the puzzle around without even realizing it. "Do you remember the necklace Mama wore all the time then? The silver one?"

"I think so, yeah. Why?"

"Did you give it to her?"

He sighed. "No, I didn't."

"Do you know where it came from?" she asked.

"I don't know, Ollie. It was probably a gift, I guess. Maybe *he* gave it to her."

Olive swallowed hard. She didn't need to ask which "he" Daddy was talking about. It was the mystery man, the other man, the man Mama supposedly left them both for.

But what if it wasn't true?

"I think it would be best," Daddy said, "for you to forget all about that necklace."

Olive could feel the silver pendant against her chest. She wanted to reach up and touch it but didn't want to give Daddy any clues.

"I think you've got other things you need to be concentrating on right now." He looked at her, his brow furrowed like he had a bad headache coming on. "School starts next week," he said at last.

"I know," she said, her mouth suddenly dry. She'd been trying hard not to think about it.

"Things are going to change around here this school year." He was breathing harder now, his face red. He looked like a man ready to stroke out. "You think you've been fooling your old man here, but you haven't. I've gotten the calls. The letters. Your report card. I know how much school you missed last year. How many assignments you missed. You passed ninth grade by the skin of your teeth, Ollie. I even went up and had a meeting with the principal and your guidance counselor."

"What?" she gasped.

"They understand that last year was tough for you. That there were *extenuating circumstances*. But things have to change, Ollie. This year they won't be so easy on you. They know you can do better. *I* know you can do better."

"Daddy, I'm sorry. I didn't mean . . ."

He shook his head slowly, like his neck was sore and his head was so, so heavy. "I don't want apologies. I just want to see that this year it'll be different. That you'll go in there and bust your ass. Make up for last year. You'll go in there and make your mama and me proud."

He looked at her, eyes rimmed with red.

"Yes, sir," she said.

"Know what else?" Daddy said now, the sledge swinging in his hand like a heavy pendulum. He wore his stained leather work gloves, so worn that his index and middle fingers poked through on the right hand. "I think you should stay the hell out of Rosy's. I don't want you talking to that Sylvia Carlson anymore." He spat out the name like it left a bad taste in his mouth. "Stay clear of her. She's half in the bag most of the time. If there was any clubbing going on, Sylvia probably put your mama up to it. I wouldn't be at all surprised if Sylvia's the one who introduced your mama to—" He stopped himself here, his face reddening under the pale layer of plaster dust.

Olive finished the sentence in her own head: *Him.*

Him again. The man Mama ran away with.

She almost asked the question that came into her head then, the question she'd been asking herself again and again since she'd found her mama's necklace: *What if that's not what happened? What if Mama didn't run off with some man she'd met in a bar?*

But the answers to those questions were almost more difficult, more painful to imagine, than thinking that her mama had been unfaithful, had a boyfriend on the side whom she took off with.

"Let's get back to work," Daddy said, turning from Olive, swinging his hammer as hard as he could into the wall, sending the plaster flying, smashing right through the thin wooden strips of lath. He pulled his hammer back, hit the wall again and again, with so much force, so much anger, Olive thought he might bring the whole house down around them.

FLOORS AND TRIM

CHAPTER 29

Helen

"Are you sure about this?" Helen asked as she followed Riley through the door of the old Hartsboro Hotel. Everything about this felt strange and slightly dangerous. There was no way the old Connecticut Helen would have let anyone drag her to a creepy run-down hotel to sit with a bunch of strangers and try to make contact with the spirit world. It seemed like the opening of a bad horror movie.

The sign in the front said that it was an antique shop now. They stopped in the lobby, beside the old front desk, like they were waiting to check in, waiting for someone to pass them one of the old keys that still hung on hooks on the wall.

"Like I said, it can't hurt, right?" Riley told her, voice low. "Dicky hosts these spirit circles every Wednesday, and they're open to whoever comes by. Maybe if Hattie or Jane or Ann has a message, they'll be able to get it to you through the circle."

Helen was hesitant. She was still struggling to figure out the logic of all of this, because it seemed like *if* something was going to happen, wouldn't it happen back at the house? The house and the objects in it were what drew them back. How was coming to some dusty old hotel five miles away from the bog, where you had to pay twenty bucks to sit around in a candlelit circle with strangers, going to help? But still, she was desperate to make contact again. Since she'd seen Ann's spirit for that brief moment a few weeks ago, there had been nothing.

Riley seemed determined to give this approach a try, and Helen had to admit she was curious about the spirit circle: what it would be like, who might be there. What sort of people were desperate enough to talk to the dead that they'd come to something like this?

Me, she thought. *I'm their target audience.*

"Have you been before?" Helen asked Riley.

"Once or twice, but it was forever ago," Riley said. "You just have to promise you won't tell Olive we did this. She'll think we've both totally lost it, and right now I think you and I are pretty much the only stable things she's got in her life."

"And you have to promise not to ever tell Nate," Helen said.

"It's our secret then," Riley said.

Riley had handled Nate, telling him that she was whisking Helen away for a girls' night out. "Come on, all work and no play makes Helen a dull girl. I'll take good care of her," Riley had said. "I promise."

The three of them had spent the day installing the hardwood floor in the living room. It was salvaged maple, and Helen was thrilled with it: each scratch and nail hole gave it character—a warm charm that new flooring could never achieve. Even Nate agreed that the extra work to get the old boards fitting together and flush was worth it. And Riley had gotten them a great price on it. Riley had also found them a few hundred square feet of wide pine boards from an old silo that they were going to use for the upstairs floors. Nate was thrilled that they were now under budget on flooring.

Now Helen followed Riley up the hotel stairs (which didn't feel all too sturdy) and down a carpeted hallway. They passed doors to old hotel rooms, most closed, but the open ones were packed full of junk: broken furniture, racks of moth-eaten clothing, rusting bedsprings.

At the end of the hall was a set of double doors. Above them, an old sign read: BAR AND LOUNGE.

Riley went through, Helen behind her.

The room was dark and smelled of scented candles, musty incense, and maybe marijuana. There was a long wooden bar just in front of them with a mirror behind it and a row of empty stools in front. To their right, a wall of windows that had been covered with heavy curtains. To their left, a group of people sat in a circle, candles burning all around them: on the floor, on the mantel of the fireplace they sat in front of, on tables and empty chairs. They were talking in low voices. Riley led Helen over. The floor was covered with a tattered throw rug. The furniture was beat-up, the upholstery full of holes. There were six people in the circle, and now all twelve eyes were on Riley and Helen.

"Hi, Dicky," Riley said.

"Nice to see you, Riley," he said.

"This is my friend Helen."

The man she spoke to nodded, looked up at Helen, eyes locked on hers. The skin on the back of her neck prickled.

"Welcome," he said. "Take a seat." He was tall, Helen guessed in his early fifties, and had an angular, weathered face with small gray-blue eyes and a large mustache. He was wearing jeans, a button-down shirt, cowboy boots with pointed toes. Then Helen noticed his large leather belt and the holster attached to it. The man had a handgun strapped to his waist.

What did a man who talked to ghosts need with a gun?

She thought the best idea was to take Riley's hand and drag her the hell out of there. But it was too late. Riley had taken an empty seat and was pointing at the last vacant chair, letting Helen know she should take it.

They'd been waiting with two empty chairs. Like they'd been expecting them.

Helen settled in, looked over at Dicky and tried to imagine him as the little boy who had lost his father to the woods, to the white deer. What had little Dicky seen that day? How long had he chased after his father and the deer, calling out, desperate?

The woman to Dicky's left leaned over and whispered something to the old man next to her. He had large eyes and ears with tufts of hair growing out of them. Helen thought he looked like a great horned owl. The owl man nodded.

"Before we begin," Dicky said, "let's all take a minute to remember that the communication we all seek with those who have passed doesn't begin and end here, in this circle."

The owl man nodded, gave a low "Mm-hmm."

Dicky cleared his throat and continued. "I reckon you could say learning to read signs from the spirits is a little like learning to speak another language."

This got him more nods of agreement.

"It's about picking up on patterns, learning to be more receptive to the signs we get from our departed ones every day. We've all gotta be on the lookout for those patterns. You all know the stuff I mean: dreams we have again and again, numbers that come into our lives over and over, a song on the radio, an image we can't shake. Reality . . . it ain't random." He shuffled his feet in the pointy-toed boots. "The spirits, they have the power to manipulate the world around us.

To send us signals. It's up to us to keep our eyes open. To listen to what they've got to say."

Was it Helen's imagination, or was Dicky looking right at her when he said this?

"I keep seeing that pileated woodpecker in my yard," a man Helen recognized from the pizza and sub shop said. "It was my brother's favorite bird. I'm sure it's him."

There was a general murmur of agreement from the group, followed by more discussions of coincidences, serendipitous moments, and signs they'd all received: repeated license plate numbers that were actually a code, voices with important messages picked up on the static in between radio stations, recurring dreams.

Helen said nothing.

Dicky looked at her. "Tell me, Helen, have you experienced anything like this?"

She squirmed, looked at Riley, who gave her a little nod.

"Well," Helen began, "I do find myself waking up at the same time in the night. Three thirty-three." She didn't tell them she woke up and saw ghosts. Though she was sure this was exactly the sort of crowd that would be eager to hear such a thing, she wasn't willing to trust this detail to a group of strangers.

The old woman beside her nodded. "It's the spirits waking you. That's a powerful number. The number three is the number of communication. Of psychic ability. It's the number of mediums."

She looked at Helen, gauging her response. "What happens when you wake up, dear? Do you see any visions? Have any particular feelings?"

"No," Helen lied. "I just go back to sleep."

The woman nodded. "Stay up next time. Stay up, keep your eyes open, and listen. If they're waking you up again and again, there's a reason."

More murmured agreement from the group. Helen felt everyone studying her.

"We can begin," Dicky said. He reached out, took the hands of the two people sitting on either side of him, and then the whole circle joined hands. Helen took Riley's hand in her right and held the old woman's hand in her left. The woman's hand felt light and fragile and fluttered slightly like a small bird in Helen's hand. Dicky closed his eyes and bowed his head, and the others did the same. Helen tilted her head down but kept her eyes wide open, watching.

"We bring only our best intentions into the circle," he said.

"We bring only our best intentions into the circle," the others echoed.

"We open our hearts and minds to those we can feel but cannot see," Dicky said.

"We open our hearts and minds to those we can feel but cannot see," the group echoed.

"We ask the spirits to join us here in the room, to come forward."

This time, there was no repeated refrain. The musty room was still. All Helen could hear was the others breathing.

"Are there any spirits here among us now? Give us a sign," Dicky called.

There was a loud rap that came from somewhere behind Dicky, near the old fireplace. Helen jerked her head up, searched the shadows.

"Welcome," Dicky said, smiling, eyes still closed. "Come forward. Do you have a message for us? A message for anyone here?"

There had to be another person in the room. Someone hiding behind the wall, listening. Someone playing ghost. Giving these people what they'd come for.

Disappointment flooded through Helen. It was a sham. These people couldn't really call the spirits.

The old woman sitting next to Helen squeezed her hand tighter. "I'm getting something," she said, her voice a dull crackle. "It's a message for Kay."

A middle-aged woman in a red sweater leaned forward, said, "For me? Who is it? What do they say?" Her hair was a washed-out blond; her skin looked yellow and sickly in the candlelight. She had on thick blue eye shadow all the way up to her eyebrows.

"It's your sister, Jessa."

"Oh!" Kay said, eyes wide open, excited. "What does she say?"

"She wants you to know she loves you. And she says . . . she says she's sorry."

"Ohh!" Kay exclaimed, tears filling her heavily made-up eyes, running down her yellow cheeks. "Oh, Jessa! You don't need to be sorry. I forgive you! Tell her I forgive her!"

She was sobbing now.

The old woman beside Helen smiled. "You've made her so happy, Kay. She's so relieved."

Jesus, thought Helen. *What a complete crock of shit.* It seemed cruel, heartbreaking, really, taking advantage of people like Kay, people in grief who didn't know any better, who clearly had unfinished business with the dead. She imagined that if she had stumbled into this group right after the death of her father, when the rawness of her pain had left her ripped right open, these people would have had a field day with her. And she probably would have bought it all, too. Because she was so desperate to talk to her father one more time, to say the good-byes she felt she'd been cheated out of.

"There's another presence here," Dicky said.

"Oh yes, there is," said the old woman beside Helen. She turned to Helen. Her face was etched with deep wrinkles. "It's a message for you, dear."

"For me?" Helen asked.

The old woman nodded, closing her eyes. She held tight to Helen's hand, giving it a squeeze. "Oh! She's a strong spirit, this one."

This was too much. Too goddamned much. She should never have listened to Riley, should never have tried this. She wanted to stand up and walk out, but politeness kept her there, holding hands, eyes closed, thinking, *This will be over soon and then I can get the hell out of here and never come back.*

Her head was starting to ache. The incense and candles were too sweet and cloying, the scent filling the back of her throat, making it feel like it was closing, getting tighter and tighter.

"It's a woman, but she won't identify herself. She says you know who she is. She says . . . she says there's someone you've got to find. I think it's someone related to you? No, no, that's not it. The person is related to *her.* That's who you've got to find."

Riley gave Helen's hand a hard squeeze.

"She says you have to hurry. You're running out of time," the old woman said, tightening her face into a grimace.

"Is there more?" Riley asked. "Does she say how to find this person?"

"Wait! She's got another message," the old woman said, opening her eyes, giving Helen's hand another squeeze. "This one's just for you and you alone. Close your eyes, dear. Close your eyes and listen with your whole self. She's trying to come through to you."

Helen closed her eyes, took in a breath, tried to forget where she was, how much her head was throbbing. She felt a breeze, imagined she was outside, near the bog.

She heard one short sentence, one command, spoken clearly in the grinding glass voice she'd come to know: *Save her.*

Helen nearly opened her eyes but kept them clamped shut, concentrated on breathing in and out.

The room, and everything in it—the smell of the incense, the breathing and shuffling of the people around her—seemed to retreat. Helen was in the bog. She saw a white deer—Nate's white deer, so elegant and strange—then something shifted, and suddenly *she* was the white deer. And she was being chased, hunted. She ran through the woods to the bog, and where her hooves struck the ground, pink lady's slippers sprang up. Dragonflies circled around her, the hum of their wings a song, a terrible warning song that turned into Hattie's ground-glass voice: *Danger. You are in danger.*

Then she was in the center of the bog, and there was the sound of a gun going off. And she felt the bullet hit her chest, her white deer chest, and she sank into the bog, going down, down, down.

Helen's eyes flew open, heart thumping madly, mouth dry and cottony. But she could smell the bog all around her. Hear the buzzing song of the dragonflies. *Danger. You are in danger.*

Her eyes locked on Dicky's gun.

"I have to go," Helen said, standing, letting go of the old woman's hand, pulling away from Riley, who was giving her a worried look.

"You can't break the circle," Dicky warned.

Helen moved away on shaky legs. "I'm sorry," she said.

"Please," the old woman called. "You can't be afraid of what they show you."

Helen hurried out of the room, bumping into chairs, banging through the door and down the stairs, Riley behind her, calling, "Helen, wait up!"

.   .   .

The lights in the trailer were off, so they sat in Riley's car, smoking a joint.

"You gonna tell me what happened in there?" Riley asked, face full of concern. It was eerily similar to the way Nate had been looking at her lately. Helen kept her eyes fixed on the dark windows of the trailer, thought it was a damn good thing Nate hadn't seen her big freak-out at Dicky's.

"Nothing," Helen said. "Just my fucked-up imagination. God, that place gave me the creeps. And those people, it's like they're feeding on other people's needs and misfortune, you know?"

Riley said nothing, then at last said, "I'm sorry. We shouldn't have gone. I didn't know it would be like that."

"It's not your fault. But doesn't that Dicky guy give you the creeps? I mean, why does he carry a gun everywhere? Was he expecting civil unrest during the spirit circle?"

Riley smiled. "You're right. He's kind of a yahoo. We're just used to it, I guess."

They were quiet as they finished the joint. The windows in the car were down, and Helen could hear frogs calling in the bog, smell the dark rich scent. She looked at the trailer, thought of Nate sleeping obliviously inside, surrounded by his nature guides, his carefully rendered drawings of their dream house. She knew she should go in, crawl into bed beside him, find comfort in his warm familiarity.

But that's not where she wanted to be.

She turned back to Riley. "I heard Hattie's voice," Helen said.

"At Dicky's?"

"Yeah."

"What'd she say?"

Danger. You are in danger.

"She said, 'Save her.'"

"Save who?"

"This relative I'm supposed to find, I think. The one the old lady was talking about."

Riley frowned at her, bit her bottom lip. "Anything else?"

"She said . . . I'm in danger."

"Helen, maybe you should stop, you know?"

Stop? Helen couldn't believe that Riley, of all people, might suggest such a thing.

"I can't. I don't know how to explain it, but I can't. Hattie wants me—no, she *needs* me to do this."

Riley was silent, staring at Helen. "But did you ever stop to think that maybe she doesn't have your best intentions at heart? Or maybe she's just fucking with you."

"Why? Why would she do that?"

"I don't know, Helen. Because it's fun. Amusing. Because she can."

"No." Helen shook her head. "She's not, Riley. I know it—she hasn't led me astray yet. She needs me, I can feel it."

Riley studied Helen for a moment.

"All right. Whatever you say. Just be careful, okay? Just remember that things aren't always what they seem."

. . .

Helen turned off the computer, rubbed her eyes, and closed her little notebook, the notebook she'd come to think of as the "Mystery of Hattie" notebook. She'd been searching online for nearly two hours, and all she had to show for it was a name for Ann's daughter. Samuel Gray and Ann Whitcomb Gray had had two children: Jason, born in August 1968, and Gloria, born in April 1971. She found a copy of Gloria's birth certificate—her middle name was Marie, and she was born at 3:40 p.m.—but nothing beyond that. There were hundreds of hits for both Jason Gray and Gloria Gray, and she didn't have any other information to narrow things.

Nate was still out cold in the bedroom and hadn't so much as stirred when Helen had come in and turned on the lights in the trailer.

She looked at the table in the corner where his laptop was set up. It was open and showing the green-tinted images from the three outdoor cameras set up in the yard. Helen went over to look at them. There was nothing out there, no movement at all, only the trees, the trailer she and Nate were tucked safely inside, and the dark unfinished house looming above it.

The windows of the trailer were open and all Helen heard were the usual night sounds: the occasional croak of a frog from down by the bog, a lone barred owl, crickets.

She noticed Nate's wildlife journal tucked against the laptop and opened it up. There was the first entry: the great blue heron in the bog. And then the porcupine, a male and female cardinal, a red squirrel. Then the sketch Nate did of the deer after his first sighting of her, the day he fell in the bog back in July. His drawing was remarkably lifelike—his art skills seemed to be improving with each sketch. She turned the page and found more drawings of the white deer and copious notes about his observations. She continued to flip through and felt her stomach harden into a knot. Page after page was full of sketches of the white deer and messily scribbled notes that seemed to make less and less sense as she went along. The notes said things like "Her eyes change color—tapetum lucidum?"; "went out into the middle of the bog and vanished"; "tracks disappeared."

There were detailed accounts of sighting after sighting all summer long: where she came from, where she went.

One note said: "It's a game we play. Like a child's game of tag."

Helen continued to turn the pages with trembling fingers.

His book was nearly full and over 90 percent of it was sketches of and notes about the deer. Close-ups of her face and eyes. Notes on her approximate height and weight.

"My god," Helen muttered, sure she was looking at the diary of a man unwound, a man completely obsessed. She felt sick to her stomach.

Then she got to the last page with today's date at the top: "She was waiting for me today at our usual place. She was clearly annoyed that I was late. She looked at me as if to say, *Please don't keep me waiting again.* Then she took off, running so fast that I could not possibly follow."

CHAPTER 30

O live

 SEPTEMBER 10, 2015

Olive had been dreaming about Hattie for the past few weeks. Since she'd put Mama's necklace on. Dreaming not just about Hattie but that *she* was Hattie. She was standing in front of her house by the bog. Then she heard men and dogs coming for her.

The dreams ended the same: with a noose around her neck and her hanging from the big white pine.

She woke up at midnight on the living room couch and was totally disoriented: she thought she was still Hattie, waking up in the little crooked cabin.

"You okay?" her dad said, standing over her. He was in boxers and a T-shirt. His hair was ruffled and his eyes were puffy.

"Yeah, bad dream," she said.

"You screamed in your sleep," he said. "Scared the hell out of me. Woke me up out of a sound sleep. I came tearing out here thinking something . . . I don't know what."

"Sorry." She rubbed her face and shook her head, trying to rid herself of the dream.

"Then when I got out here, you were talking in your sleep."

"Yeah? What'd I say?"

" 'I'll always be here,' " he said. "That's what you said."

Olive got chills.

"You sure you're feeling okay, Ollie?" Daddy said. He put a hand on her forehead, like she might have a fever. "You don't look right."

"I'm fine, Dad," she said. But she was anything but fine.

"If you're sick tomorrow, I can call Riley, see if she can come hang out with you."

"No, Dad, I'm fine, really."

"Things going okay at school?"

"They're fine," she said.

The truth was, even though she was only a few days in, the year was off to a better start. She hadn't cut so much as a single class. She showed up prepared, did all of her homework.

"Okay, let's both go back to sleep," Daddy said. "Don't go having any more bad dreams."

"No more bad dreams," she said. And she meant it. Because no way was she falling back to sleep.

She waited until it was quiet upstairs, then she went into the kitchen and grabbed a flashlight, shoved it into her backpack. She snuck out the back door, crossed the yard, and walked through the woods to the bog, following the path that started at the edge of her yard by the hollow tree. She stopped there, checked the hollow, foolishly hoping that there might be a message inside. Only pine needles and a wood louse.

The night was cool and moonlit. There was a dampness to the air that clung to her.

She got to the bog and found it covered with a fine mist. She thought she saw a figure on the other side, over by where Hattie's house once stood. She shone her light across the water, then made her way along the edge toward the stone foundation, but there was nothing. No one.

Still, she felt she wasn't alone.

She took her necklace off, watched it swing in the moonlight.

She hadn't attempted to communicate with Hattie like this since that first time. It had freaked her out too much. Made her feel half crazy. And, if she had to admit it, she was a little afraid of whatever answers Hattie might give her.

"Are you here, Hattie?" Olive asked, holding the thin leather cord that the silver *I see all* pendant dangled from.

It began to swing in a slow and steady clockwise direction.

"Am I going crazy?" she asked.

The pendulum held still.

"What am I even doing out here?" she said, more to herself than to Hattie. She was about to put the necklace back on, to give up trying to communicate with Hattie, when the silver circle at the end of the string swung forward, back and forth.

"What does that mean?" she asked. The pendulum just kept swinging out in a forward motion. Weird. She took a step forward.

Yes, the pendulum said, moving clockwise again. Then it went back to moving straight back and forth, only off to a slight left angle. Taking a chance, she took another step in the direction the pendulum was pulling her.

"You want me to follow you?"

Yes.

Olive started to walk, straight at first. Then the necklace swung to the left, and Olive started walking to the left. She was heading out toward the middle of the bog. She'd explored the bog enough to know where the deep places were, but still, it was dark and she felt a little nervous about stepping into a spring.

Then, all at once, the necklace stopped, holding perfectly still.

"Why'd we stop?" Olive asked. "Is there something here?"

The silver circle moved clockwise again.

Olive slipped the necklace back over her head, shone her flashlight down at the ground. She didn't dare hope, did she? Could it be the treasure? Could Hattie have decided to show her where it was?

Then she got down on her knees and began to dig. She didn't have a shovel or trowel, so she used her fingers to rip away the grass and peat. She kept the flashlight on the ground beside her, the beam flooding the area where she was digging.

Maybe it wasn't the treasure but a small piece of the treasure. A little taste. Proof that it was real.

She hadn't gone down far when her fingers touched something hard. Something flat. Something metal.

The top of a box maybe?

A treasure chest?

Heart pounding, Olive scraped at the mud faster, more frantically. Her fingers were getting torn up, but she dug and scraped until she was able to find the edge of the metal object and pull it out into the light.

An old ax head, pitted with rust.

"Nice," she said sarcastically. Then she turned, looked out at the bog, and shouted, "Thanks a lot, Hattie. Just what I always wanted!"

She threw it into her backpack and went back home, exhausted and discouraged, her jeans and sneakers soaked through, angry with Hattie for getting her hopes up and giving her nothing but a rusty old ax head.

She changed out of her wet things into a dry T-shirt and pair of sweatpants and lay back down on the couch.

She dreamed of the ax.

That it was cleaned up, sharpened, and she was using it to chop wood.

But then it wasn't wood she was chopping.

She was hacking her mother up into chunks and throwing them into the bog.

She woke up screaming.

Daddy came flying into the living room, flipping on lights.

He reached out and took her hand, looking at the filthy, bloody fingertips.

"Jesus, girl," he said. "What's going on with you?"

She started to cry. He took her in his arms and rocked her like she was a little girl again. "Shh," he said. "It's all right."

But it wasn't all right.

Maybe her father had been right. Maybe she *was* sick. Sick in the head. Or maybe it was something worse than that.

Maybe, somehow, Hattie had gotten inside her.

CHAPTER 31

Helen

 SEPTEMBER 10, 2015

Helen opened her eyes. She'd been dreaming of Nate's white deer. It had been speaking to her in Hattie's ground-glass voice.

Wake up, Helen, the deer told her. *Wake up!*

Helen blinked at the open doorway to the bedroom, half expecting to see Nate's deer there—that the creature might have somehow followed her out of her dream. But there was nothing.

Helen's head ached. Her thoughts felt slow. Foggy.

She wanted to lay her head back down and sleep, but something was wrong.

Very wrong.

"Nate." She shoved at him hard. "Get up!"

"What?" he mumbled sleepily.

"Gas," she said, the panic starting to rouse her. "Propane! I smell propane."

He sat up. "Jesus," he said, coughing. "Come on." He grabbed Helen's hand, pulled her out of bed and into the hall.

The smell was overpowering, the air thick with propane.

"Don't turn on any lights," he warned; "the spark . . ." His hand was wrapped firmly around hers as they hurried through the trailer in the dark and out the front door, into the cool night air.

Nate ran to the side of the trailer where the big white tank was and switched the gas off.

"Should we call the fire department?" Helen asked.

"I think it'll be okay," Nate said. "The front door's open. Let's let it dissipate a bit, then we can open all the windows." He looked at Helen. "How do you feel?"

"I have a headache and I'm a little dizzy, but okay," she said.

"Me, too. We got lucky. Good thing you woke up when you did."

Good thing Hattie woke me, she thought.

"What happened?" she asked.

"Must be a leak somewhere," he said.

They sat outside, holding hands, taking deep breaths.

In a few minutes, they went in and started cranking open all the louvered windows.

"Nate," she said, "when I went to bed, all these were open."

"What? Are you sure?"

"Positive. I could hear the frogs."

Soon, Nate deemed it safe enough to turn on a light. "Helen?" he called. He was standing in front of the stove.

"Yeah?"

"Come take a look at this." He was pointing at the stove. "The gas is wide open, every burner turned on but not lit."

"It wasn't a leak," Helen said, her whole body tensing.

"You didn't leave the stove on, did you?" Nate asked.

She shook her head. "I didn't use the stove at all tonight. And why the hell would I turn on all four burners? When I got home, I hung out here on the computer for a while."

And I saw your fucked-up nature journal, full of the elusive white doe.

"I'm sure I would have noticed if the gas was on then—I was, like, five feet from the stove."

"Are you sure?" Nate asked.

"Of course I'm sure!"

"Then what . . ."

"Someone came into the trailer," Helen said, the panic returning, replacing the relief. "After we went to sleep—someone came in here, turned on the gas, and closed the windows."

"But how . . . who . . . ?" His voice trailed off, then he jumped up. "The cameras would have caught them! We'll see who it is! Have evidence."

He went over to his laptop and blinked at it miserably. "The cameras have all been disconnected," he said. He tapped the keys. "The recordings from tonight are all gone. There's nothing here. It's been wiped clean."

"We need to call the police," Helen said. She was already dialing 911.

.   .   .

A state trooper pulled into their driveway twenty minutes later. He was an older man in his early sixties, with a ruddy complexion, and introduced himself as Trooper Bouchier. He listened to their story. Helen let Nate do most of the talking, fearing that her voice would tremble. The trooper looked at the front door, the windows, and the gas stove. He watched patiently while Nate showed him his computer with feed from the outdoor cameras.

"See," Nate said. "All the footage from tonight has been wiped clean."

Trooper Bouchier nodded. "And why do you have all these cameras, exactly?"

"For wildlife," Nate said.

"Wildlife?" the trooper echoed.

Nate nodded. "Deer, coyotes, owls. That kind of thing."

"I see," Bouchier said in a tone that suggested he didn't see at all. Then he turned to Helen and asked, "And you're sure you didn't use the stove at all before you went to bed?"

"I'm positive. And I'm sure all the windows were open."

"And what time was this?"

"Late," Helen said. "Near one."

The trooper nodded. "And you'd been out with a friend before this?"

"She and her friend Riley had a girls' night," Nate explained. He turned to Helen. "Where'd you go, anyway?"

"Oh, you know," Helen said, wondering how much trouble you got in for deliberately lying to the police in a situation like this. "Just out for a bite to eat and drinks."

"So you'd been drinking?" the trooper asked.

"No," she said. "I mean, yes, I, uh, had one glass of wine."

He nodded.

"Any drugs?" he asked. She wondered if her eyes were still red and glossy from the pot.

"No," she said.

The trooper and Nate were both studying her. Now Nate looked like he was doubting her, too. Like maybe she'd gotten good and wasted with Riley and then . . . closed all the windows and cranked open all four burners on the stove before passing out?

"So what now?" Helen asked, trying to hide her irritation. "Are you going to dust for fingerprints or something?"

"No, ma'am," Trooper Bouchier said with a small smile. "I'll write up a report."

"A report?" Helen said. "That's it?"

"Mrs. Wetherell, Mr. Wetherell—there's no sign of a break-in, no sign of a crime," the trooper said.

"Someone did this!" Helen said, losing all hold on her composure. "Someone came in here and turned on the gas and closed the windows! We could have died!"

"Mrs. Wetherell," the trooper said. "It's just as likely that it was an accident. Maybe you . . . bumped against the stove and didn't even realize it. It's a very small kitchen you've got here. And the windows— well, you wouldn't be the first person in the world to do something on autopilot late at night and forget about it later, now would you? One night, after a few beers, I ate all the leftover meatloaf—wasn't I mad the next morning when I went to make myself a sandwich for lunch? Said to my wife, 'Where on earth did you—'"

Helen broke in. "Sorry, let me get this straight—you're not going to do anything because you don't believe us."

"Helen—" Nate began.

"What?" she snapped. "That's what he's doing. Absolutely nothing."

"I'll write up a report," the trooper repeated, smiling that small, amused smile again. "And of course, if there's another incident, you be sure to let us know."

"We appreciate it," Nate said.

"Great," Helen muttered. "Very helpful."

CHAPTER 32

O live

 SEPTEMBER 10, 2015

Olive rolled over on the couch and opened her eyes. She smelled coffee. And pancakes. Her dad never made breakfast. The only one who did was . . . Mama!

Olive leapt off the couch and ran to the kitchen.

"Morning, sleepyhead," Riley said, smiling at her.

Olive blinked at her aunt, who stood in front of the stove, flipping pancakes on Mama's big cast-iron griddle. She had on Mama's pink apron.

"I thought we could have a nice breakfast, then I could give you a ride to school."

"Where's Dad?"

"He had to go into work early. They're starting a big repaving job."

Olive helped herself to coffee.

"Your dad said you had a rough night," Riley said.

Olive shrugged. "A couple bad dreams, that's all. Did Dad call you? Is that why you're here? 'Cause I'm fine, really."

"He's worried about you, Ollie."

"I just had a nightmare—it's fine. Everyone has nightmares sometimes, don't they?"

"What about?"

Olive looked down into her milky coffee. "I don't remember."

Riley put pancakes on a plate and set them on the table. Olive sat down and reached for the maple syrup. She wasn't really hungry, but she dove in with a smile. "These are delicious!" she said.

Riley sat in the chair across from her. She watched her carefully, frowning. "The truth is, I'm concerned about you, too." A lump formed in Olive's throat, making it hard to swallow.

"But everything's good," Olive said, between bites of pancake. "I mean, it's just the very beginning of the school year, but things are going okay. I actually like my classes so far."

"Your friend Mike came to see me," Riley said.

"What?" Olive set her fork down, her hands clenched into fists. How could he? She would kill him for this.

"Now hang on," Riley said. "Don't get all mad at him. He did the right thing. He's worried about you, Olive."

"Mike's always worried about something. He exaggerates and panics and gets all freaked out at the slightest little thing!" Olive said.

"He told me you found your mother's necklace in the bog over the summer."

Shit! Shit, shit, shit. Should have known that chickenshit traitor would tell.

She hesitated, wondering what the chances were of Riley believing her if she lied.

"Is that true, Olive?"

"Yeah, I found it in the bog. That silver necklace she was wearing all the time before she left."

Riley nodded. "I know the one you mean."

"Mama called it her *I see all* necklace."

Riley smiled, but it was a sad smile. "Yeah, she did. I remember."

"The chain was broken," Olive said.

They were both silent for a moment.

"Where's the necklace now?" Riley asked.

Olive felt it there, resting against her chest, tucked safely underneath her T-shirt and hoodie. She thought of pulling it out and showing it to Riley, but she was embarrassed. She worried Riley would think it was silly, a little pathetic even, to be wearing her mother's necklace.

"I hid it. Someplace safe."

Riley looked at her and Olive had this idea then that her aunt had X-ray eyes, could see just where the necklace was. It seemed to give a warm pulse against her skin, a pulse that her aunt might be able to somehow detect. But that was impossible.

"Mike also says you went to see Dicky Barns because you heard your mom might have been going to his spirit circles?"

"Yeah, I went to the hotel and it was way creepy. I heard Mama might have gone there, but Dicky said she never came to any of his séances or whatever they are. That the only time he ever saw her was at the store when Mama was working."

Riley looked at Olive across the table. "You believe him?"

Olive thought about what she'd heard Dicky say on the phone, her plans to go back there on Sunday. She couldn't tell Riley. No way would Riley let her go.

"Yeah, I believe him," Olive said, shrugging. "And being in there, talking to Dicky, I've gotta say I can't imagine Mama ever being part of that place. She and Daddy always made fun of Dicky. I think she was looking for the treasure, and trying to find out about Hattie, but no way was she going to Dicky Barns and his ghost club for clues."

Riley nodded. "Yeah, I agree. Your mom doesn't think much of Dicky. I can't really imagine her going there either."

Olive picked up her fork and went back to her pancakes.

"Have you shown the necklace to anyone else?" Riley asked.

"No."

"So your dad doesn't know you found it?"

"Uh-uh," Olive said around a mouthful of pancakes. She swallowed, had a glug of coffee. "Mike thought I should show him—Mike also thought maybe I should take it to the police. Like it might be a clue or something. But like I said, he tends to get all panicky and overexaggerate stuff."

Riley was quiet a minute.

"Do you think I *should* bring it to the police?" Olive asked, setting her fork down again. "Just to see what they think? I mean, it's not like my dad ever filed a missing person's report or anything like that."

"I think . . ." Riley paused a second. "I think that we should wait. See what we can figure out on our own first. Bringing the police in, having them asking questions, bringing up all the boyfriend stuff— think what that would do to your dad."

"Riley, what if Mama didn't run off with some guy? What if something else happened to her?"

"Sweetie," Riley said, giving Olive that familiar look of pity she so hated. "I think there's still a good chance that your mom really did run off with a boyfriend. Sometimes the simplest, most obvious explanation is the right one."

Olive frowned. "I just have a bad feeling. And I keep having these stupid bad dreams."

Riley nodded, reached across the table, and put her hand on top of Olive's. "What are the dreams about, Ollie?"

"They're about Hattie mostly. But sometimes they're about Mama too. About something bad happening to her."

"Tell me about them," Riley said.

Olive got a chill, shook her head. "I don't really remember," she said. No way was she going to tell her the gory details. Riley would take Olive to the nearest shrink.

Riley was quiet again. She gave Olive's hand a squeeze, then pulled her own hand away. "Do you remember the last time you saw your mom?" she said, her voice low.

"I've been driving myself nuts thinking about it, trying to remember every detail. I know she hadn't been around a lot. She was working, or hanging out with friends or something. So I don't remember exactly the last time I saw her. But I remember the last time I heard her."

Riley looked at Olive, puzzled. "Heard her? Did she call you?"

"No. But I heard her and Daddy arguing. It was the middle of the night. Mama hadn't been home when I'd gone to bed, so I think she was just coming in. I was up in bed, but I woke up because they were right here in the kitchen, right below my room. And they were yelling."

"About what?"

"I couldn't hear what they were saying, but Daddy was really mad. I think he even threw something. There was a crash. Then the door banged open. Mama must have left. When I got up in the morning, Mama was gone. Daddy was sitting at the table drinking coffee like it was any other morning. Mama didn't come home again after that."

Olive looked right at Riley. And what she saw freaked her out completely.

Riley looked scared. But then she seemed to try to pull herself together, to look more normal. Olive could still see worry in her eyes.

"Ollie, how about you come back to my place after school today. Stay there with me a few days while we try to figure out what to do, okay?"

Olive thought about it. Thought about leaving her dad alone in the house.

"No," she said. "Dad needs me."

"But Ollie, if you—"

"No. Don't you get it? Things are going good for us lately. Dad's happy school's starting out so well. And we're nearly done with my room. If I leave and go stay with you, he'll be all worried and weirded out. I've gotta stay."

"Okay," Riley said. "You stay. I'll do a little poking around, see what I can turn up about what your mom might have been up to those last few days. See if I can find out anything about guys she was seeing."

"So you think maybe she *didn't* run off with some guy?"

"I don't know what I think," Riley admitted. "But I want you to promise me you'll stop playing detective, okay? And don't say anything to your dad. Leave it to me. If I can't turn anything up in a couple of days, we'll go talk to the police together, okay?"

"Deal," Olive said.

Riley took her hand and gave it a squeeze. "Now run upstairs and get dressed. I don't want you to be late for school."

CHAPTER 33

Helen

 SEPTEMBER 10, 2015

"What happened last night with the propane—that's some serious shit," Riley said, voice low so that none of the customers would hear. Helen had driven to the salvage yard after lunch to tell Riley the latest—that now she believed someone had tried to kill her and Nate.

"I know. That's why I called the police."

"You called the police?" This time Riley forgot to lower her voice, and a young couple looking at stained-glass windows turned their way.

"Yeah, but I see now that it was a mistake," Helen whispered. "The cop thought I'd left the stove on, that I was too drunk or flaky or whatever to be remembering right. And I bet word's getting around town that we called—the kid down at Ferguson's probably heard it on his scanner, and by now, I bet the whole town knows."

"So what did the cop do?"

"He didn't do shit, to be honest. Just wrote up a report. He said there was no evidence of a crime. It was just our word, my word really, and that doesn't exactly carry a whole lot of weight around here. Shit, even Nate was looking at me like maybe I accidentally turned on the gas and closed all the windows and somehow forgot . . ."

Riley blew out an exasperated breath, pushed her blue bangs away from her eyes. "What if it was Hattie?"

"Hattie?"

"What if . . . what if it was her who turned that gas on last night?" Riley asked.

Helen shook her head. "No, I told you—she's the one who woke me up, I'm sure of it. And I've been thinking. What if it's not some asshole from town who wants me to go because I'm the new witch of the bog? What if it's because of the research I'm doing? Maybe there's something about Hattie's family I'm not supposed to find out."

"But what?" Riley said. "What would be worth killing you over?"

"I have no idea. But the one thing I know, the one thing I truly believe, is that I should listen to Hattie. I think she's guiding me. She needs me to find someone. And I've got to hurry. The stunt last night with the gas really drove home that point."

"I don't know, Helen. I don't like this. This is scary shit."

"I have to keep looking. Try to find Ann's children. I learned her daughter's name: Gloria Gray. She was born in 1971, so she'd be forty-four now. I found her birth certificate but nothing else. She just kind of disappears. Fades into the thousands of possible Gloria Grays out there. The newspaper story covering the murder and the woman I met who runs the antique shop said that the children were sent to live with relatives. I need to figure out where they went, who took them in."

Riley nodded, her face full of worry.

Helen looked at her watch. "I should get back to Nate. He doesn't know I'm here. I was just supposed to make a quick run for finishing nails and more putty."

"Just be careful," Riley implored. "You and Nate both."

. . .

Helen pulled into the driveway and saw a beat-up red pickup parked there. Then she spotted Nate sitting on the steps of the new house with Dicky Barns. They were each holding a can of beer.

"Oh shit," Helen mumbled, hurrying out of the truck, carrying the bag from the building supply store.

What the hell was Dicky doing here?

Nate gave Helen a cold glance. "Helen," he said. "Your friend Dicky brought back your phone." Nate held it up to show her.

"My phone?"

Dicky nodded. "You must have dropped it last night."

Helen held her breath.

"When you visited Dicky's ghost-summoning circle," Nate said, staring at her. His face was a blank slate.

She said nothing. Nate continued. "Dicky's been telling me about his weekly gatherings. And about his father. About the white deer and Hattie."

"I should go," Dicky said, standing up, draining his beer, and carefully setting the empty on the step. "I just wanted to make sure you got your phone and that you were all right."

"Thank you so much, Dicky. I'm fine. I'm . . . I'm sorry about last night."

"No worries. Hope to see you again. We meet every Wednesday at eight," he said.

"Thank you," she said again.

"Thanks for the beer, Nate," he called as he got into his pickup. They watched him drive off.

Nate reached for the six-pack, cracked open another beer. Pabst Blue Ribbon. It was what the new frugal Nate drank these days.

Helen braced herself for what might come next.

"I have *never* in my life felt like such a complete idiot," he said finally, his voice low but furious, enunciating every word too clearly. "Holy fuck, Helen, how do you think it looked when this guy pulls up and introduces himself, tells me he met you at a fucking ghost-hunting circle?"

"I'm sorry. I—"

"You lied to me, told me you and Riley went out for dinner and drinks. Not to mention lying to the cop last night!"

"I didn't lie. Not exactly," Helen said, scrambling. "I just left some parts out because I thought you'd get mad."

"I can't imagine why," he said, voice thick and harsh with sarcasm. "You said you were going for a girls' night out on the town. I was imagining karaoke and cosmos, not summoning the dead. You went because of Hattie, right? You're so obsessed with this woman, this woman you've never met, who died almost a hundred years ago, that you go and sit down with a bunch of nutjob strangers to try to conjure her up?"

"I thought they might—"

He held up his finger in a *but wait, there's more* gesture.

"Tell me about the mantel, Helen," he said.

"What?"

"I've been thinking. First the beam, then the bricks. I thought it was great at first, that you were incorporating pieces of history into our house, repurposing materials."

Really? Then why'd you argue with me about it every step of the way? she thought, but stayed silent.

"But it's *weird,* Helen. Your insistence on bringing home objects connected to these women who died in terrible ways. So, who did the mantel belong to, Helen? What's the real story behind it? I wondered when you brought it home but didn't ask. But now I've got to know."

"I—"

"Tell me the truth, Helen. Please. Or are you just going to lie to me again? It must be getting pretty easy by now." He looked so crushed.

She felt a horrible weight bearing down on her. Guilt. How had it come to this? How had she become a woman who could do something like this, sneak around and lie to her own husband, the man who was once the great love of her life, the man she once shared every secret thought with?

Because he doesn't understand, a little voice whispered. *He never has.*

"Okay. The mantel belonged to a woman named Ann Gray. She was Jane's daughter. Hattie's granddaughter."

Nate clenched his jaw. "Yeah, I figured. But let me guess. There's more to it than that, right? She died in some really horrific way?"

Helen thought of lying. She did. But Nate would look online and learn the truth in a few quick keystrokes. She sighed and nodded.

"It was a murder-suicide. Her husband shot her, then himself."

He laughed in a sickening *I can't believe this is happening* kind of way. "So the mantel—this mantel that you just had to have, that we had to do a major redesign for—for our new home, our new life together that we left everything behind for, it came from the house where the guy shot his wife and then himself?"

"I—" she stammered. "I'm sorry," she said, truly meaning it. Feeling it in her gut. "I know it sounds crazy and terrible, but it's not. I didn't mean to lie. I was just afraid. You get so annoyed, angry even, when I talk about Hattie and Jane."

"Do you blame me, Helen? I mean, really? Think about it. How is it that they've become more important to you than I am?"

"They're not more important, Nate. How can you think that?"

How could she explain it? This feeling she had, uncovering little pieces of truth about these women and the lives they led. It was like Hattie wanted her to find them. Hattie was guiding her, helping her to bring them all together like this, these generations of Breckenridge women. And now to save one of them.

"It's just been this amazing experience," she confessed. "To make these discoveries. To feel so connected to the past. To find these objects tied to these women, generations of Breckenridge women. It's like . . . like I was meant to find each object, led to them somehow, and I—"

"Don't give me this New Agey destiny bullshit," he interrupted. "You sound like that wacko Dicky talking about all that the spirits have to teach us."

"I don't think—"

"You're turning our house into this fucked-up museum of Hattie's fucked-up family, all of whom seemed to die in horrible ways! Some people move into a haunted house, but you, you want to *build* a haunted house, Helen. How fucked up is that?"

He took a few long swallows of beer, tilting the can way back. Then he wiped his mouth with the back of his hand and stared at her accusingly.

She'd never seen him this angry, this spiteful. His whole face seemed to change. The dark circles beneath his eyes made them look sunken deep in his skull, small and beady. His hand holding the beer can trembled slightly.

She thought, absurdly, of Ann's husband. Of what it had taken to break him, to turn him to act in the violent way he had. He must have loved her once, back before something snapped inside him.

Was everyone capable of such evil? Of doing such a terrible thing?

A few months ago, Helen would never have believed herself capable of lying to Nate. And if anyone had told her Nate would talk to her in such an angry way, look at her with such loathing, she never would have believed it.

Other people's lives were like that. Not theirs. They were different.

They loved each other. He'd written her a poem about the night they'd met, a beautiful poem that had won her over completely. They had their differences, sure, but she didn't remember him ever even losing his temper before Vermont.

"Shit, Helen," Nate continued. "Are you going to charge admission at Halloween? *Welcome to Helen's Haunted House: enter if you dare!*"

She didn't speak.

"Do you have any idea how totally fucked up this is? You're obsessed. It's a sick, unhealthy obsession. I think you need help. Seriously. And I don't mean help from Dicky and his spiritualists. I think it might be time for therapy. For someone to help you figure out where this need you have for these things is coming from."

She didn't say anything, just stood, concentrating on trying to keep breathing.

"Your father wouldn't have admired this. He would have been horrified."

This was more than she could stand. She barked out a cold laugh. "You're one to talk. You've got your own fucked-up little obsession, don't you?"

"I don't know what you're talking about."

"I saw your nature journal, Nate. You've filled the entire fucking thing with notes on that deer. If that's not an obsession, I don't know what is."

He opened his mouth to speak, to defend himself, but she kept going before he got a chance.

"Have you been keeping track somewhere in one of your little spreadsheets of how many hours you spend looking for your white deer? Of the money you've sunk into it—the top-of-the line infrared cameras, the cables, the bags of deer food and salt licks? While you bitch and moan about being over budget. And you haven't even gotten a single clear picture yet, have you?"

"No, but I will. The deer is *real*, Helen. An actual flesh-and-blood creature. Unlike these ghosts you're apparently trying to summon."

"You know what I can't help but wonder? If maybe your need to do all this research and gather all this proof about the deer is because part of you worries that maybe, just maybe, Riley was right. Maybe that deer really is the ghost of Hattie Breckenridge. And you refuse to accept that possibility, so you're determined to prove her wrong."

"That's absurd," Nate said.

"You write about her like she's a human being, Nate. Like she's got magical abilities. Like you have some kind of special relationship. Like she's your fucking mistress!"

He turned from her, reached down, grabbed the remaining three beers. "We're done here."

He walked away, down to the trailer, where he slammed the door so hard the whole sad little tin building seemed to shake.

CHAPTER 34

O live

 **SEPTEMBER 11, 2015**

"Dammit!" Helen said when she missed the nail, smashed her finger with the hammer.

"You okay?" Olive asked.

"Fine," Helen said, shaking her finger. "I just need to take a break for a minute."

Helen looked tired, worried, and, all of a sudden, way older. There were dark circles under her bloodshot eyes and her skin was pale and pasty looking—Olive could see the blue traces of veins underneath.

They were in the house, putting up the trim around the last of the windows. Olive was holding the boards while Helen nailed them in place. Then she used a nail set to sink them, and Olive covered the holes with dabs of wood putty.

Nate had gone into town to pick up more caulk and primer. Olive was relieved he'd taken off because things were weird and awkward. Nate and Helen were barely speaking—just giving each other measurements and passing boards back and forth. Olive could tell they were really pissed off at each other. Maybe that was why Helen looked so worn out.

Olive imagined she didn't look all that much better than Helen—she hadn't gotten much sleep last night. She'd tossed and turned in bed, thinking about her talk with Riley at breakfast and how frightened Riley had looked. About her promise to stop looking into things, to stay safe and leave things to Riley. And their plan to maybe go to the police.

When she did sleep, she dreamed it was her own hand ripping the necklace from her mother's throat. Then choking her.

She woke up damp with sweat, heart thumping. She jumped out of bed, downed three cups of sweet, milky coffee, and skipped breakfast entirely—the idea of solid food turned her stomach. On her way to catch the school bus, she stopped by the hollow tree and thought about dumping the necklace back in there but found she just couldn't part with it.

She'd come to Helen's straight from school, not even heading home first to drop off her backpack. She didn't want to be alone. Not even for a minute.

Olive looked at the stack of books on the kitchen counter: *Ghosts and Hauntings; Witches in New England; A Guide to Haunted Vermont; Spells, Hexes, and Curses; A Witch's Guide to Spell Casting.* The one on top was called *Communicating with the Spirit World.*

She set down the tub of wood putty, reached up, touched the necklace under her shirt. Then she picked up *Communicating with the Spirit World* and started flipping through it, not really reading, just skimming. She came to a passage that made her stop. She felt goose bumps form on her forearms and a chill on the nape of her neck. She read it out loud, slowly:

A spirit will sometimes attach itself to an object. Often this happens with an item the spirit had a strong personal connection to in life.

A spirit can also attach itself to a living person.

This can become quite troublesome, even dangerous. If you are experiencing missing time, blackouts, or nightmares, or find yourself acting in ways that are not normal for you, it may be that a spirit has taken hold of you.

Helen chuckled. "Pretty crazy stuff, huh?"

"Helen, do you think that's possible? That a spirit can attach itself to an object or a person? And, like, make them possessed or something?"

Helen smiled. "I think those books have a lot of strange ideas, some based in reality, some not so much. But me, I've come to believe there's more to this world than meets the eye, so I try to take it all in with an open mind."

"But if there was a haunted object and you carried it around, could it make you do things that you normally wouldn't do?"

"Some might believe it would. But I think that an object, even a haunted one, can only have the power you give it. You can choose what effect it may or may not have on you."

Olive thought over what she'd said. She believed her mom's necklace had some sort of power. But maybe it was also kind of cursed. Maybe that was where her nightmares came from.

Or maybe they came from something far worse.

"And what about a spirit attaching itself to a person?" Olive asked, her throat dry, voice crackly. "Do you think that ever actually happens?"

Helen leaned forward, brushed a chunk of unruly hair back from Olive's forehead. "I don't think that's anything you or I have to worry about."

Olive swallowed hard, forcing a *you're absolutely right* smile. "Do you think I could borrow some of these books?" she asked.

"Sure. They're mostly library books. I keep checking them out, then returning them, then checking them out again. They're due again in another week, but I'm done with them."

"I can bring them back to the library for you," Olive said.

"Great," Helen said. "They're yours. Hey, how's the treasure hunting going?" Helen gave Olive a tired-looking smile. "Found anything yet?"

Let's see, I found my mom's necklace, so now I think she didn't run off with a guy at all and that maybe something else happened, maybe something bad; I found the same image chalked on the floor of this creepy old hotel where my mom maybe used to go have séances with this totally weird dude who thinks he's a cowboy; oh, and I found out I can communicate with a dead lady, except sometimes she messes with me and shows me a rusty old ax head instead of treasure.

"I've found stuff. Not the actual treasure, but other things," Olive said. "Actually, I brought you a present." She went and got her backpack, unzipped it, and pulled out the rusty old ax head. "I found this the night before last. It was over at the other end of the bog, near where Hattie's house used to be. I've found lots of stuff over there—a few old coins, a cast-iron pot, nails and hinges, and a horseshoe. But this ax head is way cool, isn't it?"

She got an image from one of her recent nightmares: hacking at her mother with an ax.

Please take it, she thought now, feeling queasy. *I never want to see this thing again.*

Helen reached out, took the rusted metal ax head. "It sure is."

"I bet it was hers," Olive said. "I bet it was Hattie's."

"You could be right," Helen said, looking it over. "I'm no expert on ax heads, but it certainly looks very old."

"So old the wooden handle rotted away. It's a hewing ax. You can tell because of the wide blade on the head. I looked it up," she said, and Helen smiled at her.

"I bet Hattie used it to shape the logs when she built her little house," Olive said.

Helen nodded.

"I want you to have it. I thought maybe you could clean it up, sharpen it, get a new handle. You'll have a nice ax for splitting kindling and stuff. Maybe you can even use it to help you build your house. Shape a piece of lumber or something. Like Hattie did."

"Are you sure?" Helen said.

"Absolutely," Olive said.

Helen leaned over and hugged her. "Thank you, sweetie," she said. "It's an amazing gift."

And being there, held tight in Helen's arms for two seconds, gave Olive a sudden jolt of happiness, of comfort.

"You okay?" Helen asked, and Olive realized she was close to crying.

"Fine. Totally." But she wasn't fine. Anything but. "Just thinking about Hattie."

"What about her?"

"How happy she'd be to know that someone had her old ax and was going to fix it up and use it again. It's almost like . . . I know it might sound weird, but it's like bringing a little piece of her back to life in some way. Does that make sense?"

Helen nodded. "Yes. It makes perfect sense. And I agree completely."

Helen

 **SEPTEMBER 12, 2015**

Helen soaked the ax head in vinegar overnight to loosen the rust, then went to work in the morning, cleaning it with a wire brush and sandpaper.

She and Nate had decided to take the weekend off from building.

"On Monday, we'll get back on track and finish up the house," Nate said, all businesslike, barely making eye contact with her. "We can polyurethane the floors, get the walls and trim primed. I'll call the building supply place and order the roof shingles first thing."

"Okay," she'd agreed.

"Cold weather's coming," Nate reminded her. "We don't want to be in that trailer when the first snow hits. And we don't want to have to move in here when it's still a construction zone."

"Agreed," Helen said.

Nate went off into the woods with his camera and field guides. She drove to the hardware store and bought a handle for the ax head, a special file, and a round hockey-puck-like stone to sharpen it.

Helen spent the day in the yard, working on her ax—removing the rust, sharpening it, and rehanging it by following instructions she'd found online. It was satisfying work, and by late afternoon, she had a beautiful ax. An ax with history. Hattie's ax.

.   .   .

Helen was sitting on the front steps of the house, sipping a bottle of beer and admiring her handiwork, when Nate came up the path from the bog.

As he got closer, she could see he was wet and filthy, his clothing muddy and torn in places. His hair, badly in need of a trim, stuck up at odd angles.

Who looks like the crazy one now? Helen thought, hating herself for thinking it.

"What's that?" he asked, staring at the ax.

"It's a hewing ax," she said, holding it out so he could see better.

"Where'd it come from?" he asked.

"Olive found an old ax head somewhere out in the woods and gave it to me." She was careful not to mention Hattie or her house, or the possibility that the ax had once been hers. "She knows I like old things. I spent the day fixing it up—it's good as new!"

He nodded, then reached to take the camera off from around his neck. "Great. You need to see this," he said.

"What is it?" she asked.

"I got it," he said with satisfaction.

"Got what?"

"A picture! Of the deer. I followed her into the woods, trailed her all morning, and at last, I caught up, got close enough to get some good shots."

He turned the camera, pushed some buttons, looked down at the screen on the back. "Look," he said.

His hands were trembling, just slightly. His nails, she noticed, needed trimming. There was dirt underneath them.

Helen peered at the tiny screen on Nate's Nikon, trying to make out what she saw, which was little more than a white blur in front of trees—but a blur that didn't seem deerlike at all. It was tall, narrow. As if he'd shot it from the front and the deer was coming right at him, charging him.

"It looks more like a person than a deer," Helen said, squinting at the image, trying to make sense of the blurry white form. Were those ears? Or was that hair?

Nate jerked the camera away, looked at the image himself, puzzling over it.

"No," he said, thrusting the camera at her again. "Look, it's obviously a deer." He forwarded to the next picture, this one even blurrier. In it, a white figure (or maybe just a flash of reflected light?) seemed to be darting behind a tree. Again, it was tall and narrow—not a deerlike shape at all.

"I believe you," Helen said. "I believe you saw it."

"I'm not asking you to take me at my word, Helen! I'm asking you to acknowledge the fucking proof right in front of your eyes!"

His voice had an edge she wasn't used to. The sound of a man at the end of his rope. Was this how Ann's husband had sounded that last day?

Helen took a long swig of her beer and said nothing.

Nate let out a slow breath and said quietly, "Do you or do you not see a deer in this picture?"

She thought of lying, of saying, *Yes, of course I see it.* But that's not what she said. "I see something. But really, Nate, it doesn't look much like a deer to me."

He hung the camera back around his neck and stomped down to the trailer, went in, and slammed the door hard behind him.

Riley stopped by not long after and Helen showed her the ax. Nate hadn't come out of the trailer and Helen wasn't about to go down.

"It was a gift from Olive. She found it with her metal detector out in the bog. We think it might have been Hattie's."

"Wow," Riley said, picking up the ax, touching it almost reverently. "Hattie's ax! What an incredible find!"

"Took me all day and a dozen YouTube videos to get it cleaned up and in working order, but it didn't turn out half bad."

"It's beautiful," Riley said, handing the ax back to Helen.

Helen nodded, asked, "Want to walk down to the bog?"

"Sure."

Helen left the refurbished ax in the house, leaning against the wall under the beam between the living room and kitchen: her latest gift for Hattie.

It was dusk and the late-season crickets were chirping away as they made their way down the path, Helen in the lead. She loved going to the bog at twilight and how sometimes, now that it was getting cooler, like this evening, there was a layer of mist hovering over the water, and Helen was sure she could see it move as if it were taking shape, pulling itself into the form of a woman in a dress. They walked over to the stones of the old foundation and each took a seat. Riley pulled out a joint and lit it, inhaling.

"Is something up with Olive?" Helen asked. "She seemed a little . . . off when I saw her yesterday. She okay?"

"She's real worried about her mom," Riley said. "Has she talked to you about it at all?"

"No. Not a peep."

"She has this idea that maybe her mom didn't run off with some guy like everyone says. That maybe something else happened."

"Do you think that's a possibility?"

"No . . . I mean, I don't know." She was quiet a second, eyes on the mist over the bog. "Maybe something scared her off."

"What do you mean?" Helen asked.

"Olive said that just before her mom took off, she heard her parents having a really bad fight down in the kitchen. There was a big crash. Like it got physical."

"What . . . you think your brother might have hurt her?"

"I can't imagine it. He loves her so much. But years ago, when Dustin was drinking all the time, he was a mess. Sometimes he'd get kind of crazy. Never hurt anyone else, just himself, but . . ."

"Riley, if you think—"

"No," Riley interrupted. "What I really think is that Lori took off with one of her boyfriends. Maybe Dustin found out she was cheating on him and they fought and that was the last straw for her. She got the hell out and didn't look back."

"Poor Olive," Helen said. "It's awful that she's going through this."

Riley passed her the joint, and they were silent for a minute, smoking, looking out at the bog.

"I still can't believe she gave me that ax," Helen mused.

"I love the ax," Riley said at last. "But I'm not sure keeping it is such a good idea."

"What? Why?"

"It's just starting to worry me. You collecting all these things with such morbid histories."

"You sound just like Nate," Helen snorted.

"It's like . . . you're opening a door," Riley said.

"Yes!" Helen said. "That's exactly the point."

"But when you open a door, who knows who or what you might be letting in," Riley said. "Not to mention the fact that you're really pissing your husband off. And worrying him."

"Huh?"

"He called me at the shop this morning."

"Really? What did he say?"

"He thinks your interest in Hattie and her family and all these objects is a bit . . . unhealthy. He asked me to please stop helping you with it—and he definitely doesn't want me to take you back to Dicky's any time soon. I heard all about how Dicky came by with your phone and told Nate about our visit there."

"Yeah. Nate was pretty pissed," Helen said.

Riley nodded. "But it's not just that he's mad, Helen. He's worried you're losing your grasp on reality."

"And do you agree with him? Do you think I've gone round the bend?"

"I think . . ." Riley paused. ". . . that it's a dangerous game you're playing. Blurring the lines between the past and present, the dead and the living."

"I hear what you're saying, but all I can say is that I've never felt so strongly compelled to do something. And I can't do it without you. Will you help me?"

There was a long pause.

"Of course," Riley said at last. "What is it you need?"

"There's only so much I can find myself online, especially with Nate looking over my shoulder all the time. Maybe if we both go back to the historical society and search through all the databases you guys have access to there, use the microfiche reader to go through old newspapers, search through all the birth, death, and marriage records, you can help me put together a solid family tree for Hattie. Try to track down who Gloria and Jason went to live with and what happened to them."

"Okay," Riley said. "I know Mary Ann's been reorganizing things in there since she got back from North Carolina. I think she's pretty much got the place put back together—and there's even a new computer. I'm working tomorrow, but I'm free the day after. Monday. We'll get in there and see what we can find."

CHAPTER 36

O live

Olive studied the books Helen had let her borrow—the library books she'd been reading up at the new house and a couple more Helen had down in the trailer.

"Just don't take anything in the books too seriously," Helen had warned.

"I totally get it," Olive assured her. "And don't worry, I'm not going to start trying to do spells or conjure demons or anything. I just find all of it interesting, you know? Reading what other people believe."

In one of the library books, Olive found a whole chapter on communicating with the dead by using a pendulum. It said a spirit could help you find lost objects using a pendulum. Also answer divination questions. The book suggested making a chart with possible answers to questions you have and then asking the spirit to point the pendulum to the correct answer.

Olive was flipping through one of the books on witchcraft when she came across a section on magic symbols.

She actually gasped, like some stupid girl in a horror movie.

There, on the page, was a design that was nearly identical to Mama's necklace: a circle with a triangle inside it, and inside that, a square with another circle in it. Olive read the words below it:

Squaring the circle is an important symbol used in ancient alchemy. To square a circle was thought to be an impossible task, uniting shapes that are not meant to come together. The circle represents the spirit world; the square, the physical world with its four elements. Some believe the triangle represents a door in which the dead, or possibly even demons, can walk through.

"Holy shit," Olive said.

A door the dead (or demons) can walk through.

She thought of the symbol chalked on the floor of Dicky's hotel. Was that what they'd been doing there? Trying to open an actual door to the spirit world?

And what if they'd succeeded?

Who, or what, might have come through?

"Ollie?" Daddy came into the living room in his work clothes.

Olive jumped.

"I've gotta go to work. Break in the water main over by the high school. Getting time and a half, though," he said with a wink.

"Okay," she said.

"What're you reading?" he asked, looking down at the books. "Something for school?"

"Not exactly," she said.

He scowled when he saw the titles.

"Where did these come from?" he asked, weirdly angry all of a sudden. His jaw was clenched and he was breathing through his nose like an angry bull. "Did Riley give them to you?"

"Aunt Riley? No," she said. Olive thought. She didn't want to get Helen in trouble. "I borrowed them. From the library. See?" She turned the book on its side so he could see the sticker on the spine with the call number on it.

"I don't want them in this house. I don't want to see another witchcraft book in this house again. I won't have it."

"Again?" she asked. Then, "Did . . . Mama have books like these?"

His face hardened even more, like he was turning to stone. Becoming a statue man. "I want them gone, Olive." He forced the words out through his clenched jaw. "In fact, here, I'll take them and drop them off at the library myself on my way to the school." He grabbed them, held them tightly in his dirty hands.

"But, Daddy, you—"

Library books clutched to his chest, he turned and went out of the living room, his body rigid, his boots stomping too loudly on the unfinished plywood floor.

FINISH WORK

CHAPTER 37

Helen

 **SEPTEMBER 13, 2015**

LAST CHANCE

The words were written on the front door of the new house. Fortunately, they'd been written in charcoal, so they were easy to clean off. There was a piece of burned wood on the front step that had been used to write the message.

Helen worked to scrub the words away before Nate could see. She scrubbed hard and fast, heart pounding, sweat beading on her forehead.

She was running out of time. She could feel it, could feel Hattie whispering to her.

Hurry. You are in danger.

Was the burned wood a warning, too? A reminder of what had happened to Hattie's mother, to Hattie's crooked house, to the schoolhouse, to Jane at the mill?

Whoever was leaving the messages wanted her gone.

How far would they go to drive her away?

Would there be another gas leak? A fire next time?

If Helen and Nate stayed, would they wake in the trailer one night to the smell of smoke, to flames licking at the walls?

"What are you doing?" Nate asked when he walked up to the house.

"There's a smudge on the door," she said, polishing it with a rag.

"It's Sunday," Nate said. "I thought we agreed to take the day off."

"Definitely," Helen said. "Just tidying a little."

"Did you turn off my cameras?" he asked.

"What? No."

"It's odd," Nate said. "They were all switched off. I didn't get any pictures from about midnight on last night."

"Strange," Helen said. Whoever had come and left the message on the door hadn't wanted to be seen.

"I'm going for a hike," he said.

Helen nodded. "Great. I think I'll see if I can get into the historical society to do a little research," Helen told him.

He frowned but said only, "You're not going to bring back any more haunted objects, right?"

"Just research, I promise," she told him. "Enjoy your hike."

. . .

Helen knew she couldn't wait. She called Mary Ann Marsden and asked if she could possibly let her into the historical society. She explained that she was a friend of Riley's.

"I know it's a Sunday and I hate to ask, but I'm just so eager to get started on my research."

Mary Ann chuckled and said she'd be glad to open the historical society. "I get out of church at noon and I can meet you there right after. I don't have anything planned for the afternoon, so I'm more than happy to help."

. . .

Mary Ann was an elderly woman in a polyester pantsuit the color of lima beans. She wore a huge enameled flower brooch pinned to her lapel, so heavy Helen was amazed its weight didn't pull the poor woman over. She had on dark red lipstick that had run into the creases of her upper lip, making them look like veins.

"So you're Riley's good friend, eh?" she asked, as she unlocked the door and let Helen in.

"Yes, I'm Helen. I so appreciate you letting me in like this."

Helen followed Mary Ann inside, watched her flip on the lights and shuffle over to the desk. All the plastic totes and cardboard boxes that had covered every surface on her last visit were gone. The place looked neat and tidy. The bulky, antiquated computer Riley had used was on a table in a back corner. A sleek new computer rested on the main desk.

"So, you're interested in the Breckenridge family?"

"Yes, that's right. Last time I was here, Riley showed me a painting of Hattie. I was hoping I could get another look at it."

She didn't expect the painting to yield any new clues, but she longed to see it, to be held in Hattie's gaze once more. She thought it would be a good way to start her research—would bring her luck if Hattie was actually watching over her.

"Of course," Mary Ann said, turning to go back to the cabinets. She opened drawers, pulled paintings in and out.

"Well, that's odd," she muttered.

"What is it?"

"It doesn't seem to be here," Mary Ann said. "At least, it's not where it should be. When something's loaned out, there's a pink sticker that goes where the painting should be. But there's no painting and no sticker." She turned back to the desk, picked up a big three-ring binder and flipped through it. "When we loan paintings out, we have a form that we use. And we have a logbook when anything gets borrowed. But there's nothing here."

"So do you think the painting could have been stolen?"

Mary Ann laughed. "Stolen? Oh dear, no. I can't imagine why anyone would want to steal a painting of Hattie Breckenridge! Not when we have other, much more valuable things here—silver, old coins, jewelry even."

"So what do you think happened to it?"

"Well, maybe it just got put away someplace unusual. Or someone might have borrowed it and not done the proper paperwork. Or we misplaced the paperwork. I can't imagine, really. We have several volunteers. I think the first step will be checking in with each of them."

She looked at the wooden cabinet, at the blank spot in the pulled-out drawer where Hattie's painting had been.

"I'm sorry I can't help you with the painting—what else are you looking for?" Mary Ann asked.

"When I was here with Riley, we found a couple of photographs of Hattie—an old school picture and a couple taken at a town picnic when she was a young woman. Do you know if there might be any others?"

Mary Ann nodded. "We have the final picture taken of Hattie," she said.

"Final picture?"

"Of the hanging," Mary Ann said. "Surely Riley showed it to you."

Jesus. A photograph of the hanging? It didn't seem possible.

"Um, no. We missed that one somehow."

"Ah," Mary Ann said, standing, going over to a tall black file cabinet. "It's in our special collection. Maybe Riley hasn't seen it herself." She opened a drawer, started looking through files. "Let's just hope that hasn't gone missing, too." Mary Ann chortled a bit.

Helen secretly wished it had.

"Oh, here we are," Mary Ann said, sounding almost giddy as she slipped a file folder out of the cabinet. She opened it up. Inside, it was lined with two sheets of paper. Between the sheets of paper, an old black-and-white photograph.

Helen cringed, had to force herself not to look away.

"Who would take a picture like this?" she asked.

"We're not sure who the photographer was," Mary Ann said.

Helen moved closer, studying the photograph. It was centered on a large old tree full of thick, heavy branches.

She looked at the picture, thought of how there was a piece of that very tree in her house.

Beneath the tree in the old photo, probably three dozen people were gathered, all turned toward the camera, posing. Some were smiling. Some looked down at the ground. It looked like it could have been a picture taken at a town dance or country fair—Hartsboro's finest gathered in celebration. Some wore dusty work clothes and looked as though they'd come straight from plowing the fields or shoveling coal into a steam engine. Others were in suit and tie, the women in dresses with their hair neatly fastened.

And above them, their kill.

Hattie Breckenridge hung by a thick rope from a high branch. Helen could make out the noose around her neck. She wore a white dress that was dirty, stained. Her shoes were caked with mud. Her eyes were closed, her face placid. There was a woman right below her—a woman with light hair. She was smiling and holding something in her hands, something that seemed to glint in the light.

"What's that woman got?" Helen asked, leaning in.

"I'm not sure," Mary Ann said, squinting down. Helen saw a magnifying glass on the desk and reached for it. She studied the photograph through it and could see what it was: a necklace. Helen peered closer, and though it was hard to make out, she was sure it was the same necklace with a strange design Hattie had been wearing in the portrait: a circle, triangle, and square all tucked inside each other.

"Who's this woman?" Helen asked, pointing to the woman holding Hattie's necklace like a trophy, a sickening smile on her face that seemed to say, *The witch is dead.*

"I believe that's Candace Bishkoff. Her daughter, Lucy, had been killed in the fire. The story goes that she's the one who led the townspeople to Hattie's that afternoon."

"Bishkoff? Are any of her relatives still around?"

"Why sure. There are plenty of them. They own the pig farm and smokehouse—Uncle Fred's Smokehouse—you know it?"

She nodded. "I've driven by."

Mary Ann carefully replaced the photo in its folder and rubbed her hands together excitedly. "Well! Enough of that! Let's get started with that research! What exactly are you looking for?"

"I'm trying to trace Hattie's family tree, to find any living descendants she may have."

I'm trying to save one of them.

Helen continued. "I know she had a daughter, Jane . . ."

"No one knows what happened to Jane," Mary Ann said sadly, shaking her head. "She disappeared soon after the hanging and was never heard from again."

"Actually, I'm fairly certain she went up to Lewisburg and eventually married a man named Silas Whitcomb. They had two children, Ann and Mark. Jane was killed in a fire at the Donovan and Sons Mill when the children were young. Her daughter, Ann, later married a Samuel Gray—they lived over in Elsbury. Samuel and Ann had a son, Jason, and a daughter, Gloria. Samuel and Ann were killed . . . a murder-suicide, and the children went off to live with relatives."

"My goodness," Mary Ann said. "You certainly have learned a lot! You should come volunteer here. We could always use someone with good research skills!"

"I'd love to. Maybe once the house is finished and I have more free time—right now, I'm looking for any other family. And I'd like to know what happened to Jason and Gloria—who they went to live with, where they are now."

Mary Ann was amazingly adept at using both the computer and

microfiche reader. In fact, she was a much faster typist than Helen—
her fingers flew across the keyboard.

Together, they looked through genealogy websites, public records,
census data, and old newspapers. Helen's eyes got bleary and she felt a
little queasy from flipping through page after page of birth and death
records in state newspapers on the microfiche reader. She read articles
about the mill fire that killed Jane, about Ann's murder.

The first thing they discovered was that after Jane's death, Silas
Whitcomb remarried and had four more children, giving Ann and
Mark half siblings, each of whom then married and had children.

Through Mary Ann's skillful navigation of public records, they
learned that Mark Whitcomb moved to Keene, New Hampshire, and
married a woman named Sara Sharpe in 1965. They had three daughters: Rebecca, Stacy, and Marie. Mary Ann pulled up copies of birth
certificates for all three.

"Riley can help me with this tomorrow," Helen said after they'd
been working for nearly two hours. "I don't want you to have to be
here all day."

"Oh, I don't mind at all," Mary Ann said. "I'm actually enjoying
the detective work. I had no idea that Hattie Breckenridge had left
such a legacy. It's fascinating that there are living relatives out there
somewhere, isn't it?"

"Absolutely," Helen said.

"You know," Mary Ann confessed, "I always thought it was unfair—
the way people treated Hattie, the way the whole town talks about her
still. I don't think it's right, to vilify a person like that."

Helen smiled at her. "That's part of what's pulling me to do this
research. I want to know her side of the story."

Helen took a break and ran across to the general store to get them
sandwiches, cups of coffee, and a box of raspberry Danish.

"I brought us provisions," she announced when she got back.

"I've got some information on Samuel Gray here," Mary Ann
said, eyes on the computer screen. "He was one of eight siblings, and
his mother, Eliza Gray, lived until 2002. She was in Duxbury, so the
kids could have gone to her."

Helen reached into her bag for her notebook to start writing down
the list of names they came up with, but her notebook wasn't there.

"Damn," she muttered.

"Everything all right?"

"Sorry, I thought I had my notes with me, but I guess not."

She must have left the notebook back at home. By the computer there, maybe. Careless. If Nate found it . . . but he wouldn't find it, would he?

Mary Ann found her a blank legal pad. Helen started to write down the names and dates of birth of every family member they'd found whom Jason and Gloria might have gone to live with.

"I don't want to make things more difficult," Mary Ann said, "but I think it's important to remember that they might have been taken in by a distant cousin, the sister-in-law of an aunt or uncle—anyone."

In the end, after she and Mary Ann had been at it for over four hours (and had polished off their sandwiches along with all the raspberry Danish), she had a long list of aunts and uncles, great-aunts and great-uncles, cousins, in-laws. She had four pieces of paper taped together on which she'd sketched a rough outline of Hattie's family tree—the branches twisted and tangled, heavy with names.

.   .   .

Helen flicked on her turn signal when the smiling cartoon pig on the Uncle Fred's Smokehouse sign came into view. Under the pig sign hung another that said: BACON, SAUSAGES, HAM. There was a low single-story building with a green metal roof and an awning that said simply: MEATS. Behind it, a small shed with a metal chimney that sweet hickory smoke poured out of.

Helen walked through the door of the shop, where there was a large refrigerated case full of smoked meat: sausages, hams, thick slabs of fatty bacon. Helen's stomach felt a little queasy—it was all too much, the sweet smoky smell, the fatty cuts of pork, rinds red from smoke. The rest of the shop was full of knickknacks tourists might buy—stuffed toy moose with ILOVERMONT T-shirts, maple syrup, local hot sauces, jellies and jams, quilted pot holders, beeswax candles—all of it seemingly covered with a thin layer of greasy dust. An old metal fan sat in a corner, chugging, doing its best to stir the thick air.

"Can I help you?" asked a young woman behind the counter. Helen guessed she was still in high school or maybe college. She didn't look old enough to drink legally, but she was wearing a Long Trail Ale T-shirt and so much eye shadow and mascara that Helen was amazed the girl could keep her eyes open.

"I'm not sure," Helen said. "I'm looking for family of Candace Bishkoff."

"Candace?" the girl asked, looking up at the ceiling, thinking. "I don't think I know any Candace, and I know pretty much all the Bishkoffs. My boyfriend, Tony, he's a Bishkoff." She smiled at Helen, proud to be showing her allegiance to this clan of the smoked meat Bishkoffs; maybe one day she and Tony would get married, and their children would grow up and learn the secrets of brining and sausage making.

"Candace would be dead by now," Helen explained. "She was around back in the early 1900s."

"Oh," the girl said. "You're talking old-time Bishkoffs. That's the cool thing about this family—they've been around here for-ev-er!"

Helen nodded. "Is anyone from the family around at the moment? Anyone who might know anything about Candace?"

"Sure, hang on a sec; let me get Marty for you. Marty knows everyone."

"Oh, great! Thanks," Helen said.

"No prob," the girl chirped, going through a back door and calling, "Marty! MAR-TY!"

Soon, the girl was back, followed by a gray-haired man who shuffled in in worn overalls. He was thin and gangly and reminded Helen of a scarecrow who had come to life and just climbed down off his post. His face and neck were patchy with stubble, like he'd tried to shave but missed huge spots. His eyes were rheumy.

The girl took her seat behind the counter, stared down at her phone and started typing on it.

"Help you?" the old man grunted.

"I hope so. You're Marty?"

He nodded.

"Nice to meet you. I'm Helen. I was looking for someone who might know something about a woman named Candace Bishkoff?"

He nodded. "She was my grandmother."

"Did you . . . did you know her?" Helen pictured the woman from the photograph, young then, holding the necklace, smiling a victorious smile.

"She died when I was young, but I remember her some, yes. She taught me to play checkers. No one could beat that old lady. I mean no one."

Helen believed that.

"Lived to be ninety-nine years old," he said. "Almost a century. Imagine that."

"That's wonderful," Helen said. "This might sound odd, but I'm wondering about a piece of jewelry your grandmother might have owned. A necklace with a circle, triangle, and square."

He nodded. "I know the one you mean."

Helen's heart jumped. She'd been right.

"Do you have it? Is it still in your family? I'd love to have a look at it."

He shook his head. "We sold it. A little over a year ago. Lady came in here, just like you, asking all sorts of questions about it. She offered cash. Three hundred bucks. A lot of money to pay for an ugly old necklace, if you ask me," he said.

"Three hundred bucks?" the girl behind the counter asked. "Really?"

The man nodded.

"Well, maybe it was really old and valuable, like a relic or something. Something that belongs in a museum," the girl suggested. "Maybe it was really worth way more than that and that lady took you for a ride."

"I don't think so," the man said. "And to be honest with you, Louise and I, we were happy to get rid of it. Louise used to say that necklace was cursed."

"Why would she say that?" the girl asked.

"Because it once belonged to Hattie Breckenridge."

"No kidding?" the girl said. "The witch? The one that got hung out by the bog?"

Marty nodded, ran a hand over one of the straps of his overalls.

Helen winced as she remembered the photograph: the smiling crowd gathered at the base of the tree while Hattie swung up above them. The witch was dead.

She looked at Marty, thought, *Your grandmother did that. She was there. Her smile was the biggest, the most satisfied.* Helen felt her own throat tighten, as if there were an invisible noose around her neck.

"Do you know the name of the woman you sold the necklace to?" Helen asked, forcing the words through the knot in her throat.

"Of course I do," Marty said. "Small town like this, I knew just who she was. It was that Lori Kissner girl. The one who took off and left her husband and daughter."

"Oh, I know who you mean," the girl said. "Her daughter's a real freak. I feel bad for her, what with her mother running around with all different men and the whole town knowing it—but Olive's a freak."

"Olive?" Helen echoed, unable to keep the surprise out of her voice.

"Yeah." The girl shrugged her shoulders. "The kids at school all call her Odd Oliver."

CHAPTER 38

Olive

 SEPTEMBER 13, 2015

She couldn't get the phrase "deep shit" out of her head, because that's just what she was in.

Olive was trapped in Dicky's old hotel.

She'd snuck into the hotel a little before six o'clock. She didn't know what time the others were coming, but she wanted to make sure she was there in plenty of time. The front door was unlocked and she slipped inside, looking around the old lobby.

She had planned just what she'd say if Dicky caught her. She'd say she'd lost a bracelet, her very favorite one, one her mama who was gone now had given her, and the last time she remembered having it on was the day she visited Dicky. *I've looked everywhere else and this is the only place it could be,* she'd tell him. *I'm so sorry for bothering you like this, but that bracelet is real important to me.*

But, to her relief, she didn't need to use her excuse. Not right away, anyway. There was no sign of life in or around the lobby. Just a single pillar candle burning in a holder on the front desk. It was a total fire hazard, surrounded by mountains of junk mail and papers.

She heard laughter coming from upstairs.

She knew this was just plain stupid. She shouldn't be here. She should be home watching TV or putting up drywall. Daddy was out working on the water main break (it was the second day of working on it, and if they didn't get it fixed, there would be no school tomorrow because that whole area of town had no water).

This is stupid, she told herself. *I should turn around and go home before I get caught.*

But still, she found herself climbing the stairs, as if the voices up there were a magnet pulling her. If there was any chance at all that she could learn anything about Mama, she needed to try. And Dicky and his friends obviously knew something. She crept slowly up the stairs, repeating the made-up story about the bracelet in her head, preparing herself just in case she was caught. When she was all the way up at the top, listening, trying to figure out where the voices she heard were coming from, the front door downstairs banged open and a man called up, "Dicky?"

Olive froze. There was silence for about ten seconds, and Olive scurried farther down the hall, which proved to be a good choice, because she could hear the new visitor start up the stairs.

"Where're you at, Dicky?" the man called.

Olive looked at all the closed doors to the old guest rooms. No time to try each knob on the off chance one might be open. She went down the hall and into the lounge, where she'd been on her last visit. Familiar territory.

"Where the hell are you guys?" this new voice called out from the hall. This man's voice, now that he was closer, sounded familiar to Olive, but she couldn't place whom it belonged to.

"Third floor," Dicky called back from up above. "But we're coming down."

Olive was standing against the wall beside the door, listening, trying to slow her racing heart. The lounge was dark, the old tattered shades over the arched windows drawn. The room had a stinky, acrid smell, like burned hair. She heard footsteps coming down the curved wooden steps from the third floor, where Dicky lived. It sounded like hoofbeats during a stampede. It was impossible to tell how many people he had with him: Two? Twenty?

Then they were coming her way.

Footsteps and voices, laughter.

Crap. They were coming to the lounge! Of course they were.

She looked around, frantic. There was nowhere to run, no back door or escape hatch. No closet. Only a bunch of broken chairs. Windows with tattered curtains. The fireplace. Could she fit inside it, climb her way up and out the chimney like Santa Claus? Not likely.

She hurried over to the bar, got behind it, and ducked down.

Please don't let them come behind the bar, she thought. She remembered the tequila and the glasses, prayed no one wanted a drink. She tried to make her body as small as she could, concentrated on disappearing into the wood of the bar, being invisible. She was good at holding still, at not making a sound. She'd honed her skills during years of hunting with Daddy. Only now she felt like the hunted rather than the hunter.

They gathered in the hall, a jumble of voices and footsteps, calling out greetings to each other: "Hullo there," "Long time no see." Then they tumbled into the lounge, and it did sound more like tumbling than walking, like a river breaching its banks, spilling over.

Olive listened hard, tried to pick out the distinct voices, to count the number of people.

They made small talk, discussing the weather, work, baseball. Some of them lit cigarettes—Olive could smell the smoke. Every now and then, someone new joined them and the greetings would begin again. They all discussed whether someone named Carol was coming, and some of them seemed very distressed by the possibility that she might not be.

"We all need to be here," Dicky said, clearly agitated. "It won't work if we're not all here. I thought I made that clear."

The talk moved back to boring things—someone told a story about seeing someone named Bud in the supermarket and how good he looked considering he was now missing half his liver; someone else talked about how to make the lightest angel food cake you've ever tasted.

Olive held still and listened. Her legs went to sleep under her, but she didn't dare move. The light coming in around the cracks in the heavy window drapes got dimmer as the sun set. The talking went on and on, and Olive started to wonder if there had been any point at all in coming here for this. The room filled with cigarette smoke. At last, Carol arrived with a story about car trouble.

"Are we all here, then?" a man with a high-pitched mouse squeak of a voice asked.

"Yes," a voice Olive recognized as Dicky's answered.

"And we've got the diary?" a woman asked.

"No," Dicky said. "Not anymore."

"Well, where is it?" asked the woman.

"Hidden," Dicky said. "It's back at Lori's. In the shed. Don't worry. Everything's been taken care of."

Olive's mind whirled, thoughts spinning like a pinwheel. What diary? Hidden in the shed at her house?

"It doesn't sound to me like things have been taken care of at all," another woman said. "Lori's girl is poking around. The newcomers are asking questions, digging things up."

"Well, that's why we're here, isn't it?" Dicky asked. "To ask for guidance. For protection."

"We need more than guidance!" a man argued. "We need to stop that girl and those people building on Hattie's land!"

"Plans are in place," Dicky said. "But now we need help from the other side."

There was a murmur of agreement.

"Well, then, let's begin," a man with a deep, gravelly voice said.

More footsteps, the rustle of fabric. The sound of chairs being pulled back and rearranged. There were a few soft murmurs from the group gathered. Olive could make out Dicky and thought a couple of the other voices might be familiar, but she couldn't place them.

These are people you've probably been seeing in town your whole life, she told herself.

The murmurs built to a hum. A hum that filled the room and sounded, to Olive, almost insect-like, as if she were suddenly in a hive of bees, a nest of some sort of strange winged creatures droning. Above the buzz, a single voice rose: Dicky's voice, loud and sure, speaking with his fake Texas twang: a rodeo cowboy turned preacher.

"Spirits of the east, of the north, of the west and south; creatures of water, air, earth, and fire, we call upon you. We compel you to open the door."

Then the hum changed, morphed into a chant:

As above, so below
The door is opened
Let the worlds unite
Let the spirits walk among us

Olive's skin prickled.

"Hattie Breckenridge, come forward," called a man.

"We give ourselves to you," said another.

"We offer ourselves to you," said a woman.

"We are your faithful servants."

And then the voices rose up together—"Hattie, Hattie, Hattie, Hattie"—until a single voice called out, Dicky saying, "Come to us, Hattie. We ask you to join us, your faithful servants. Come and guide us. Show us the way."

The room got brighter, the smoke more intense.

Olive pictured the chalk marks on the floor, imagined them opening up like a magic portal and Hattie Breckenridge crawling through.

This she had to see.

Slowly, as quietly as she could, Olive crawled out from her hiding
spot behind the bar, peering around, keeping her body hidden.

The group was standing in a circle in front of the fireplace, around
the chalk circle drawn on the floor. The symbol that matched her
necklace.

The door to the spirit world.

Olive counted nine people. There were candles lit all around the
room—on the mantel, the floor—and incense burned in little brass
bowls (the things she'd taken to be ashtrays the other day), filling the
air with thick, sweet smoke.

Above the mantel, the black cloth had been removed to reveal not
a mirror at all, but a painting. It was a portrait of a woman with long
dark hair and dark eyes. She wore a red dress and had a necklace on—
and it wasn't just any necklace: it was the very same one Olive herself
was now wearing.

The necklace seemed to thrum beneath Olive's shirt, buzzing like
a tuning fork.

Even from Olive's hiding place, the woman's gaze was mesmerizing, enchanting. Olive felt the woman was looking right at her,
seeing inside her, and that she was trying to tell Olive something,
something important.

Maybe just *Give me my necklace back, or else!*

And she knew this was Hattie, though she'd never seen a picture,
never heard what Hattie had looked like, never heard people say she'd
been beautiful. The way people talked about her, Olive had imagined
a cruel, twisted face, fangs, a few warts maybe.

But this, this was the true Hattie: radiant, glowing like cool moonlight.

This was Hattie who'd once lived in a little crooked house at the
end of the bog. Hattie who was hanged for witchcraft. Hattie, whose
necklace Olive now wore.

Olive shifted her gaze from the painting down to the circle of
people standing below it. They had drifted apart, made an opening,
and a woman came out of the shadowy back corner to the left of the
mantel and made her way into the center of the circle. She was moving slowly, dancing through the thick smoke. She had long dark hair,

a white dress. And on her face, a white deer mask. It was strangely realistic, with real fur, a black nose, shiny black eyes.

The white doe.

Olive held her breath.

Hattie?

Had they really conjured the actual spirit of Hattie Breckenridge, who was now moving among them, in the center of their circle?

As Olive watched this spirit woman move, there was something spookily familiar about the dance she did: step, step, shimmy; step, step, shimmy. Then Olive looked down, peeked through the legs of the people who stood in a circle, chanting, "Hattie, Hattie, Hattie," and saw the woman's feet.

She wore ivory-colored shoes with silver beads embroidered across the toes in a flower shape and straps that fastened with tiny silver buckles.

Olive clasped her hand over her mouth to keep from making a sound, from crying out, "Mama!"

CHAPTER 39

H elen

Helen was trying to put the pieces together: Olive's mother paying $300 for Hattie's necklace, then running off, never to be heard from again. And what the girl had said about Olive: *Odd Oliver.* Helen's heart nearly broke. She needed to talk to Olive, to ask if she knew anything about the necklace her mother had bought, find out if she'd ever mentioned it. It wasn't too late—she'd call Olive tonight, invite her over for hot cocoa to talk.

But her plans slipped away when she walked into the trailer.

Nate was sitting at the kitchen table, looking down at something. At first, she worried it was another warning message: *LAST CHANCE.*

But this was far worse.

Helen froze in the kitchen, wishing she could turn around and run.

Nate was pale, shaking. He had the ax next to him. And Helen's notebook—full of all she'd learned; all she'd experienced with Hattie, Jane, and Ann; all the things she had lied to Nate about over and over—was there, open on the table.

Helen stepped back. "Nate?"

She thought of Ann being shot dead by her husband in their living room. What did it take to make a person snap, to pick up a gun (or an ax) and come after the one he loved?

"What did she look like?" he asked. He croaked the words out, like a frog calling from the bottom of the well.

"Who?"

"Hattie. When you saw her in the kitchen. And later, in the house. What did she look like?"

He reached down, rested a hand on the ax handle—the new hickory handle Helen herself had bought for hanging the ax.

"I—" Helen scrambled, unsure what to say. Perhaps deny it all, tell Nate that he was right, that there was no such thing as ghosts, she knew that now. Tell him she must have imagined it.

But hadn't she done enough lying?

Nate rose, holding the ax. His eyes were glassy, bloodshot. "What did she fucking look like, Helen?" he shouted.

"Nate," Helen stammered, taking a stumbling step backward, toward the still-open door, estimating the distance between Nate and herself.

"Did she have black hair?" Nate asked, wrapping his fingers around the ax handle now. "Dark eyes? A little shorter than you are?" He was looking at Helen but also beyond her, like the figure he was describing might be right behind her, watching.

Helen nodded, taking another step back, knowing she must be close to the door. She held one hand in front of her, palm out in an *it's okay, let's calm down* gesture. With her other hand, she reached back, feeling for the doorway.

"I saw her," Nate said. "Jesus, I must be going crazy, because I swear to you, I actually saw her."

He collapsed back down in the kitchen chair, let the ax slip from his hand, slumped forward, put his arms up on the table, and buried his face in them.

Helen went to him. She put a hand on his arm. "Tell me," she said. "Tell me exactly what you saw."

Tell me what she did to you.

He lifted his head. "I was out in the woods, tracking the deer. I know you think I'm crazy, but she's real, Helen. But now I think . . . oh god, I don't know what I think."

"So you were in the woods. Is that where you saw Hattie?"

"No." He shook his head. "I was walking in circles for what felt like hours. She knew I was following her. It's something she does. A game she plays? Then the circles got wider, and soon, I was following her along the edge of the bog. Only . . . it was different."

"Different how?"

"Maybe I somehow stumbled onto another bog? Or another part of the bog. An area we haven't explored yet."

Helen nodded but knew there was no other bog. No other part of the bog.

"What did you see there, Nate?"

"There was a house. A little cabin. A ramshackle thing. Crooked, leaning to the left." He looked at her and she nodded again, encouraging him to continue. "There was a chimney with smoke coming out of it. And the door was open. My doe . . . I mean, the doe, the white doe I'd been following, she walked right in. I couldn't quite believe what I was seeing, but I knew I had her then. She was trapped. I got my camera ready and ran, ran toward the cabin. But when I got there . . ."

"What?" Helen asked. "What, Nate? What happened?"

Nate pushed his chair back, stood up, rubbing his face.

"There was no deer inside. But there was a woman just inside the front door. A woman with dark hair and eyes. She was wearing a white dress. And the way she looked at me, Helen . . ." He paused, his eyes locked on Helen's. In them, she saw pure terror. His voice shook. "It was like she knew me, Helen. Like she'd been waiting for me."

O live

Mama! It was Mama there, dancing in the center of the circle.

But how? Why?

Olive's mind scrambled for explanations and for an idea of what she was supposed to do next.

If only she had a cell phone, like every other fourteen-year-old kid on the planet, then she could sneak back behind the bar, call or text her dad and Aunt Riley, tell them she'd found her mom, to hurry up and come quick.

But she didn't have a phone and she was stuck here, in this old bar and lounge at Dicky's hotel.

Think, she told herself.

Olive thought about tracking a skittish deer when hunting, how you had to keep it in your sights and follow carefully until you had the perfect shot, until just the right moment.

Her one and only shot with Mama was trying to get her alone, to talk to her one-on-one.

"She speaks!" one of the men said, as if reading Olive's mind.

"Hattie, speak to us!" a woman said. "Tell us your secrets. Tell us what it is we must know. Tell us what it is we must do."

These people sounded ridiculous, hokey, but even though it sounded like something from a cartoon, they seemed serious, and it scared the hell out of Olive.

The group moved closer to the deer-headed woman (Mama!), encircling her, listening.

But Olive didn't hear a thing, only the hum of the group, the sound of her mother's feet shuffling across the floor in the fairy-tale slippers.

And a whisper. Just the faintest hint of a whisper.

She had to get closer.

The possibility of hearing her mother's voice pulled on her like a superpowered magnet, luring her out of her hiding place.

Olive spotted a small, tattered red love seat just ahead of her and started to crawl for it, sure that the group was fixated on Mama in the mask. And the room was dark. She could move through the shadows.

"Guide us, Hattie," a man said. "Show us the way."

Olive scuttled forward on all fours, moving fast—too fast. Her right foot struck a ladder-back chair she hadn't even seen in the dim space. It tipped backward, balanced for a second, and then crashed to the floor just behind her.

The humming stopped, the circle opened, everyone turned to look her way.

And there was Olive.

Caught on her hands and knees, like a large and foul bug in the center of the room. And she felt as vulnerable as an insect, something that could easily be squashed and put out of its misery.

"Who the hell is that?" asked the man with the mouse voice.

Her mother leaned forward, the eyes on the deer mask gleaming, flickering in the candlelight. The group circled her more tightly, protectively.

Dicky put his hand on the gun in his holster. Olive didn't wait to see what might happen next: she sprang to her feet and bolted for the door.

"Come back here!" Dicky shouted, and there was the sound of footsteps behind her, like hoofbeats, but she didn't slow, didn't dare to turn around, just yanked the heavy wooden door open and ran through it, flying down the carpeted hallway, past the closed doors of long-abandoned guest rooms, taking the stairs three at a time, landing in the front hall, speeding by the front desk and out the door into the night.

She jumped off the porch, the dressed-up mannequins watching like frozen sentries, unable to stop her. The front door banged open again behind her, Dicky shouting, "Stop right there!" There were other voices behind him, shouting, desperate.

"Don't let her get away!"

"Lori's kid! I can't believe it!"

"Stop her!"

Heart jackhammering inside her chest, she tore off around the corner of the building, searching for the shadows, for darkness, running up the hill, staying off the road, cutting through backyards and toward the woods. They were following her still—she could hear their footsteps, their gasping breaths. But she was faster, younger, nimbler; she moved like a jackrabbit through the night, her eyes on the woods in front of her at the top of the hill.

Was her mother behind her, part of the group chasing her now? She wanted to look, to turn around and see if she could catch a glimpse of the white deer mask, but didn't dare.

She sprinted the last of the way up the hill, pushing herself harder than ever before, leg muscles screaming, lungs gasping. Finally she reached the safety of the trees, smelled the rich, loamy forest scent. She zigzagged expertly through the trees, jumping over rocks and roots, her eyes fully adjusted to the dark.

She ran on, heard Dicky somewhere behind her, far off now. "Goddamn it, we lost her!"

A female voice (her mother's maybe?) said something faint, but Olive was sure she could make out the words: "For the best."

CHAPTER 41

H elen

 SEPTEMBER 13, 2015

Helen stood in the kitchen, stunned. Nate had seen Hattie. She'd brought him to her house. Helen had a worried, sick feeling in her stomach: What had Hattie done to him there? Was this going to be like those stories in old folktales about a woman so mesmerizing, the poor man couldn't resist and went to her, kissed her, had some kind of supernatural sex with her?

"Did she speak?" Helen asked. "Did you? What happened?"

What did she do to you?

She held her breath, waiting.

"I took her picture," he said.

"You . . . photographed her?"

He nodded. "And as soon as I did, it was all gone—the house, the woman, the deer. I was standing alone at the other end of the bog. It was like I'd imagined the whole thing. But it seemed so goddamned *real*."

"What does the picture look like?" Helen asked, though she knew how he would answer.

"Like nothing. Like pure light was shining through the lens. Just one overexposed blur." He looked down at Helen's notebook again. He had it open to the passage where she talked about seeing Hattie for the first time in the kitchen. "Do you think it was her?" Nate asked.

"I do."

"And these other women you've written about, Hattie's daughter, her granddaughter—you've really seen them, too?"

Helen nodded.

Nate looked down at Helen's notebook, touched it. "It's because of the objects in the house? That's why they come?"

"I think that's part of it. I think the objects help them to come, but I think they come for other reasons."

"What reasons?"

"I think they want to be together again. And . . . and I think they want something from me. From us, Nate. From our house."

"Our house?" He gave her a helpless, perplexed look.

She nodded, paused. "I think they want these objects in our house so that it can be a gathering place, a safe space for them all to come back to. Somewhere between our world and theirs. An in-between place."

"In-between place?" he echoed in the dull monotone of someone in shock, someone who was dealing with more than he could handle. But she had to go on, to tell him the rest.

"But there's more than that. I think they want us to help them."

"Help them how?" Nate asked.

"There's someone they want me to find. A living descendant of Hattie's."

"Who?"

"I'm not sure, but whoever it is, I think she's in danger."

He stared at her, not knowing how to respond, doing his best to process what she was saying, to take it all in.

Helen reached out, put her hand on his arm. "We've got to help her, Nate. That's what Hattie wants. What all this has been for."

CHAPTER 42

Olive

She ran home, cutting through the woods and people's backyards, staying off the streets because she didn't want to risk being seen if Dicky and his friends had gotten in their cars to look for her. The moon was nearly full and she had good light to navigate by. Once she was back in her yard, she went straight into the workshop—an old, leaning eight-by-ten wooden shed that stood on the other side of the driveway from the house. Heart thumping, skin prickling with cold sweat, she grabbed the old twelve-gauge Winchester her daddy used for duck hunting. All of their other guns were locked up in the gun safe in the dining room. But Daddy had been cleaning the twelve-gauge, so it was in the shop, on the workbench.

She didn't know if Dicky and his gang of wackos would come after her, but she wanted to be ready if they did.

She felt around on the workbench until she found the flashlight her dad kept out there and flicked it on. The batteries were low and the light it cast was dim.

She found her father's waxed-canvas duck hunting bag and opened it up, grabbing a box of ammo.

Then she started to search the shed for this diary she'd heard them talk about tonight. Hattie's diary, maybe?

She checked the shelves, the toolboxes, the old apple crates full of junk. No diary. She found old batteries, taps and buckets for sugaring, spools of wire, boxes of nails, old tire rims, but nothing resembling a diary. She spotted the giant pink tackle box her mother had used for her brief foray into beading. A few years back, Mama had decided it would be fun to make beaded jewelry and sell it at craft fairs and the farmers' market. She spent a small fortune on supplies, then made only a few of pieces of jewelry (which she kept herself or gave to Riley—she didn't sell any) before losing interest. Mama was fickle like that. Things held her interest only so long, then she was chasing after something new.

Olive reached up and lifted the tackle box down from the shelf, set it on the worktable, and opened it up. The top drawers were full of tiny compartments of beads all sorted by color and size. There were spools of nylon cord for stringing the beads and clasps, closures, and hooks. At the bottom of the main compartment were her tools: a small hammer, tweezers, pliers of all sorts. And underneath these, a leather-bound book.

Olive pulled it out and flipped through it, recognizing her mother's tiny, sloped letters, her careful penmanship.

It was her mother's diary! Not Hattie's, but Mama's.

Olive had had no idea that Mama had kept a diary. The first entry was dated January 1, 2013.

Olive flipped through the pages. There was something so wonderful and comforting about seeing her mother's writing, touching the pages her mother had touched, reading her thoughts.

Many of the early entries were boring everyday stuff: hours she'd worked at the market, how annoyed she was with her boss, a funny story a customer told her.

Then things took a turn for the interesting. She was writing about Hattie, about the treasure. Mama was clearly searching for it.

About a month before she disappeared Mama wrote:

I feel Hattie leading me to it, bringing me closer all the time.

In another entry, she wrote:

If I can find the necklace, I'll find the treasure. The necklace is the key.

On June 12 of last year, she wrote:

I hate lying to Ollie about all this, but I'm doing what has to be done. It's the only way to keep her safe. I see that now. I've seen how desperate the others are, the lengths they'll go to to find the treasure. "There is no treasure," I tell my girl. "There never was. It's just a silly story people tell." I wonder if she believes me. My Ollie Girl, she's my bright shining star, and something tells me she sees right through my lies.

On June 14, she wrote:

I've got it! I've got the necklace. It took a huge chunk of my savings, but money is no object now. If this works the way I believe it will, we'll soon be rich beyond our wildest dreams!

Then another entry, the second to the last, dated June 28 of last summer, the day before she disappeared.

I have found the treasure! I left it in the ground where it was for safe-keeping for the time being. I have made a map and hidden it well so that I won't forget its exact location. But I no longer believe I am safe. I must move carefully. I must get Olive, dig up the treasure, and go quickly.

Then, the following day, the final entry of the diary, written in fast, sloppy letters, the ink badly smudged:

Dustin is watching my every step. He keeps asking me what I've been up to, what I've been so secretive about. "Nothing," I tell him. The other day, when we were arguing, he grabbed my arm and twisted it hard, leaving a ring of bruises. He said if I'm not careful, I'll end up with a lot worse than a hurt arm. "Sometimes people disappear," he told me. "People who keep secrets." My heart jolted. I've never been so frightened.

Olive's hands were shaking. Her mouth was dry and sour.

What had her father done?

Outside, a car pulled into the driveway, the headlights spilling over the shed. Olive flipped off her flashlight, stood in the dark, listening. A car door opened and closed. Footsteps, then the front door of the house banging open and shut.

Should she run?

No. If she ran, she'd never discover what had really happened to her mother.

Olive grabbed the shotgun, loaded it, and started very slowly toward the house.

CHAPTER 43

Helen

 SEPTEMBER 13, 2015

Nate was looking over Helen's notes from the historical society while she paced the tiny kitchen in the trailer.

"Okay, so this Gloria Gray would be Hattie's great-granddaughter. You think she's the one in danger?"

Helen nodded. "I do. But the only record we could find was her birth certificate. I know that after her parents died, she and her brother were sent to live with family. So that's a list of all the relatives Mary Ann and I could find, people they might have gone to stay with."

"It's a long list," Nate said.

"I know," Helen admitted. "But I've got to try."

Nate nodded. "Okay. Get your laptop and phone. Let's start trying to find these people, see if we can track down Gloria."

. . .

At first it seemed hopeless, trying to find out what might have happened to Gloria Gray. Nate used Helen's laptop (his was in the corner, streaming the feed from the wildlife cameras) and she took notes and made calls when they were lucky enough to find a phone number. She left several voice mails. Nate sent emails and Facebook messages, trying to convey how urgent it was to hear back as soon as possible without sounding crazy or desperate.

Helen was overwhelmed, feeling more and more like this was an impossible task. She thought of how it seemed as if she'd been led to find Jane and Ann—why would she hit a dead end now?

"Wait a second," Nate said. "What's the date of birth for Gloria's brother, Jason?"

Helen looked down at her notes. "August 22, 1968."

"I've got an obituary," he said.

"You're kidding!"

"He died in 1987, from injuries sustained in a motorcycle accident."

"Shit," Helen said. "He was so young."

"He was living in Keene, New Hampshire. He'd just graduated from high school there the year before. And listen to this: 'Jason was predeceased by his parents, Samuel Gray and Ann Whitcomb Gray. He is survived by his sister, Gloria Whitcomb. He is also survived by his uncle and aunt, Mark and Sara Whitcomb, and his cousins, Rebecca Whitcomb, Stacy Whitcomb, and Marie Whitcomb.'"

"Wait a second," Helen said, turning the laptop to get a better look. "His sister is listed as Gloria *Whitcomb?*"

"That's what it says," Nate said, pointing out the line in the obituary.

Helen's mind whirred. "They must have gone to live with their uncle Mark and Gloria changed her last name."

"But why did she change her name and Jason didn't?"

"Hell if I know, but let's do a search for any Gloria Whitcombs in New Hampshire."

Helen glanced at Nate's laptop, streaming the live feeds of his cameras: views of their trailer, yard, and new house with a glowing green cast. She was sure she saw movement: a figure leaving the house, moving so fast it seemed to fly across the yard, into the woods, moving down toward the bog.

"Okay, got something," Nate said.

"What is it?" she asked, moving over to stand behind him, squinting down at the screen while he read.

"Listen to this, it's a wedding announcement from 1998 in the *Keene Sentinel:* 'Gloria Whitcomb, of Keene, New Hampshire, and Dustin Kissner of Hartsboro, Vermont, were united in marriage on June 2 at St. James Episcopal Church in Keene. The bride is the daughter of Mark and Sara Whitcomb of Keene. The groom is the son of Howard and Margaret Kissner of Hartsboro, Vermont.'"

Dustin Kissner.

The name pinged in Helen's brain.

"That's Olive's father," Helen said.

Nate typed more, brow furrowed. "Yup. Current address is listed as 389 Westmore Road. That's Olive's place. So is Gloria Olive's mother?"

"No, her name is Lori, I'm sure of it."

"Could Lori be short for Gloria?"

"Oh god, I guess you're right. But . . . she disappeared last year," Helen said quietly.

"Disappeared?" Nate asked.

"Rumor has it she ran off with a man, but Riley was telling me that Olive thinks maybe something else happened. Riley seemed a little worried, too. She seemed to think that maybe her leaving had something to do with Dustin. That he'd scared her."

"What? Like he threatened her in some way?"

"Nate," she said, "what if he . . . what if Olive's dad did something to Gloria? Hurt her. Or worse. And what if Olive found out?"

"Helen, you don't know—"

"Maybe it's not Gloria I'm supposed to find and save," she said. "Maybe it's Olive."

CHAPTER 44

O live

 SEPTEMBER 13, 2015

Her father was standing in the kitchen, wearing his town work shirt with his name stitched over the chest pocket. DUSTIN.

Dusty, his friends called him.

But his friends didn't come around anymore. Not since Mama left. Not since they started their endless renovations. The knocking down of the walls, the piles of dust, the drywall and tape and compound and holes in the ceiling and floors.

"What are you doing with the gun, Olive?"

It was his serious, no-bullshit *I'm the dad here* voice. He called her Olive only when he was scared or angry or both.

She pulled the diary out of her back pocket, dropped it on the worn kitchen table.

"I found this in the shed," she said.

He glanced down at it but kept his eyes on her, on the gun that was pointed at him.

When there's a gun in the room with you, you give it your full attention.

Daddy looked tired. Thin. The dark circles under his eyes made him look like a raccoon man. "Put down the gun and we can talk, Olive," he said, his voice like the chatter of an anxious coon. *Danger. There's danger here.*

"Do you know what this is?" Olive asked, nodding at the book.

"No," he said. "I've never seen it before."

"Mama's diary," she said.

His face twitched slightly. "Lower the weapon, Olive," he said.

"Did you know she was keeping a diary?"

He shook his head. The little color he had left his face, until he was as pale as the walls.

"I read it, you know. Can you guess what she wrote?"

He was silent, thinking, his jaw clenching, eyes on the gun. "Is it about the other men?" he asked finally.

She laughed. "You know what? I don't think there ever were any other men. I think that was entirely your paranoia. Or maybe just you trying to cover your tracks."

"Cover my tracks?"

"You know what's in this diary? You know what she wrote? She wrote that she was *afraid* of you." Olive swallowed hard, looked at her father. Her father, who taught her to shoot and to follow the rules of a hunter: respect your weapon; never fire on a target you're not sure of; never let an animal suffer; never, ever aim a gun at a person unless you intend to use it. "Why's that, Daddy? Why would Mama be afraid of you?"

"Afraid of me?" he said, voice low, raspy, like he was in danger of losing it altogether.

"I read the diary," she said. Her hands were hot and sweaty on the gun. She kept her finger on the trigger. "Don't lie to me."

She looked around the room, saw the torn-open walls, the missing floorboards. The constant state of destruction and demolition she lived inside. Then she understood. She finally figured out her father's obsession with deconstructing the house. She felt like a cartoon character with a lightbulb going off over her head. "You've been looking for her map and the diary, haven't you?" she said.

"What map?"

"The map to Hattie's treasure. You thought she must have hid it in the house. Hid it somewhere good, somewhere no one would look. And the diary, that might prove what you did."

He looked pained, his face proof of the expression "The truth hurts."

"I—" he stammered, unable to come up with any more words.

"But you never found them, did you?"

He didn't answer.

"I know you hurt her," Olive said.

"Hurt her?" He staggered back as if the weight of her words had struck him in the chest. "Where on earth did you get that idea?"

"That's what Mama wrote in her diary. That you hurt her. And you threatened to make her disappear."

He was leaning against the counter now.

"She said that?" The words came slowly. "Why would she have said that?"

"You tell me, Dad."

He shook his head. "I have no idea. I never hurt your mother or threatened her in any way. I would never dream of it." He seemed to sink deeper into himself, to be taking up less and less space. The incredible shrinking man.

It was hard for Olive to believe that her father was lying—he looked so genuinely confused and hurt. But why would Mama have written those words in her diary?

Her father's eyes moved from Olive and the gun to the kitchen window. "There's someone out there," he said.

"What?" Keeping the gun on him (was it a trick, something he was doing to divert her attention so he could get the gun?), she glanced out the window.

Daddy was right. She saw movement. She thought at first it was Dicky Barnes, that he'd come for her. Dicky and his band of spirit-calling witches were the last thing she needed right now.

But it wasn't Dicky.

She saw the white dress, the glow of the white deer mask in the cool blue light of the moon.

Daddy stood looking out the window, blinking in disbelief at the deer head with white fur, long snout, glossy black eyes. "What the hell is that?" he asked.

But Olive was already at the kitchen door, throwing it open, watching the figure dart off across the yard toward the tree line.

"Mama?" she cried. The figure stopped, turned back to look at Olive, the white mask seeming to glow. Then she turned away again and ran off into the woods. "Mama! Please! Wait!"

CHAPTER 45

Lori Kissner

 JUNE 29, 2014

The others knew. She was sure of it.

She'd gone to the circle tonight, just as she did each week, as she'd been doing for the past six months now, and stepped into the center of the group right on cue, playing Hattie, channeling. She wore the white dress, the black wig, her beaded shoes, and, tonight, as the perfect finishing touch, Hattie's necklace.

The others believed she had a gift.

She heard Hattie's voice as no one ever had before.

She heard it and she let it speak through her.

It was like she invited Hattie inside her, let her take over her body and mind, her tongue and mouth, let her say and do what she pleased.

She did have a gift.

And now, now she understood why.

She'd done the research. She'd been to the mill in Lewisburg and learned what had happened to Hattie's daughter, Jane. And eventually she'd learned that Jane had had two children, Ann and Mark, and that Ann was none other than Lori's mother, and Mark was Lori's uncle, the one who had taken them in after the "tragedy."

Before Ann's death, she had said little about her own mother to Lori. Of course, Lori understood about keeping the past a secret. She'd kept her own past a secret all her life. When she moved in with Uncle Mark and Aunt Sara, she reinvented herself—started going by Lori and asked to have her last name legally changed to theirs. As if leaving the past, and all the pain that came with it, behind could ever be that easy.

Lori told no one about how she'd watched her father shoot her mother, then himself. She just told people, "My name is Lori Whitcomb. I grew up in Keene. My mom and dad are Sara and Mark Whitcomb." What happened in Elsbury, when she was little Gloria

Gray, was long ago and far away—and she liked it that way. Perhaps she shouldn't judge her mother for never teaching her children her own mother's name and the gruesome details of her death.

And now, years later, Lori told no one of what she'd learned about her true family history. Family tradition, after all. It was a powerful secret she kept, that she was related to Hattie by blood.

At first, Lori had believed that maybe she did have a gift. Maybe she was touched, as Hattie had been. Maybe it ran in the family, passed down to each generation of women.

Then she realized the truth.

Any power she had, any gift of divination or secret knowledge—it all came from Hattie. She knew things because Hattie spoke to her.

And now the words Hattie spoke were words of warning.

Be careful, Hattie whispered to Lori in her dreams. *You're in danger.*

And now, now that she'd found the treasure, actually found it with Hattie's help and blessing, she felt the walls closing in. All their eyes were on her, searching.

"Any updates?" they'd asked. "Any sign of it yet?"

"No," she lied. "Nothing yet."

She hadn't wanted to come to the circle tonight at all. She wanted to stop going to the weekly gatherings altogether. To drop out of the group. To pass on her role as Hattie to someone else. But that would look suspicious. So she played along.

. . .

Once Lori put the necklace on, started wearing it day and night, hidden under her shirts, the visions and dreams truly started.

She dreamed of Hattie's house again and again. Of Hattie stacking rocks for the foundation after her family home had been burned down, her mother killed.

Lori took out the necklace, looked down at the design, at the circle, triangle, and square that were the door to the spirit world. The door with the eye inside. A symbol that Hattie had been able to see things in both worlds, had the gift of sight.

Lori started going out at night so she wouldn't be seen. She told Dustin she was going out to see friends, to see a band, any excuse she could think of. She wanted to surprise him with the truth. To bring that treasure home and say, *This is my secret. This is what I've been hiding.*

The digging was hard. She'd have to bring a change of clothes with her so she wouldn't come home soaking wet and filthy. The worst part was trying to put things back in a way that made it look like the area hadn't been disturbed. The last thing she wanted was a hiker or teenage stoner coming out, seeing the recent excavations, and getting curious. Rumors of Hattie's buried treasure had gone on for generations—most people didn't believe it, but still, treasure hunters came poking around from time to time.

The necklace and dreams brought her closer to the treasure.

After nearly two weeks of digging almost every night, she'd found it last night! A crumbling wooden box. Inside that, a metal box with rusted hinges and catches. She broke it open with the spade of her shovel—inside were jewelry, gold coins, old bills, all wrapped in waxed canvas. It was real. As much as she trusted Hattie to lead her, she couldn't quite believe that it was here, that she could touch it. She gingerly picked up a gold bracelet—were those rubies? Garnets? She put the bracelet back, nestled among other things that glinted and sparkled. She blinked down stupidly at the treasure, unsure of what to do next. It was nearly two in the morning. The box was too big; there was too much to carry back on her own easily. She decided to rebury it and come back again soon, once she'd thought things through and made a plan.

She carefully put it all back in the ground, changed into dry clothes, then walked home and slipped into bed beside Dustin. He didn't stir.

.   .   .

Tonight, as she drove home from the spirit circle, she knew time was running out. The others were suspicious. They'd be watching her, keeping a close eye. She needed to go back and get the treasure soon—tonight! She'd do it tonight. She'd go home, change into old clothes for digging, pick up Dustin's canvas duffel bag, and go get the treasure. Then she'd bring it home, hide it. She'd show Dustin, of course, and together, they'd figure out what their next move should be.

Heart pounding, shaky with adrenaline, she turned off the headlights as she pulled into her driveway and up to the dark house. She opened the front door slowly, crept into the hall.

The kitchen light came on.

Dustin was waiting for her.

"Where have you been?" he asked. His eyes were rimmed with red. From the smell of him and the empty bottle of Jim Beam on the kitchen table, he'd be in no shape to go in to work in the morning. And no shape to start an argument with.

She would tell him now. Tell him everything. "I—"

"And where have you been every damn night? Last night you didn't get in until two in the morning. Now look at you—creeping in just before midnight, all dressed up, fancy shoes on."

"Dustin, there's something I need to tell you," she said.

"Who is he?" Dustin demanded.

"What? There is no he," she said.

"Half the town knows it," he said. "How do you think it feels to go in to work, have the guys whispering about what a dumbass I am because my wife is sleeping around and I don't even have a fucking clue?"

"Dustin, I've never been unfaithful, how could you even—"

"I'm not going to be the dumbass anymore," he snarled. He stood up from the kitchen table, stumbling a bit. "You know what I keep thinking about? How back when I asked you to marry me, you took your time answering—you weren't sure—and me, I needed you to say yes. I needed you to say yes because I didn't want to live without you. I loved you that much."

"I loved you, too, Dustin. I love you still."

"Get out."

"But, Dustin, I—"

"Get the fuck out of my house! Go on! Before your daughter wakes up and finds out the truth about her slut of a mother!"

Then he slapped her across the face so hard she staggered backward, fell over.

Dustin stood over her, face red, fist raised.

In that moment, she didn't know him at all.

CHAPTER 46

Helen

 SEPTEMBER 13, 2015

Olive was Hattie's great-great-granddaughter. Helen could hardly believe it.

Helen called Riley, but the call went to voice mail. "I found Gloria Gray. You're not going to believe who it is. Call me as soon as you get this!"

"Helen, maybe we should wait," Nate said. "Or go to the police first."

Helen laughed. "The police? You mean Officer Friendly, who couldn't give a shit when someone tried to gas us to death? And what are we going to tell them? That a ghost told me to find Lori Kissner? They already have me flagged in the system as a crazy person, I'm sure."

"I don't know . . . I—"

"I'm going to Olive's right now to talk to Olive. And to Dustin. Are you coming or not?"

They got in the truck, Helen behind the wheel. She threw the truck into reverse before Nate even had his door closed.

"Jesus, Helen, slow down," Nate said as she hit the gas, backing up, spinning the wheel to get them turned around, headlights illuminating their decrepit trailer, the motion-activated camera at the edge of the yard near the woods.

Helen ignored him and barreled down the driveway, barely slowing when they got to the road and she yanked the wheel to the left, the truck fishtailing a bit.

"We're not going to be any help to Olive or her mom if we're pinned in a wrecked truck," Nate reminded her.

"I've *got* it, Nate," she said. He was quiet.

The headlights turned the road into a brightly lit tunnel of thick trees, the vegetation reaching for them, everything feeling very alive, very much like it wanted to overtake them.

Three-quarters of a mile down the road, they came to the dented mailbox at the end of a long, steep drive. KISSNER was painted on the side in white paint.

Helen turned up the drive, the truck bouncing over the washouts and ruts.

They could see the house at the top, all the lights on.

"Looks like they're home," Nate said.

They pulled in behind a half-ton Chevy pickup. Helen cut the engine, reached for the door handle. Nate leaned over, put a hand on her arm.

"Hey," he said. "Let's play it cool in there, huh? Maybe Gloria— Lori—really did run off with someone. We don't have the whole story. Maybe no one needs saving at all."

"Yeah, maybe," she said, opening the door and jumping out, but she knew he was wrong.

Olive was in danger. She could feel it all around her. She could practically hear Hattie's voice screaming at her through time and space: *Save her!*

Helen ran for the front door. It stood open.

"Wait," Nate ordered, catching up to Helen, pulling her back, and going in first. "Hello?" he called. "Olive? Dustin?"

Helen was right behind him. They were in a stripped-down front hall with plywood floors, bare stud walls. The living room was to their right, the kitchen to the left. All the lights were blazing. There was a table saw set up in the living room, sheets of drywall leaning against the wall, tools everywhere.

"God, it looks like our house—what's he doing?" Nate said.

Helen shook her head. "Olive said they were doing some renovations. I had no idea . . ."

Nate crossed the living room, jogged up the stairs. Helen stood in the living room, heard his footsteps up above, heard him calling out, "Hello?," and then he was back downstairs.

"No one's here," he said.

Helen checked the bathroom and the kitchen—both rooms had half-finished walls, exposed wiring and plumbing. The kitchen door was open, and Helen stepped through it, looked around the yard. She was sure she'd heard something, a voice calling. Nate came outside and stood beside her, started to speak. She shushed him.

"Did you hear that?" she asked, and right away, she was the crazy lady again, the woman who heard screams in the woods, saw ghosts.

"No," Nate said. "I didn't, but—"

And then a voice cut through the darkness. A man's voice, angry and not too far off.

"Ollie!" he yelled. "Ollie, get back here!"

O live

 SEPTEMBER 13, 2015

"Ollie!" Daddy called behind her. "Ollie, get back here!"

Olive ran with the shotgun held tight in both hands, kept it firm against her body, barrel pointing up to the left.

Never run with a gun, Daddy always told her, but if there was ever a time for breaking the rules, this was it.

She got to the edge of the yard, passed the old hollowed-out maple she and Mama used to leave gifts for each other in. The place she'd hidden the necklace she now wore.

Mama was ahead of her, just a blur of white moving through the trees like a deer-headed ghost.

And it was like chasing a ghost, so much so that Olive wondered if maybe this wasn't her mother, if it really was Hattie.

But why would Hattie be wearing her mama's special fairy-tale shoes? Even in the dark, from a distance, she could make them out— could see the sparkling light from the flower-shaped beading on top.

Her mother was moving surprisingly fast, considering that she was wearing her good shoes and her vision must be encumbered by the mask.

But then again, Mama knew this path by heart. She'd been walking it for years and, like Olive, could probably do it with her eyes closed.

Olive knew where they were going, where the path led.

They looped through the woods, up the hill, then back down, the figure ahead moving easily over the roots and rocks, navigating the path perfectly in the moonlight.

Daddy, on the other hand, was off behind them, struggling to catch his breath, tripping on fallen trees, stumps, roots. Olive heard him cursing each time he went down. And he was calling for her. "Ollie! For God's sake, wait up!"

But she did not slow. She made her way past ghostly white paper birch trees, white pine, maple, and aspen. She did not want to lose Mama (or was it Hattie? Hattie who'd found a way back and was now wearing Mama's magic shoes as she ran through the woods toward the bog?).

Olive saw the lights of Helen and Nate's trailer through the trees as they skirted around the back edge of their property. Olive imagined them tucked safely inside, Nate watching his wildlife cameras, Helen reading about spirits and hauntings. Olive wondered if Nate's camera might catch a glimpse of them running through the woods, if he might see the pale mask of her mother and think his albino doe had come back once more, taken human form now.

"Mama!" Olive cried out again, her voice breathy, choked sounding.

But what if it's not Mama? a worrying voice asked.

What if it's really Hattie and she's leading you out into the bog to kill you?

But she didn't believe that. She knew in her heart (didn't she?) that Hattie would not hurt her.

Olive could hear the call of frogs coming from the bog, the trill of crickets singing their early fall symphony.

The trees thinned, were replaced by cedar and larch, and the air changed as she got closer to the bog. The rich green bog smell filled Olive's nose; she could practically taste it on the back of her throat. At last, she broke through the trees, her feet hitting the quaking, quivering surface of the peat, sneakers soaking wet. The bog was layered with a thick blanket of mist that seemed to glow green, to move and reshape itself. Olive came to a fast stop, not far from the ruined stone foundation that was once Hattie's house.

But where was Hattie?

Not Hattie, she reminded herself. Mama. It was Mama she was chasing.

But where was she?

Olive held still, clutching the gun as she gasped to catch her breath and scanned the bog, eyes searching for movement in the mist. She saw no movement. And now, strangely, the air had gone quiet. Too quiet. The whole bog was holding its breath, waiting to see what might happen next.

Where did she go?

It was as if the figure had disappeared into thin air.

Now you see her, now you don't.

Poof.

True magic.

Maybe she'd been chasing a ghost after all.

"Mama?" Olive called. Then, drawing up the courage, she called out hesitantly, "Hattie?"

Her father came bursting through the trees behind her, his breathing as loud as a freight train, his hair going in crazy directions, his shirt untucked, his tan work boots sinking in the ground. He staggered like a drunk man, a man unsure of the ground underneath him. But he came toward Olive at a steady clip. "There you are!" he said. "I thought I'd lost you."

She raised the gun in his direction.

"Stay back," she warned.

But it turned out she didn't need to warn him.

Because the deer-headed woman appeared behind him, slipping out of the trees, something in her hands—a large rock—that she raised up just behind Daddy.

And Olive thought, for one brief second, that she should cry out, should warn him, but he was the enemy here. So she just watched as the woman (Mama! she was being saved by Mama!) brought the rock down against the back of his skull.

He fell to his knees, then forward, facedown, motionless. Limp as an old rag doll.

CHAPTER 48

Helen

"Helen!" Nate called behind her. "Wait! Where are you going?"

"After them," she said. She continued on the path she'd found in the woods, working her way along as quickly as she could, navigating by the light cast by the nearly full moon in the sky above.

"But it's dark and we don't know these woods," he said. "You've gotta trust me, Helen. I've been lost in them myself. It's easy to get turned around, even in daylight."

She thought of the story of Frank Barns, who'd chased the white doe into the woods and was never seen again. Of George Decrow pulling his wife, Edie, out of the bog.

"But Olive's out here. And that man yelling—someone's after her, maybe her father. We've gotta help her."

She'd never been so sure of anything before.

There was only one thought flooding her mind: *Olive. You've got to save Olive.*

She scrambled over fallen trees, around rocks. The trees were thick here, shading out the light of the moon, making it harder to see. She caught her toe under a thick root and went tumbling, her fall broken by the thick leaf litter. Her mind raced. Panic built, pulsating, making her heart race faster.

No. She was not going to let this happen, to let herself be paralyzed by her own emotions.

"Helen, slow down," Nate said. "You don't want to break an ankle out here."

She pushed up on her knees, took Nate's hand when he reached for her.

"Do you see anything?" she asked, voice low, taking a deep breath, trying to center herself. "Or hear anything?"

He shook his head. They stood in the dark, holding hands, keeping very still, listening.

She thought she heard something way off to the left. Sticks snapping, a low grunt. "Is that them?" she asked.

"I don't know," he said, practically whispering. "It could have just been an animal."

She broke away from Nate and pushed off in the direction of the sound she'd heard.

She walked blindly now, hands in front of her, no longer on any clear path, the trees and shrubs thickening around them. Branches reached out to claw at her face; her legs got tangled, feet caught up on roots and rocks.

"Helen," Nate said. "I think we should turn around. Try to find our way back. We're not any good to Olive lost in the woods."

But which way was back? She could no longer see the lights from the house.

And Olive was out there somewhere.

"Let's go back," Nate said. "Call the police. Report the empty house with doors open, the yelling in the woods."

Helen began patting her pockets for her phone but knew it was no good. It was still in her purse in the cab of the truck.

"Do you have your phone?" she asked.

"Dammit. No. We flew out of there in such a hurry that I left it on the kitchen table."

If they wanted help—professionals with flashlights and dogs and guns—to find Olive, they had to go back.

"Okay," she said. "So which way is back?"

"This way, I think," Nate said, starting to walk.

"But didn't we come from the other direction? Didn't we pass that huge leaning tree on the way here?"

"No, it's this way," he told her.

So Helen followed, knowing that they were getting more and more lost with each step.

They walked in silence for a few minutes, Helen following Nate, her eyes on his back, his pale T-shirt leading the way.

But she was letting the wrong person guide her. She understood this. She dropped back a bit from Nate.

"Hattie," she whispered. "Help me. Help us. Help us find Olive."

She took in a deep breath, tried to clear her mind, to listen for a voice, a signal.

Come on, Hattie, don't fail me now.

But the only voice that came was Nate's from up ahead.

"Helen," Nate said, voice low. "Look!"

He pointed out ahead of them into a stand of trees growing close together, looking darker than the rest of the woods.

And there, standing just in front of it, watching them, looking almost as if she'd been waiting, was Nate's white doe.

She was full-sized and her fur was bright white, her eyes dark and glittering as she watched them, her ears perked, listening. She held perfectly still and seemed to give a silvery shimmer in the moonlight. She was like a creature from a dream.

"Oh, Nate," Helen said in a trembling whisper. "She's beautiful." She said it as if the deer were something Nate himself had created: a work of art he was sharing with her.

"Come on," he said, taking her hand. "She wants us to follow her."

CHAPTER 49

O live

"Mama?" Olive said, lowering her gun, taking a step toward the woman in the mask and her crumpled, motionless father.

"Oh, *Olive,*" the woman in the deer mask cried, pulling the mask away from her face, letting it fall to the ground.

"Riley?" Olive said, blinking at her aunt in disbelief.

"You're okay now, Ollie," Riley said, coming forward, gently taking the gun from Olive's hands, laying it on the ground beside the white deer mask before encircling her in a tight, almost crushing hug. "Thank God you're all right!"

Olive pressed her face against her aunt's shoulder, her nose mashed against the stiff fabric of her white dress. She smelled like the incense that had been burning at Dicky's hotel.

"It was you?" Olive asked. "Back at the hotel."

"Yes," Riley said.

"But I don't understand," Olive said, the disappointment hitting her like a wall, knocking all the air out of her. "Where is Mama?"

The hug got tighter. "Oh, Olive, I think I know. Maybe I've known all along but haven't wanted to believe."

"She's dead, isn't she?"

Riley broke away from the hug but still held Olive's arms tight. She looked into her eyes. "I think so, Ollie."

"And Daddy . . ." She could hardly bring herself to say the words. "He . . . he killed her?"

Riley nodded slowly.

"But why?"

"I don't know, Ollie," she said, studying Olive's face in the moonlight. "Maybe because he found out she was having an affair?" She paused. "Or maybe she told him she was going to leave him?" Riley said. She brushed the hair away from Olive's face. "I don't think we'll ever know for sure."

"She found the treasure," Olive said.

Riley seemed to hold her breath. "She did. And I think he knew it. But she wouldn't tell him where it was. Maybe that was the last straw."

Olive said nothing, just tried to imagine the scene as it might have unfolded: Mama and Daddy arguing, him accusing her of being unfaithful, her saying she was leaving, that she could afford to now. And he'd want to know how and maybe she'd told him, told him just to piss him off, to prove that she'd been right all along—the treasure had existed and she'd found it. *So where is it?* Daddy would have asked. *Where is this treasure you're going to use to start a new life with your new boyfriend?* And she wouldn't tell him. And then . . . then what? Had he struck her? Shot her? Strangled her? Had it been an accident somehow, a shove that he hadn't meant to be so rough with? Or had it been cold, premeditated murder?

Olive thought of the fight she'd heard early that morning. How it had ended with a crash. Had she heard her mother's voice again after that?

Olive looked at her father's crumpled body on the ground behind them. He looked like a small and ruined thing. Hard to believe he'd been capable of such a horrific act.

"Do you know, Ollie?" Riley asked. "Did your mama tell you where she hid it?"

She put a hand on Olive's shoulder, squeezing gently at first, but then a little too tight.

"You two were always so close," Riley said, putting her second hand on Olive's other shoulder. "She must have said something. Or left you a note? A sign."

Olive shook her head. "No," she said, her throat growing dry.

"Have you been getting messages, too?" Riley asked.

"From Mama?" Olive was confused.

"No! *From Hattie.* Your mother found the treasure because of Hattie. Hattie would send her messages. Sometimes in dreams. You said you'd been dreaming about Hattie. What has she shown you?"

"I don't know. I—"

"Think!" Riley demanded.

Olive tried to squirm away, but Riley held her tight, pulling her closer, her arms now wrapped around Olive.

"Don't you get it? How special you are?" Riley said, tightening her grip even more. "Your mother didn't understand, either. Not at first. But she was *chosen*. Chosen by Hattie. Hattie gave her powers, gave her the ability to see things beyond what any normal person can see. I didn't understand at first. I kept asking myself why. Why Lori of all people? She didn't even want the gifts Hattie gave her. I thought it was so unfair, infuriating. But now I finally understand. It was right there under my nose the whole time, but I never put it together."

"Put what together?"

"They're related! Lori was Hattie's great-granddaughter."

"What?"

"It's true. You and your mother have Hattie's blood running in your veins. Do you understand how special that makes you? That's why you've been dreaming about her—you're connected by blood. Tell me what you've dreamed, Ollie."

"I . . . I don't remember," Olive said.

"Think, dammit!"

And as Olive tried to squirm out of her aunt's grasp, she did think.

She thought of how her mother had pulled away from Riley in the last days before she left, had refused to go out with her and how they'd fought.

She thought of her mother's diary, of the final entry, how the writing was messier, more hurried. Was it possible that her mother hadn't written it? That someone else had?

She thought of looking through her mother's closet and how the only pair of shoes missing was the beaded ivory slippers. Of how that meant she'd been wearing them when she left the house for the final time.

"How did you get my mother's shoes?" Olive asked.

Riley looked at her a second, her face tense. Then she smiled, but it was a sickening *I'm about to tell you a big lie and you'd better believe it* sort of smile. "She gave them to me."

Olive kicked at her aunt, dug her fingernails into Riley's arms.

"Help!" she screamed, thinking if she screamed loud enough, Helen and Nate would hear, would come running.

Riley pulled Olive closer, spinning her, wrapping one arm around her neck, holding her other hand over her mouth.

"Shh, Ollie. Calm down. You're okay. Everything's going to be okay."

But as she spoke, her arm tightened around Olive's neck.

"Please, Aunt Riley." Olive wheezed out the words with what little air could get through.

"Shh, my special, special girl," Riley cooed, pulling her arm even tighter.

CHAPTER 50

Helen

 SEPTEMBER 13, 2015

Hattie Breckenridge was choking Olive.

Not the faint ghost of Hattie, but an actual, physical Hattie.

They were standing not twelve feet away from Helen, by the wrecked foundation of Hattie's house, and Hattie was behind Olive, holding her, the crook of her elbow against Olive's throat.

The moon cast a bright light, fully illuminating the scene in the bog.

They'd been following the doe, jogging along behind it through the woods. It would get far ahead of them, nearly out of sight, then stop and wait for them to catch up before moving on. When Olive's scream pierced the silence, the deer broke into a run, Helen and Nate right behind her. She'd heard Nate stumble, fall to the ground with a "Shit!," but hadn't turned back. Helen followed the deer to the bog, and as she stood at the tree line, she saw Olive and Hattie about four yards away. A man was crumpled on the ground beside them.

Helen sprinted up behind the figure in the white dress with the long dark hair. She got to her, grabbed her hair, screamed, "Let her go!"

But the dark hair came off in her hands.

A wig.

And under it, a bare neck with a circular snake tattoo.

"Riley! What the hell are you doing?"

Helen grabbed Riley's shoulders, pulling her back. Olive dropped to the ground, gasping. Olive looked up and Helen saw she was wearing the necklace: Hattie's necklace, the circle, triangle, and square glinting in the moonlight.

"You!" Riley screamed at Helen. "Why couldn't you have just gone away? Left before it was too late?"

Riley swung at Helen, catching her right in the bridge of the nose, sending her reeling backward, the pain bright and blinding. She sank down to her knees on the bed of wet, spongy moss.

"Helen!" Nate yelled. He sounded far away.

Riley stood over Helen. "Why couldn't you have just given up? Gone back where you came from!" She kicked Helen hard in the side, sending her toppling over from the pain and force of it.

"Hattie," Helen said, half in answer to Riley's question, half calling to her, hoping she would come and save them.

"Hattie! It's all about Hattie. She comes to you people and you don't even want her to! You don't even try. And why you, Helen? You're not even related. You're nothing. No one. Just a former history teacher who happened to put up a haunted beam. A beam *I gave you*. She would never have come to you if it wasn't for me!"

Riley stepped back, positioning herself to kick Helen again, but stood frozen, a strange statue in a white dress, eyes focused out on something in the middle of the bog.

The white doe. The animal stood, seeming to hover over the surface of the bog, her white fur as pale and glimmering as the stars above, her eyes an iridescent silver.

The doe was moving toward them, slowly at first, then full-on charging right at Riley, head down.

"Hattie?" Riley said, putting her hands up in front of her, in what Helen thought at first was a *stop now* protective gesture, but she was wrong—Riley was opening her arms to the deer, calling her closer, waiting to embrace her.

Olive struck Riley on the back of the head with the butt of a shotgun. Riley sank to her knees beside Helen on the boggy ground, dazed but conscious. Olive quickly turned the gun around, training it on her aunt.

"Hattie?" Riley said plaintively.

But the deer was gone.

CHAPTER 51

Lori

 **JUNE 29, 2014**

Dustin stood over her, swaying like a snake.

"Get out before I do something we'd both really regret," he spat.

Lori scrambled to her feet, left, got in her car, and drove aimlessly for an hour or more. She was moving on autopilot, numb and frightened. Not sure what to do or where to go.

She circled back through town, saw the lights at Rosy's still on, and looked through the window to see Sylvia cleaning up. She knocked on the window, and Sylvia let her in, gave her a full glass of whiskey.

"Can I stay with you tonight?" Lori asked.

Sylvia kept pouring whiskey and Lori kept drinking, saying too much to her old friend.

She spent the night with Sylvia and made a plan. She got up at dawn, head pounding and stomach heaving from all the whiskey she'd had. She snuck out of Sylvia's and drove home.

She wrote Dustin a note and stuck it under the windshield wiper of his truck:

> *D—*
> *I love you with all of my heart. I would never be unfaithful. Soon, you'll understand everything. I have a surprise. Something that's going to change everything. Meet me in the bog at midnight, by the foundation of Hattie's house. I'll show you what I've been up to every night.*
> *All my love,*
> *Lori*

She went to the mall, walking around like a zombie, then wandered into the movie theater, where she paid ten bucks for a matinee she barely paid attention to and a box of popcorn that tasted greasy and

stale. After the movie, she drove to a truck stop out on the highway—
a place she and Dustin used to come when they first moved back
here. Exhausted, she pulled in between two semis and slept in her car
awhile, then woke up and had a big steak and eggs meal.

 **JUNE 30, 2014**

Just after midnight, she was in the bog, waiting. She'd left her car
in the driveway of the Decrows' old place, right next to their abandoned trailer.

She paced around the edge of the bog, waiting.

A figure appeared at the other end, tromping through the bush,
shining a flashlight here and there.

"Dustin!" she called. "Over here!"

But it wasn't Dustin.

It was Riley.

Had Dustin sent her instead?

"What are you doing here?" Lori asked.

"Dustin doesn't want to talk to you," Riley said.

"Didn't he get my note?" Lori asked.

"My poor little brother. He's a mess, you know. He called me this
morning, sobbing, drunk, asked me to come over. When I got there,
I saw the note under his wiper. I thought it was best not to upset him
any more by showing it to him."

"Riley, why would you—"

"He says you've been cheating on him for a long time. Everyone
knows it. You know how it is in this town—how easily rumors spread.
I tell a few people I've seen you go home with a stranger at the bar,
that Dustin told me you're cheating—and suddenly the whole town
knows."

"But . . . that's bullshit," Lori said softly. She shifted her weight,
the peaty ground beneath her feet far from solid. Perfect, really, when
nothing else felt solid anymore, either. "Why would you tell people
that?" Her voice was high, tears pricking her eyes.

"Perfect Lori's not so perfect, is she? Isn't it time everyone saw it?"

"I never . . . I never claimed to be perfect."

"Maybe not. But Dustin always saw you that way."

Riley reached into her shirt, pulled out a gun. Not just any gun. It was Dicky's six-shooter.

"I borrowed this," Riley said with a grim smile. "Tell me, Lori, what's the big surprise? What were you going to show Dustin?"

"Nothing," Lori said, taking a step back. "I just wanted to see him, to tell him we could work things out."

Riley laughed. "You can't bullshit me. How dare you even try? After everything I did for you. Bringing you to Dicky's? Helping you develop your gift, your connection to Hattie?"

"I . . ."

"You found it, didn't you? You found Hattie's treasure. She led you to it, right? Where is it?"

"There is no treasure. Not that I've found, anyway."

"If you tell me, I'll let you live."

Now it was Lori who laughed. "Really? So now you're going to kill me? Over some fantasy, some legend? Come on, Riley. I know you better than that."

"Do you? Maybe you just think you do."

"What's that supposed to mean?"

Riley brushed her blue bangs away from her eyes with the hand that wasn't holding the gun. "I never did get what Dustin saw in you."

"We . . . we love each other."

"You don't even know him! Not like I know him! You don't even know half the shit we went through when we were kids, everything I did for him, everything I fucking sacrificed for him." She waved Dicky's gun around, keeping it pointed at Lori, who stood frozen.

Lori thought of the years she'd spent with Riley, going out drinking, listening to bands, going to yard sales and flea markets. *The Lori and Riley Show,* that's what Dustin called them. They told each other everything.

But now, now Lori realized she hadn't known her sister-in-law at all. It had all been an act. A ruse.

"I tried to tell Dustin you were no good for him," Riley went on. "But it just pushed him away, pissed him off. So I did what I had to do. A full-on about-face. I made you my new best friend. And suddenly Dustin and I were close again."

Lori shook her head in disbelief.

"Where is it?" Riley asked. "Where's the treasure?"

"For God's sake, Riley, I'm telling you—there isn't any."

"It's not just for me. I'm doing this for Dustin. And for Olive. You, you'll leave town quietly and swear to never come back. I'll take the money and use it to take care of Dustin and Ollie. Take care of them like you never could. You were never good enough for them, you know that, right?"

"Please, Riley."

Riley rocked back on her heels; the tattoos on her bare arms seemed to writhe each time she moved, lit up by the moon.

"It was never fair, that she came to you." She glared at Lori with such hatred that Lori felt she'd already been shot. "I was the one who called to her first! The one who tried hardest. Promised to be her faithful servant, to dedicate myself to her in exchange for the treasure." She began moving closer to Lori, waving the gun, gesturing with it. "I've practiced witchcraft and divination for years and *she chose you,* a complete novice! Can you explain that? Why people are always choosing you? Dustin chose you, even Hattie Breckenridge chose you over me. Why would that be?"

She was so close now that the gun was nearly touching Lori's chest.

"I . . ." Lori thought of telling the truth. That she was related by blood, that that's why Hattie had come to her. "I'm—"

"Where's the fucking treasure?"

The barrel of the gun was pressed against her chest now. She was sure that Riley wouldn't pull the trigger. Hell, it probably wasn't even loaded. Dicky never kept it loaded. That's what he'd told her, anyway. Lori put her hand on the barrel of the gun, tried to pull it down, aim it away from her, from either of them, before someone got hurt.

The gun went off with a deafening explosion, so much louder than Lori would have ever believed possible. And Riley, the look on her face just then wasn't one of jealousy or rage, but only genuine surprise.

And the flash was so bright that it seemed to light up the whole bog, and there, over Riley's shoulder, stood a tree Lori had never seen before: a massive old tree with many thick branches, and from one hung the body of a woman—a woman who was reaching for her now, who had floated away from the tree and was taking Lori's hand, saying, "Shh. It's all right. Come with me now."

CHAPTER 52

H elen

 SEPTEMBER 14, 2015

The police in their dive suits, with rubbery skin as slick as seals', moved through the bog, carrying the body wrapped in black plastic, wound round and round with silver duct tape. They'd just pulled it out of the deepest part, the pool at the heart of the bog where water lilies floated like tiny yellow stars on the water. The police trudged their way clumsily through the peat, crushing delicate pitcher plants, sedge, low blueberry bushes, their feet sinking with each spongy step. It was like walking on the surface of another planet.

Helen watched from solid ground, holding her breath.

Other searchers continued to move around and through the bog in wet suits, chest waders, or fluorescent vests, radios squawking. A terrible invasion.

One of the cops slipped, nearly dropping the body. He cursed quietly, righted himself, adjusted his grip, but the plastic was slippery, his footing unsure.

Dragonflies darted through the air, shimmering, jewel colored. Frogs sang. A red-winged blackbird flew low, landing on a small cedar tree on the other side of the bog, watching the invaders with curiosity.

The trees, and all the creatures in them—the chattering squirrels gathering food, the black-capped chickadees, and the angry blue jays—watched, too. Behind Helen, on the east side of the bog, was the clearing where she and Nate lived. In the clearing stood their nearly finished house: their dream house, their haunted house, a home for the dead and the living. A place where Hattie and her family could gather.

An in-between place.

Nate had gone out to do errands: get the oil in the truck changed, pick up bar and chain oil for the saw.

"Come with me," he'd said. "You don't need to stay and watch."

But he was wrong.

She did need to stay.

She needed to watch Lori's body be pulled out.

Olive and Dustin weren't watching, either. They were back at the hospital, waiting for news. Dustin had regained consciousness on the way to the hospital and had been diagnosed with a concussion, but no fracture, and admitted for observation. Olive hadn't left his side.

"I hate to think that my mother's been down there this whole time," Olive had said when Helen was with her in the hospital cafeteria last night. "It just seems so . . . so lonely."

But Helen didn't think so. No, she didn't think Lori would be lonely down there at all.

Because she wasn't alone down there.

Be careful of the bog, Nate always told Helen. *Stay close to the edge.*

But the bog always drew her in.

Come closer, it seemed to whisper. *Come share my secrets.*

It had such an acidic, rich, mesmerizing smell—a primordial scent, she imagined. And it was such an otherworldly place, a landscape unlike anything she'd ever seen.

Some nights, she just sat at the edge, watching, listening, imagining she could see lights, the vague outline of the old house that once stood on the other side.

Hattie's house.

The past and the present, all that had happened and all that was happening now—she felt it all layered in this place; not just layered but deeply entwined, like the roots of the biggest trees.

She thought of everything that led her here: her father's death, Nate's belief and determination, a dream. A dream of a place where she'd feel she belonged. Where she was meant to be.

And she'd found it.

Maybe with a little help, but she'd found it.

.   .   .

Another searcher in a dive suit who'd been floating around in the pool at the center of the bog waved his arms. "There's something else down here!" he called. "More remains. Skeletal."

Others closed in, moving toward him slowly, carefully.

And Helen wanted to scream, to warn them. To say, *Leave those bones alone. They belong here. They're as much a part of this place as the bog itself.*

A man beside her mumbled something into a radio.

Another, a volunteer fireman she recognized from the general store, said, "It ain't safe in that bog. Not with Hattie's ghost out there."

Helen turned away, knowing Hattie's ghost wasn't out in the bog.

She knew just where the spirit of Hattie Breckenridge was.

She was back at Helen's house with the others, waiting.

CHAPTER 53

O live

 JUNE 8, 2016

Olive was back near the old foundation of Hattie's house. She didn't come out to the bog much these days. It was too hard to come and think about Mama. About what had happened to Mama.

But still, even though she stayed away from the bog, the bog was with her. It filled her dreams, her waking thoughts, too.

Especially after Dicky Barns came to visit her last week. He brought a note from Aunt Riley, who was safely locked up at the women's correctional facility up in South Burlington. "Your aunt asked me to deliver this to you," he said.

"My daddy says I'm not supposed to have any contact with her. Our lawyer says so, too," Olive said.

"Don't shoot the messenger," Dicky said, handing her the paper, then turning to go. He stopped a minute, turned back. "I had no idea, you know. None of us did. We all thought Lori had run off with a man, like Riley said."

Olive had heard all of this in court. She'd heard how Riley had taken Dicky's gun without Dicky knowing. And how Riley had taken Mama's diary, brought it back to the group of people who made up Dicky's circle, hoping it might have clues about where the treasure might be. But then, when Olive went to Dicky's and started asking questions, Dicky panicked and asked Riley to put the diary back. That was when she'd written the last passage, the one meant to incriminate Daddy.

Dicky looked down at his pointy-toed boots now. "Olive, I'm so sorry for all of this. Your mother, she was a special lady. She had a lot of gifts, but I guess you don't need me to tell you that."

Olive watched him walk away, shoulders slumped, looking so much smaller than he usually did. And gone was the gun in the tooled leather holster. The gun Riley had taken from Dicky and used to kill Olive's mother.

She read Riley's note:

> *Dearest Ollie,*
>
> *The treasure is real. You know that, right?*
>
> *It's in the bog. It has to be. Your mother was going to show it to your dad that night. She asked him to meet her there.*
>
> *Don't stop looking. You deserve to find it.*
>
> *I'm sorry. More sorry than you will ever know. There's no real explanation or excuse for the things I've done. What happened with your mother—it really was an accident. I never intended to shoot her. I just wanted . . . I guess I wanted impossible things. I wanted to be the one that Hattie chose. I wanted to see her, to hear her voice, to taste her power. I thought maybe if I had the treasure, it would make me close to her, too. But that wanting, that need—it was blinding and it made me lose everything I ever cared about. Including you.*
>
> *Find the treasure, Ollie. Ask Hattie. She'll show you. I have no doubt.*
>
> *All my love,*
>
> *Riley*

Now Olive stood by the old foundation, looking out over the bog.

Birds and dragonflies darted through the air. Frogs sang. The pink lady's slippers were plentiful this year, as if Hattie had been dancing in circles around the bog.

On the other side, she saw the path that led up to Helen and Nate's house, finished now. Helen was probably out working in the garden. And Nate off at work at the Nature Center. Last week, when they'd had Olive and her dad and even Mike over for dinner, Helen had shown Olive her new tattoo: a delicate pale pink lady's slipper on her forearm. Her tribute in ink to Hattie.

Mike loved the tattoo. And Helen and Nate loved Mike.

"*Cypripedium reginae,*" Mike said when he saw it. Olive rolled her eyes but smiled at him, feeling weirdly proud of her smart, dorky best friend.

"Where have you been hiding this guy?" Nate asked, and Mike

made a quirky response about hiding in plain sight, which led to a long discussion between Nate and Mike on all the animals that used camouflage and the different forms of camouflage, both of them throwing around terms like "disruptive coloration," "background matching," "countershading," "mimicry."

Mike's hair had grown out from the buzz cut he'd worn his whole childhood, and he'd grown half a foot in the last six months. Even Olive's dad seemed to be looking at Mike in a whole new way, calling him "son" and inviting him to stay for dinner most nights after Olive and Mike had been working on homework together.

Olive and her dad, with Helen and Nate's help, had finished the renovations of their house. They'd put up the final drywall, laid down flooring, painted, and put away all of their tools. Sometimes Olive saw her dad looking at the walls and could tell he was thinking about changing things again. She'd take his hand, walk over to the framed photos they'd put up of Mama: the three of them on holidays and birthdays, Mama and Daddy on their wedding day. Nothing they did—changing the house, finding the treasure, even—would bring her back. But she was with them still. Olive felt it. She knew her daddy did, too.

"Mama would have loved this house just the way it is," Olive would say.

. . .

Olive stood in the bog now, wearing her mother's necklace—*Hattie's necklace*. The door between the worlds.

She took it off, let it dangle on the thin leather cord.

"Show me, Hattie," she said. "It's time."

And she felt it. Felt it in her heart. That it really was time. That Hattie was ready to show her now.

And the silver pendant started moving, pulling to the left. She walked a few steps, then the necklace changed direction and so did she. Step-by-step, she followed the path the necklace laid out. Hattie's path. She stepped over the pink lady's slippers that seemed to be leading the way. The path, accented with the wild pink orchids, led right to the back corner of Hattie's house. Then the necklace began to twirl in fast clockwise circles.

"Here?" she asked.

Yes, the necklace said. *Yes.*

Maybe it was another trick; she'd dig up another ax head, an old pot or sink maybe.

She laid the necklace down on the ground, began pulling back rocks. Tested with her metal detector and got a strong signal.

She kept digging, moving rocks.

Until her shovel hit something hard.

She reached down, felt a piece of wood and, behind it, the edge of a heavy metal box.

Beside it, Hattie's necklace glinted up at her in the sunlight, the eye in the center watching.

I see all.

Acknowledgments

This book would not exist were it not for Dan Lazar, Anne Messitte, and Andrea Robinson, who asked me to write my own version of a haunted house story. Thanks for encouraging me to take this journey and for all the insights you gave me along the way. Many thanks to the whole spectacular team at Doubleday. And to Drea and Zella, who always go along for the ride, whether they necessarily want to or not (even when it involves exploring old stone foundations and getting soggy feet tromping through bogs!)—I love you guys.

About the Author

Jennifer McMahon is the International Thriller Writers Award–winning author of eight novels, including the *New York Times* bestsellers *Island of Lost Girls, Promise Not to Tell,* and *The Winter People.* She graduated from Goddard College and studied poetry in the MFA Writing Program at Vermont College. She lives in Vermont with her partner, Drea, and their daughter, Zella.